MIDNIGHT PROMISES

SHERRYL WOODS

THORNDIKE PRESS
A part of Gale, Cengage Learning

GALE
CENGAGE Learning®

Detroit • New York • San Francisco • New Haven, Conn • Waterville, Maine • London

Copyright © 2012 by Sherryl Woods.
The Sweet Magnolias Series #8.
Thorndike Press, a part of Gale, Cengage Learning.

Thorndike Press® Large Print Romance.
The text of this Large Print edition is unabridged.
Other aspects of the book may vary from the original edition.
Set in 16 pt. Plantin.

LIBRARY OF CONGRESS CATALOGING-IN-PUBLICATION DATA

Woods, Sherryl.
 Midnight promises / by Sherryl Woods. — Large print ed.
  p. cm. — (The Sweet Magnolias séries; #8.) (Thorndike
Press large print romance)
 ISBN 978-1-4104-5036-4 (hardcover) — ISBN 1-4104-5036-8 (hardcover)
 1. Large type books. I. Title.
PS3573.O6418M54 2012
813'.54—dc23   2012016043

Published in 2012 by arrangement with Harlequin Books S.A.

Printed in the United States of America
1 2 3 4 5 6 7 16 15 14 13 12

Dear Friends,

From the moment I first wrote about struggling single mom Karen Ames in *Feels Like Family,* a book in the original Sweet Magnolias trilogy, readers wanted to know much, much more about her and her romance with sexy, caring personal trainer Elliott Cruz. Since they were on their way to the altar by the end of that book, I thought the story was over.

Recently, though, it seemed to me that romance and conflict don't always end when marriage vows are spoken. And when Elliott's dreams for their family collide with Karen's past struggles, well, there's a whole new story to be told. You'll find that story right here in *Midnight Promises* as this couple faces the same questions that so many married couples face. Maybe the answers and compromises they find will be solutions for some of you, too.

You'll also get to spend some time with what I like to think of as the "Senior Magnolias" — three vibrant, lively older women who create their share of laughter and poignant moments during this book and the two yet to come this summer.

I hope you'll enjoy being back in the world

of the Sweet Magnolias. As always, I'd love to know what you think. You can email me at Sherryl703@gmail.com or become a fan on Facebook and join in the conversation there.

All best,
Sherryl

PROLOGUE

The bride wore a cocktail-length, off-the-shoulder gown in shimmering off-white satin and an antique lace mantilla — a family heirloom — reluctantly provided by her soon-to-be mother-in-law.

At the front of the small Roman Catholic church in Serenity stood the man who'd changed Karen Ames's mind about love, convincing her that the past was just that, over and done with. He'd promised her enduring love, a true partnership, and he'd shown her those traits time and again during their long courtship.

At a tug on her skirt, Karen leaned down to look into the excited face of her six-year-old daughter, Daisy.

"When are we getting married?" Daisy asked, practically bouncing up and down in anticipation.

Karen smiled at her eagerness. After too many years with no father figure around,

Daisy and Mack had fallen as deeply in love with Elliott Cruz as Karen had. And in many ways, it was his kind and generous relationship with her children that had convinced Karen that Elliott was nothing like her first husband, a man who'd abandoned them all, leaving behind a mountain of debt.

"I want to be married to Elliott," Daisy said with another tug in the direction of the altar. "Let's hurry."

Karen checked her four-year-old son to assure that Mack hadn't stripped off the tie she'd put on for him earlier or managed to douse his new suit with soda. She also assured herself that the wedding rings were still firmly attached to the pillow he would carry down the aisle.

Dana Sue Sullivan, her boss, friend and matron-of-honor, touched a hand to her shoulder. "Everything's good, Karen. How are your nerves?"

"Dancing a jig," she responded candidly. "And then I look inside and see Elliott waiting there, and everything settles."

"Then keep your eyes on him," Dana Sue advised. "And let's get this show on the road before these two leave without us."

She glanced down at Daisy and Mack, who were already inching from the foyer into the church.

At some signal Karen didn't even notice, the organist began to play for their entrance. Daisy took off down the aisle almost at a run, scattering rose petals with enthusiasm. Then, at some whispered comment, she grinned, glanced back at her mother and slowed to a more sedate pace. Mack was right on her heels, his expression solemn, a tiny frown puckering his brow until he'd safely reached Elliott's side.

Dana Sue followed, winking at her husband who was sitting at the front of her church, then smiling broadly at Elliott, who was running a nervous finger under the collar of his shirt.

Karen took a last deep breath, reminded herself that this time her marriage was going to be forever, that she'd finally gotten it right.

She lifted her gaze until she met Elliott's, then took that first confident, trusting step down the aisle into the future that promised to be everything her first marriage hadn't been.

1

Now that fall was just around the corner, Karen Cruz was experimenting with a new navy bean soup recipe for tomorrow's lunch at Sullivan's when sous-chef and friend Erik Whitney peered over her shoulder, gave an approving nod, then asked, "So, are you excited about the gym Elliott's going to open with us?"

Startled by the seemingly out-of-the-blue question, Karen spilled the entire box of sea salt she was holding into the soup. "My husband's opening a gym? Here in Serenity?"

Obviously taken aback by her puzzled reaction, Erik winced. "I take it he hasn't told you?"

"No, he hasn't said a word," she responded. Unfortunately, it was increasingly typical that when it came to the important things in their marriage, the things they should be deciding jointly, she and Elliott didn't have a lot of discussions. He made the decisions, then told her about them later. Or, as in this case, didn't bother informing her at all.

After dumping the now inedible batch of soup out, Karen started over, then spent the next hour stewing over this latest example of Elliott's careless disregard for her feelings. Each time he did something like this, it hurt her, chipping away at her faith that their marriage was as solid as she'd once believed it to be, that he was a man who'd never betray her as her first husband had.

Elliott was the man who'd pursued her with charm and wit and determination. It was his sensitivity to her feelings that had ultimately won her over and convinced her that taking another chance on love wouldn't be the second biggest mistake of her life.

She drew in a deep breath and fought for calm, doing her best to come up with a reasonable explanation for Elliott's silence about a decision that could change their lives. It was true that he did have a habit of trying to protect her, of not wanting her to worry, especially about money. Maybe that was why he'd kept this news from her. He had to know she'd react negatively, especially right now.

They were, after all, planning to add a baby to their family. Now that her two children from that previous disaster of a marriage — Mack and Daisy — were both settled in school and on an even keel after the many upheavals in their young lives, the timing finally seemed right.

But between Elliott's fluctuating income as a personal trainer at The Corner Spa and her barely above-minimum-wage pay here at the restaurant, adding to their family had taken careful consideration. She'd wanted never again to be in the same financial mess she'd been in when she and Elliott had first met. He knew that. So where on earth was the money to come from to invest in this new venture of his? There was no savings for a new business. Unless, she thought, he intended to borrow it from their baby fund. The possibility sent a chill down her spine.

And then there was the whole issue of loyalty. Maddie Maddox who ran the spa, Karen's boss, Dana Sue Sullivan, and Erik's wife, Helen Decatur-Whitney, owned The Corner Spa and had made Elliott an integral part of the team there. They'd also gone way above and beyond for Karen when she'd been a struggling single mom. Helen had even taken in Karen's kids for a while. How could Elliott consider just walking out on them? What kind of man would do that? Not the kind she'd thought she'd married, that was for sure.

Though she'd started out trying to rationalize Elliott's decision to keep her in the dark, apparently the strategy hadn't worked. She was stirring the fresh pot of soup so vigorously, Dana Sue approached with a worried frown.

"If you're not careful, you're going to puree that soup," Dana Sue said quietly. "Not that it won't be delicious that way, but I'm assuming it wasn't part of your plan."

"Plan?" Karen retorted, anger creeping right back into her voice despite her best intention to give Elliott a chance to explain what had been going on behind her back. "Who plans anything anymore? Or sticks to the plan, if they do have one? No one I know, or if they do, they don't bother to discuss these big plans with their partner."

Dana Sue cast a confused look toward Erik. "What am I missing?"

"I mentioned the gym," Erik explained, his expression guilt-ridden. "Apparently Elliott hadn't told her anything about it."

When Dana Sue merely nodded in understanding, Karen stared at her in dismay. "You knew, too? You knew about the gym and you're okay with it?"

"Well, sure," Dana Sue said as if it were no big deal that Elliott, Erik and whoever else wanted to open a business that would compete with The Corner Spa. "Maddie, Helen and I signed off on the idea the minute the guys brought it to us. The town's been needing a men's gym for a long time. You know how disgusting Dexter's is. That's why we opened The Corner Spa exclusively for women in the first place. This will be an expansion of sorts. We're actually going to be partnering with them. They have a sound business plan. More important, they'll have Elliott. He has the expertise and reputation to draw in clients."

Karen ripped off her apron. "Well, isn't that just the last straw?" she muttered. Not only were her husband, her coworker and her boss in on this, but so were her friends. Okay, maybe that meant Elliott wasn't being disloyal, as she'd first feared, except, of course to her. "I'm taking my break early, if you don't mind. I'll be back in time for dinner prep, then Tina's due in to take over the rest of the shift."

A few years back, she and Tina Martinez, then a single mom struggling to make ends meet while she tried to fight her husband's deportation, had split the shifts at Sul-

15

livan's, which had allowed them both the flexibility they desperately needed to juggle family responsibilities. Karen was still thankful for that, even though they were both working more hours now that their lives had settled down and Sullivan's had become a busy and unqualified success story.

Though she'd thought mentioning Tina would reassure Dana Sue that she wasn't going to be left in the lurch, Dana Sue's expression suggested otherwise.

"Hold on a second," she commanded.

Then, to Karen's surprise, she said, "I hope you're going someplace to cool off and think about this. It's all good, Karen. Honestly."

An hour ago, Karen might have accepted that. Now, not so much. "I'm in no mood to cool off. Actually I'm thinking I just might divorce my husband," she retorted direly.

As she picked up steam and headed out the back door, she overheard Dana Sue say, "She doesn't mean that, does she?"

Karen didn't wait for Erik's reply, but the truth was, her likely response wouldn't have been reassuring.

Elliott had been totally distracted while putting his seniors' exercise class through its paces. Usually he thoroughly enjoyed working with these feisty women who made up for in enthusiasm what they lacked in physical stamina and strength. Though it embarrassed him, he even got a kick out of the way they openly ogled him, trying to come up with new reasons each week to get him to strip off his shirt so they could gaze appreciatively at his abs. He'd accused them on more than one occasion of being outrageously lecherous. Not a one of them had denied it.

"Honey, I was one of those cougars they talk about before they invented the term," Flo Decatur, who was in her early seventies, had told him once. "And I make no apologies for it, either. You might be a little out of my usual range, but I've discovered recently that even men in their sixties are getting a little stuffy for me. I might need to find me a much younger man."

Elliott had had no idea how to respond to that. He wondered if Flo's daughter, attorney Helen Decatur-Whitney, had any idea what her irrepressible mother was up to.

Now he glanced at the clock on the wall, relieved to see that the hour-long session was up. "Okay, ladies, that's it for today.

Don't forget to get in a few walks this week. A one-hour class on Wednesdays isn't enough to keep you healthy."

"Oh, sweetie, when I want to get my blood pumping the rest of the week, I just think about how you look without your shirt," Garnet Rogers commented with a wink. "Beats walking anytime."

Elliott felt his cheeks heat, even as the other women in the group laughed. "Okay, that's enough out of you, Garnet. You're making me blush."

"Looks good on you," she said, undisturbed by his embarrassment.

The women slowly started to drift away, chattering excitedly about an upcoming dance at the senior center and speculating about who Jake Cudlow might ask. Jake was apparently the hot catch in town, Elliott had concluded from listening to these discussions. Since he'd seen the balding, bespectacled, paunchy Jake a few times, he had to wonder what the women's standards really were.

Elliott was about to head to his office when Frances Wingate stopped him. She'd been his wife's neighbor when he and Karen had first started dating. They both considered her practically a member of the family. Now she was regarding him with a worried look.

"Something's on your mind, isn't it?" she said. "You were a million miles away during class. Not that we present much of a challenge. You could probably lead us without breaking a sweat, but usually you manage to show a little enthusiasm, especially during that dancing segment Flo talked you into adding." She gave him a sly look. "You know she did that just to see you move your hips in the salsa, right?"

"I figured as much," he said. "Not much Flo does surprises or embarrasses me anymore."

Frances held his gaze. "You still haven't answered my question."

"Sorry," Elliott said. "What?"

"Don't apologize. Just tell me what's wrong. Are the kids okay?"

Elliott smiled. Frances adored Daisy and Mack, though both were unquestionably a handful. "They're fine," he assured her.

"And Karen?"

"She's great," he said, though he wondered how truthful the answer really was. He had a hunch she'd be less than great if she found out what he'd been up to. And truthfully, he had no idea why he'd kept these plans for opening a gym from her. Had he feared her disapproval, anticipated a fight? Maybe so. She was rightfully very touchy when it came to finances after going through a lousy time with an ex-husband who'd abandoned her and left her with a mountain of debt.

Frances gave him a chiding look. "Elliott Cruz, don't try fibbing to me. I can read you the same way I could read all those kids who passed through my classrooms over the years. What's wrong with Karen?"

He sighed. "You're even sharper than my mother, and I could never hide anything from her, either," he lamented.

"I should hope not," Frances retorted.

"No offense, Frances, but I think the person I really need to be talking to about this is my wife."

"Then do it," Frances advised. "Secrets, even the most innocent ones, have a way of destroying a marriage."

"There's never any time to talk things through," Elliott complained. "And this isn't the kind of thing I can just drop on her and walk away."

"Is it the kind of thing that will cause problems if she finds out some other way?"

He nodded reluctantly. "More than likely."

"Then talk to her, young man, before a little problem turns into a big one. Make the time." She gave him a stern look.

"Sooner, rather than later."

He grinned at her fierce expression. No wonder she'd had quite a reputation as a teacher, one that had lived on long after she'd retired. "Yes, ma'am," he said.

She patted his arm. "You're a good man, Elliott Cruz, and I know you love her. Don't give her even the tiniest reason to doubt that."

"I'll do what I can," he assured her.

"Soon?"

"Soon," he promised.

Even if it stirred up a particularly nasty hornet's nest.

When she reached The Corner Spa at the corner of Main and Palmetto, Karen paused. She was beginning to regret that she hadn't followed Dana Sue's advice and taken a slow walk around the park to calm herself down again before arriving here to confront her husband. Even she knew it was probably a terrible idea to do it, not only when he was at work, but when she was still completely furious about being left in the dark. Nothing was likely to be resolved if she started out yelling, which is what seemed likely.

"Karen? Is everything okay?"

She turned at the softly spoken query

from her former neighbor, Frances Wingate, a woman now nearing ninety who still had plenty of spunk, even if her age was slowing her down a bit. Despite her own lousy mood, Karen's expression brightened just seeing the woman who was like a mother to her in so many ways.

"Frances, how are you? And what are you doing here?"

Frances regarded her with a perplexed expression. "I'm taking Elliott's exercise class for seniors. Didn't he tell you?"

Karen heaved a frustrated sigh. "Apparently there's quite a lot my husband hasn't been sharing with me recently."

"Oh, dear, that doesn't sound good," Frances said. "Why don't we go to Wharton's and have a chat? It's been ages since we've had a chance to catch up. Something tells me you'd be much better off talking to me than going inside to see Elliott when you're obviously upset."

Knowing that Frances was absolutely right, Karen gave her a grateful look. "Do you have the time?"

"For you I can always make time," Frances said, linking her arm through Karen's. "Now, did you drive or shall we walk?"

"I didn't bring my car," Karen told her.

"Then walking it is," Frances said without

a moment's hesitation. "Good thing I wore my favorite sneakers, isn't it?"

Karen glanced down at her bright turquoise shoes and smiled. "Quite a fashion statement," she teased.

"That's me, all right. The ultimate fashionista of the senior set."

When they reached Wharton's and ordered sweet tea for Frances and a soda for Karen, Frances looked into her eyes. "Okay now, tell me what has you so out of sorts this afternoon and what it has to do with Elliott."

To her dismay, Karen's eyes filled with unexpected tears. "I think my marriage is in real trouble, Frances."

Genuine shock registered on her friend's face. "Nonsense! That man adores you. We chat after class every week, and you and the kids are all he talks about. He's as infatuated now as he was on the day you met. I'm as sure of that as it's possible to be."

"Then why doesn't he tell me anything?" Karen lamented. "I didn't know he was seeing you every week. And earlier I found out that he's planning to open some sort of gym for the men in town. We don't have the money for him to take that kind of risk, even if he has business partners. Why would he take on something like that without even talking it over with me?"

She gave Frances a resigned look. "People warned me about these macho Hispanic men. I know it's a stereotype, but you know what I mean, the ones who just do whatever they want and expect their wives to go along with it. Elliott's father was like that, but I never thought Elliott, of all people, would be. He was such a thoughtful, considerate sweetheart when we were dating."

"Are you so sure he's keeping you in the dark deliberately?" Frances inquired reasonably. "There could be a lot of explanations for why he hasn't mentioned these things. With two children and two jobs, you're both incredibly busy. Your schedules don't always mesh that perfectly, so time together must be at a premium."

"That's true," Karen admitted. She often worked late at night, while he left for the spa early in the morning. They were sometimes like ships passing in the night. Their schedules weren't great for real communication.

"And when you do have time off, what do you do?" Frances persisted.

"We help the kids with their homework or drive them to all these endless activities they're involved in, then fall into bed exhausted."

Frances nodded. "I rest my case. There's not much time in there for the kind of heart-to-heart talks young couples need to have, especially when they're still adjusting to being married."

Karen gave her a wry look. "We've been together awhile, Frances."

"But you've only been married and living together for a couple of years. It took time for your annulment to come through. Dating is very different from being married and establishing a routine. It takes time to get in a rhythm that works, one that gives you the time alone you need to communicate effectively. I imagine Elliott's as anxious for that as you are."

There was something in her voice that gave Karen pause. "Has he said something to you? Please tell me you weren't in on this whole gym project, too. Was I the only person in town he hadn't told?"

"Stop working yourself into a frenzy," Frances said, though her cheeks turned pink as she said it. "Elliott and I did have a chat earlier, but he didn't mention a thing about any gym. Just now was the first I've heard about that. He told me that he's been putting off talking to you about something important because you're both so busy. He never got into the specifics with me."

"I see," Karen said stiffly, not entirely relieved by the explanation or by the idea that more people had been talking behind her back.

"Don't you dare make more of that than is called for," Frances scolded. "I asked him why he was so distracted in class today. He hemmed and hawed and finally admitted he'd been keeping something from you. I told him there was no good excuse for not communicating with a spouse." She gave Karen a pointed look. "Notice I said communicating, not yelling. Real communication involves listening, as well as talking."

Karen smiled weakly, duly chastised. "I hear you. But how on earth do we find the time to really sit down and have those heart-to-heart talks we used to have when we were dating? Right now we need all the hours at work we can get. And even if we could find some time, babysitters are too expensive for our budget."

"Then you'll let me help," Frances said at once, her expression eager. "Since you married and moved to a new home with Elliott, I don't see Daisy and Mack nearly as much as I'd like. They're growing like weeds. Soon I won't even recognize them."

Karen immediately regarded her with guilt. Though she'd taken the kids by often right after she and Elliott had married, the visits to Frances had dwindled as their schedules had grown more complicated. How could she have been so selfish, when she knew how much the older woman enjoyed spending time with Daisy and Mack?

"Oh, Frances, I'm so sorry," she apologized. "I should have brought them by more often."

"Hush now," Frances said, giving her hand a squeeze. "That was not my point. I was about to suggest we work out one evening a week when I'll come over and stay with them, while you and Elliott have a night out. I imagine I can still oversee a little homework and read a bedtime story or two. In fact, I'd love it." She grinned, an impish light in her eyes. "Or you can bring them to my place, if you'd rather have a romantic evening at home. I'm sure I could handle a sleepover now that they're older."

Karen resisted, despite the obvious sincerity of the suggestion. "You are so sweet to offer, but I couldn't possibly impose on you like that. You've already done way more for me than I had any right to expect. When times were tough, you were always there for me."

Frances gave her a chiding look. "I consider you family, and if I can do this for you, it would be my pleasure, so I don't want to hear any of this nonsense that it's too much. If I thought it were, I wouldn't have offered. And if you turn me down, it will only hurt my feelings. You'll be making me feel old and useless."

Karen smiled, thinking that Frances was definitely neither of those things. Chronologically her years had added up, but her spirit was young, she had dozens of friends, and she was still active in the community. She spent a few hours every day making calls to housebound seniors just to chat with them and make sure there was nothing they needed.

She nodded at last. "Okay, if you're sure, then I'll talk it over with Elliott and we'll check with you about setting an evening. We'll give it a test run and see how it goes. I don't want Mack and Daisy to wear you out."

Frances's expression radiated delight. "That's good, then. Now, I should be running along. I'm playing cards tonight at the senior center with Flo Decatur and Liz Johnson and I'll need a nap if I'm to be alert enough to make sure they're not cheating. For otherwise honorable women, they're sneaky when it comes to cards."

Karen laughed as she slid out of the booth and hugged her friend. "Thank you. I really needed this talk even more than I needed to confront my husband."

"Confrontation is all well and good," Frances told her. "But it's best not done in anger." She gave Karen's hand another squeeze. "I'll expect to hear from you in the next few days."

"I'll call. I promise."

"And when you get home tonight, sit down with your husband and talk to him, no matter the hour."

Karen smiled at her. "Yes, ma'am," she replied dutifully.

Frances frowned. "Don't say that just to pacify me, young lady. I expect to hear that the two of you have worked this out."

Clearly satisfied at having the last word, she left.

Karen watched her go, noting that there wasn't a person in Wharton's she didn't speak to or offer a smile on the way.

"She's remarkable," Karen murmured aloud, then sighed. "And wise."

Tonight would be soon enough for that talk she intended to have with Elliott. She would use the extra time to think through the situation, figure out exactly why she was so upset and find a way to discuss it all calmly and rationally over dinner. Frances had been exactly right. Yelling wasn't the mature way to resolve anything.

And unlike the passive woman she'd once been, Karen also knew that the strong, confident woman she'd become wouldn't allow resentment to simmer too long or let the whole incident slide in the interest of keeping peace. She'd deal with this head-on before it destroyed her marriage. At least she'd learned something from her marriage to Ray: what not to do.

Pleased with her plan, she paid for their drinks and headed back to Sullivan's, where Dana Sue and Erik greeted her warily.

"Oh, don't look at me like that," she said. "There are no divorce papers being filed. In fact, I never even saw Elliott."

Erik breathed a visible sigh of relief.

"Where were you, then?" Dana Sue inquired.

"At Wharton's with Frances, the voice of reason," Karen told them.

Dana Sue grinned. "Did she give you one of those sage lectures that makes you feel about two-inches tall? When she was my teacher, she could just look at me with one of those disappointed expressions and practically reduce me to tears. She was the only teacher I ever had who could pull that

Forget I said anything."

"Don't stop now," Elliott said. "Something tells me I'd better hear this."

Cal didn't look one bit happy about being the bearer of bad news. "Apparently Erik mentioned the gym to Karen today. She didn't take it well. He called me to ask if I thought he should give you a heads-up. We agreed he probably should stay out of it, that the damage had been done."

He gave Elliott a concerned look. "I gather you hadn't told her."

"Not a word," Elliott admitted with growing regret. "Just how furious was she?"

"It was bad enough," Cal admitted. "But it got worse. When she found out that Dana Sue knew as well, she stormed out of Sullivan's to head over here. Obviously she wasn't thrilled about being left out of the loop."

Elliott sighed. "So that explains it," he said. "I saw her outside talking to Frances and wondered what she was doing here, but then they left. She never came inside."

Cal grinned. "If I were you, I'd send flowers to Frances. Obviously she managed to do what Erik and Dana Sue couldn't. She calmed Karen down."

"I don't think I'll count on that," Elliott replied. He knew all too well that Karen's

off. It even worked on Helen."

"No way," Erik said, looking impressed. "I didn't think anyone intimidated my wife."

"Frances Wingate did," Dana Sue said. "She had the best-behaved students in the entire school. We didn't turn into full-fledged Sweet Magnolia hellions until later." Her expression suddenly sobered as she turned back to Karen. "So, have you stopped being mad at me and Erik?"

"I was never mad at either of you," she told them. "I knew you were just the messengers."

"And Elliott?" Dana Sue prodded.

"I still have plenty to discuss with my husband," Karen said. "But at least now I think I can do it without throwing pots and pans or those nifty little dumbbells at the spa at him."

"Word has it that Dana Sue was pretty good at turning pots and pans into weapons back in the day," Erik commented, giving Dana Sue a taunting look.

"Only because Ronnie deserved it," Dana Sue retorted, her tone unapologetic. "The man cheated on me. Fortunately he learned his lesson and I haven't needed a cast-iron skillet for anything other than cooking since then."

After a very tense afternoon, Karen suddenly chuckled. Impulsively, she crossed the room and hugged her boss. "Thank you for giving me my perspective back."

"Glad to be of service," Dana Sue said. "Now, if no one has any objections, let's get these dinner preparations underway before our special of the night is grilled-cheese sandwiches."

"On it," Erik said at once. "Thoroughly decadent chocolate mud pie coming up."

"And I'll get started frying chicken," Karen said, thankful that her relief would be here soon. "When Tina gets here, she can take over and I'll finish up salads before I head home."

At least here, she thought as she settled happily into her routine, peace and harmony once again reigned. Something told her, though, that it was just the calm before the storm.

2

Elliott had spotted his wife outside of The Corner Spa talking with Frances. When she hadn't come inside, he'd been surprised, but he'd been so busy with his packed schedule of private clients who were booked well into the evening that he hadn't had time to consider why Karen might have come by, then left without speaking to him.

It was near closing time when Cal Maddox came in to pick up Maddie, who'd stayed late to deal with dreaded end-of-the-month paperwork. On his way to his wife's office, Cal stopped to visit with Elliott.

"How'd things go with Karen earlier?" Cal asked.

Struck by Cal's oddly sympathetic expression and his dire tone, Elliott frowned. "No idea what you're talking about."

Cal immediately looked chagrined. "Oh man, first Erik sticks his foot in it, and now I'm doing the same thing," Cal said. "Sorry.

sweet nature was deceptive. When her temper stirred, it tended to simmer, then reach a boil when he least expected it. "I suspect Frances only delayed the inevitable."

Cal gave him a curious look. "I still can't believe you hadn't mentioned the gym venture to Karen. Is there some reason for that?"

"I haven't had time to get into it with her," Elliott said in frustration. "Apart from the fact that Karen and I barely see each other lately, there were a lot of issues the group of us had to consider. I wanted to be sure it was a go before I broached the subject with her. You know her history, Cal. Money's a big deal to her, and risk scares her to death. I didn't want her to panic for no reason."

"So, you kept quiet to protect her?"

Elliott nodded ruefully. "It made sense to me at the time."

Cal gave him an understanding look. "I get it, but a piece of advice? In this town, it never pays to keep secrets, because if even one other human being knows, sooner or later everyone will know. Remember how it went over with Dana Sue when she discovered Ronnie's plans for the hardware store? Or how well Sarah took it when she figured out that Travis had big plans for a radio station and wanted her to be a part of that? These Sweet Magnolia women like to be in on things from the get-go. They don't like to be blindsided."

"Karen's never really hung out with the Sweet Magnolias," Elliott said, but he understood Cal's point.

"She spends all day with Dana Sue and with Helen's husband," Cal reminded him. "She works out here and sees my wife all the time. Maybe she doesn't go to margarita nights, but trust me, she's a Sweet Magnolia. With women this tight, it's an all-inclusive we're-sticking-together mind-set."

Elliott nodded. "I hear you. I guess I'd better get home and face the music. Something tells me this is going to cause one of those uncomfortable conversations about me following in my father's macho footsteps. I'm afraid my sisters have been a little too chatty about my father's my-way-or-the-highway approach to marriage. Ironically, every one of them married men just like him. I pride myself on not being a thing like my father, but after this little episode, something tells me I'm going to have a tough time selling Karen on that."

laughed. "Good luck."

anks," Elliott said. "I suppose it

wouldn't hurt to double that order of flowers."

When Elliott walked in with a huge bouquet of brightly colored, fragrant lilies, Karen knew someone had filled him in on what had happened earlier at Sullivan's. And they said women were terrible gossips, she thought, with a rueful shake of her head. The men in this town — at least those married to Sweet Magnolias — were thick as thieves, and they all had big mouths. She and Elliott might be on the periphery of that group, but the effect spilled over.

"Who told you?" she inquired, even as she drew in the sweet scent of the flowers, then found an old florist's vase for them. She had quite a few, thanks to Elliott's frequent and thoughtful gifts. She was pretty sure he had the local florist on speed dial. Most of the time, though, flowers weren't meant to get him out of a jam. He was just a considerate guy who excelled at the impulsive, romantic gesture.

He gave her an innocent look. "Told me what?"

"That I flipped out earlier? Did Erik call to warn you before I even got over to the spa?"

"Erik didn't call." He chuckled. "At least

he didn't call me. He called Cal to see if he *should* warn me. They agreed he should stay out of it."

"But then Cal came by to pick up Maddie and filled you in himself," she guessed. "It figures."

"The Serenity grapevine is a miracle," he agreed. "It functions quite nicely even without resorting to modern technology. This may be the only town in the country not addicted to text messaging." He crossed the kitchen to stand close, his hands on her waist, his breath warm against her cheek. "So, exactly how much hot water am I in?" he whispered in her ear.

She wasn't crazy about the amusement threading through his voice, even as he asked what should have been a very serious question.

"Enough," she told him.

Sadly, she wasn't entirely oblivious to his tactic. Elliott could seduce her in less time than it took to call for pizza, which she'd done just before his arrival. He now seemed intent on nuzzling her neck, which was usually just a prelude to more fascinating foreplay. She frowned at him before he succeeded. "You are not going to distract me, p that this minute."

b what?" he inquired, his chocolate

espresso eyes once more filled with an attempt at innocence she wasn't buying. "I'm just saying hello to my beautiful wife after a long day."

"No, you're not," she chided. "You're hoping to coax me out of being mad at you because you know perfectly well if you can manage to get me into bed, I'll completely forget what I'm mad about." She regarded him intently. "Not this time, Elliott. I mean it."

He sighed and backed up a step, obviously disappointed but accepting her decision that seduction was off the table for the moment. "Where are the kids?"

"They're not here to save your hide, either. Your mom is keeping them at her house for enchiladas."

His expression immediately brightened. "Mom made enchiladas? We should go over there."

"Not on your life. She'll save any leftovers for you," Karen said. "You and I are having pizza and salad and a very long talk. Depending on how that goes, we'll decide if you're picking the kids up tonight or staying over there with them."

For the first time, he seemed to really get just how upset she was. An expression of alarm crossed his face.

"Just because I forgot to mention the whole gym thing to you?"

She frowned at his characterization. "You didn't 'forget' to mention anything, Elliott," she said quietly, annoyed by the tears that immediately sprang to her eyes. She turned away, hoping he wouldn't see just how emotional she was. She wanted so badly to remain calm and cool so they could discuss this rationally without her dragging all her baggage into the discussion.

Pretending to focus on the salad dressing she'd been making when he'd arrived, she said, "You deliberately chose not to discuss it with me because you didn't think my opinion mattered or you were afraid I'd try to veto the idea."

"That's not how it was," he protested.

"It's exactly how it was." She turned and faced him. She gave up on fighting the tears and allowed them to flow unchecked. "How are we supposed to make our marriage work, Elliott, if we don't talk about something that's going to change our lives? From what little I know, even I can see that this gym is a big deal. You're obviously right at the center of it. Do you have any idea how much it hurt that so many other people already knew about it and I knew nothing?"

"I'm sorry," he said at once. "I really am.

It's an incredible opportunity, Karen. I'd never be able to do something like this totally on my own. I was trying to work it through in my head, figure out if we could really make it happen."

"And you didn't consider that poor brainless me might have any thoughts about that?"

He looked genuinely shocked by her bitter words. "Don't be crazy, *querida.* You know how much your opinion matters. You're everything to me."

His use of the endearment touched her heart as always. "I thought I was," she said softly, brushing impatiently at the tears she couldn't seem to stop.

"Ah, don't cry," he pleaded, pulling her into his arms. "Please, don't cry. You know it tears me up inside, especially when I'm the one at fault."

After holding herself stiff for a moment, Karen sighed and allowed herself to relax. This caring, adoring side of Elliott was the one she'd fallen in love with. That's why it was all the more shattering when he did something thoughtless like leaving her totally out of the loop on this decision.

"Can I tell you about it now?" he pleaded. "Will you listen and keep an open mind?"

She nodded slowly, not letting go of him.

41

"I can do that." Then she lifted her head and held his gaze. "But this kind of thing can't keep happening, Elliott. When it comes to the big things — or even the littlest ones that affect our family — we decide together. That's what we agreed. Otherwise we're doomed."

"I know you're right. I promise to be more considerate," he assured her. "I thought I was saving you from worrying unnecessarily about something that might not even be feasible. I guess I thought I had more time to work out the details."

She gave him a wry look. "In Serenity?"

He laughed. "Yeah, that's what Cal said. The truth is, though, that we've only been talking about this for a few weeks now. At first it was nothing more than an idea that a couple of the guys tossed out over beers one night after we played basketball. I wasn't even sure it would go anywhere. There was no reason to mention it."

"But it's gone way beyond the talking stages now, hasn't it? And still you said nothing," she said, seeing the excitement in his eyes die and hating that she was putting a damper on his enthusiasm. What else could she do, though? There were serious questions that needed answers.

"I've Tom McDonald's run some numbers. Ronnie Sullivan's looked at a few pieces of property."

"Not with Mary Vaughn, I hope," she said, thinking of how Dana Sue didn't trust her husband anywhere near the Realtor, even now that Mary Vaughn had been happily reunited with her ex-husband and they had a second, late-in-life child together. Mary Vaughn had a bad habit of going after Ronnie whenever she sensed he might be vulnerable. In theory, she'd given up. In practice, who knew?

Elliott smiled at her reaction. "I believe they have been suitably chaperoned on every occasion," he said. "Between a new baby and trying to train Rory Sue to become a Realtor, Mary Vaughn has plenty on her plate these days without going after Ronnie again." He shook his head. "You women have really long memories, don't you?"

"When it comes to the way she pursued him for years, we do," Karen confirmed. "Something for you to remember in case there are any old flames of yours lurking about that you've neglected to mention."

"None," he said swiftly.

She patted his cheek. "Good to know."

Before he could continue to fill her in on the plans for the gym, their pizza arrived from Rosalina's. Karen put her salad on the table, poured a couple of glasses of wine, and then they sat at the kitchen table. After she'd taken her first bite of pizza, she noticed Elliott's gaze on her.

"What?" she asked.

"I know the reason for this intimate little dinner wasn't exactly romantic, but I have to admit, it's very nice to have my wife entirely to myself for a couple of hours with no little potential interruptions underfoot."

She smiled at the heat in his voice and the unmistakable desire in his eyes. He'd always been able to make her feel incredibly special and desirable with exactly that look. Even now she let it get to her and take the edge off her earlier anger.

"Then it's a good thing Frances has offered to give us a night just like this one every week," she told him. "If we can get your mom on board, too, for another night, maybe we'll have the time we need to get ourselves back on track."

"Do you really think we've been that far off track?" Elliott asked, clearly thrown by her choice of words.

"Far enough," she told him candidly, then added, "You know what destroyed my first marriage. Ray got us into terrible debt that I knew nothing about, then bailed on me. He didn't even stick around long enough to help dig us out of financial ruin. That was all on me. All I could think about when I heard about this gym was that the same thing was happening all over again. I know it was irrational, but it was like this terrible flashback and I couldn't help panicking, Elliott."

Though he had every reason to be offended by the unjust comparison, he merely leveled a look into her eyes. "First of all, I will never be irresponsible about our money," he assured her. "And second, no matter how hard things get or how many disagreements we have, I will never bail on you. When I married you, it was forever, *querida*."

Karen heard the sincerity behind the promises, knew that he meant them with all his heart, but history had taught her that even the best intentions weren't always enough. The proof would be in what happened in their relationship from here on out.

Though he'd seen the anger die in Karen's eyes and felt certain the worst was over, Elliott also knew his wife well enough to know that he needed more time to make amends. While she was in the kitchen cleaning up, he made a quick call to his mother.

"*Mamacita,* can you keep Daisy and Mack

with you for the night?" he asked in an undertone.

"Of course," she said at once. "And why are you whispering?"

"I'm not sure how Karen will feel about me farming them out with you."

Immediately on high alert, she said, "Are the two of you fighting about something? I had the sense when she called earlier and asked if I could keep them a few hours longer that she wasn't hoping for a romantic evening with her husband."

Elliott knew better than to drag his mother into the middle of any problems he and Karen might be having. The two women had come to an uneasy truce, and it wouldn't take much for it to be lost. "Will you keep Daisy and Mack, Mama? Please."

Apparently she understood that she would learn no more about his reasons for asking, because she immediately said, "Of course. Shall I see that they get to school in the morning? They have clothes here. Your sister can pick them up and take them. Adelia's children go to the same school."

"If you wouldn't mind, that would be great," he said. "*Gracias,* Mama."

"*Da nada.*" She hesitated only a moment before adding, "And, Elliott, whatever is wrong, make it right."

46

"I intend to," he said at once.

He hung up, then went into the kitchen where he took the dish towel from his wife's hands. "Sit," he said. "I'll finish cleaning up."

She regarded him with amusement. "Let's see now. The trash has been thrown out. The dishes are washed. Just what is it you intend to do?"

"I'll finish drying the dishes," he said at once, backing her up until she was trapped between him and the counter. "And then I plan on having dessert."

"Dessert?" she asked, her eyes widening, her breath hitching. "What exactly do you have in mind? There's no ice cream in the freezer. I checked. You and the kids ate the last of it."

"But you're here," he said. "I can't imagine anything tastier, *querida*."

His softly spoken words lit a fire in her eyes. "Shouldn't you be going to pick up Daisy and Mack?" she asked. "They shouldn't be out too late on a school night."

"They're being safely tucked into bed at my mother's right this minute," he assured her. "And since it seems we're past the point when you intend to banish me to spend the night over there with them, I was hoping we could make the most of having the rest of the night to ourselves." He searched her face. "You have forgiven me, haven't you?"

"Mostly," she conceded.

"But not entirely?"

"I'm going to need proof that you've learned your lesson," she said.

"I doubt I can come up with the proof tonight," he lamented.

"True. Only time will tell."

He ran a finger along her jaw, felt her pulse scramble. "And until then?"

Slowly, her arms circled his neck, and she molded herself to him. The way they fit together was enough to have his blood pounding.

"Until then," she said slowly, her lips touching his, "we can try this whole dessert thing and see how it goes."

He smiled against her lips. "I already know how it's going to go," he told her. "I'm going to make love to my wife until she screams and begs for more."

She leaned back and regarded him with amusement. "I *never* beg."

"Bet I can change that," he said, already dipping his hand inside her panties, watching as her eyes drifted closed and her body responded to his touch.

Even when her breathing turned shallow and her skin glowed with a soft sheen of perspiration, to her credit, she didn't beg.

Instead, she clung to his shoulders, wrapped her legs around his waist and kissed him until he was the one ready to beg for mercy.

As he walked to the bedroom with her in his arms, he thought for the thousandth time how lucky he was to have found her. She was sugar to his spice, sweetness to his passion.

And, then, just when he least expected it, she turned the tables on him, showing him unexpected heat that took his breath away. The give-and-take between them, at least in this area, was the kind that every man dreamed of.

As for the other give-and-take, the kind of communication and sharing that kept a marriage solid, he still had work to do on that, as today had shown. But for this, to keep this woman happy and content in his arms forever, he'd do whatever it took.

Karen still had questions, a lot of them, in fact, but just as she'd noted earlier, Elliott had a way of making her forget everything except the way it felt to be the center of his world.

She'd been terrified of the passion he stirred in her when they'd first met. She

49

hadn't been ready to let herself fall so completely, head-over-heels in love, not when her experience with marriage had been so disastrous. She'd kept Elliott at arm's length, had almost lost him because of it, in fact. In the end, though, it had been Frances who'd made her see that he was her second chance.

She'd had a lot of second chances back then. Helen had negotiated one for her at Sullivan's when Dana Sue had been about to fire her. Helen had also rushed to the rescue when stress had brought Karen close to an emotional breakdown that could have cost her the children. Helen had taken in Daisy and Mack, seen to it that Karen got the support she needed, then reunited them when the time came.

Then, during that terrible time when she'd been at her absolute lowest, she'd met Elliott, a man not only strong, but quietly confident, persistent and with a generous, open heart. While he'd built up her physical strength during workouts at the spa — a gift from Helen, Dana Sue and Maddie — he'd also built up her battered ego whenever she'd let him.

It had been so hard for her back then to trust that what he'd felt for her so quickly could be real. She hadn't trusted her own feelings at all. And when his mother and sisters had objected strenuously to his involvement with a divorced woman, she'd seized it as the perfect excuse to run.

Thank God, he hadn't let her run far. Surprisingly, the love between them had given her the confidence to face down his mother, to win her over and make her, if not a friend, at least an ally.

Now, lying beside him in bed, still warm from their lovemaking, she felt his gaze on her.

"What's on your mind, *querida?*" he asked, studying her intently as his hand rested on the curve of her hip. The touch was gentle, possessive.

"Just thinking about how we got here," she admitted. "How did you know we belonged together?"

He smiled at the question. "The first time I saw you, you stole my heart," he said simply. "You were in my blood."

"Why didn't I know it that first instant, too?" she wondered. It had always bothered her that he'd been so sure, while she'd been so scared.

"You did," he corrected.

"Absolutely not," she argued.

His smile spread. "People only run so hard when they're afraid, *querida*. And they are only afraid of feelings so powerful they can't control them."

She met his gaze, laughing. "Now, you're just being smug."

"No, I am being smart and right," he teased. "Admit it. You were at the very least in lust with me from that first day at the spa. You didn't want to be, but you were."

Still chuckling, she nodded. "Okay, I'm like every other woman in there. Maybe I was just a little in lust." She studied him. "But it was more than that for you, and I still can't figure out why. What did you see in me? I was a wreck back then."

"You were like no wreck I'd ever seen before," he said. "You were beautiful and vulnerable and I wanted to be a part of making you strong again."

She lifted an arm, flexed her biceps, then sighed. "Still not so strong."

He tapped her chest. "It's your heart that's strong again."

"You can say that after the way I freaked out today?"

He smiled. "You stood up to me, didn't you? You said your piece, insisted on answers. You didn't back down."

"Not until you got me into this bed, anyway," she said.

"We're not here just so I can distract you,"

he said. "If you have more questions, I'll answer them until you're satisfied."

She grinned at that. "The questions can wait," she told him. "I'd rather you satisfy me again the way you did a little while ago."

His eyes darkened at once. "With pleasure," he murmured. "Always with pleasure."

3

Frances could not for the life of her recall where she'd left her apartment keys. They weren't on the hook by the kitchen door where she usually left them, or on the counter, none of the obvious places. If she was late getting to the senior center, Flo and Liz were going to worry. She'd always been the most punctual of all of her friends.

She searched high and low, digging in the bottom of her purse, under the sofa cushions, checking in the bathroom, on her dresser. She eventually found them in, of all places, the freezer. She must have put them in there when she'd been getting her lasagna dinner out. Holding the ice-cold keys in her hand, she frowned. Didn't they say that one of the first signs of Alzheimer's was leaving things in odd places? Just the thought was enough to frighten her.

"Stop it this minute," she told herself sternly. "Don't make a mountain out of a molehill. It's not as if you do something crazy like this every day."

She tried to put the entire incident out of her mind, but over cards at the senior center, she mentioned it to Flo and Liz, forcing herself to laugh about her absent-mindedness. To her shock, neither of them seemed to share her amusement. In fact, the look they exchanged was clearly worried.

Liz, who was only a few years younger, reached for her hand. "Frances, I don't want to alarm you, but maybe you should get this checked out."

Frances bristled. "How many times have you forgotten where you put your keys?"

"Plenty," Liz conceded. "But I haven't once found them in the freezer, or anyplace else particularly odd, either."

Frances regarded her oldest and dearest friend with dismay. "What are you trying so hard not to say? This isn't just about the keys, is it?"

"No, it's not," Liz said. "You've said and done a few things lately that haven't made a lot of sense. I've noticed. So has Flo."

Flo nodded.

"And you've been talking about it behind my back?" Frances asked, knowing that her indignation was misplaced. They were her friends. Of course, they'd be concerned. Of course, they'd compare notes, rather than risk offending her by mentioning some incident that might mean nothing.

"Neither of us was sure it amounted to enough to say anything to you," Liz said gently. "We agreed just to keep a closer eye on you. Now that you've noticed yourself that something's not quite right, well, maybe it would be best to see a doctor."

Frances felt as if the bottom of her world had just fallen out. Alzheimer's? Not a one of them had mentioned the word, but it was clearly the elephant in the room. It was the cruelest of all diseases in so many ways. She'd seen it rob friends of their memories and, worse, take them away from their families long before they were physically gone. She'd always thought it heartbreaking.

"Don't panic," Flo said, now holding tightly to Frances's other hand. "We'll go with you to the doctor. And I've been reading up on Alzheimer's on the internet. There are new medicines that can help. That is, if you even have it. Let's not get ahead of ourselves. We're all getting more forgetful every day. Maybe this is nothing more than that."

"Absolutely," Liz said, then gave Frances

a sympathetic look. "Whatever you're dealing with, we're here for you. That's a given, okay? You're not in this alone."

"Will you promise me that whatever the diagnosis, you won't say a word to anyone in my family?" Frances pleaded. "I'll decide when the time is right for that. I don't want them worrying unnecessarily or rushing over to Serenity to have me locked away in a nursing home."

Neither of her friends agreed immediately.

"What?" she demanded. "Have you already spoken to Jennifer or Jeff?"

"Absolutely not," Liz said. "But if I think the time has come that they must know and you haven't told them yourself, I can't promise that I won't. I'll push you to do it first, of course, but I won't allow something terrible to happen to you because of negligence on my part."

Frances turned to Flo. "And you?"

"I'm with Liz on this," she said. "We'll respect your wishes as long as you're doing well and are safe. And it's not just about you, you know. Your daughter, son and grandchildren would want to know if there is a problem. They'll want to have as much time with you as possible."

Frances sighed. They were right, as usual.

"Fair enough," she said reluctantly. "But

we're probably worrying over nothing. Sometimes putting the keys in the freezer is just a sign of having too much on my mind, not a sign that I'm losing it." She thought of her conversations earlier with Elliott and Karen, her deep concern for these two young people who mattered as much to her as her own children. That probably explained it. Her mind had been on their problems, nothing more.

"Of course," Liz agreed as Flo nodded.

"I think I'll head home now," Frances said, suddenly more exhausted than she'd been in ages.

"I'll drive you," Flo said at once.

"I can still walk a few blocks," Frances said irritably. "I'm not likely to get lost in a town I've lived in all my life."

Liz gave her a chiding look. "She's taking me home, too. It's right on our way."

Frances gave Flo an apologetic look. "Sorry for overreacting."

"It's understandable," Flo said. "Any of us would be scared to even consider something like this might be happening to us."

Frances knew that was true. As they'd aged, she and her friends had discussed every illness known to man at one time or another, but it seemed the greatest dread centered on this one.

But while she appreciated their empathy, there was one thing they could never comprehend. It was happening to her, not them. And theorizing was very different from the blind panic that had set in tonight.

It was morning before Elliott finally set aside the time to lay out the detailed plans for the gym for Karen. They'd definitely gotten sidetracked the night before.

He'd called his first two clients to push back their appointments and was in the kitchen making breakfast when Karen wandered in wearing one of his old shirts and nothing else. His mouth went dry at the sight of her. He wondered if she'd always have the power to take his breath away.

She wrapped her arms around him from behind. "Do you know how sexy you are when you're standing in front of a stove?" she asked, resting her cheek against his back.

"You'd be attracted to anyone who fixed you a meal after you've spent your days in the kitchen at Sullivan's," he teased.

"Nope, it's you. You're this gorgeous guy who looks like a cover model with abs of steel and here you are, all bare-chested and wearing one of my aprons. You just can't get much sexier than that." She grinned. "It takes quite a man to go with the ruffles, you know."

He laughed. "One of these days I need to buy one of those manly barbecue aprons," he replied. "If our friends ever catch me looking like this, I'll never hear the end of it. There's fresh orange juice in the refrigerator, by the way."

"You really do pamper me," she said, releasing him. She poured two glasses and set them on the table. "When was the last time we had a quiet breakfast, just the two of us?"

"Before we got married, I think. It's been way too hectic since then."

"How'd you pull it off this morning? You're usually long gone by now."

"I rescheduled a couple of clients."

"Were they furious?"

"No, which was a good lesson for me. I can make more time for us if I put my mind to it."

"So can I," Karen said. "We need to do it more often. It's good for the soul." She poured herself a cup of coffee, took a sip and winced.

"Too strong?" he asked.

She laughed. "You can't help it. I think it's in your genes that coffee's no good unless it makes your hair stand on end. I'll dump in half a carton of milk and it will be fine."

When he'd set their plates of healthy egg-white, veggie omelets and whole-grain toast on the table, he sat down across from her. "Okay, here's the deal on the gym. It'll be a division of The Corner Spa. In addition, there will be six partners, all of us with equal shares."

"Who?" she asked.

"Cal, Ronnie, and Erik, plus Travis and Tom McDonald, and me."

"How much money do you have to put up?"

"We're still finalizing all that, but I'll be making only a minimal financial investment compared to them," he said. "My contribution will be mostly sweat equity. The way I understand it, that's the way it was when Maddie went into partnership with Dana Sue and Helen on the spa. I'll run day-to-day business operations under Maddie's oversight — at least initially — and continue seeing my personal-training clients."

Karen looked surprised. "You're willing to let Maddie boss you around?"

Elliott chuckled. "What do you think she does now?"

"It's not the same. You're an independent contractor, not a spa employee. If you got ticked off at her, you could take your clients to Dexter's. And speaking of those clients, are you just going to abandon them?"

"No, of course not. I'll still do the senior classes at the spa and see my regular clients. I'll just have to lighten the number of hours I spend there, so I can spend the bulk of my time at the gym. And they're talking about hiring someone to be at the gym whenever I'm not, so the place can be open longer hours. It's a win-win, Karen. We stand to make out nicely financially with a share of any profits, plus I'll be able to handle more clients since I can work with men there and still keep the women clients I have at the spa."

"So, there's no real financial risk at all," she concluded, looking relieved.

Elliott knew he could let her go on thinking like that, and, in his mind, it was mostly true, but after what had already happened, he knew he couldn't let the comment pass.

"I do have to put up some money," he reminded her. "An initial, short-term investment to get things off the ground."

She frowned. "So there *is* a risk?"

"Come on. You know none of us would be doing this if we thought it was risky, but sure, any new business can face unexpected pitfalls."

"How much money, Elliott?"

"We're still working that out."

She held his gaze. "How much?" she repeated, obviously sensing that he was being deliberately evasive.

"Ten thousand, maybe fifteen," he said eventually, then watched as alarm registered in her eyes.

"Our savings for the baby?" she asked, her voice shaking. "All of it?"

"I know to you it sounds like a lot."

"It *is* a lot. It's all we have."

"But the payoff," he began, only to have her cut him off.

"*If* there is a payoff," she said direly. "What if there isn't?"

Elliott felt his temper begin to fray. "Do you have no faith in me? You're my wife. Shouldn't you believe in me at least as much as Cal, Ronnie, Erik and the others do?"

"It's not a matter of not believing in you," she insisted. "It's our savings, Elliott. What about having a baby? I thought that mattered to you."

"We'll still have a baby, and we'll have more money than ever to support it," he insisted.

"Only if this works out the way you envi-

63

sion it," she said, looking as if she were near tears.

"It's going to work out," he insisted. "Have a little faith."

"I want to," she said, her expression miserable.

"Just think about it," he pleaded. "Talk to Maddie or Dana Sue. Ask Erik. You trust him, right? They all have confidence in this."

"I suppose I could do that much," she conceded with obvious reluctance. The wheels in her mind were clearly still turning. "What if it goes belly-up, Elliott? Are you protected then?"

"I'll have to check with Helen, but I think so."

"Make sure of it, Elliott. What if there's some humongous lawsuit or something?"

"We'll have liability insurance," he assured her. "Stop worrying. Helen will protect us. You can count on that."

"You know I'd trust her with my life," she said. "After all, she took in my kids when I couldn't take care of them a few years ago. There's nobody I trust more."

"Then hash all of this out with her. If you're not reassured that it's all good, we'll keep discussing it until you are. I don't want you panicking, Karen. But you also need to understand that this is our big chance to get ahead."

"I get that," she said, sounding resigned but not yet convinced.

He searched her faced. "You and me, we're okay?"

She met his gaze. "We're okay," she said, though slowly.

"You don't sound very convincing. What's that about?"

"The issue is bigger than the gym, Elliott. We haven't been communicating, not the way real partners should. And I know you try, but I don't think you really understand how panicked I get about money."

"Didn't I just say that I get it?" he asked in frustration.

"But then you ignore it," she argued. "Promise me when it comes to things that are important, we'll do a better job of communicating."

"We were communicating very well through most of the night," he replied, trying to spark a smile.

"That's not what I mean, and you know it. You never told me you were seeing Frances at those classes for seniors. You know how much she matters to me. It just makes me wonder how many other things you've kept from me. Your father —"

"My father has nothing to do with this,"

he said curtly, bristling at the unfair comparison. "As for me keeping anything from you, that's a bit of an overstatement, don't you think? We hardly ever spend any time together. Sometimes days go by before we have a real conversation. By then, I've forgotten things I meant to tell you. Don't make a big deal out of it."

She looked so hurt by his dismissive tone that he relented at once. And deep down he understood her point. "I'll try to do better," he promised. "I know that communication is almost as touchy a subject with you as finances. I shouldn't have kept the whole gym thing from you, even to protect you from worry. And, believe me, I do get the money thing. I may not have lived through anything so drastic, but I saw for myself the toll it took on you."

"Thank you. And, as I told you last night, Frances has promised to help us find more alone time. If we can manage these breakfasts occasionally, too, maybe things will get better."

"Of course they will," he said. He would see to it, because no one had ever mattered more to him than this woman who'd been through such terrible times when they'd met and now had blossomed into a formidable companion, lover and wife. She was his

66

heart, and he'd do whatever it took to see that she always knew that. If only he could be sure it would ever be enough.

When Karen arrived at Sullivan's, she found Dana Sue in a frenzy.

"What's going on?" she asked at once. "Where's Erik?"

"Sara Beth's sick and Helen's in court, so he has to stay home with Sara Beth," she answered from inside their walk-in freezer. "I tried to reach Tina to see if she could come in early, because he's taught her most of the dessert recipes by now, but she's not available until this afternoon."

She walked back into the kitchen, her cheeks pink from the icy freezer. "Can you believe there's not even a stupid pie left in there? I guess we're just going to have ice cream on the menu, at least for lunch."

"What about brownies?" Karen asked. "Those are easy enough. You used to make them all the time until Erik got all territorial about desserts. If you can make those, I'll get started on the specials. We'll keep them simple for lunch. How about those ham-and-cheese panini Annie convinced you to put on the menu? Calling them glorified grilled-cheese sandwiches was pure genius. And maybe the walnut-and-cranberry chicken salad? I made that pot of navy bean soup yesterday, so it's all set to go."

Dana Sue sighed, her relief evident. "Thank you for bringing me back down to earth. I have no idea why I panicked there for a minute."

"Because you're addicted to that schedule you keep posted on your office wall," Karen teased. "Deviations make you a little crazy."

"Are you suggesting I'm a control freak?" Dana Sue asked, though her eyes were twinkling.

"I know you are," Karen replied, just as Ronnie walked into the kitchen.

"I hear there's a crisis," he said, pausing to give his wife a thorough kiss. "You don't look as crazed as you sounded on the phone. Are things better?"

"Definitely better," Dana Sue said, "but it was Karen, not you, who made me sane."

"Then you don't need me to pitch in, after all?" Ronnie asked, looking relieved.

Dana Sue grinned. "Given that we don't serve pancakes at Sullivan's except for Sunday brunch and they're your only specialty, I have no idea why I called you in the first place."

"Because just the sight of me calms you down," he suggested.

Dana Sue laughed. "Yes, I'm sure that's it."

"I could go over and sit with Sara Beth, if you really need Erik in here," he offered. "I've got help at the hardware store till mid-afternoon."

"No, we're going to be fine. Karen came up with a plan."

"Then I'll go back and run my own business," he said, winking at Karen. "Call if you sense she's falling apart again."

After he'd gone, Karen regarded Dana Sue with envy. "I love that he was willing to drop everything to run to your rescue."

"Elliott would do the same for you," Dana Sue insisted as she began to assemble the ingredients for the brownies. "How'd things go last night, by the way? Did you two work out your differences about the gym?"

"I'm not entirely reassured that we're not getting in over our heads financially," Karen said. "We're not in the same place the rest of you are, so to me his share of the initial investment seems huge. When I said that, though, he got all defensive and implied I don't have any faith in him." She regarded Dana Sue in frustration. "It's not that at all."

"No, it's your past history talking," Dana Sue said. "I'm sure he gets that."

"He says he does," she said, then shrugged. "We'll see. And I'm still not crazy about him not talking to me about it. He knows that, though, so I guess we'll have to see if he leaves me out of the loop again."

"I doubt he did it intentionally," Dana Sue said. "Men just don't think like we do. They like to work out all the details, consider all the angles, anticipate our objections, then present us with what they consider to be a foolproof fait accompli."

"Are you okay with that?" Karen asked.

Dana Sue laughed. "Hardly. Control freak, remember? Only Helen has me beat on that front. And maybe Maddie."

"But you and Ronnie found a way to work through that, right?"

"Ronnie and I have been together — and apart — and together again for a lot of years now. It has not been all smooth sailing, Karen. You know that."

She paused while stirring the brownie batter, her expression sad. "When I found out about him cheating on me, even though he swore it was only once and a moment of total stupidity, I hated him. I didn't trust him from here to the corner. I wanted him gone, and Helen, bless her heart, saw to it that he went. In retrospect that might not have been the best thing, especially for Annie."

She shrugged. "But we found our way back to each other in the end. I knew when we were kids that he was the guy for me and even when I was the most furious, a part of me couldn't stop loving him. I guess that's what people mean when they talk about soul mates. Nothing really tears them apart, at least not for long."

Karen nodded. "Is it possible to find your soul mate the second time around? I sure didn't find him in Ray."

"I think we all saw something special between you and Elliott right from the beginning," Dana Sue said. "So, yeah, if I had to guess, I'd say he's your soul mate. Doesn't mean he's perfect." She gave Karen a pointed look. "Or that you are."

Karen laughed. "Believe me, I get that. You know what's amazing, though? Elliott seems to think I am."

"Oh, boy!" Dana Sue said, laughing. "Then the man is definitely a keeper. Cut him all kinds of slack, you hear me."

Karen heard what she was saying. She even knew Dana Sue was probably right. But she also knew if Elliott continued to leave her out of the important decision-making, especially if there were financial

71

consequences involved, there was no way she'd be able to let it slide.

Elliott finished up with his last client of the day in late afternoon. He was anxious to pick the kids up from his mother's, where they went after school, get them home and fed and then hang out and maybe have a nightcap with his wife. He already knew about the crisis at Sullivan's, knew she'd be running late and would need something to unwind. After last night and their talk this morning, he'd resolved that instead of crashing as usual, he'd be there for her at the end of a long day. It was one more attempt to fix what was wrong between them.

When he arrived at his mother's, though, he found his older sister sitting on the front stoop, her expression despondent as the kids — hers and his — ran around in the yard.

"Everything okay?" he asked Adelia, trying to gauge her mood.

"Fine."

"Where's Mama?"

"She went out, thank goodness. She was asking too many questions." She said it with a pointed look at him.

"Ah, so no one's supposed to notice that you look as if you just lost your best friend?" he suggested.

"Exactly."

"That might go better for you if you managed to put a smile on your face," he said lightly.

"Bite me," she retorted. "Now that you're here, I'll take my kids and go."

Frowning, he reached out and caught her hand. "Adelia, what's wrong? Seriously."

"Everything," she retorted bitterly. "Seriously."

Before he could pursue that, though, she called out to her children, loaded them into the car and drove away. Elliott stared after her. It wasn't like Adelia to bite his head off. His other sisters might be moody from time to time, downright impossible at times, but Adelia had always had it together. She'd married Ernesto Hernandez right out of college, had their first child seven months later. The other three had come with barely ten months between them. He'd expected her to be worn out, but she seemed to glow with motherhood, at least until recently. Now she was starting to look every one of her forty-two years.

"Are we going home now?" Mack asked, sitting down beside him and interrupting his thoughts.

"We arc," Elliott said, getting to his feet, scooping up the seven-year-old and tossing him in the air until he giggled.

"Me, too," Daisy pleaded, looking up at him with eyes as big as saucers and so much like her mother's that it made him smile.

He grinned at her. "Young ladies don't get tossed in the air," he teased. "They're sedate and quiet."

"Not me," she said impudently. "I'm going to be just like Selena."

The reference to his oldest niece had him shuddering just a little. Selena, at twelve, was not only a tomboy on the verge of adolescence, but already showing a wild streak that was going to keep Adelia and Ernesto on their toes for some time to come.

"No," he corrected. "You are going to be Daisy, your own unique, special person, little one. You do not need to copy anyone else."

"But Selena's really awesome," Daisy protested. "She's already got her first bra."

Elliott might be able to handle the self-described cougars at the spa and their outrageous comments in relative stride, but he was pretty sure Daisy's outspoken ways were going to be the death of him. "It'll be a few years before you need to be thinking about bras, young lady."

"But Selena says boys only like girls with big boobs," she parroted, then regarded him

74

with a perplexed expression. "What's that mean, Elliott? Do you think she's right?"

"It means Selena needs to get her priorities straight," he said, resolving to mention just that to his sister. At the very least his niece needed to be more discreet in her conversations with Daisy, who was only nine, for heaven's sake. She ought to be thinking about dolls, not boys and bras. He had a feeling that was only wishful thinking, unfortunately.

"Can we drive out to McDonald's again tonight?" Mack pleaded, always eager to head for the fast-food place that had sprung up in the next town a few years back.

Elliott winced. He'd gotten into the bad habit of taking the kids there because it was easier than making a meal they both liked, even though he knew Karen hated them having fast food. It went against his code, as well, but sometimes best intentions got lost to expediency.

"Not tonight, buddy. We're having spaghetti and salad."

"But I hate salad," Mack whined.

"And spaghetti will make me fat," Daisy said. "Selena said so."

"Selena doesn't know what she's talking about," Elliott said. "And you'll like this salad, Mack. Your mom made it."

Mack still didn't look impressed, but he didn't argue. And once they were home, he ate both the salad and the spaghetti as if he were starving. Daisy picked at both.

"May I be excused?" she asked eventually. "I have homework."

"You can be excused, when you've finished your dinner," Elliott said firmly.

"But —"

"You know the rules," he said. "Mack, do you have homework?"

"Just spelling and math. I did it at Grandma Cruz's house."

Elliott had his doubts. "Could I see it, please?"

To his surprise, the math problems were completed and correct. He ran through the spelling words with Mack, who got every one of them right.

"Those were easy," Daisy said snidely.

"Were not," Mack said, clearly ready for a fight.

"Enough," Elliott said, interceding. "Mack, go grab a shower and then you can watch TV for an hour before bed." He looked at Daisy's plate, then nodded. "Good job. Finish your homework and then you can take your bath and head for bed."

"I want to wait up for Mom," she protested.

"We'll see," Elliott told her. "Now, scoot."

Only after they were both gone did he breathe a sigh of relief. He'd adored Daisy and Mack from the moment he'd gotten involved with Karen, but being a stepfather was still a challenge. Their personalities had already been well-formed when he'd come into their lives, and he still wavered between stern disciplinarian and outsider.

He'd mentioned adopting them early on, but Karen had seemed oddly resistant to the idea, so he'd let it go. He supposed it didn't really matter, as long as both children knew he loved them as if they were his own. And after some initial hesitation, his mother had welcomed them into her life as full-fledged grandchildren to be enveloped in hugs and fed an endless supply of chocolate chip cookies. His nieces and nephews treated them as cousins. It sometimes seemed he was the only one who felt uncertain about his role in their lives.

Just when he was starting to fret about that yet again, Daisy emerged from her room, walked into the kitchen and threw her arms around him in the kind of impulsive gesture that was increasingly rare now that she was growing up.

"I love you," she whispered against his chest. "I wish you were my dad."

Holding her close, Elliott felt his eyes sting with tears. "I am your dad in every way that matters, little one. You can always count on me."

She gazed up at him with those big eyes of hers. "Will you come to the father-daughter dance at school with me? I wasn't going to go, because I don't even know where my dad is, but if you'd come, it would be okay."

He saw the surprising hint of fear in her eyes and knew she'd wondered if she was overstepping somehow, yet more evidence that even after all this time, their roles weren't so clearly defined.

"I'd be honored," he assured her, deeply touched by the invitation.

"Do you think it will be okay with Mom?"

The question gave him pause. He could only assume Karen would be fine with it. Surely she wouldn't want Daisy to feel left out on such an important occasion.

"I'll talk it over with her," he promised. "When is this dance?"

"Next Friday," Daisy told him. "I have to get a ticket tomorrow."

"How much do you need?"

"Just ten dollars."

Elliott gave her the money, then promised, "I'll speak to your mother tonight." He studied her expression. "Is that why you wanted to wait up? Did you want to speak to her about this first?"

She nodded. "Sometime she gets sad when I ask about things like this, like she feels bad that she's disappointed me." She regarded him earnestly. "But she didn't. It's not her fault Daddy went away. And besides, she found you."

"The next best thing, huh?" he said, a wry note in his voice she probably didn't understand.

"Not the *next* best," she replied, then added adamantly, "The *very* best."

And with that, Daisy captured yet another piece of his heart forever.

4

Despite his best intentions, Elliott fell asleep on the sofa before Karen got home from work. In the morning, both he and Karen overslept, and in the ensuing rush to get Daisy and Mack off to school, he never did have a chance to talk to her about Daisy's school dance. After that, it slipped his mind.

It was two days later, again over a rushed breakfast, when Daisy was the one who mentioned it to her mother.

"I'm going to need a new dress for the dance, Mom," she said.

Karen regarded her with a perplexed expression. "What dance?"

"The father-daughter dance next Friday." Daisy turned an accusing look on Elliott. "Didn't you tell her?"

"Sorry. I forgot," he admitted, chagrined by the omission. "Your mom and I will talk about it after I drop you and Mack off at school, okay?"

Daisy gave him a panicked look. "But we're going, right? You promised. I already bought the ticket."

"We're going," he assured her, avoiding Karen's gaze as he said it.

As soon as he'd driven the kids to school, he returned home to find Karen waiting for him at the kitchen table, a cup of coffee in hand and a frown on her face. It was obvious she was ticked off . . . again.

"Please don't make too much of this," he said. "Daisy told me about the dance a couple of nights ago. She was so afraid she wouldn't be able to go, but I said I'd take her. We both intended to discuss it with you first, but I fell asleep. You didn't wake me when you came in and I just forgot."

She sighed. "I see."

It was evident she was still upset. What he couldn't be sure about was why. Was it the fact he hadn't discussed it with her or because he was overstepping by agreeing to go? Too many conversations these days seemed to be minefields for which he held no map.

"Okay, Karen, I can tell you're not happy about this," he began. "Does it bother you that I agreed to go to a father-daughter dance with Daisy? Was I out of line to agree?"

She shook her head at once. "Of course not. What bothers me, once again, is that you didn't mention it to me."

"I just explained what happened."

"And I understand how easy it is for things like this to slip through the cracks," she admitted. "I really do. I don't know why I let it make me so crazy. It's a dance, for goodness' sakes. And I can see how badly she wants to go. Elliott, I'm sorry for turning it into some kind of issue. I really am."

He watched her closely and, despite the careful words, realized that there was more going on. It finally dawned on him what it was. "This dance involves buying a fancy dress," he said with sudden understanding. "A dress that's not really in our budget."

She nodded. "That's definitely part of it. I know the whole money thing worries me way too much, Elliott. You're nothing like Ray. We've even been able to save for a baby, but the dress on top of the whole gym thing? It's like the straw that broke the camel's back. I guess it's just a knee-jerk reaction, but I don't know how to respond any differently when these unexpected expenses come up. Panic just crawls up the back of my throat and I can't seem to stop it."

Though money had never been plentiful in his own family, Elliott and his sisters had never wanted for anything. It was harder for him to grasp just how terrible things had been for Karen, especially after Ray had walked out on her. She'd been in danger of being evicted from her apartment more than once, in danger of being fired from Sullivan's because she'd had to bail on her job too frequently due to crises with the kids that she'd been left alone to handle. Because of the debt Ray had left behind, she'd teetered at the edge of bankruptcy. It had taken all of her emotional resources and her energy to avoid it.

When they'd married, she'd insisted they plan their combined budget down to the penny and obsessed over every expense that had exceeded their projections. He understood her need to feel in control, but he also understood that with kids they needed wiggle room for things like this dance.

"We have a contingency fund," he reminded her.

"For emergencies, not a dress."

"For Daisy this amounts to an emergency," he said reasonably. "Going to this dance really matters to her. It's not about a party. It's about having a dad."

Karen met his gaze, looking chagrined. "I know you're right."

He was struck by a compromise. "Why

don't I ask Adelia if Selena has some party dresses she's outgrown?" he suggested. "That child has a wardrobe fit for a princess. Since Daisy idolizes her, maybe she won't feel as if she's being given a hand-me-down dress. What do you think?"

Karen's expression immediately brightened. "That's perfect."

"You don't think Daisy will be disappointed about not going to shop for a dress with you?" he asked.

"Maybe a little," she admitted. "And so will I, but this is the way it needs to be. Check with Adelia and see what she says."

"Will do," he promised, dropping a kiss onto her forehead. "One more crisis averted."

"Do you think there will ever be a day when there isn't one?" she inquired plaintively.

"With two kids and the hope for more, it's not likely," he told her candidly. "But life is unpredictable. That's what keeps it interesting."

She laughed. "Sometimes I'd like things to be a little less interesting."

"Why don't we talk about that over dinner tomorrow? Something simple that won't break the bank," he suggested impulsively. "I can give Frances a call, see if she's available. How about you? Are you off?"

She nodded. "As far as I know."

"Then it's a plan," he said. "Love you."

She smiled as he kissed her. "Love you, too."

He was counting on that love to help them weather these rough patches. Big or small, it didn't seem to matter, because each one was a test, and he intended to see to it that they passed. Anything less was unacceptable.

Frances had been delighted when Elliott had called to ask her to sit with Daisy and Mack. These days any distraction was a good one. She hadn't been able to push the whole conversation with Liz and Flo out of her mind for long. She had, however, successfully avoided making that call for an appointment with her doctor. Each time one of them reminded her of her promise, she brushed them off. She was feeling just fine now, and there hadn't been any more disturbing incidents. She convinced herself they were all worrying over nothing.

She did, however, ask Elliott to pick her up. "I don't much like driving at night anymore," she confessed. Left unsaid was the fact that she found the new suburban neighborhood just outside of Serenity where they'd bought their small home confusing with its many cul-de-sacs. It was difficult enough to navigate in the daytime. At night, for anyone unfamiliar with the street names, it was impossible.

She was ready for him when he arrived, a box of freshly baked cookies in her hands. Elliott smiled when he saw them.

"You do know their mother's a chef, don't you?" he teased.

"And when was the last time she had the time to bake cookies at home?" Frances replied. "I know your mother probably has a batch ready for them after school, but Daisy and Mack love my oatmeal-raisin cookies."

"So do I," Elliott said, giving her a wink. "Last time you sent them over, I gained two pounds."

She gave him a wry look. "Two pounds? Lucky you. I usually gain five if I don't ration them out."

"The kids are really looking forward to seeing you tonight," he told her. "And Karen and I are incredibly grateful that you're willing to sit with them for a couple of hours."

"It's my pleasure," she assured him. "I miss them. Just be sure to fill me in on the rules, so I don't let them get away with any mischief. I haven't forgotten how sneaky children that age can be. They tend to torment substitute teachers and babysitters by trying to stretch the boundaries."

"As if you're ever likely to let them get away with that," he teased. "I know your reputation. You're probably a better disciplinarian than either one of us."

"That was a long time ago. I'm a softie now," she said. "Especially when it comes to those two." She sighed. "They're getting so big. I remember when Karen first moved in across the hall. They were little more than babies. Times were so tough for her then."

"And you were a godsend," he said. "I'm not sure how she would have managed without you. Seems to me, you're rushing back to our rescue now."

Frances regarded him curiously. "Are things still not quite right, then?"

"Mostly they're fine," he said at once. "We're adjusting, that's all."

"You do realize that's what marriage takes, don't you? You have to constantly adjust as your family grows and priorities change. Being rigid can be the kiss of death."

"I wish Karen understood that," he said. "I understand why she feels the need to keep such a tight rein on expenses and such. I don't even disagree. I just see her worrying herself sick over every dime, and I don't know how to reassure her that we're in good shape. She sees the bank statements and writes the checks, same as I do, so she knows that."

"Knowing it intellectually and coming from the emotional place she's been are two different things," Frances reminded him. "Cut her a little slack. Every month that the bills are paid and you're all fed and happy will reassure her. The fact that you understand why she worries will help you keep this in perspective. It would be a shame if her past caused problems for you in the present."

"I won't let that happen," Elliott vowed as he pulled into the driveway.

Frances reached over and touched his arm. "I'm counting on you to make her happy, Elliott. She took a huge leap of faith when she allowed herself to fall in love with you."

He nodded. "I know that, and I intend to do my best never to let either of you down."

"Just for that, I'll see that the kids leave at least a few of these cookies for you," she promised.

Karen stood in the doorway as she and Elliott were about to leave for their midweek date, her gaze on Frances, who was on the sofa with Daisy on one side and Mack on the other. As they munched on cookies, they vied for a chance to fill her in on their lives, their words tumbling over each other as Frances chuckled.

"Look how much they adore her," she whispered to Elliott. "They're so lucky to have her in their lives."

"I think she counts herself as the lucky one," he said. "It's such a shame that her grandchildren don't get here to visit very often. She was meant to be surrounded by kids. Her students used to fill that void, but she's been retired a long time now."

As they drove into town for a casual dinner at Rosalina's, Karen voiced the concern that she'd kept to herself for a while now. "How much longer do you suppose we'll have her?"

"There's no way of predicting such a thing," Elliott said. "We just have to be grateful for every minute we do have."

"I think she's slowing down, though. I never noticed it before, but tonight she just seemed a little tentative to me."

Elliott frowned. "Tentative, how?"

"I'm not sure I can explain it. Even though she's been to the house before, she seemed a little uncertain about where things were. Didn't you notice that? And just having you pick her up was a change. Usually she drives herself everywhere."

"She told me she doesn't like driving after dark anymore. A lot of people her age have vision problems at night. The streetlights and headlights bother them. And let's face it, our neighborhood isn't the easiest to navigate."

"I suppose that's all it is," Karen said, then regarded him with a grin. "Enough doom and gloom and trying to anticipate something that's in God's hands. You and I are actually having a date night. How amazing is that?"

He gave her a slow once-over that had her blood stirring. "A date night, huh? Does that mean we get to park and make out before I take you home?"

She grinned at him. "Depends on how good this date is," she said. "Do you still remember how to woo me?"

He winked. "I'll definitely give it my best shot, especially with that payoff you hinted could be mine." He reached for her hand, brought it to his lips even as he kept his eyes squarely on the road. After the kiss, he rested her hand on his thigh, covered by his hand. She felt the involuntary bunching of his muscle, the heat of his skin. It made her feel not only very feminine but powerful, knowing the effect she had on him.

After Elliott pulled into a parking space and cut the engine, he turned to her. His expression stern, he said, "Remember, no trying to figure out the secret ingredients or trying to sneak a peek into the kitchen. This is a date, not an undercover op to check out the competition."

Karen chuckled. "I figured out all of Rosalina's secret ingredients years ago. I don't do any culinary spying here. I can just relax and enjoy my meal."

"Ah, so it's only in the restaurants in Charleston and Columbia I have to worry about what you're up to when you claim to be going to the restroom," he teased. "And whether you're more interested in the food than in me."

"I will always be more interested in you than anything," she assured him, then added thoughtfully, "Unless somebody happens to have the perfect chocolate soufflé on the menu. I'd love to get a handle on that one."

"Don't let Erik ever hear you suggest that his isn't perfect," Elliott warned. "The man's pastry skills are supposedly legendary, at least around South Carolina."

"Pies, cakes, cobblers, I'll give him all of those," Karen said. "But making a soufflé is an art. And if you'll think about it, Sullivan's doesn't have it on the menu, not ever. It's because Erik knows his isn't perfection. I'd love to surpass his skill at just one thing someday."

"Google it," Elliott suggested. "Find the finest chocolate soufflé maker in the state, and I'll take you there."

She regarded him with amazement. "You would, wouldn't you?"

"If it would make you happy, anything," he said. "Don't you know that by now?"

She smiled. Mostly she did, but it didn't hurt being reminded of it every now and then.

Date night was a huge success all around. Karen felt revived after an entire evening with her husband with no crises. The kids pleaded with Frances to spend the night, so Karen found her a nightgown and settled her into the guest room. Frances promised to make them all French toast for breakfast, before sending everyone off on their busy days.

When Karen crawled out of bed in the morning, she found Frances in the kitchen, already dressed. She'd gathered the ingredients for French toast, something she'd made as a regular treat for the kids when they'd lived next door. Now, though, she was just standing there regarding everything with a vaguely perplexed expression.

"Frances?" Karen said softly, trying not to startle her. "Is everything okay?"

Frances jumped slightly, her expression filled with dismay. "Oh, my goodness, dear, you scared me. I didn't hear you come in."

Karen gave her a hug. "You looked a little distracted."

"I suppose my mind wandered there for a minute. I'm perfectly fine."

Though her words were reassuring, something still felt wrong to Karen. Trying to act casual, she slipped past her and started the coffee, then asked, "How about some help? I could whisk the eggs, cinnamon and milk together for you."

Her offer seemed to trigger something for Frances. "Absolutely not," she said briskly. "I've been making French toast for years. I can handle it."

But despite her confident words, she seemed to hesitate as she went to work, her movements deliberate as if she was giving extra thought to what she was doing.

In the end, the French toast was perfect, and the kids gobbled it up with noisy exuberance. Elliott, who normally stuck to healthy egg whites or a high-fiber cereal in the morning, ate his share of the breakfast treat, as well.

As soon as the dishes were in the dishwasher, he offered to drop the kids at school. "Frances, why don't I drop you off, too?"

"I'll take her," Karen said, wanting a little more time to see if she could pin down why things seemed so off with Frances on this visit. "I need my fair share of Frances's attention before we let her get back to her normal routine." She looked at her friend. "Is that okay? Are you in a rush? I'll be ready in a half hour."

"Actually I think I'd better go with Elliott," Frances said, avoiding Karen's gaze. "I have things to do this morning."

Karen saw the lie for exactly what it was, an excuse to evade Karen's questions.

"Sure, if that works better for you," she told the older woman. "Next time maybe you can stay with us for the weekend. We'd all love that, wouldn't we, Daisy and Mack?"

The enthusiastic chorus of responses from the kids brought a smile to Frances's lips. "Then that's exactly what we'll do," she said readily. "Mack, you can teach me how to play that video game you were telling me about. And, Daisy, I'm going to want to hear all about the father-daughter dance

94

you're going to with Elliott."

Elliott urged them all to the door, then cast a last curious look back at Karen. "Everything okay?" he murmured.

"I'm honestly not sure," she said, not even trying to hide her frustration. "You'd better go, though. We'll talk about it later."

He kissed her, his lips lingering against hers. "Great date," he murmured against her mouth, a wicked sparkle in his eyes.

"Coming home was even better," she replied, thinking of how tenderly he'd made love to her before they'd fallen asleep wrapped in each other's arms.

He grinned. "Yeah, it was." He cupped her chin in his hand, held her gaze until heat stirred. "I'll call Adelia today about the dresses, or would you rather do it?"

She gave him a wry look. "Asking your sister for a favor? We're not quite there yet. She still hates me."

"She doesn't hate you," he protested. "She's just overly protective of me. I'll call."

Just then, someone in the car hit the horn to urge him to hurry. Elliott chuckled.

"I'd better go before one of the kids decides they're old enough to take the car for a spin."

"Not to worry. Frances would never allow them to get away with that," Karen said, but even as she spoke the words, she wondered if they were true. She'd seen signs that Frances was changing, and, though she had no idea just what those signs might mean, she suspected it couldn't be anything good.

Elliott called his older sister at midmorning during a break between his spinning class and his jazzercise class. She answered the phone with the same harried, impatient tone she'd had at his mother's a few days earlier.

"Things sound less than cheerful at the Hernandez *casa* this morning," he said lightly. "What's going on, Adelia?"

"Nothing," she said, her tone clipped. "Why are you calling?"

"Actually I need a favor," he said, "for Daisy."

"Of course," she said at once. Though she might not have totally welcomed Karen into the family, she had opened her arms and her heart to Daisy and Mack. "What does she need?"

"You know about the father-daughter dance at the school?"

"It's all Selena's talked about," she said. "She says it's lame, but she's still begged her father to take her. Ernesto's not thrilled, but he's agreed. Now it's up to me to keep

him from backing out at the last minute and disappointing her. Are you taking Daisy?"

"She asked me to," he said.

"I'm so glad. I was afraid she was going to feel left out."

"The thing is, she needs a fancy dress. Our budget's pretty tight these days."

"And Selena has a whole closetful of dresses," Adelia said, immediately understanding. "Why don't I pick out a few and bring them by the spa? She can try them on at home tonight."

"You could just take them over to Mama's if that would be easier," he suggested.

"And have Selena notice and make some thoughtless comment about Daisy getting her hand-me-downs? Bad idea."

"Of course," Elliott said, wishing he'd thought of the potential for hurt feelings. "I'll be here the rest of the day. Drop them by, anytime. You can use the spa while you're here, maybe have a workout."

Silence greeted the offer. "What's that supposed to mean? Are you suggesting I've put on a few pounds?"

Elliott had the sense he'd just inadvertently wandered into another of those minefields the females in his life were known for. "I would never suggest such a thing," he said quickly. "Has Ernesto said somethin

97

to you?" If so, he'd have a little chat with his brother-in-law about showing some respect to his wife. So what if she was carrying a little extra weight from those close-together pregnancies? Those were Ernesto's babies she'd been carrying.

"Ernesto seems to have a lot of opinions lately," Adelia said with rare bitterness. "I've stopped listening."

Now Elliott *knew* he was smack in the middle of the minefield. No matter where he stepped, there was danger. "Want to talk about it?" he asked carefully.

"I do not," she said tersely. "I'll be by later with some dresses."

Taking his cue from her, he let the matter drop. "Thanks."

She hesitated, then said in a quieter tone, "It's sweet, what you're doing for Daisy."

"It's not sweet. I just don't ever want her to miss out on things because her dad's not around," he said.

"And that's sweet," Adelia insisted again. "When are you and Karen going to have a child of your own?"

It was a question she, their sisters and their mother had been asking regularly practically since he and Karen had said, "I do."

"When the time is right for us," he said

he always did. Telling her simply to mind her own business was useless.

At least this answer seemed to silence her, though not for long, he realized, when she asked, "And when will that be?"

"Adelia, as my oldest sister, you will be among the first to know," he assured her. "Right after Mama."

"I want to be first," she teased. "Who taught you everything you know about girls? Who else protected you from the bullies at school?"

"Not you, for sure," he said, laughing. "You were all talk, and almost got me in more trouble than I could handle with that sassy mouth of yours."

She laughed, the first genuinely carefree sound he'd heard since the conversation began. "It made you strong, didn't it? And you were a huge hit with all the girls because I told you what women like."

"I suppose that's one way of looking at it. See you soon."

"Te amo, mi hermano."

"I love you, too."

Even though his sisters had the ability to drive him crazy in less than a heartbeat, he couldn't imagine his life without them. He wanted Karen to benefit from being surrounded by all that love, as well, but it had been slow going so far. Though their open hostility toward her had faded, his sisters' caution was still firmly in place. One of these days he'd have to find a way to bridge that gap.

Karen had her share of friends, counted on them as she would family, but he knew from a lifetime of experience that the support of love and family made all life's problems just a little easier.

5

Elliott walked into the gym at school with Daisy on his arm. Karen had piled her daughter's light brown hair on top of her head in an arrangement of curls. The dress they'd chosen together was pastel pink satin that seemed to bring out the color in her cheeks and made her eyes sparkle. Or perhaps that was the excitement of attending her first real dance.

She stood in the doorway, looking around with an awed expression at the tiny white lights that decorated potted trees, the disco ball hanging from the ceiling that sent out shafts of color as it spun, and the usual colorful streamers that turned a big empty space into something special.

"It's beautiful," she said softly, turning to him with delight shining in her eyes.

"You're beautiful," Elliott told her sincerely. "You look very grown up. I think you may be the prettiest girl in the room."

"Not really," she said, though she looked pleased. "Are Selena and Ernesto here yet?"

"I don't see them," he said, scanning the room, which was already crowded with young girls and their fathers. The excitement was at a fever pitch, as was the noise level.

When the disc jockey began to play a slow song, Elliott looked down into Daisy's hopeful face. "Would you care to dance?"

"Really?" she asked, sounding breathless with anticipation.

"That's why we're here, is it not? I imagine I can still make it around the floor a time or two without stepping on your toes."

He showed her where to put her hands, then counted for her as she awkwardly tried to follow his lead. At the end of the song, she took a deep breath. "I'm glad it's you and not a boy," she said, her expression filled with frustration. "I'm no good at this. I'll never have a date."

"You'll get the hang of it long before you're old enough to go on your first date," he promised just as he spotted Ernesto and Selena coming their way. His brother-in-law looked oddly out of sorts.

"How'd Daisy talk you into being here?" Ernesto asked, his tone sour. "You wouldn't catch me near this place if Adelia hadn't raised a fuss."

Elliott caught the shadow that passed over Selena's face at her father's thoughtless words.

Instead of talking back to her father, though, she whirled on Daisy. "That's my dress!" she announced in a voice loud enough to carry to several nearby girls, who immediately giggled. "Mom must have dug it out of my throw-away pile."

Elliott frowned at his niece. "Selena, enough!" he said sharply since Ernesto seemed to have no interest in correcting his daughter. "You're deliberately trying to embarrass your cousin."

"She's not my *real* cousin," Selena said nastily. "And you're not her *real* dad."

At Selena's cruel words, Daisy looked stunned, then burst into tears and ran from the room. Elliott hesitated only long enough to give Selena a disappointed look. "I thought your mother had raised you to be kinder than that," he said quietly. He held his brother-in-law's gaze. "And you have nothing to say about this kind of behavior?"

Ernesto only shrugged. "What can I say? She's her mother's daughter."

Elliott shook his head, wondering not for the first time what on earth was happening to his sister's marriage. "I'll deal with both of you later."

He took off to find Daisy. She was pushing ineffectively at a locked door at the end of the corridor.

"Niña," he said quietly. "Little one, I'm sorry."

"I want to go home," she pleaded, turning her tear-streaked face toward him.

"And I will take you, if that's what you really want," he told her. "But sometimes when people misbehave as badly as Selena did in there, the best thing to do is hold your chin up high and show people that you're better than that."

"But everybody's laughing at me," Daisy said, her eyes filling once more with tears. She regarded him with bewilderment. "I thought we were friends. Why would she be so mean?"

Elliott wondered about that himself. "I don't know," he said honestly. "But I think perhaps she is very unhappy tonight."

Daisy looked intrigued by his response. "How come?"

"I'm not sure," he said, not wanting to suggest that Ernesto had let her down. "But I think she took her own unhappiness out on you. That was very wrong, but perhaps you will be the bigger person and find it in your heart to try to understand and forgive her."

Daisy seemed to consider his words for a very long time before she met his gaze and asked with a sniff, "Do I have to?"

Elliott had to turn away to hide a smile. "No, little one, you don't have to, but I hope you will. Despite what happened here tonight, we're still family."

She sighed heavily. "Okay, I'll think about it." She met his gaze. "But I still don't want to go back. Please, can we go?"

"Why don't we go to Wharton's for ice cream?" he suggested. "How about that?"

She gave him a wobbly smile. "Ice cream would be good."

On the way to Wharton's, she wiped away the last of her tears and turned to him. "Before Selena said all those things, I had a good time, Elliott. Thank you for taking me."

"Anytime," he assured her. "And I had a good time, too. Next year's father-daughter dance will be better. I promise."

And first thing in the morning, he intended to get to the bottom of whatever had made his niece behave in such an uncharacteristically rotten way. His brother-in-law might be comfortable letting it slide, but he most definitely was not.

"Selena said what to Daisy?" Karen asked, her expression stunned when Elliott described the awful scene at the dance. "Why would Selena do such a thing? Daisy adores her. She must have been crushed."

"At first, yes," he admitted. "But a hot fudge sundae seemed to go a long way toward making her feel better."

"At least this explains why she went straight to her room when you got back here just now and didn't answer when I asked about the dance."

"She felt humiliated, no question about it," he admitted, looking chagrined. "For my niece to do such a thing . . ." He shook his head. "Honestly, though, I'm more worried about Selena right now. Something was not quite right with her tonight. I got the sense that Ernesto had no desire to be there and had made that plain to her. Maybe his insensitivity explains why she was so mean to Daisy."

"That's no excuse," Karen said.

"Of course not," Elliott agreed, for once not taking his family's side. "I think there's a lot more to the story. Adelia hasn't been acting herself lately, either. I'll get to the bottom of all of it tomorrow. And, trust me, Selena will apologize."

"A forced apology won't mean much," Karen said.

"But it is necessary, nonetheless," he said with conviction. "People in this family do not behave in such a way." He gave Karen an apologetic look. "I'm so sorry the night was ruined for Daisy. I wanted so badly for it to be special, a memory she could cherish."

Karen could see how upset he was that a member of his family had caused her distress. "As you said, the sundae went a long way toward fixing things. I'm sure it will all blow over."

He hesitated, then said, "There is one thing Selena said that I think we should discuss, something we could correct."

Karen frowned at that. "Why is it up to us to correct anything that Selena said out of spite?"

"Because we can," he said simply. "She said Daisy wasn't her real cousin and that I wasn't her real dad. We've talked before about me adopting Daisy and Mack, but we haven't made a decision. Maybe it's time we did."

Karen nodded distractedly. The subject of adoption had come up in passing before.

She'd let it slide, though she wasn't entirely sure why. Tonight, though, she simply couldn't focus on such an important topic.

"We'll talk about it," she said, "but not now. I need to check on Daisy."

Elliott's sigh hinted at his exasperation, but she ignored it. Tonight Daisy came first. She was still seething over what had happened. At least this once Elliott hadn't rushed to take his niece's side. Sometimes, she thought, he wore blinders where his family was concerned. There had been a few occasions when Adelia, his other sisters and even his mother had been just as careless of her feelings. Thankfully, though, that was mostly in the past.

As she stood to go to her daughter, she leaned down and kissed him. "Thanks for taking such good care of her."

"It's my job," he said simply.

She found Daisy in bed with the covers pulled up high. The dress, which had been the cause of tonight's incident, was in a heap on the floor.

"You should have hung this up," Karen said lightly, picking it up and putting it on a hanger.

"Why? I'll never wear it again. I don't want it here. Give it back to dumb Selena if she cares about it so much. And I don't want to go to Grandma Cruz's after school anymore, not if Selena is going to be there."

Karen sighed at the stubbornly determined note in Daisy's voice. She sat on the edge of the bed, still holding the dress as she met her daughter's gaze. "We'll discuss where you'll go after school another time. I'd rather focus on what happened tonight. Maybe I can help you to understand it."

"Selena's just selfish, that's all."

Karen shook her head. "You don't mean that."

"Yes, I do."

"You know, don't you, that what Selena said most likely wasn't about the dress at all?"

"What then?"

"Elliott seems to think her dad wasn't very excited about taking her to the dance, not the way Elliott was so happy to be there with you. I suspect Selena was jealous."

Daisy sat up, her eyes wide. That her idol might have been jealous of her clearly intrigued her. "Of me?"

Karen nodded. "You know that Elliott adores you. It made him feel great that you asked him to take you to the dance. Ernesto seemed to think it was a chore or a duty he couldn't get out of. I'm sure that hurt Selena's feelings. Can you understand that?"

Daisy's expression turned thoughtful. It was a lot to ask of a nine-year-old that she try to grasp the impact of an adult's hurtful actions.

"I guess," she said eventually.

"Then maybe you can think about focusing on how lucky you are to have Elliott as a stepdad and consider forgiving her," Karen suggested.

"Maybe," Daisy said grudgingly.

Karen leaned down to hug her. "Just think about it. Good night, angel. I'm sorry your first dance wasn't everything you wanted it to be."

"It started out okay," Daisy admitted. "Elliott was teaching me to dance."

"He's got some very nice moves on a dance floor," Karen said, smiling at the memory of dancing with him at their wedding.

"All the other girls were watching him," Daisy admitted. "I think they all wanted to dance with him."

"I imagine they'll have a lot of questions for you on Monday morning," Karen said. "But you'll have to tell them he's taken, that he belongs to your mom."

Daisy giggled. "Mom!"

"Well, it's true," Karen said.

"I think he's the best stepdad in the whole

world," Daisy said.

"I think so, too," Karen said softly. The very best.

And when she weighed that against the petty annoyances that had come between them lately, there was absolutely no contest. The day she'd found Elliott had been the luckiest of her life. When the going got tough — and there was little doubt that it would again — she needed to remember that.

Elliott usually barely managed to squeeze out a half hour for lunch on Saturdays, but this week he turned his eleven o'clock appointment over to the spa's other personal trainer and headed to his sister's, determined to get to the bottom of whatever was going on in her household these days.

When he drove up to the large home Ernesto had built on a wooded acre of land outside of Serenity, he heard the kids splashing in the pool around back. Normally he would have circled around to greet them, but today his only goal was to get Adelia alone for a heart-to-heart conversation.

Just as he was about to ring the doorbell, the front door was flung open and Ernesto brushed past him, a scowl on his face. From inside the house, he heard Adelia shouting

111

after him not to bother coming home.

Elliott closed his eyes, muttered a prayer for guidance, then walked inside to find his sister alone in the kitchen slamming dishes into the dishwasher, tears streaming down her face. He walked up behind her and put his arms around her.

"Tell me," he commanded.

She turned to him, her expression stricken. Wiping ineffectively at her tears, she tried to force a smile. "I didn't know you were here. How'd you get in?"

"Your husband kindly left the door open as he left," he said wryly. "I heard, Adelia. I heard you tell him not to bother coming home."

She waved off the comment. "People say things like that all the time. I didn't mean it."

"It sounded to me as if you did."

"Oh, what do you know? You're still in the honeymoon phase. What do you know about marital fights?"

He smiled at that. "Karen and I have had our share."

"And gotten past them," she said, her tone brisk. "Ernesto and I will, as well. Now, let me pour you a cup of coffee. I have some of Mama's cookies here, too." She frowned then. "Why aren't you at the spa? I thought

Saturday was one of your busiest days."

"It is, but I thought we needed to talk about what happened last night."

She frowned, looking genuinely mystified. "Last night? Did something happen at the dance? Selena didn't say a word. Neither did Ernesto."

"I'm not surprised," Elliott said. "It wouldn't show either of them in the best light." He described the scene at the dance. "Selena deliberately humiliated Daisy in front of all their classmates."

"I am so sorry," Adelia said at once, her expression heartsick. "I'll deal with this right now. Selena's behavior was totally unacceptable. Poor Daisy. My heart breaks for her."

She was about to call Selena in from the pool, but Elliott stopped her. "I think the more important question may be why she was so upset that she lashed out in the first place."

When she didn't immediately answer, he prodded, "Adelia?"

Adelia sighed heavily. "I suspect you can blame her father for that. Ernesto didn't want to go. Just as I'd feared he might, he invented some sort of important business meeting and intended to bail at the last minute. I stepped in and insisted that he couldn't disappoint his daughter like that. I'm afraid Selena overheard us arguing. She knew her father was ready to choose business over her, that he didn't care if he let her down."

"Has that been happening a lot lately?" he asked, holding her gaze. "The fighting, I mean."

She blinked and looked away. "We'll work things out. We always do," she said, almost by rote. It sounded as if she'd been using the same words to try to convince herself for some time now.

"Have you talked to Mama about whatever's going on?" he pressed.

She gave him an incredulous look. "Are you crazy? And listen to her lectures on how it's all my fault if things aren't a hundred percent rosy in my marriage? You know how Mama is. She believes all husbands should be treated like kings, even if they're acting like asses."

Elliott smiled at her assessment. "True enough," he said. "She was certainly devoted to our father, no matter how unreasonable he was being."

"Trust me, Papa was a bastion of reason and calm compared to Ernesto."

There was a bleak note in her voice that Elliott found worrisome. "Adelia, is he bul-

114

lying you? Abusing you?"

She closed her eyes, her cheeks pink with embarrassment. "Nothing like that. I'd never allow it. For all of my weaknesses, I do have enough pride not to tolerate such disrespect."

"I hope not," he said, still concerned. "I'd straighten him out if he ever raised a hand to you."

Adelia almost smiled at his vow. "I know you would, and I love you for it."

"Would you like me to stay and have a talk with Selena myself?"

She shook her head. "No. I'll handle it. There's no need for you to witness the tantrum she's likely to throw when I tell her she's grounded for the next month."

Elliott was startled by the severity of the punishment his sister intended. "A month?"

She shrugged. "Anything less is just an inconvenience. Believe me, a month is the only thing that gets her attention."

"Maybe what she needs more than punishment is reassurance that her parents are going to work harder to get along," Elliott suggested.

Adelia gave him a sad look. "I try not to make promises I'm not sure I can keep," she said as she walked him to the door.

Elliott wanted to stay, wanted to wipe the

sorrow from his sister's eyes, but he wasn't the one who had the power to do that. And it was increasingly apparent that the man who held that power didn't care.

"Is Frances going to be looking after Daisy and Mack tomorrow night by any chance?" Dana Sue asked Karen on Monday.

Karen regarded her boss with surprise. "I hadn't planned on it. I'm off tomorrow, remember? I'll be home with the kids."

"Let me rephrase," Dana Sue said, sounding more like Helen, when she was cross-examining a reluctant witness. "*Can* Frances take care of the kids tomorrow night?"

Puzzled, Karen shrugged. "I'd have to check with her, but probably. What's this about? Do you need me to work after all?"

"Nope. The guys — except for Erik, who'll be in charge here — are all getting together for basketball and more talk about the gym, so the wives decided we deserve to have a margarita night. It's been ages since we've had one. We want you to come."

"I thought margarita nights were some sort of sacred ritual for the Sweet Magnolias," Karen said. She'd certainly never before been invited.

"And we think you should officially be one of us," Dana Sue said with a grin. "If

Elliott's going to be in business with some of us and our husbands, then you should be included when the girls get together."

"Really?" Karen said, surprised by the hint of wistfulness that had crept into her voice. She'd always wondered about those mysterious nights Dana Sue, Maddie, Helen and their friends spent together. She'd never given two figs about the margaritas, but the strong bond of their friendship was something she'd desperately envied. She'd been on the receiving end of that support system from time to time and understood its value.

"Really," Dana Sue assured her. "And before you get all weird and panicky, there are no secret rites or oaths, other than what happens at margarita nights stays at margarita nights."

Karen grinned. "I can do that."

"Then tomorrow night at seven at my place."

"What can I bring?"

"Not a thing. I fix the guacamole. Helen makes the margaritas, and since they feel that we now need more food to sop up any alcohol, Maddie, Jeanette, Annie, Raylene and Sarah take turns bringing other food. Believe me, Maddie will see that you're assigned your turn. She's going to be thrilled about putting another chef into the rotation. Aside from me, Raylene's the only one with any real creativity in the kitchen."

Karen thought of the progress Raylene had made in overcoming her agoraphobia. There'd been a time not that long ago when all margarita nights had to be held at her house to accommodate her terror of leaving the safety of her own home.

"Raylene's really better now, isn't she?" she asked Dana Sue. "It's hard to believe she's the same person. I see her at her dress shop and out with Carter and his sisters all the time now."

Dana Sue smiled. "Just one of the many miracles we've been blessed by in this town."

Karen started back to work on the salads for the day's lunch, but eventually curiosity got the better of her. She glanced over at Dana Sue. "Why now, Dana Sue? Is it just because you don't want me to feel left out?"

Dana Sue, who could always be counted on for candor, said honestly, "That's part of it, no question about it. But for a long time, your life was so complicated with Helen keeping your kids so you wouldn't lose them and your future working here so insecure, we didn't think it was a good idea to blur the boundaries any more." She smiled. "Just like Raylene, you're not the same person you were a few years ago. We all like you. We always have. Now, though, I think it's more as if we're all meeting on level ground."

"As equals," Karen suggested.

Dana Sue laughed. "That's sounds so incredibly stuffy and narrow-minded of us, but in a way, yes. I'm sorry if that hurts your feelings."

Karen shook her head. "Actually, to the contrary, it makes me proud to know how far I've come in getting my life together. I was a mess a few years ago. And even without me being an official Sweet Magnolia, you all helped me. I'll always be grateful to you for that."

"And now we'll get to find out if you can hold your tequila any better than the rest of us," Dana Sue said.

Karen thought of how little she drank, because she didn't like the lack of control that came with alcohol or the wasted expense of buying it. "Something tells me I'm going to be no competition on that front. I'm a weakling in the margarita department. Will that be a problem?"

"Nope," Dana Sue assured her. "It'll just leave more for us. But if you turn down my killer guacamole, we just might have to reconsider."

"Now *that* will never happen," Karen said, laughing. She hadn't been married to Elliott all this time without learning how to handle plenty of spice.

6

Frances was delighted to be spending the evening with Daisy and Mack. For one thing it was much less stressful than evading questions from Flo and Liz about whether or not she'd made an appointment with her doctor. They were getting tiresome.

Even though she was where she wanted to be — away from the prying eyes of her friends — she was grateful that Daisy and Mack had plenty of homework to keep them occupied. For some reason trying to keep up appearances these days was exhausting. She was relieved to be able to simply sit and glance through the magazines she'd brought along or to watch TV.

She was startled when she glanced up and found Mack standing in front of her, his expression a mix of dismay and embarrassment. She'd seen that look often enough in her classrooms over the years to have a pretty good idea this was about homework troubles.

"Is everything okay, Mack?"

He shrugged.

Frances had to hide a smile. Even at seven, kids had a lot of pride. "How's your homework going?" she prodded. "All finished?"

He shook his head, his cheeks turning even pinker. "I don't get my math problems." He gave her a pleading look. "Could you help me? Subtracting's hard."

Though she was pleased to be asked, she wondered if she'd be any help. "I can certainly try," she said. "And if I can't, I imagine Jenny can."

His expression turned puzzled. "Jenny? Who's that?"

Frances blinked, then shook her head and gave an embarrassed chuckle. "Did I say Jenny? I meant Daisy. Jenny's my granddaughter. She lives in Charleston." Jenny had been named for her mother, Frances's daughter, Jennifer.

Mack's face lit up. "I remember her. She used to come to visit. Sometimes she even spent the weekend."

"She did," Frances confirmed. "What a wonderful memory you have!" At the moment, she envied him.

"She was bigger than Daisy, though," he

said, looking perplexed again. "How old is she?"

Frances felt as if she were slogging through mental mush as she tried to recall. "She must be fifteen now." Or was she older? Had Jenny gone off to college? Or was that Marilou? And why couldn't she keep them straight? There were three girls, she remembered that much. Jennifer had so hoped for a boy that last pregnancy, but there'd been another girl. On the teacher salaries she and her husband earned, they'd decided a fourth child simply wasn't in the cards.

Darn! If she could remember all that, why couldn't she keep the names and ages straight?

The answer, of course, was obvious. This was another of those troubling mental glitches. It was a good thing Flo and Liz weren't around to witness it. Their pleas that she make that doctor appointment would become even more strident.

"Sit beside me and show me those math problems," she said, rather than dwelling on her earlier slip.

Finally confident that he wasn't going to be judged, Mack eagerly crawled up on the sofa beside her and showed her his paper. Thankfully, the problems were fairly basic subtraction, something she *hadn't* forgotten.

Once he'd finished the math to her satisfaction and had shown her his other homework, he ran to get Daisy for the milk and cookies she'd promised them both before bed.

"Have you finished your assignments, Jenny?" she asked as she poured the milk.

"You mean Daisy," Daisy said, regarding her curiously. "Jenny's someone else."

"Her granddaughter," Mack supplied.

"Sorry," Frances apologized. "I don't know where my mind is tonight."

Mack gave her a broad grin. "Maybe me and Daisy should look for it."

"Daisy and I," she corrected automatically, then added, "And I wish you would. Let me know if you find it."

Because it was getting harder and harder to pretend that everything was just fine.

Karen gazed around Dana Sue's living room at the group of women gathered there. She knew them all, but seeing them like this, relaxed and bantering about their lives, their husbands and their work surrounded her with a warmth she'd never experienced before. She had the feeling that these women shared the most intimate details of their lives without fear of judgment.

"Have we scared you off yet?" Maddie

asked, slipping into the space beside her on the sofa. "No topic's sacred when the Sweet Magnolias get together."

Karen laughed. "I can see that. Is it the margaritas, or are you all just so comfortable with each other that anything goes?"

"A little of both, I suspect," Maddie said. "You know Helen, Dana Sue and I have been friends since we were in grade school together about a million years ago. There are very few secrets left among us. Jeanette started joining us after she came to work for us at The Corner Spa. Annie, Sarah and Raylene were all high school friends, but a whole different generation. Helen and I practically helped to raise Annie because she was always underfoot, along with my kids. Now, of course, she's married to my son."

"I think that's what I love the most," Karen admitted, "seeing two generations, especially a mother and daughter, getting along like best friends. I wish I'd had a chance like that with my mother."

"Has she passed on?" Maddie asked, her expression sympathetic.

"Passed out more than likely," Karen said, unable to keep a note of bitterness from her voice. "I accepted a long time ago that we'd never have a good relationship."

"Mother-daughter bonds can be tricky under the best of conditions. Helen and Flo certainly have their moments," she revealed, eyes twinkling. "And my mother —"

"She's the famous local artist — Paula Vreeland, right?" Karen asked, remembering.

"She is, and we've had our ups and downs over the years," Maddie admitted. "But Raylene's the one who had a really difficult relationship with her mother. You should talk to her sometime about how hard it's been for her to make peace with that. The circumstances were different, but clearly both of you have been affected by what happened."

"Maybe I will," Karen said.

Maddie's expression turned more serious. "Have you and Elliott worked out any issues over the new gym? I'm so sorry we inadvertently created tension between you."

"Not your fault," Karen said at once. Because she wasn't quite ready to open up about how terrified she was about his financial commitment, she forced a smile. "We'll figure things out."

"I'm sure you will," Maddie said. "He does adore you, you know."

Karen smiled. "So I hear."

Maddie frowned at her glib choice of

words. "You don't believe it?"

"Of course I do," Karen said a little too quickly. "Every marriage has bumps, right? And the first years are the trickiest."

"No question about it," Maddie confirmed. "Just so you know, we're all glad you're here tonight. If you ever need to talk, we're all good at listening. Sometimes we can even keep our advice to ourselves, if that's what you'd prefer."

Karen looked around, hearing the others all pitching in with opinions about whether it was time for Sarah and Travis to get serious about having a baby. She turned back to Maddie. "Really?" she inquired skeptically.

Maddie laughed. "I promise. It may kill us, but we can do it."

Just then Karen's cell phone rang. She glanced at the caller ID and saw it was coming from home. "I need to take this," she told Maddie.

She slipped out of the room as she answered. "Daisy, is everything okay?"

"I'm not sure, Mom. Can you come home?"

"Of course I can, but what's going on?"

"It's Frances. She's been acting a little weird all night. Confused, kinda."

"Confused in what way?"

"I had to show her where the bathroom is, and she keeps calling me Jenny. That's her granddaughter."

Alarm bells went off, even though the mistaken name might have been an innocent slip of the tongue. Alone it might have meant nothing, but not remembering where the bathroom was in a home she'd visited quite recently was certainly worrisome. In addition, Karen had seen signs that something was off with Frances on her last visit. The combined incidents were definitely troubling.

Besides, if something didn't feel right to Daisy, then Karen needed to get home now.

"I'll be right there," she promised. "I'm sure everything's fine, but I'm glad you called."

"Hurry, Mom. It's kinda freaking Mack and me out."

Karen was about to make her excuses when she suddenly realized that she had no way to get home. Elliott had dropped her off and planned to come back to pick her up after his evening with the guys. A glance at her watch indicated that wouldn't be for another hour at least.

As she walked back into the living room, Dana Sue regarded her worriedly. "Everything okay?"

128

"There could be a problem at home. I need to try to reach Elliott and see if he can come get me."

"Don't bother him," Raylene said at once, already on her feet. "I'm tonight's stone-cold sober designated driver. I'll run you home."

"Are you sure? I'd really appreciate it."

"Not a problem," Raylene said, then turned to the others. "No one budges or says anything scandalous until I'm back, okay?"

"Not a word," Sarah teased. "We'll just talk about you."

Raylene made a gesture indicating what she thought of the teasing.

Once in Raylene's car, Karen could barely concentrate on anything other than the fear in Daisy's voice.

"Want to talk about whatever's going on?" Raylene asked gently.

Karen shook her head. "It's probably nothing. You know how kids' imaginations get the better of them. Daisy was just a little concerned that something might be going on with the babysitter."

Raylene looked startled. "Frances?"

Karen had forgotten for a moment that everyone in Serenity knew everyone's busi-

129

ness, or at least a good chunk of it. She nodded.

"Is she ill?" Raylene asked.

"Daisy seems to think something's just off with her tonight. I figured if my nine-year-old is worried, I should be, too."

"I agree," Raylene said as she turned into the cul-de-sac where Karen lived. "Want me to come in while you check on her, just in case it's anything serious?"

Though Karen wanted to say yes just to have the moral support, she knew it would humiliate Frances if another person showed up and there was no crisis. She shook her head.

"I'll be okay. If there's a real problem, I'll call Elliott. He can be here in a few minutes. Thanks for offering, though."

"Anytime," Raylene said readily. "People were amazing when I was having all my problems with a crazy ex and suffering from agoraphobia. I'm eager to return the favor in whatever way I can."

"Thanks." Karen hesitated, then thought of what Maddie had said about her and Raylene having a few things in common. "Maybe we can grab coffee sometime in the morning before you open up your boutique. Erik makes the best in town, and I can sneak you into the kitchen at Sullivan's. It's

a well-known secret that Annie and a few others slip in there before we open just for his coffee."

Raylene grinned. "I've heard that. Count me in. I'll try to get by one morning later this week."

"Tell everyone I enjoyed tonight. I'm sorry I had to bail so early," she said as she exited the car.

Raylene waved as Karen practically ran to the house. Despite Karen's insistence that she could handle whatever she found inside, Raylene waited in the driveway. That simple gesture of support showed Karen once again the value of having the kind of solid friendships she'd been missing.

Karen had barely entered the house when Daisy materialized. The concern on her face faded at the sight of her mother. Karen gave her a hug.

"Everything okay?"

Daisy nodded, casting a surreptitious glance over her shoulder toward the living room. "She seems fine now. I probably shouldn't have bothered you."

"No, you did exactly the right thing. And it's past your bedtime, so run along. I'll spend some time with Frances and make sure she's okay. Try not to worry."

Despite Karen's reassuring words, Daisy still looked worried. "She's always been like our unofficial grandma, you know. I don't want anything bad to happen to her."

"Neither do I," Karen replied. "We'll try to make sure it doesn't. Now, scoot, sweetie. I'll stop by to tuck you in as soon as I've checked in with Frances."

In the living room, the TV was on, the volume low. Frances's eyes had drifted closed. Karen flipped off the TV, then sat down in a chair across from her. Silently, she studied the face of this woman who'd been like a surrogate mother to her or maybe, given her age, a grandmother. Her own mother might have been a mess, but Frances had been a rock, her support unwavering, even when Karen had thought she was going to completely fall apart and lose everything — her marriage, her home, her job and, worst of all, her children.

Frances looked peaceful as she dozed. Her color was good. Karen tried to reassure herself that a few slips of the tongue might not mean a thing. There might be a reasonable explanation for being slightly confused about her surroundings, as well. She also knew it could all be symptomatic of more, a ministroke, perhaps, or, far worse, Alzheimer's. That would fit with what she'd observed when Frances had tried to make French toast on her last visit.

Please, not that, she prayed silently. Watching this strong, wonderful woman slip away by degrees would break her heart.

Just then Frances's eyes blinked open. For a moment, she looked confused, but then she managed a faint smile. "I must have fallen asleep on the job. I'm so sorry."

"Don't be," Karen said. "Everything's fine."

"How long ago did you get home?"

"Just a few minutes ago."

Frances glanced at her watch. "It's early. I've heard about those margarita nights. They usually go on till all hours."

"Maybe everyone's just getting too old to hang out really late during the work week," Karen said, unwilling to admit she'd left early to check on Frances. "How was everything here?"

"Fine. I helped Mack with his math homework, then we all had milk and cookies and the two of them went off to bed."

"You should have gone into the guest room and gotten some sleep yourself," Karen said, still studying her with concern. "I hope they didn't wear you out."

"Heavens, no. I'm still up to solving a little bit of math, at least for a second grader. I'm not sure I'll be up to it once they start doing algebra. I couldn't do that very well even in my prime."

"Neither could I," Karen said with a laugh. "I sure hope Elliott can."

"Is he home yet? I should probably head home," Frances said.

"I'm not sure when he'll finally wander in. I got a ride home with Raylene. Why don't you stay here tonight? I put a clean nightgown out for you again, and there are toiletries in the guest bathroom."

Frances hesitated, then finally nodded. "Maybe that would be best," she said. "And if you don't mind, I think I'll head in there right now."

"Sure," Karen said. "Good night, Frances. Thanks for staying with the kids tonight."

"It's been my pleasure, as always."

After she'd gone, Karen stared after her. There'd been nothing amiss in their conversation, no hint of confusion. Even so, she couldn't shake the sense that Daisy's concern had been justified. For the second time, she resolved to keep a closer eye on Frances. If something else happened, as difficult as it might be, she'd have to have a heart-to-heart talk with her.

Elliott was relieved to find Karen already

asleep when he got home from his evening with the guys. Once she'd texted him that she'd gotten a ride home with Raylene, he'd stayed on at Cal's so they could all go over the numbers for the gym one more time. Though he shouldn't have been since he'd provided the figures for the equipment himself, he'd been shocked by just how expensive the start-up was likely to be.

Ronnie had been the first to notice his stunned reaction. "Elliott, are you having second thoughts?"

He had shaken his head, though that response had obviously been belied by his expression.

"You know the rest of us can pick up the difference between our original projections and these figures," Travis McDonald had said.

"That's right," his cousin Tom had agreed. "It's a solid investment, Elliott. We're all going to get our money back and then some. Just look at how profitable The Corner Spa has been."

"But it filled a niche for women," Elliott said, playing devil's advocate. "Dexter's was no competition. And the services they offered couldn't be matched anywhere in the region outside of Charleston or Columbia, and they were more expensive there. Do you

135

really think men will abandon Dexter's, dump that it is, just because we're cleaner and our equipment is newer?"

"Absolutely," Cal said at once.

"Even though we're going to have to charge more for a membership?" Elliott persisted. "It's still a tough economy out there, guys. Women will always squeeze a little out of the budget to pamper themselves. Men may figure they can get by with going for a run. The high school track and the path around the lake are free."

"I hate to say it, but he has a point," Ronnie said. "Maybe we're the only men in town desperate for this."

Cal shook his head. "I did an informal survey as part of the business plan, remember? I talked to the dads of all the kids I coach, and eighty percent of them said they'd use a facility like this if it were convenient and memberships were reasonably priced. Come on, Elliott. Why are you getting nervous now? You know this is going to work."

"I want to believe it will," Elliott admitted. "But then I see the look on Karen's face when she realized I planned to invest our baby fund to make it happen."

Shock had spread across his friends' faces.

"Your baby fund?" Ronnie echoed.

Elliott nodded. "We've been saving to make sure we can afford to have a child together. Karen insisted we needed to be financially prepared for all the expenses that come with a new baby, and I really get where she's coming from."

"Oh, boy," Tom murmured. "I get it, too. I had no idea how much paraphernalia one tiny little person could need till Jeanette started stocking our nursery."

The others agreed.

"Then we'll just pick up the slack, all of it," Travis said. "I have investments from my baseball salary that aren't earning diddly these days. I might as well put that money into something I believe in."

"I can come up with more, too," Tom offered.

Elliott frowned at them. "I appreciate the offers, guys. I really do, but absolutely not. I need to pull my own weight financially if we're going forward. Otherwise, I'll never feel as if I've earned a stake in the business."

"But you're talking about taking money out of your savings for a baby," Travis protested. "That's no good."

"It'll just postpone things a little longer," Elliott insisted, knowing that Karen wouldn't see it that way. She was going to be furious, but what could he do? He couldn't be the charity partner. Pride wouldn't allow it. He'd find some way to make her see reason.

Unfortunately, right this second, even after pondering it for the entire drive home, he still had no idea what kind of valid argument he could offer that would keep her from blowing a gasket.

Adelia had gotten her wish. Ernesto hadn't been home for four days now. Ever since he'd stormed out Saturday with her words warning him not to come back ringing in his ears, he'd stayed away. The kids were beside themselves, and she was all out of explanations. The only one she had wasn't something she intended to share with their children, that he'd taken refuge with the mistress he'd been seeing for months now. Much to her humiliation, she'd forced herself to drive over there on Sunday and had seen his car parked outside of her home. The car had been there again on Monday night and Tuesday.

They couldn't go on like this. In her heart she knew it wasn't going to get better. Their marriage had been disintegrating long before he'd gotten involved with this latest woman. She was, in fact, the fourth, maybe

138

even the fifth, in a string of mistresses he'd made no real attempt to hide from Adelia.

She was sick of the embarrassment, sick of making excuses for his absences, sick of ignoring the scent of perfume on his clothes.

And yet, she'd been raised to believe that the man was the king of the household. If there were problems in a marriage, it was more than likely through some fault of the wife. How often had her mother ingrained that message in her head? Add to that her mother's strong sentiments about divorce, and it left Adelia exactly where?

It was ironic really. She'd been among those in the family quick to judge Karen when Elliott had first brought her into their lives. Just as her mother had been, she'd been vocal about the inappropriateness of him being with a divorcee. Eventually Karen had won over his mother, first with her unmistakable love for Elliott and then with her willingness to go through the church's annulment process.

Adelia had been a tougher sell. She still kept Karen at arm's length, most likely because she was terrified that she wouldn't be half as strong about getting herself out of her own mess of a marriage. Now, with things in her life coming to a head, she could see how badly she'd misjudged Karen's misfortune.

She was sitting at her kitchen table pondering that when she heard the tentative knock on the back door. She opened it to find Karen on her doorstep.

"Why are you here?" she snapped out before she could stop herself.

Karen merely smiled. "As welcoming as always, I see," she said.

Wincing, Adelia drew in a deep breath. "I'm sorry. I'm in a nasty mood and you were the first person to cross my path. Please, come in. I could probably use some civilized company to help me remember my manners."

Karen, her expression undaunted, which was a change from the past, stepped inside, then held out Selena's party dress.

"I thought I should return this," she said.

Adelia regarded her ruefully. "You probably should have cut it to shreds. I can't believe my daughter behaved so badly. Is Daisy okay? I haven't let Selena go by Mama's after school. I didn't want to take a chance on those two getting into it again." She shrugged. "Besides, Selena's grounded for a month and that shouldn't include any of Mama's after-school treats."

Karen smiled. "I appreciate your concern for Daisy's feelings." Her expression turned serious. "How is Selena? Elliott's been worried about her, too."

Now, there was a complicated mess, Adelia thought. If anything, Selena's state of mind was even more precarious with Ernesto absent.

"She'll be fine," she said eventually.

"And you?" Karen asked hesitantly.

Adelia frowned. "Why would you ask about me? What did my brother blab to you?"

"It wasn't blabbing," Karen replied with a frown. "He's concerned, that's all."

"Well, there's nothing to be concerned about," Adelia insisted. "Ernesto and I will always have our ups and downs. He's a volatile man, and, as I'm sure you've noticed, I have a temper of my own."

Karen nodded. "I know we're not exactly friends, Adelia, though I'd like us to be closer for Elliott's sake. Still, I am a halfway decent listener, and thanks to what I went through with my first husband, I have some experience with a troubled marriage. At the least I could be a sounding board, if you ever need one."

"I have sisters and a mother," Adelia replied, then cringed at the dismissive sound of her words, as if Karen didn't measure up on whatever scale she used for who qualified to listen. "Sorry. I didn't mean that the way it came out. I do appreciate the offer."

Karen shrugged. "It's always on the table." She leveled a surprisingly steady look into Adelia's eyes. "And you might want to keep in mind that I may have a perspective they don't have, given their quick tendency to make judgments."

Startled by Karen's perceptiveness, Adelia chuckled. "You get that, do you?"

"I was on the receiving end of it," Karen reminded her. "Believe me, I get it."

"I'll keep that in mind," Adelia said, meaning it. She sensed that one of these days she was going to need an objective ear as she poured out all the problems in her marriage. Karen might be the very best person to hear her complaints. She looked her in the eye.

"I think maybe I've misjudged you," Adelia said quietly. "I'm sorry for that."

"And maybe I kept my defenses in place for too long around you," Karen said, giving her hand a squeeze. "We both love Elliott, and he sees something special in both of us. That ought to give us a starting point, don't you think?"

Adelia smiled. "Actually I do."

Karen looked pleased. "Well, I'd better run. I'm due at Sullivan's. I'm working the late shift today. Give Elliott a call. Maybe you all could take the kids out for dinner together on neutral turf this evening. I'm thinking McDonald's. He thinks I don't know he takes Daisy and Mack there, but I know all about it. Never trust a seven-year-old with a secret."

For the first time in what felt like an eternity, Adelia laughed. "Tell me about it."

In fact, that's what scared her about the current situation that her own children would go blabbing to everyone that daddy hadn't been coming home. And when that news leaked, all hell was likely to break loose in her family.

7

Elliott's suggestion that they have dinner at Rosalina's again on the Saturday after margarita night caught Karen by surprise.

"It's all arranged," he assured her. "Mama said she'd keep the kids overnight and take them to church Sunday morning."

"But you're usually exhausted on Saturdays," Karen replied. "And I have to work during the day, so I'll probably be beat, too. Are you sure you want to go out? We should probably spend the evening with the kids."

"They love spending the night at Mama's, and I want some private time with my wife," he'd told her. "We've both had a busy week, and we vowed to make time for each other, didn't we? I'm determined to stick to our plan."

She'd acquiesced because it was obviously important to him that he keep his word about making these so-called date nights more frequent.

Now that they were at Rosalina's, though, she wondered about the wisdom of coming on a Saturday. It had been so long since she'd been out on a Saturday night, she'd forgotten what it could be like. The friendly place was filled with families and teenagers on dates. The noise level was crazy. She met her husband's gaze.

"If you were counting on quiet and romantic, I don't think this is the place," she said.

"Anyplace with you is romantic, *querida*. This will be fine."

Surprised that he wanted to stay, she shrugged and followed him to an available booth. When he sat beside her, rather than across from her, she chuckled. "I think I'm beginning to see your strategy. If it's noisy, you have the perfect excuse for sitting practically on top of me and whispering in my ear."

He laughed. "Caught me," he said unrepentantly.

They placed an order for salad, pizza and icy mugs of beer, then settled back into the booth, Elliott's arm draped around her shoulder. She slanted a look at him.

"Okay, mister, what's really going on?"

He tried his best to look innocent, but he couldn't quite pull it off. Eventually, under her unrelenting gaze, he gave up.

"We need to talk about the gym," he confessed.

Karen stilled at his somber tone. "You haven't said much about it since you all got together the other night. Is there a problem?"

A part of her honestly hoped there was. Maybe if the others called it off, she and Elliott could move forward with their own plans for increasing the size of their family. Even as the thought crossed her mind, though, she knew how selfish it was. This business venture obviously meant a lot to him and, he clearly believed, to their family's future.

Elliott took a sip of his beer, then nodded. "I don't think it's a big problem, but you might."

That didn't sound good, she thought, though she was trying to remain at least neutral until she heard the rest. "Just tell me."

"The start-up figures are finalized, and they're a little higher than we anticipated," he admitted.

"How much higher?" she asked tightly, already seeing that this conversation was likely to deteriorate faster than a match burned out. "And what does that mean for you? You're already talking about using almost everything we have in savings, Elliott."

"We have a little more," he said, holding her gaze. "And we have some equity in the house."

Her heart honestly seemed to stop in her chest. "You can't be serious," she said incredulously. "You want to take all of our savings *and* get a second mortgage on the house? Not a chance, Elliott. I mean it. That's our home. I won't let you put it at risk."

"It's just a few thousand dollars extra," he argued. "It'll be short-term. We'll put that money back in within a few months, tops."

She continued to regard him with disbelief. "It's not just about a few thousand dollars. It's our home! Our safety net! After what Ray did, how could you give serious thought to doing anything like this? You know how many times I came close to being evicted and out on the streets with two kids. You know how close I came to having to declare bankruptcy. What would make you think I'd ever consider anything that might put my family in that position again?"

"Just hear me out," he pleaded.

"No," she said, trying to push him out of her way so she could leave. Unfortunately he was like a block of granite, close to impossible to budge. Since she couldn't leave, she settled for reminding him, "My name is on the deed to the house right along with yours. The bank will never okay a loan without me signing off on it, and I won't. I promise you, Elliott, I won't do it."

She could hardly bear to look at the hurt in his eyes when she said it, because she needed to cling to every ounce of anger coursing through her. Someone in this family needed to be sensible, and obviously it was up to her.

"Karen, be reasonable. We agreed to talk about these decisions. That doesn't mean you get to make them unilaterally."

"Nor do you."

He sighed. "True, but if you would just listen, you'd see that this whole thing is solid. Cal's done some market research."

She lifted a brow. "He's talked to some of the dads from school, I imagine."

Elliott winced, proving the accuracy of her guess.

"My point is that there's a need for this gym. What we're putting into it is a pittance compared to the rewards."

"The *potential* rewards," she corrected. "There's nothing certain when it comes to business, Elliott. Serenity's not a huge town.

The economy's still weak. People don't have a lot of disposable income."

"I'm sure people said the same thing to Dana Sue when she wanted to open Sullivan's in a town where Wharton's burgers were considered the equivalent of haute cuisine," Elliott replied. "And look at what Ronnie's done with his hardware business, even though the last hardware store in that space was failing. He had a unique vision and he made it work."

She couldn't argue with either example, but they didn't change her mind.

"Still not convinced?" he guessed. "Then take a look at The Corner Spa. Maddie, Helen and Dana Sue had zero experience with running a spa, but it's got a statewide reputation. This gym will have me. I've spent years in the fitness business. I know a lot of people. I have a reputation for knowing what I'm doing."

Since she could tell he wasn't going to let her escape until he'd had his say, she tried to relax. "Elliott, I'm not questioning your expertise as a personal trainer. I've seen the results you can get for myself, after all. This isn't about believing in you."

He cupped a hand under her chin and forced her to meet his gaze. "Yes, it is. Opportunities like this don't come along every day, Karen. Can't you please take this leap of faith for me? For us?"

She heard the plea in his voice and wanted desperately to give him her full support, but how could she? What if they were ruined? She wasn't sure she could go through anything like that again.

"I want this for you," she said, trying to make him understand. "If I had a crystal ball and could see into the future and know that this was going to be a huge success, or even a solid break-even business, I'd back you a hundred percent. But life doesn't work that way."

"You're letting fear overrule reason," he accused.

"I probably am," she agreed candidly. "I just don't see another choice. Maybe I could live with you using the last of the savings, but not the equity in our house. That's a deal breaker for me. If the others have so much faith in this, let them pick up the slack. As you said, most of them have thriving businesses. Their financial lives are more stable than ours."

"They offered," he admitted.

"Well, there you are," she said, feeling an overwhelming sense of relief. "There's a solution. I'm not single-handedly destroying your dream."

"No," he said wearily. "Just my pride." He stood up then. "I need to go for a walk. I'll be back before our food comes."

"Elliott!" she called after him, but he either didn't hear her or, more likely, ignored her.

She sat there in a daze, wishing she could just walk out but knowing that wasn't an answer. As difficult as this conversation had been, they'd needed to have it. And, amazingly, she'd learned something about herself, something that almost brought a smile to her lips. She'd held her own. That alone was worth celebrating.

She only hoped she didn't lose her husband because of it.

Elliott paced the jammed parking lot at Rosalina's for ten minutes, pausing only to slam his fist into the hood of his car from time to time, hoping to work off his temper.

Karen was right. He knew she was, at least from her perspective. He'd handled this all wrong from the beginning. Maybe if he'd brought her into the conversation from the outset, when Erik and the others had first approached him with the idea, she'd be more predisposed to be enthusiastic.

What was he supposed to do now? He wasn't going to walk away from this. Every time he got together with the guys, his excitement grew. Despite his own devil's-advocate stances the other night, he was convinced the gym would be successful as long as they managed their investment and their expenses prudently.

But as determined as he was, he also knew he didn't dare go behind Karen's back and seek out a loan against their home. Even he could see that not only would the deception destroy all trust between them, but it probably would be financially foolish.

"You look like a man who's just had a very uncomfortable conversation with his wife," Cal said as he approached Elliott in the parking lot.

Elliott sighed. "You have no idea."

Cal laughed, though the situation was hardly worthy of amusement. "I think I do. Maddie and I had just sat down across the room when we spotted you. I could tell it wasn't going well and had a pretty good idea about why." His expression sobered. "Elliott, if this project is going to put stress on your marriage, maybe we need to rethink it."

"No," Elliott said. "I want to do this. I think it's my chance to do something bigger than just exercise classes or personal training. I love working with people, but having a business, a club in which I have a personal stake, could ultimately give Karen and me the financial stability she's desperate for us to have. It's ironic really that she's so afraid of the short-term risk, she can't see the long-term potential at all."

"Can you blame her?" Cal asked reasonably.

"Of course I don't blame her," Elliott said in frustration. "I know exactly where she's coming from. Ray burned her. He burned her bad." It suddenly struck him that Cal had said something about Maddie. He hadn't seen her out here, though. "Where's Maddie, by the way?"

"I left her in there talking to Karen. Maybe she's had time enough to get through to her. Want to go back in and check? I don't know about you, but I'm starved, and I doubt either one of them will bring us take-out here in the parking lot."

Elliott regarded him with surprise. "Maddie's ticked off, too?"

"She thinks we're a bunch of male dolts who've mishandled this from the beginning, so she's in there sympathizing."

Elliott smiled. "I'm definitely a dolt, but I don't think you deserve a share of the blame."

Cal draped a friendly arm over his shoulders. "I told you, Sweet Magnolias stick together. They may love us to pieces individually, but collectively, they can turn on us in a heartbeat if they think one of us is out of line. You, my friend, have made things tough on all of us. Once the word spreads about tonight — and believe me, it will — most of the wives won't be speaking to their husbands out of solidarity with Karen."

"And yet you're still speaking to me," Elliott said.

"Because I've been there, done that," Cal said sympathetically. "So have all the others. We've become very good at commiserating. This is going to work out, Elliott. We'll find a way."

"Short of figuring out how to hit a delete button on Karen's memory of her first marriage, I don't know how," he said bleakly.

"Let the women work their wiles," Cal suggested. "They're behind this idea, too, after all. We might have to sit back a bit and wait, but I think reason will eventually kick in."

"You're an optimistic man," Elliott said with a disbelieving shake of his head.

"I won Maddie despite very long odds, didn't I?" Cal said. "She was against marrying me. The entire school system opposed our relationship because she was the mother of one of the kids I coached and ten years older than me to boot. The whole town was in an uproar." He grinned. "Look at us now, married and the parents of two kids of our own, plus her three. How could I be anything other than optimistic about things always working out the way they're meant to?"

It would have been nice, Elliott thought, if that optimism had been contagious. Instead, he went back into Rosalina's wondering if anyone there would even be speaking to him.

Karen had been startled when Maddie slid into the booth opposite her just after Elliott had walked out. She'd been even more surprised by her first words.

"Men can be utterly insensitive, can't they?" Maddie had asked.

Karen regarded her with surprise. "You heard us?"

Maddie shook her head at once. "Not the words, but I could guess at the content. Cal told me about the gym's projected budget being higher than anticipated. I imagine Elliott brought you here tonight to fill you in, hoping you wouldn't kill him in a public place."

Despite her very sour mood, Karen

couldn't help laughing. "I imagine that was exactly his strategy."

"He seemed to be in one piece when he walked out of here," Maddie commented.

"Probably because I was too stunned to figure out what weapon I could use to pound some sense into his thick skull."

"Too bad these restaurants are all non-smoking now," Maddie said. "Ashtrays are usually heavy enough to work."

Karen gave her an odd look. "Why have I never noticed before that you have a slightly bloodthirsty streak?"

Maddie looked oddly pleased by the comment. "I know. Isn't it great? I think it's a reaction to all those years I was way too passive in my first marriage. Cal seems to encourage the feisty side of my nature."

"Elliott usually does the same with me," Karen confided. "I think he's regretting that tonight. He's very unhappy that I put my foot down about risking our house to get more money to invest in the gym." She gave Maddie a plaintive look. "I'm not being unreasonable, am I?"

"I certainly don't think so, but this isn't my marriage or my house."

"Would you have agreed?"

"Have you seen that giant mausoleum I live in? It was the Townsend family home, which I joyfully received on loan in the divorce settlement. If I could put that place at risk, I'd do it in a heartbeat, but that's revenge, not practicality talking. It would make my ex a little crazy if he saw the family jewel on the auction block. I'd actually be far happier in one of those new developments where you are, someplace where everything's new and doesn't break down if you happen to look at it cockeyed."

"You could sell it and move," Karen suggested.

"Not without an okay from my ex. It's basically only on loan to me till our kids are grown. Thank Helen for that deal. She's quite a negotiator when she's fighting for a friend." She sighed. "Only a couple of more years till Katie, the youngest of my kids from my first marriage, is off to college, and then the Townsend house and I can part ways forever. Both Cal and I will be happy to see the last of it, but it's been good that Ty, Kyle and Katie were able to stay there, especially when the divorce was tearing them apart. Staying in the home they'd always known gave them a sense of stability."

The pizza Karen and Elliott had ordered came then, and she and Maddie dove into it. All but a single slice was gone by the time

Cal returned with Elliott in tow. Elliott glanced at the nearly empty pizza pan. "Dinner?"

"It was delicious," Maddie said. "I have no idea why I never thought of adding jalapeños before."

Elliott shook his head and glanced at Cal. "I think we're on our own." He eyed Karen cautiously. "May we at least sit with you?"

"Sure," she said, calmer now that she'd had a conversation with someone sane who wasn't trying to badger her into going against her convictions.

Just as the two men were about to sit, though, Maddie held up a hand. "This is a gym-free discussion zone for the time being," she announced. "Agreed?"

Cal and Elliott exchanged a look, then nodded.

"Good," Maddie said. "Because indigestion is not on the menu. The jalapeños are about as much stress as my system can handle. Besides, date nights are supposed to be about fun and relaxation."

Karen regarded her with surprise. "You all plan date nights?"

"Of course," Cal said. "If we didn't, I'd never see my wife."

"How many times a week?" Elliott asked, even as he turned his gaze to Karen.

"I aim for seven," Cal said, grinning. "With that many I figure I'm bound to get lucky at the end of the night at least once."

Maddie nudged him with an elbow. "Stop it. We try for two and are thankful if we pull off one."

"We've just started trying to work them into our schedule," Karen admitted. "We had our first one a couple of weeks ago. Tonight's the second one."

"And here we are intruding," Maddie said, as if they'd turned up at the table uninvited and interrupted some private moment, rather than intervening in what had obviously been a fight.

"We were in need of friendly referees," Elliott said. "I'm grateful you were around."

"Me, too," Karen said, glancing at her husband. There was no mistaking the concern in his eyes. He was obviously still worried about their disagreement, though whether it was because they'd fought or because she'd differed with him, she had no way of knowing.

Already lying in bed, Elliott watched Karen as she undressed and slipped on a silky negligee that she wouldn't be wearing fifteen minutes from now, if he had his way. She'd been quiet on the way home, but he was hopeful that they could maintain the truce Maddie had insisted on at the restaurant.

When she'd finished in the bathroom and crawled into bed beside him, he reached for her.

She pulled away. "We need to talk," she protested.

"Not tonight," he replied just as firmly. "We both said a lot of things earlier. Now it would be best if we just slept on them and talked again in the morning when our minds are clear."

"My mind is clear right now," she argued. "And I haven't changed it." She turned her back to him and moved as close to the edge of the bed as she could to keep distance between them.

He sighed at that. Obviously make-up sex wasn't in the cards. He stared up at the ceiling and tried to figure out what to do next. How could he possibly get through to her how important this gym was to his identity as a man and, equally important, to their future?

"Elliott?"

The whisper sounded half asleep and, if he was hearing correctly, a little scared.

"What, *querida?*"

"You won't go behind my back and get

the money, anyway, will you?"

He hated that she thought so little of him. "No, I will never go behind your back. You should know me better than that."

"It's what your father would have done, though, isn't it?"

He thought about that for a minute. Truthfully, he couldn't deny it. "More than likely."

"And what would your mother have done?"

"She'd have accepted his decision as head of the household," he said.

She rolled toward him then and, in the moonlight streaming into the room, he saw the tracks of tears on her cheeks. "I don't think I could do that," she said.

Though a part of him wished it could be so simple between them, that his word would always be gospel, he knew better than to expect it. He wasn't his father, and she, heaven help him, was nothing like his mother.

"I would never expect it of you," he reassured her. "We're partners, Karen. We'll work through this together."

"But I don't see how," she said. "You have your needs and I have mine. They're not the same."

"We have one overriding need that is the

same for both of us," he corrected. "We love each other and we believe in this marriage, so we will do whatever it takes to make it work." He studied her worriedly. "I'm right about that, aren't I? This disagreement hasn't shaken your faith in us?"

"It's scared me," she admitted. "I don't see how we can both get what we feel so strongly about."

At the moment, Elliott had no idea about that, either, but they would. Somehow they would, because anything less was unacceptable.

Only a few days after his confrontation with Karen over his part in financing the gym, Elliott was back with the guys going over details. They were all determined to move forward, and their offers to pick up any financial slack were still on the table. So far, though, he'd insisted he would find a way to pay his own share.

The basketball game tonight had given way entirely to a business meeting at Ronnie's where they could spread out all their information and hash out a final business plan. Elliott had apparently been a little too quiet because eventually Ronnie directed a look at him.

"Is Karen still having a problem with your

part in this?" Ronnie asked.

"Not with the concept," Elliott said, embarrassed to have to admit even that much.

"It's the money thing, isn't it?" Travis guessed. "I'm telling you, don't let that become an issue when it doesn't have to be. If we split up that final investment among the rest of us, it'll be fine. I'm game. How about the rest of you?"

All of the men nodded at once.

"No," Elliott said yet again. "I won't be the charity partner."

"You do know Maddie would cut your heart out if she heard you refer to yourself like that," Cal said. "Keep in mind she put in sweat equity, not cash, at The Corner Spa. Every penny of the start-up money came from Helen and Dana Sue."

"It's not the same," Elliott said stubbornly.

"Because he's male and a Latino," Ronnie said wryly. "No disrespect, but do you intend to let pride keep you from building a business you're more qualified than anyone in this room to run? We're counting on you to make this place a success. Without you, we have an idea, but no gym, no expertise. I'd say that deserves a break on the financial contribution."

"I agree," Travis said.

The others echoed their agreement.

Elliott wanted to seize the opportunity they were willing to give him, but it just didn't sit right. "Give me a few days, maybe a week. Let me see if I can't put something together. I'll feel better if I've paid for my share. Otherwise I won't feel right about participating in the profits. I'll feel like an employee."

Tom, who'd been mostly silent up until now, finally spoke, his expression thoughtful. "What if we make it a loan?" he suggested. "You can pay us back that extra investment out of your share of the profits. It would be strictly a business arrangement with a generous deadline to allow for any hitches in getting into the black. You wouldn't have to put up any collateral the way you would at the bank. Would Karen go for that?"

Elliott was tempted. It was a more than fair solution. He wouldn't even have to tell Karen about it since nothing they owned would be at risk. "Let me think about it," he said eventually.

"And talk it over with your wife," Ronnie advised, apparently guessing that he was considering keeping the arrangement quiet.

Elliott smiled. "And here I was just thinking I could avoid that."

"Not if you're smart," Cal said. "She's going to wonder how you pulled it off to move forward, and whatever she imagines will probably be a thousand times worse than the truth."

Elliott sighed. "You have a point. I'll get back to you all at our next meeting."

"And in the meantime, I'm going to sign that lease that Mary Vaughn keeps waving under my nose," Ronnie said. "That's how much confidence I have that we're moving forward."

"Hold off on that," Elliott pleaded. Because if word of that signed lease got around town before he had another heart-to-heart with Karen, the likely explosion would pretty much kill whatever good will he'd managed to reclaim between them.

8

"Mom?"

Adelia turned to her twelve-year-old daughter, already anticipating another tantrum. Selena had been throwing them regularly from the moment she'd been grounded. They'd gotten worse since Ernesto hadn't come back home. Though she understood why her daughter was so angry, dealing with the outbursts calmly was another matter.

She studied Selena's face, but for once what she saw there was fear, rather than defiance.

"What is it, *niña?*"

Selena frowned. "I'm not your little one. I'm almost a teenager."

"You'll be my baby until I'm a hundred and you're almost eighty," Adelia told her.

Selena looked horrified. "That's awful."

"But true. It's the way moms are wired. Now, tell me what's on your mind."

Selena looked everywhere but directly at her. "Are you and dad getting a divorce?" she asked eventually.

Adelia had known it was only a matter of time before one of the kids asked the question. She'd also known it was likely to be precocious, outspoken Selena. The younger children seemed to accept Adelia's increasingly feeble explanations that their dad was tied up with business. Not a one had questioned why that meant he wasn't home at night.

"You know how this family feels about divorce," she said carefully to Selena. "We're Catholic. We don't believe in it."

Selena didn't look convinced. "Deanna Rogers is Catholic, but her parents are divorced."

"Some people take the teachings of the church more seriously than others. Divorce is a very personal decision."

"You mean Grandma takes them seriously," Selena said. "We hardly even go to church on Sundays. She goes to Mass practically every day."

"With a family like ours, she has a lot to pray about," Adelia said, smiling. "She's hoping to save us all."

Selena grinned. "Do you think she prayed about what I did to Daisy?"

"Oh, I'm sure of it," Adelia told her. "Even I prayed for guidance over that."

For the first time since the incident, what appeared to be genuine guilt spread across her daughter's face. "I'm sorry," she said in a small voice. "I'm really, really sorry. I don't know why I was so mean."

"Want to hear my theory?" Adelia asked, relieved to have the door finally opened by her daughter in a way that suggested she might actually listen.

Selena nodded and pulled out a chair at the kitchen table, where they'd had so many after-school talks through the years.

"I think maybe you were jealous," Adelia told her.

"Of Daisy?" Selena said incredulously. "She's practically still a baby."

Adelia smiled. "But that night she had something you desperately wanted. She had someone at the dance with her who really wanted to be there, your *Tio* Elliott. I think your father's attitude, his reluctance to go with you, hurt your feelings, and you lashed out at Daisy because of it."

Selena sighed heavily as Adelia's words lingered in the air.

"You could be right," Selena admitted. "I guess I was too scared to yell at Dad when I figured out he didn't want to be there with me, so I took it out on Daisy."

"Then maybe the next time you apologize to her, you could sound as if you really mean it," Adelia suggested gently. "What you said that night was deliberately cruel. You know how much your cousin idolizes you." She gave Selena a pointed look. "And she *is* your cousin. Understood?"

Selena's cheeks flushed with embarrassment at the unvarnished assessment and the stark reminder of her most cutting comment. "She probably hates me now. Uncle Elliott, too."

"She might," Adelia said candidly. "But you're family, and she adored you not that long ago. I think if she believes you're really sorry, she'll give you another chance. As for your uncle, he's disappointed in you, but he could never hate you."

"Could I call her now? She's probably still at Grandma's. I know the phone's off-limits, but maybe this could be an exception," she said hopefully.

"I think it could be," Adelia agreed. "But ten minutes. No more. I'm not lifting the grounding."

"Yeah, I figured," Selena said, sounding resigned.

She was about to walk out of the kitchen, when Adelia shook her head. "Use the phone in here," she commanded.

"You don't trust me to make the call and say what I promised?"

"Sorry, *niña*. You're going to have to earn back my trust."

"I guess it's kinda the same thing with Dad," Selena said, suddenly sounding way too grown-up. "He'd be grounded, too, if that worked with grown-ups."

If only it did, Adelia thought. But she wasn't sure there was a fit punishment for the humiliating way her husband had been treating her. Selena didn't need to know that, though.

"Make that call. Then you can get back to your room and finish your homework," she said.

"Will Dad be home for dinner tonight?"

"I doubt it."

Selena frowned. "Is he ever coming home?"

"He'll be back," Adelia said with a confidence she was far from feeling. The real kicker, though, was she was increasingly unsure if she wanted him here.

Karen had taken on extra shifts at Sullivan's for the past week. She was doing it partly for the overtime pay, but also because on some level she was hoping to avoid another battle with Elliott over the money for the gym. It had been days since they'd had a chance to have a private conversation at home. This morning at breakfast, she'd heard the impatience in his voice after she'd told him she'd be working late again tonight.

"You don't need to worry about the kids, though," she'd told him, as if caring for them was the issue. "It's Saturday night. They have sleepovers planned with their friends."

"Wouldn't that make it the perfect night for us to spend an evening to ourselves, then?" he'd asked, his tone reasonable.

She couldn't even meet his gaze as she'd responded. "We need the extra money, Elliott, especially if you're still planning to dip into our savings."

"That's one of the things we need to talk about. I've worked things out. I'll still need a chunk of our savings to invest, but there's no need to take out a loan on the house."

He'd said it as if that had ever been a viable option.

"Good to know," she'd replied, unable to keep a hint of irony out of her voice.

Elliott had looked as if he'd wanted to get into another argument right then and there, but she fled, claiming she was already late for work.

171

She knew, though, that they couldn't avoid the topic forever.

Now that she was at Sullivan's, she could finally relax. She even managed to push the whole gym controversy and the tension at home out of her head as she worked on lunch prep.

Dana Sue had encouraged all of them to experiment with recipes, and Karen loved doing that. After working at a country-style diner outside of town where the menu had been limited mostly to burgers, shakes and fried foods, she enjoyed trying out different herbs and unusual combinations of ingredients.

Though the Sullivan's menu promised a new Southern cuisine, Karen had discovered all sorts of ways to update the traditional recipes. Dana Sue actually thought she had a real knack for it. It was the first time anyone had ever encouraged her culinary skills, and she basked in the warm and frequent praise.

She'd just finished a new variation of mac and cheese, a comfort food they often used as a side dish, when Dana Sue stepped into the kitchen.

Ignoring Erik, who was focused on icing a red velvet cake for today's dessert list, she called out to Karen, "Can you take a break?

I'd like to see you in my office."

Karen's stomach sank as she followed her boss to the tiny room that served as her office. It also served as storage for paper products and anything else they didn't know where to hide. She managed to squeeze through and moved a stack of files from the one extra chair, then sat.

"Is something wrong?" she asked Dana Sue nervously. They'd had way too many discussions in the past about absences or mistakes for Karen to assume Dana Sue was about to utter anything other than a reprimand, especially since she'd insisted on privacy. If it were anything else, she would have talked in front of Erik.

"Not with your work," Dana Sue reassured her at once. "You're doing great. I love some of the innovations you've tried for the menu. It's you I'm worried about."

"Why?"

"You've worked an extra shift almost every day this week."

"Tina needed some time off," Karen said at once.

Dana Sue held her gaze. "Is that it? Erik and I have picked up the slack for Tina before, especially on the slow week nights."

Karen couldn't help wondering if this was about the overtime pay. "I didn't think

173

you'd mind, and I could use the extra money."

"It's not about the money, and we're always grateful for another pair of hands. You'll be a godsend tonight. I'm just wondering if you're hiding out here to avoid going home." She held up a hand. "I know that's a personal question, and you don't have to answer, but frankly, I feel a little responsible for the tension between you and Elliott. I don't think any of us realized how much friction the whole gym plan might cause."

Karen released her pent-up breath. "To be honest, in some ways I know I'm overreacting, that it's pushed one of my hot buttons, and I can't begin to look at it rationally. I know how badly Elliott wants to do it and how hurt he's been that I don't seem to have enough faith that it will be successful." She gave Dana Sue a plaintive look. "I have no idea how to get past that. I'm making him miserable. We're barely speaking, mostly because . . . you're right, I have been hiding out here."

"I thought so," Dana Sue said. "That won't solve anything. You know that."

"Of course I do. I just don't know what else there is we could possibly say that would change anything."

174

"You won't know unless you try. As I understand it, the guys came up with what they think is a win-win solution the other night. Has Elliott told you about that? I don't know the details, but Ronnie seemed to think it would allay your concerns."

Suddenly Karen regretted not allowing Elliott to tell her about it. She'd shut him down every time he'd tried. This time she couldn't blame him for leaving her out of the loop. It was probably time for that to stop. She met Dana Sue's concerned gaze.

"I was going to work for Tina tomorrow, but she said she could handle the shift if I wanted it off after all," she told Dana Sue. "Would that be okay? I think I need to spend some time with my husband."

Dana Sue grinned, looking very pleased with herself. "Then my work here is done. I know it might feel like a busman's holiday, but you could bring Elliott here for Sunday brunch on the house, if you'd like to turn it into a special occasion."

Karen nodded slowly. "He might like that, and heaven knows, we could use a nice meal at someplace with more ambience than Wharton's or Rosalina's. Thank you. The kids are at sleepovers tonight. I'll see if they can hang out till tomorrow afternoon, so we'll have privacy for a real heart-to-heart, adult conversation."

"I'll reserve a table for you, then," Dana Sue promised.

"I'd better get back and check on my jalapeño mac and cheese." Karen grinned. "If I did it right, it ought to bump up drink sales."

"Or send our water bill soaring," Dana Sue teased. "I can't wait to try it."

As Karen left the office, she felt more hopeful than she had in weeks.

"But we always have Sunday dinner with my family," Elliott protested when Karen told him about Dana Sue's offer. "It's a tradition to go there after church. You know how much my mother counts on all of us being around her table at least once a week."

Karen had managed to avoid plenty of those occasions by claiming she had to work. Since the offer to eat free at Sullivan's would have been such a rare treat, she'd been sure Elliott would readily forego his mother's command performance just this once.

"It's one time," she pleaded. "And we need this, Elliott. You know we do."

"I've been saying we need to talk all week. Why would you pick the one day of the week when it's impossible?"

176

"It's not *impossible,*" she retorted.

"Okay, maybe not. I just don't want to disappoint my mother. And if she finds out you had time off and chose to go to the restaurant where you work for a meal rather than joining the family, she'll take it like a slap in her face."

Unfortunately, Karen knew that was exactly how her mother-in-law would view it. She heaved a resigned sigh. "Fine. We'll go to your mother's," she said, already regretting that she'd given up the shift at work.

"We'll go over to the lake after," he said, clearly trying to make amends. "The kids can run off their excess energy, and we'll be able to sit quietly there and talk."

"On a Sunday, when every family in Serenity has the exact same idea?" she asked skeptically.

"I'm trying to compromise," he said in frustration.

She met his gaze. "I know you are, but so am I."

He tucked a finger under her chin until she met his gaze. "We'll get better at it," he promised, moving his hand to caress her cheek.

"I should have remembered how hard marriage can be," she told him. "The funny thing is, I would have done whatever it took

177

to figure things out and save my marriage to Ray, scumbag that he turned out to be. He bolted without giving us any chance at all to work things out."

"Does that mean you intend to fight for our marriage even when it gets hard?" Elliott asked.

She reached up and put her hand over his where it still rested against her cheek, her eyes locked with his. "With everything in me," she assured him.

"And I'll do the same, *querida. Te amo.*"

"I love you, too," she whispered, stepping into his open arms. "With all my heart."

The one thing Elliott hadn't considered when he'd insisted they go to his mother's house on Sunday was that it would bring Daisy and Selena into contact for the first time since the dance. Adelia had kept Selena home that first Sunday and after school. They'd caved in to Daisy's pleas to stay away after that. He knew the two girls had spoken on the phone, but until they saw each other, it was hard to know if the matter had truly been resolved, especially since Daisy had said nothing, at least to him, after that conversation.

As they drove over to his mother's, he glanced into the rearview mirror. Daisy was gazing out the window, ignoring her brother's chatter, her expression pensive.

"You okay, Daisy?" he asked.

"Uh-huh," she murmured without looking in his direction.

Next to him, Karen frowned, obviously picking up on her daughter's mood and guessing the reason for it.

"You're not worried about seeing Selena, are you?" Karen asked quietly. "I thought things were better after she made that phone call the other day."

Daisy shrugged. "I guess."

There was no doubt in Elliott's mind that the matter wasn't resolved as he'd hoped. Unfortunately, despite having sisters, he only rarely understood the workings of the female mind. He cast a helpless *what-now* look toward Karen.

Karen turned in her seat. "Sweetie, tell us what's going on. Whatever it is, we'll help you figure it out."

Daisy frowned at that. "Why do *I* have to figure it out? Selena's the one who was mean. Now everybody at school is teasing me, and it's all because of her." Her voice rose as she spoke, and tears started to fall.

Karen turned to Elliott. "Maybe we shouldn't do this," she began, but he was already shaking his head.

"Postponing this will only delay the inevitable," he told her. "They're cousins. They have to work through the problem, and the only way to do that is face-to-face."

"I don't think it's that simple," Karen argued. "Not if the other kids are using the incident to say more hurtful things to Daisy. Maybe we should speak to the principal."

"No!" Daisy protested, looking alarmed. "It's bad enough now. I don't want to be a big old tattletale. I just don't want to have to spend time with Selena at Grandma Cruz's house, too. Everyone there will just take her side, the same way they do at school."

"You know better than that," Elliott said, trying to reassure her. "I've been on your side from the beginning, haven't I? And Adelia punished Selena."

"What about Ernesto?" she complained. "He didn't say anything, and he was right there when it happened."

Elliott wasn't sure quite how to answer that. He wondered if Ernesto would even be there today. He doubted it. From what he'd seen and heard recently, Ernesto had been making himself scarce ever since he'd brushed past Elliott and left home a couple of Saturdays ago. Though Elliott had wanted to talk to Adelia about it, his sisters had advised him to stay out of it. They were convinced the couple would eventually work things out, because that's what people in their family did.

He wondered, though, if his mother was aware of the strain in that marriage. He knew Adelia would do everything in her power to keep it from her. Would that extend to somehow convincing Ernesto to show up today to keep up appearances?

"Don't worry about Ernesto," he advised Daisy eventually as they pulled into a parking spot up the street from his mother's house. "There will be plenty of other people around today. If anyone upsets you, you can stick close to me. I'll protect you."

Daisy grinned. "You used to tell me that when you'd read me scary stories before bed, back when I was little."

"I meant it then, and I mean it now. You can always count on me," Elliott assured her.

Daisy might not be his biological daughter, but she was the daughter of his heart, and no one would ever harm her on his watch again, especially not a member of his own family, not even inadvertently.

As soon as they walked into the chaos that was the Cruz family home on a Sunday, Karen noticed that Adelia was not in her usual spot in the kitchen helping her mother with the meal. Karen lingered in the kitchen only long enough to offer a greeting and her willingness to help, which was automatically rejected. She might be a cook in the region's finest restaurant, but she didn't measure up to Cruz standards.

As soon as she'd been dismissed, she went in search of the one sister-in-law with whom she'd developed at least a tentative bond recently. She found Adelia sitting on the patio in back, watching the husbands toss around a football. She noticed that Ernesto was not among them.

Karen gestured toward a chair beside her. "Is it okay if I join you?"

Adelia shrugged. "I'm lousy company," she warned.

Karen grinned. "Is that why you were banished from your usual spot in the kitchen?"

To her surprise, Adelia actually chuckled. "To be honest, I'm avoiding Mama."

"Because Ernesto isn't here and she's going to want to know why?" Karen guessed.

"Got it on the first try," Adelia said, lifting a glass of wine in a toast. It didn't seem to be her first.

"Want to talk about it with an unbiased

third party?"

The last trace of Adelia's smile faded. "Nothing to talk about."

Karen merely nodded and fell silent. She understood more than most the need for privacy in a crisis, especially among family members like these, who shared every little detail of each other's lives. While emotional support was a given, the hovering and judgments could be more than a little overwhelming.

"You're not pushing for information," Adelia said eventually.

"It's your business," Karen said simply. "If you decide you want to talk, I'm here. If not, it's okay." She held Adelia's gaze. "You do know that I've been where you are. I'm the only one in the family who has been."

Adelia shook her head. "From what I know about your marriage, as awful as it was, it doesn't come close to the travesty that is mine," she said bitterly, a tear leaking from her eyes to spill down her cheek. She brushed at it impatiently, then stood up. "I can't do this. I need to get out of here."

Before Karen could think of what to say, Adelia was gone. A moment later, a car started out front.

"Did Adelia just take off?" Elliott asked,

183

suddenly appearing in front of her, his expression filled with concern.

Karen nodded.

"What did you say to her?"

"It wasn't anything I said," Karen said, instantly on the defensive. "She's very unhappy right now."

"I'd better go after her," he said, tossing the football to one of his brothers-in-law.

Karen reached for his hand. "Don't. I think she needs to figure this out for herself."

"She needs to know we're here for her."

Karen smiled at that. "I think that's part of the problem. She's not ready for the family call-to-arms."

Elliott sighed and sat down in the chair Adelia had vacated. "You're probably right. Seeing her so miserable, though, makes me want to hunt down Ernesto and punch his lights out."

"I have a hunch Adelia might appreciate that," Karen said, "but it's probably not a good idea. When people take sides, if there's a reconciliation down the road, sometimes it's hard to forget all the angry words that were spoken or the punches that were thrown."

Elliott reached for her hand. "Marriage is

way more complicated than I ever imagined."

"That's because all you really thought about was the steady sex."

He looked shocked by her teasing comment. "That is not true," he protested. "I thought about a thousand and one things I would love about spending my life with you."

She met his gaze, seizing the opening to try to get back to the emotions that had brought them together. "Tell me."

"I thought about holding you in my arms at night. I thought about waking up beside you and looking into your beautiful eyes. I thought about having a child with you, raising a family with you. I thought about sitting in rocking chairs when we're old and talking about all the memories we've made."

"The possibility of disagreements never crossed your mind?"

He grinned. "No, only the thought of make-up sex." He heaved a dramatic sigh. "I was actually looking forward to that."

She laughed. "And here I've denied you that."

He winked at her. "But I'm still hopeful, *querida*. Maybe even tonight if I play my cards right for the rest of the day. What do you think?"

Her heart filled to overflowing by his earlier words, she nodded. "I think there's a very good chance of that."

Sex might not be the answer to all their problems, not by a long shot, but in his arms, she always remembered how safe and cherished he could make her feel. Sometimes that was enough to make it easier to get through the rough patches.

9

Karen kept a very close eye on Daisy and Selena during dinner, but saw no evidence that the two girls remained seriously at odds. If anything, the ordinarily vocal Selena seemed quieter than usual. Karen couldn't help wondering if it was because her father had never shown up and her mother had disappeared before the meal, rather than any awkwardness between her and Daisy.

Adelia's abrupt departure without an explanation had set the family's tongues wagging. It was the hot topic over Mrs. Cruz's tamales.

"There is something wrong," Mrs. Cruz speculated. "Something is not right with Adelia for her to just leave without a word to any of us."

"And where on earth is Ernesto?" Elliott's sister Laurinda asked, keeping her voice low in at least a passing attempt to keep Selena from overhearing. Selena and Daisy were at the main table in the dining room. The younger children were eating at a picnic table on the back patio, out of earshot of the conversation.

"That's what I'd like to know," Carolina chimed in. "He hasn't shown up here on Sunday in quite a while now."

"Enough," Elliott commanded quietly, slanting a quick look toward Selena to make his point.

Unfortunately his sisters didn't take the hint. The speculation continued. Suddenly Selena stood up, her complexion pale.

"He's gone!" she shouted. "Stop talking about it, okay? My dad moved out, and I don't think he's ever coming back."

Shocked silence greeted the announcement. Selena ran from the room with Daisy on her heels. Karen was about to follow, but Elliott was on his feet before she could even put her napkin on the table.

"See what you've done," he scolded his sisters as he took off after the girls.

As soon as he'd gone, the men began offering their own opinions, most of them in total support of Ernesto, which was pretty much what Karen would have expected. After a few minutes of listening to them berate Adelia as a shrew who drove her husband out of the house, she'd had all she could take. Worse, not one of the sisters, or even Mrs. Cruz, rose to Adelia's defense. This was the macho boys' club mentality at its worst, and these women were letting them get away with it.

With the volume of the discussion turned high and none of the attention focused on her, Karen left the table and went in search of Elliott and the girls. She found him sitting quietly in the grass at the far edge of the backyard with a sobbing Selena in his arms and Daisy next to them. Karen dropped down beside them and rested a comforting hand on Selena's back. Slowly the girl's sobs quieted.

Elliott gave her a grateful look, then nodded toward the house. "Are they still going at it?" he mouthed over Selena's head.

She nodded back.

"Selena, sweetheart, why don't we get your brother and sisters and head over to your house?" he suggested.

Selena sniffed and looked up at him. "What if Mom's not there either?"

"Then we'll hang out until she comes home, okay? But I have a feeling we'll find her there."

"Okay," Selena said eventually. "I don't want to go back inside Grandma's, though.

Can I wait in the car?"

"Of course," Elliott said at once.

"I'll wait with you," Daisy offered.

"Me, too," Karen said. She had no desire to go back inside and risk putting her own two cents into the current discussion. She doubted her opinion was one they'd want to hear. "Elliott, you can round up the kids, right? And grab my purse."

"Under control," he said readily.

A few minutes later, Elliott's van was packed with kids. When they arrived at Adelia's, at the sight of Ernesto's car in the driveway, most of her children spilled out of the car and raced toward the house. Only Selena hung back, obviously reluctant to face whatever might be happening inside.

Karen totally understood. She exchanged a look with her husband and murmured, "You can't come up with enough money to bribe me into going in there. How about you?"

"I'd rather eat dirt, but I have to go in just to make sure everyone's okay. If you want to wait here, believe me, I get it."

"I'm staying with Karen," Selena said, then gave her a pleading look. "If it's okay?"

"Of course it is," Karen said, giving her hand a squeeze.

"I want to go in," Mack said from the back.

"No," Karen said at once. "As soon as Elliott gets back, we're leaving."

At her words, Selena stood a little taller. Suddenly she looked a little too grown up and weary for her age. "Then I might as well go with Elliott now," she said in a resigned tone.

Elliott held out his hand and clasped hers. "Come on then."

Daisy was oddly silent as they left.

"I'm surprised you don't want to go with Selena," Karen said to her. "You could run in with them for just a second, give her a little moral support."

Daisy shook her head. "I don't like Ernesto. I'm sorry he's back."

Surprised by the reaction, Karen studied her daughter. "Is this about what happened at the dance?"

Daisy's expression turned stubborn. "I can't say."

"What does that mean?" Karen asked, frowning. "Has he done something else? Daisy, if you saw something or heard something, it's okay to tell me. In fact, it's important that you speak to an adult if another adult does something upsetting or inappropriate."

191

"I *told* you I can't say," Daisy repeated, looking miserable.

Karen was torn between getting to the bottom of whatever Daisy had seen or heard and allowing her to keep the promise she'd obviously made to someone, Selena more than likely. In the end, though, she needed to know the truth.

"Sweetheart, this is not one of those situations you can keep secret, no matter what sort of promise you might have made," Karen said. "You need to tell me. What did Selena tell you? Or was it something you saw or heard yourself?"

Daisy remained silent awhile longer, obviously struggling with her own barely developed moral compass. "Selena told me," she said eventually. "It's something she's not supposed to know. That's why she said I had to keep it a secret."

"Not from me," Karen said firmly.

"Make Mack get out of the car and I'll tell you," Daisy said at last. "If he hears, he'll blab to everyone."

"I won't tell," Mack protested, looking mutinous. "And I'm not getting out of the car."

"Just for a minute," Karen told him, understanding Daisy's need to keep whatever information she held as quiet as possible. "Please. Otherwise there will be no ice cream at the lake when Elliott gets back."

Mack scowled at his sister, but ice cream was too rare a treat to risk missing out on it. He climbed out of his booster seat and slammed the car door behind him.

Karen noted her daughter's pinched expression and waited. She knew Daisy was still weighing loyalty against a parental command. Finally, she whispered, "Selena says Ernesto has a girlfriend, that he's been staying at her house."

Karen had to work hard to keep from gasping, not only at the news, but at the idea that Ernesto's twelve-year-old daughter knew such a thing about her father. Though she didn't doubt for a second that it might be true, she couldn't imagine even Ernesto being so indiscreet.

"Maybe Selena misunderstood something," she suggested.

Daisy shook her head adamantly. "She saw them together. They were kissing."

"Where?"

"Right in front of the girlfriend's house, I guess. Selena was walking home from the school bus stop. Ernesto's car was in the driveway. They were outside, kissing in the car, and then they went in together, holding hands. Selena said even though she's grounded, she snuck out later and went back at night. His car was still there." Daisy regarded her with worry. "You're not going to tell Adelia about her sneaking out, are you?"

Karen had a million and one questions, but she wasn't about to pursue them with her own nine-year-old. It was evident that Daisy didn't fully understand all of the implications of what Selena had told her — at least Karen hoped she didn't — but it was apparent that Selena did.

"Thank you for telling me," she said, reaching back to give Daisy's hand a re-assuring squeeze. "Now, stop worrying about it. The grown-ups will figure it all out. Just try to be more understanding with Selena from now on, okay? This is a very difficult time for her."

Daisy nodded. "I kinda get it now. I mean, why Selena gets so upset sometimes," she revealed. "She's really, really scared her mom and dad are gonna get a divorce."

Karen wondered about that. Could Adelia honestly ignore something like this, just pretend it wasn't happening, apparently right under her very nose if Selena was able to walk to this other woman's house? Karen knew she certainly couldn't, but the Cruz women had a different way of looking at marriage and different expectations about the way their men behaved. Did that extend to blatant infidelity?

She was still pondering that when Elliott and Mack climbed back into the car.

"Everything okay in there?" she asked.

Elliott shrugged. "On the surface." He glanced into the backseat and, with an obviously forced note of cheer in his voice, asked, "Should we go to the lake?"

"Yes!" Mack said enthusiastically.

Even Daisy managed to muster a smile for him. "Mom said we could have ice cream."

Elliott grinned. "Then we will," he said, giving her a wink. "When your mom makes a promise, she always keeps it."

Karen found herself reaching for his hand and holding on tightly. Elliott, too, kept his promises, and right at this moment, she was more grateful for that than he could possibly know.

Elliott felt completely emotionally drained after coping with the upheaval at his mother's, Selena's meltdown and then the tension inside the Hernandez house when he'd dropped off the kids. Even with the younger kids all over their father, shouting with noisy exuberance at his return home, he'd spotted the stress on his sister's face and the way Selena had kept herself apart from the others, her expression angry. When Elliott had tried to pull Adelia aside for a private moment, she'd waved him away.

"Go," she'd insisted. "Don't keep Karen and the kids waiting."

"If you need me for anything, you'll call," he said, making it more of a command than a request. He was unable to dismiss his concern as readily as she clearly wanted him to.

"I promise," she'd said, but he knew better than to believe her. It was apparent to him she'd been keeping a whole lot to herself lately, trying to handle things on her own. That wasn't the way things were done in their family, and it frustrated him to think Adelia might need help and was too proud to ask for it.

Still, he'd left, since she'd given him no choice. By the time he drove to the small, popular lake in the center of Serenity, all he wanted was to spend a quiet hour or so sitting next to his wife and counting his blessings that their problems, as complicated as they might be, were nothing compared to his sister's.

"What happened today has taken a lot out of you, hasn't it?" Karen asked as they ate

196

their ice cream on a bench in the shade of a giant pin oak draped with Spanish moss.

"I'm worried about Adelia and that family," he admitted. "Something's seriously wrong. I think she needs backup, but she's refused my offer to help."

"That's her way, isn't it?" Karen reminded him mildly. "She knows any of you would leap to her defense if she asked. If she's not asking, there must be a reason for it."

There was something in her tone that set off an alarm bell. "Do you know something I don't?" he asked.

"Not firsthand," she said slowly. "And Daisy told me in confidence what Selena had said to her. If I tell you, you have to promise not to jump back in the car and go charging after Ernesto."

Elliott froze at her grim expression. If she feared he'd go after his brother-in-law, it had to be bad. "What?" he demanded tightly.

"Remember, this is what Selena saw and her interpretation," she cautioned. "She could have it all wrong."

"Just tell me."

"She thinks he's cheating with some woman who lives nearby. She saw them kissing, and she's slipped out of the house and seen his car over there at night. She thinks that's where he's been since he walked out on Adelia."

Elliott felt his muscles bunch as anger roared through him. "In the same neighborhood with his family?"

Karen frowned at his choice of words. "Do you think that's the only thing that's wrong about this?"

"No, of course not. I just meant that it makes it that much worse to do such a thing right under the nose of his wife and children. Do you think Adelia knows about this?"

Karen nodded. "She hasn't said a word about it to me, but I think she does. Women generally know, unless they choose not to. It would certainly explain why she's been under such terrible stress."

"Good God," Elliott murmured. "What a mess!"

He was about to stand up, when Karen put a restraining hand on his arm. "You promised not to go over there."

"We're talking about my sister. Nobody gets to disrespect her like that."

"I agree, but Adelia has to ask for your help," Karen said reasonably. "Otherwise, you'll just humiliate her. You certainly can't go rushing over there and cause a scene in front of the children."

Though it went against every protective instinct that had ever been instilled in him, he stayed where he was.

"I hate this," he said eventually.

"Me, too," Karen said, reaching for his hand.

"What should we do? Could I at least go find Ernesto tomorrow and beat him to a pulp?" he asked, half hoping Karen would agree that it was a perfectly logical next step.

She smiled. "I think you already know the answer to that."

"It's just so wrong to let him get away with it."

"I agree, but the best thing you can do is keep a closer eye on your sister and be there whenever this thing blows up. I don't think she knows it yet, but she's a strong woman, and she's not going to sit back and tolerate this forever."

Elliott thought he detected the unspoken message in what she was saying. "Divorce?"

"Can you think of another option?"

"There has to be one," he said at once. "Divorce is unacceptable."

"You would have her stay with a man who disrespects her so openly?" Karen asked incredulously. "Is that what you would have wanted for me?"

"Of course not," he said, referring only to

Karen's situation. "Ray left you. You couldn't remain in limbo."

"And Ernesto? What would you call what he's doing?" she asked pointedly.

Elliott hesitated. He saw the depths of the dilemma clearly for the first time. His family's strong faith was pitted against the reality of a marriage descending into despair. When it hit home like this, the answers were not nearly as clear or as simple as he'd always believed them to be.

On Wednesday Frances was fifteen minutes late getting to The Corner Spa for the weekly seniors' exercise class. She spotted the questioning look in Flo's eyes when she finally arrived.

Thankfully, though, Elliott turned on the CD player just then and started the dance exercises that had become everyone's favorite part of the class. With the music at high volume, Flo couldn't ask all the questions that were obviously on the tip of her tongue. By the time they were ready for a break, everyone was too out-of-breath to discuss anything.

When the class finally ended, Frances hurried to catch up with Elliott for her weekly update on Karen and the children. And, if she were being totally honest, to avoid Flo.

"Do you all need me to babysit this week?" she asked Elliott hopefully. Despite a few disconcerting moments, the time she spent with Daisy and Mack was very special to her. It filled the void that should have been filled by her own grandchildren. She felt better when she was around all that youthful exuberance and wonder.

"Honestly, I have no idea how this week is going to play out," Elliott said, his frustration plain. "We were supposed to have some time to talk Sunday when we took the kids over to the lake, but something else came up and we never got around to talking about anything we'd planned to discuss."

"Then it sounds as if you need another night out. Other than playing cards at the senior center tonight, my calendar's clear. Just give me a call if you want me to come over or want to drop the kids off at my place."

Elliott leaned down and pressed a kiss to her cheek, which drew hoots from the other women who'd lingered after class.

"Hey, no playing favorites," Garnet Rogers called out.

"And if you're looking for an older woman, I'm a better bet," Flo teased him.

Frances rolled her eyes. "Ladies, act your age."

"Good heavens, why would we do that?" Garnet responded. "The more frequently I can recapture my youth, the better I like it."

Elliott kissed Frances again, just to stir the pot, no doubt, then gave her a wink before heading for his next client.

Frances turned to leave, only to be intercepted by Flo.

"I know what you're doing," Flo accused. "You're trying to avoid me. Liz, too."

"I most certainly am not," Frances said with what she thought sounded like suitable indignation.

"You skipped cards last week."

"I had things to do," Frances said.

"And you deliberately came late today so I couldn't ask you if you've made an appointment with the doctor yet. And that private little chat you just had with Elliott was part of your strategy, too. You were hoping I'd have to rush right out of here."

"Well, if that was my strategy, it didn't work, did it?" Frances retorted.

Flo held her gaze. "You can't avoid Liz and me forever," she said quietly. "Nor can you put off making this appointment, Frances. It isn't like you to pretend everything's fine, when you know it isn't. Wouldn't it be better to know, so you can be treated and make whatever plans need to be made?"

"I think we've all overreacted," Frances said, even though she knew all too well there had been a couple of more troubling incidents, including an embarrassing moment when she'd been speaking to the preacher after church just this past Sunday and had suddenly lost her train of thought. Lots of people did that, she knew, but she'd panicked just the same. The problem was there were times, like right now after her exercise class, that she felt better than ever. Her physical stamina was remarkable for a woman of ninety. Everyone, including her own doctor whom she'd seen last year for a flu shot, agreed about that.

Flo regarded her doubtfully. "We both know that no one has overreacted. And I understand why you'd be scared."

"Not scared," Frances corrected. "Terrified."

"But isn't it better to know?" Flo repeated, obviously frustrated by Frances's stubbornness.

Frances looked directly into her friend's compassionate gaze. "Have you found any cures on that computer of yours?"

"No, but —"

Frances cut her off. "Then what difference does it really make if I find out now or a few months down the road?"

"There *are* medicines that can help for a while, at least," Flo argued. "They could buy you time to spend with your family. More importantly, you might not even have Alzheimer's. Think of the relief a proper diagnosis could bring you."

"We both know that's a long shot," Frances said.

"You're not going to do this until you're ready, are you?" Flo finally said, her expression resigned.

Frances nodded. "That's right, and it's my decision to make when that is."

Surprisingly, tears welled up in Flo's eyes. "Liz and I just want you to be all right."

"Don't you think I know that?" Frances said, giving her an impulsive hug. "You two are the best friends I could possibly have. I know you care about me, and I truly do appreciate it. One more incident and I'll see the doctor. I promise."

Flo gave her a doubtful look. "Do we have to witness this next incident for it to count, or will you keep the promise even if we're not around?"

"No matter who's around," Frances said, "I'll keep the promise."

Because even though she wanted to believe these lapses of hers weren't the first signs of Alzheimer's, she wasn't about to put anyone

204

else at risk because of her foolish refusal to accept the possibility that her health was deteriorating.

10

From the very first time Elliott had taken Karen home to meet his family, it had been clear that her relationship with Elliott's ardently Catholic mother was going to be incredibly rocky. Maria Cruz had disapproved openly of Karen's divorce. Only after Karen had confronted her and told her the details of her failed marriage had Mrs. Cruz relented and agreed that divorce had been her only option. Karen's willingness to go through the annulment process had eventually appeased her and Elliott's sisters. By the time she and Elliott had married, they'd silenced their disapproval.

Still, old resentments lingered and occasionally stirred, especially after scenes such as the one at the Cruz house on Sunday. Karen wasn't all that surprised to hear from her mother-in-law, insisting that she stop by before work, only that it had taken her so long to call.

Karen knew she probably hadn't done a very good job of hiding her disdain for her brothers-in-law the previous Sunday. She'd managed to keep quiet, but she had walked out in the middle of the family discussion in which the men were spouting some of their offensively macho, old-world nonsense.

It wasn't in her nature to stir that particular pot and try to cause some kind of feminist uprising among the Cruz women, but when she saw signs of the same behavior in Elliott, she was determined to nip it in the bud. Her sisters-in-law could manage their own lives in whatever way they saw fit.

Since Mrs. Cruz had finely tuned antennae when it came to her children, Karen wondered just what sort of lecture might be on today's agenda. Would she warn Karen against interfering in Adelia's marriage? Or was something else on her mind?

When she arrived, two of the Cruz grandchildren under the age of five were playing out front. Mrs. Cruz was waiting on the front stoop. She clapped her hands to get the children's attention.

"Inside, *niñas!*" she commanded, and though both children protested, they immediately headed inside as she'd asked.

When she'd settled them in the living room with a favorite movie, she led Karen into the kitchen, the true heart of her home. A pot of her coffee, far more palatable than Elliott's, was brewed, and there were fresh, traditional guava pastries just out of the oven.

"You are working today?" Maria Cruz asked as she poured the coffee and set a plate of the still-warm pastries in front of Karen, no doubt expecting her to eat more than one.

"I'm due there at ten," Karen said. "We have a little time."

"Then I will be direct," Mrs. Cruz said. She leveled a concerned look into Karen's eyes. "You and my son are fighting. May I ask why?"

Despite her understanding of Serenity and the Cruz family dynamics, Karen could barely keep her mouth from dropping open. It had never occurred to her that this petite, formidable woman, who was totally focused on her family, would choose to cross-examine her about something so personal. Then, again, Maria Cruz considered herself the matriarch of the family whose duty it was to keep things running smoothly, even for the children who were long since grown with families of their own. If she meddled in the other family marriages, why not Elliott's?

"Where did you hear that?" Karen asked, more out of curiosity than anything.

"It does not matter," Mrs. Cruz replied with a dismissive shrug. "Is it true? Is that why you and Elliott have asked that I take the children several times recently, so they wouldn't hear you fighting?"

Karen debated the best way to answer. "There have been things Elliott and I needed to discuss, yes, but mostly we've been trying to find some time just to be alone together. With our schedules, privacy is hard to come by. Most couples don't start their lives with two young children already underfoot."

Though she nodded in understanding, Mrs. Cruz didn't look entirely satisfied by her response. "These discussions, as you call them, are they about serious issues?" Her brow furrowed and her expression appeared genuinely troubled. "Things that could lead to a divorce?"

"Good heavens, I hope not!" Karen said. "We want the time to ourselves to work things out before they turn into real problems."

Relief washed over Mrs. Cruz's face as she sketched a cross over her chest. "It would break my heart for my son   or any of my children," she added pointedly, "to

209

be divorced."

She held Karen's gaze. "You knew our beliefs when you married Elliott. I expect you to do whatever it takes to make your marriage work."

Karen frowned. "Why is that only my responsibility? Have you said the same to Elliott?" She was a little too tempted to toss Adelia's name out there, too, but she owed her sister-in-law some discretion. Her mother-in-law might have alluded to Adelia's problems just now, but she hadn't brought the subject into the open. Karen wouldn't, either.

"Not yet, but I will," his mother said. "I wanted to speak with you first. It is always a woman's place to smooth the waters, to keep peace."

"I don't see it that way," Karen argued, determined to stand up for her own beliefs. "Men are just as responsible for the state of a relationship as the woman is." She regarded her mother-in-law curiously. "How did you deal with it when Mr. Cruz bossed you around or treated you condescendingly? I know he did, because your daughters have mentioned it. You don't strike me as a woman who would accept such treatment."

A secretive smile crossed the older woman's face. "I had my ways. Diego was never harsh or unyielding. He was a kind man, who'd grown up to believe men behaved in certain ways. I like to think I showed him that he could get better results another way."

"But you argued?"

She shrugged. "Of course. We both had tempers and strong views. But no matter how vehemently we disagreed, we always ended the day with a kiss."

"Did he recognize what a strong, capable woman you are?"

"In his way," she said with a shrug, as if it were unimportant. "But unlike you or my daughters, I was content to run this household, to put my family above all else. I had no need of another career. Only Adelia has followed in my footsteps, though she's involved in so many activities, she might as well have a full-time job."

They'd had this conversation before, so Karen refused to take offense. "There are different ways to put your family first," she said quietly. "Being responsible, working to give my children the life they deserve, is one way. Yours was another."

"Agreed," Mrs. Cruz said with a smile. "See, I've learned something from you, *niña*. Perhaps if you listen closely, you will learn something from me from time to time."

Karen laughed. "No question about it.

Your secret recipes alone have kept my husband very happy."

"Marriage is about more than keeping a man's belly full of his favorite food," Mrs. Cruz chided. "But you know that, don't you?"

"I still have a lot of lessons to learn," Karen agreed. "And I'll always hear your advice with an open mind. Anyone who raised such a wonderful man has to be very wise."

"Now you are just flattering me so that I will tell you how to make that special *mole* sauce that Elliott adores," she teased. "I believe I will keep that one in reserve for when I have a very big favor I need in return."

Karen laughed. "Elliott told me I was never going to get that recipe out of you. He says even his sisters know only that it contains a variety of peppers and maybe a hint of chocolate?" she said, hoping for a confirmation of that much at least.

"A very clever try," Mrs. Cruz praised. "But I believe I will keep that one to myself a while longer. I have to have some reason for my children to keep coming home."

"I don't think they come for the *mole* sauce," Karen told her with total sincerity as she hugged her goodbye. "They come for the love."

Mrs. Cruz kissed her enthusiastically on both cheeks. "And *that* is why you are my favorite daughter-in-law."

"I'm your *only* daughter-in-law," Karen said. And, despite this awkward conversation, it was a role in which she was slowly becoming comfortable. She wished it were as easy as being with Frances, but maybe, with time, that would happen.

She was on her way to her car when Adelia pulled up in front of the house. She frowned when she spotted Karen, jumped out of her car and crossed the lawn.

"Why were you here? Were you talking to Mama about me and Ernesto?" she demanded, alarm written all over her face.

"Absolutely not," Karen said soothingly. "Why would I do that? Your marriage is private, Adelia. You've not said a word to me about what's going on, and even if you had, I would never tell your mother."

Relief washed over Adelia's face. "Sorry. My nerves are shot. I was summoned over here by Mama, so I'm already on the defensive."

Karen chuckled.

"You find that amusing?" Adelia asked, frowning.

"I was summoned, as well. Today must be

your mother's day for solving the family marital issues."

Adelia's scowl slowly faded, and she, too, began to chuckle. "You, too?"

"Yep."

"How'd it go?"

"I think I managed to reassure her."

Adelia's momentary good humor disappeared. "I'm not sure I'm a talented enough actress to pull that off." She squared her shoulders. "But I am certainly going to try. Things are difficult enough without getting Mama worked into a frenzy."

"Good luck," Karen said, then watched Adelia walk into the house. She didn't envy her the likely interrogation that lay ahead.

Adelia would have given anything to flee her mother's house right behind Karen. She'd tried to put her mother off by claiming several meetings today, but Mama had been insistent. When Maria Cruz spoke to her children in a certain tone, they all understood that there was no room left for argument.

"Good morning, Mama," she said, forcing a cheerful note into her voice as she entered the kitchen. She made sure that her smile was bright, as well.

"Adelia," her mother said, her own expres-

214

sion solemn. "Would you like coffee?"

"I'll get it," Adelia said, trying to buy time. "And the pastries smell wonderful. Guava is my favorite. Mine never turn out as well as yours do."

Her mother simply lifted a brow at the comment. "Enough small talk," she said firmly. "We have important matters to discuss. You left this house last Sunday without a word to anyone. That was inexcusable. Nor have you called to apologize. You were not raised to behave in such a way. And then your daughter announced to all of us that Ernesto has left home. What is the meaning of that?"

"Ernesto's back home," Adelia said quickly, hoping that would be enough to cut off further questioning.

"Why did he go in the first place? You know it is your job to keep your husband content at home."

Though she'd been hearing the same tired admonition her entire life, Adelia was suddenly sick of it. "Mama, it takes two people to make a marriage work. I can't fix things alone."

"Then I will speak to Ernesto myself," her mother said at once. "Or I will have Elliott have a word with him."

"Absolutely not," Adelia snapped. "I don't

215

want the entire family involved in my marriage. It will only make things worse."

To be honest, though, she wasn't sure they could get any worse. Ernesto might be living back home, but he was sleeping in a guest room because she'd refused to allow him back in her bed straight from his mistress's. His presence was a matter of appearances only and not a first step toward reconciliation. They both recognized that. She had no idea how long they could continue to live the lie.

"You know I just want to help," her mother said gently.

Adelia released a sigh. "I know you do, but the best way is to leave us alone, Mama. I've told my sisters and Elliott the same thing."

"You're isolating yourself from the family," her mother accused.

"For now, maybe it's necessary," Adelia said. "Sometimes all the hovering is more than I can handle."

"And what about your children? Do you not want us to be there for them, either?"

"Only if you can be supportive without making comments about their father or our marriage. It's confusing enough for them, as it is."

"All the more reason to settle this quickly

and get things back on track," her mother said decisively. "You owe that to your children."

Adelia nodded agreement, because there was little choice. She wondered, though, what she owed herself.

"You're looking a little shell-shocked," Erik noted when Karen walked into the kitchen at Sullivan's. "Rough morning?"

"A duty call with Maria Cruz," she said.

He grinned. "Have you been mistreating her precious son?"

Karen lifted a brow. "Not that it would be any of your business, but no. And we had a perfectly lovely visit." Well, they had, she thought, more or less. At least it had ended on an upbeat note.

She glanced around the kitchen. "Where's Dana Sue? I didn't see her in the office when I came in."

"She went with Ronnie to look at the space we're thinking of buying for the gym. Maddie went with them, too."

Karen frowned. "You decided to buy space? I thought you were planning to lease."

"The numbers make more sense if we own, according to Maddie and Helen."

"Has Elliott gone with them?"

"I'm sure he has. He and Maddie are the ones with the real understanding of the kind of space needed."

"Is it here in town, on Main Street?"

Erik shook his head. "It's in town, but over on Palmetto, not far from The Corner Spa, as a matter of fact. Everyone seemed to think that would be another advantage, especially for Elliott, since he needs to get back and forth between the two places."

Karen hesitated for a minute. "Erik, do you need me right this second? Could I take a run over there? Fifteen, twenty minutes, no more."

He frowned at the request. "I haven't stirred up another hornet's nest between the two of you, have I?"

She shook her head, managing a weak smile. "Not this time. In fact, I was thinking maybe if I went over there, I could show my support. I've been so negative, I think Elliott might appreciate the fact that I've almost accepted this."

"Almost?"

"I still have reservations. I can't deny that, but I'm trying, Erik. I really want to be behind my husband a hundred percent. I'm not there yet, but I am trying."

"Then go," he said at once, giving her the address. "Hurry back, though. There's still a lot of lunch prep to do."

"I'm sure if I linger too long, Dana Sue will drag me back with her," Karen told him, taking off the apron she'd just donned and heading out, not bothering to grab her purse before she left.

She spotted Mary Vaughn's fancy Mercedes a block down from The Corner Spa. Since no one was outside, she guessed they were still viewing the inside of the property, another large Victorian on a street that was becoming a mix of residential and commercial. Other than The Corner Spa, most of the commercial uses were for offices for insurance agents and Realtors. Helen had moved her law practice into one of the smaller houses a few months ago, as well.

When Karen stepped inside what looked to her like a home that had been seriously neglected for a very long time, Elliott flashed a welcoming smile, which quickly faded to a look of concern.

"Everything okay?" he asked, stepping away from the others.

"Erik told me you all were looking at property," she told him. "I thought I'd come check it out for myself."

He seemed uncertain whether to take her words at face value. "That's it?"

"If this gym is going to happen, I need to

find a way to accept that and show you my support. I do have questions, though."

He smiled. "Of course you do," he teased. "You wouldn't be you if you didn't have a million and one questions. How about I answer all of them tonight? Frances is eager to babysit again. We could go to Rosalina's."

"It's a date," she said.

He gestured around as the others wandered off to another room. "What do you think?"

"It looks very sad to me," she said candidly. "Is there money to fix it up?"

He nodded. "Mary Vaughn says it's a steal, and Helen and Ronnie think in the end, even with the improvements needed, this makes more sense financially than the lease we were originally looking into. Ronnie will give us a deal on supplies for renovations and help with the work. He thinks we can do a lot of it ourselves, though we'll have to bring in Mitch Franklin and his electrical and plumbing contractors, like they did at the spa."

"It sounds expensive."

"Like I said, I have to trust Helen and Ronnie on this. They say the numbers work in our favor. I'll tell you all about it tonight."

She pressed a kiss to his cheek. "I'd better

get back to Sullivan's. I left Erik on his own."

"I'll pick Frances up on my way home," he said. "See you around seven."

When she would have taken off, he pulled her back and into his arms for another kiss. "Thank you for stopping by. It means a lot to me."

She could see in his eyes that it truly did. "I should have gotten on board sooner, for your sake."

"No more doubts?" he asked.

She sighed. "I never said that, but I'm going to work on keeping them in check."

"That's a start then," he said, looking relieved. "And I'll try to make sure to reassure you, so you have no reason to worry."

She nodded. It was one of the better deals she'd struck today.

Helen and Ronnie had prepared a comparison of all the figures for buying the house on Palmetto versus leasing space on Main Street. Elliott took those with him to dinner with Karen. Her appearance today at the walk-through had given him hope that they could move forward without it causing further dissension in his marriage.

Sitting close to her in the booth at Rosalina's, though, he was having a hard time keeping his mind on numbers. He was far more intrigued by the scent Karen wore and the heat radiating from her thigh pressed against his. She, however, seemed totally focused on the pages he'd spread out on the table. He heard her gasp and knew she'd reached the bottom line.

"Elliott, that's huge," she said, her expression shocked.

"I'm not investing all of that," he reminded her. "There are partners, remember?"

"I know, but even with six of you, there's a lot of money that won't be paid off for years. You won't be operating in the black right away, businesses never do. What if you have to keep investing more and more just to keep the doors open? Where is it going to come from? We don't have it."

He could see the panic rising in her eyes again and knew that his determination to move forward with full disclosure at every stage had probably been a mistake. He'd been lulled into a false sense of complacency by her earlier reaction to the property the group wanted to buy. Still, he also knew he'd had no choice but to reveal everything.

"There will be enough capital for a year from the initial investments," he said confidently.

"And then?"

"We're all convinced from our projections that we can be in the black by then."

"What if you're not?"

"We will be," he said impatiently. "Our estimates have been very conservative, and we have The Corner Spa's history to guide us."

She closed her eyes, clearly trying to fight down the panic. "You're sure?" she pressed eventually.

"I am," he said. "More importantly, Helen, Maddie and the others are. We're not going into this lightly, Karen. We all have a stake in its success."

"But you stand to lose more. The others have successful businesses of their own. They probably have savings to fall back on. We're just starting out." She met his gaze. "And what about a baby? How long are you willing to postpone that? I thought it was something you really wanted, for us to have a child of our own."

"I want it more than anything," he said sincerely. "You know that."

"More than this?" she asked, challenging him.

"Does it have to be an either/or thing?"

"For now, yes," she said.

"But even if you were pregnant tomorrow,

it would be nine months before the baby arrives."

"Do you have any idea how naive that is?" she said wearily. "There are doctor visits, pregnancy vitamins and other expenses. What if things don't go smoothly and I have to go on bed rest?"

"You didn't with either Daisy or Mack," he reminded her, determined to remain logical in the face of her dismay.

She scowled at him. "I was younger then. Everyone knows that risks can increase with age. What then, Elliott? We couldn't manage without my income, not with everything else tied up in this business."

He sighed and relented. "Okay, you're right. But I've told you that there will be more income. I'll have more private clients than ever." Of course, what he had yet to explain was that some of that money was committed to paying back his partners for fronting him the additional investment.

Though his reminder seemed to silence her, he could tell she wasn't totally convinced. "What?" he prodded. "Let's get it all on the table."

"You told me that you weren't going to consider tapping into the house equity," she began, holding his gaze.

"And I won't. I know how opposed you

are to that."

"Then where's the additional investment money coming from, Elliott? I know you. Your pride won't allow you not to contribute what you consider to be your fair share. Where'd you find it? You didn't ask your mother or sisters for a loan, did you?"

And there it was, he thought. "Of course not. I have no intention of dragging them into this. The other partners will float me a loan. I'll pay them back as the gym becomes profitable."

"So, you're still taking out a loan, just not on the house?" she said. "You're asking our friends for it."

"I didn't ask. They offered," he said defensively. "And they'll give me a lot of flexibility for paying it back, Karen."

"But there will be legal documents?" she persisted. "You'll owe them this money?"

"Of course."

"What if you can't pay it?"

"There's flexibility in the payback schedule," he repeated, because she obviously wasn't hearing him.

"I'm sure there were many deals that Ray convinced himself would be just as easy," she retorted bitterly.

Elliott's temper frayed. "I resent the comparison."

"I don't blame you," she said wearily. "But can you deny that I'm right?"

His heart ached at the painful memories he was stirring in her. At the same time, this was his chance to give his family the life he wanted for them. He had to seize this opportunity, and he had to do it on his terms.

"It's the best option," he told her. "And it will work out. You have to trust that I won't let you down."

She faced him, her eyes brimming with tears. "I know you'd never mean to," she whispered.

"I won't, *querida,*" he said firmly. "Never."

It was a promise he intended to do everything in his power to keep.

11

Karen was starting to feel oddly isolated. All around her the nonstop conversation was about the new gym. With all of her friends and their husbands involved directly or indirectly with the project and enthusiastically moving full steam ahead, she was the only one, it seemed, with reservations. She hated being the lone holdout, especially when it demonstrated a lack of faith in her own husband.

The papers for the property had been signed yesterday afternoon, and everyone had gathered tonight at Maddie and Cal's for a celebration. Karen had wanted desperately to beg off, but at the disappointed look in Elliott's eyes, she'd reluctantly agreed to go.

Kids were racing around the backyard, high on too many sweets. The men were filled with boundless enthusiasm for their project and clustered around plans for the renovations of the property. Karen found herself sitting alone in the shadows on the patio, wishing she could get into the spirit of the celebration, if only for Elliott's sake.

"Still not convinced?" Helen asked with her usual directness, dropping down onto the chaise longue next to hers.

Karen gave her a half-hearted smile. "I'm trying to be."

"Want some advice from someone who's watched a lot of marriages fall apart?" asked the woman who was recognized as one of the state's top divorce attorneys.

Karen wasn't entirely sure she did, but she nodded anyway. Knowing Helen, it would be impossible to keep her silent, if she felt this was something Karen needed to hear.

"First, you should know that I believe in this project," Helen said, putting the weight of her expertise as a lawyer and a business-woman behind it. "I've gone over all the angles and the numbers. I have The Corner Spa experience to gauge it by. Obviously, there are no guarantees, but I'm convinced it will be a success."

She gave Karen a conspiratorial look. "I also know something that you may not know, that none of the others know, either. Trust me, it's big news."

Karen regarded her with surprise. "If you know something that could affect how this goes, why haven't you told the guys?"

"Lawyer-client confidentiality," she said. "Today my client released me from that and said I could tell anyone who might be interested, but I've been saving it till later." She grinned. "Thought I'd make a big announcement and get my minute in the spotlight."

"Can you fill me in now, especially if you think it's reassuring news?" Karen asked, her curiosity aroused.

"Dexter's is closing," Helen revealed.

Even Karen saw how that could impact the gym project in a positive way. "Wow! I had no idea."

"No one did," Helen said. "Dexter told me he's been wanting to retire for a long time, but he knew there were men in town who counted on that dump of a gym of his. He didn't want to go till there was a viable alternative on the horizon. The minute he heard about this plan, he came to me to handle any legalities involved in closing the place down, putting the space on the market and making some changes to his will to reflect that the business was history."

Karen blinked at the news. "He's really doing it? There's no question about it?"

"None. He can't wait to get a double-wide in Florida," Helen confirmed. "He said he and his wife are eager to spend the year in the sunshine, playing bingo and going to the races and the casinos down there."

Karen felt her spirits improving for the first time since Elliott had revealed the details of the plan to her. "That really could make all the difference, couldn't it?"

"I think the new place would have succeeded, anyway," Helen said. "But, yes, this should just about guarantee it."

"Thank you for telling me. I need to find Elliott. I'm still scared by all this — he's committed for a lot of money, by my standards — but I'm definitely reassured."

Helen reached for her arm to hold her back. "One more bit of advice, if I may. It might be better to let him know you believe in him than to say you were only convinced because he won't have any competition."

Karen nodded, understanding exactly what Helen was advising. "Good point. And I do believe in him. He's never once given me any reason not to."

"It's just hard getting past what Ray did," Helen suggested. "I think Elliott understands that, too, but maybe it's time you thought about basing decisions on the man you're with, rather than the one who left."

"You're right," Karen concurred. "And the fact that I haven't driven Elliott away with all my doubts just proves he's a saint."

She found him inside, bent over the plans on the dining room table with the others. She inched in beside him. Though he gave her only an absentminded smile, he slipped an arm around her shoulders, then nodded toward the plans.

"Want a closer look?" he asked.

As if they somehow understood that this moment required privacy, the other men backed off one by one, leaving them alone.

Karen listened to Elliott's description of the space and what it would be like once it was completed, but her gaze remained on his face, not on the papers spread across the table. There was no mistaking his enthusiasm, his faith in what he was about to do.

"You're really excited about this," she said, even though it was hardly a surprise. Why hadn't she been able to accept how much it mattered to him? How had she allowed her fears to undermine her belief that she could trust this man with anything, even their money?

"It's our future," he said simply. "Maybe I didn't start our life together with such a big dream, but once it was put out there by Ronnie and the others, it seemed tantalizingly within reach. It will make all the difference for us, Karen. Maybe not right away, but in a couple of years, there will be no more scrimping, no more worry."

She smiled at his optimism. "There will always be worry. With kids and family, there always is."

"But not about finances," he insisted.

She gave his hand a squeeze. "I think maybe I'm finally starting to believe that." She met his gaze, unable to stop a grin from spreading across her face. "I have news," she told him.

He chuckled at her expression. "And where did you come by this news of yours?"

"Helen told me. She's going to fill the others in later, but I think it would be okay if I told you now."

He regarded her curiously. "Sounds as if it might be good news. Is it?"

"You tell me," she said, then added with a dramatic flourish, "Dexter's retiring and closing down his gym as soon as yours is up and running. Maybe even before."

It seemed to take him a minute to absorb the revelation, but then his eyes lit up. He picked her up and spun her around, then set her on her feet, delight giving way to dismay. "What will he do, though? I guess I never thought about driving him out of a business he's had for years. I used to go there to work out when it was the only place in town. It was run-down and disgusting, but he's a good old guy."

"Not to worry," she assured him. "Apparently he wants to retire to Florida with his wife and play bingo. You all are giving him that opportunity. It's an unintended benefit to your plans."

Elliott chuckled. "Now that's a sight I'd like to see, Dexter and a bunch of old ladies playing bingo."

"Maybe one of these days when money's not an issue, we'll pack the kids in the car and go visit," she suggested, aware even as she spoke that it was a huge breakthrough for her to look ahead and foresee the possibility of a vacation. "I wouldn't mind seeing the ocean or the Gulf of Mexico."

"And we can take the kids to Disney World," he said enthusiastically. "Just imagine how much fun they'd have."

"Don't mention it now or we'll never hear the end of it," she cautioned, though she couldn't seem to stop grinning at yet another dream she would never have dared to imagine a few years ago, or even a few weeks ago.

For the first time in a very long time, she realized she was actually looking forward with excitement, rather than back in despair, just as Helen had so recently advised.

As Adelia drove home from her PTA committee meeting at the school, she couldn't seem to stop herself from detouring a few blocks past Ernesto's lover's home. Sure enough, his car was in the driveway. The knowledge soured her good mood.

"Well, you asked for it, didn't you?" she muttered as she kept driving. Why had she deliberately tortured herself by checking? Was she a glutton for punishment? Had she somehow convinced herself that this time might be different, that he had come home to make a commitment to honor their wedding vows? He'd certainly made no such promises, which meant she was the delusional one.

Her eyes stinging with unshed tears, she walked into the house and went straight to the kitchen to get a belated dinner on the table. A few minutes later, Selena came in and found her unsuccessfully fighting tears.

"He's there again, isn't he?" Selena asked angrily. "At that woman's house?"

Adelia turned to her daughter in shock. "What do you know about that?"

"I've seen him. It's where he was staying

when he left. I snuck over there at night and saw his car," she said defiantly. "I know I was grounded, but I had to know. If you want to ground me forever, I don't care."

Instead, Adelia opened her arms and gathered her daughter close. "Oh, *niña,* these are not things you need to know about. I'm so sorry."

"But I do know, and I hate him!"

"Shh. He's your father. You don't hate him," Adelia said. No, all the hating was left to her, along with the mess he'd created. Thank goodness the other children were too young to have figured out as much as the observant Selena had.

She held Selena until she'd calmed down, then said quietly, "Get your brother and sisters. Make sure they all wash their hands. I'll have dinner ready in five minutes."

Selena's gaze narrowed. "Will *he* be here?"

"I don't know," Adelia said candidly.

"Do I have to stay at the table if he is?" Selena asked, her gaze pleading.

Adelia sighed, relenting from her usual rule that the entire family ate dinner together, no exceptions. "No. If your father comes home tonight, you may be excused and I will bring you a tray later."

And then she would spend the rest of the evening trying to figure out how she and

Ernesto were going to make things right for their children.

When Frances arrived at the town's senior center, which was set up — with a touch of irony — in what had once been a funeral home, there was a stir in the parlor, which had been set aside for card games. The few men who were there seemed to be clustered around the refreshment table, while the women were buzzing off in a corner and casting sour looks in the direction of Flo and Liz, who were the only ones actually seated at a table.

Frances took her place with them, then nodded toward the others. "What on earth has everyone in such a tizzy?"

Liz tried to keep a solemn expression, but couldn't seem to stop the chuckle that burst forth. "Jake Cudlow asked Flo out," she said, when Flo remained silent.

"Oh, my," Frances said, understanding the implications. Ever since his wife's death two years ago, Jake had been considered the hot catch at the senior center. Every widow there had her eyes on him. So far, though, he'd remained stubbornly elusive, coming to events alone and responding to the parade of casseroles offered to him with little more than polite gratitude.

She turned her attention to Flo. "How do you feel about being the chosen one?" she inquired, her lips twitching.

"As if I've suddenly become the town slut," Flo responded sourly. "I didn't ask for this. Did I take one single tuna casserole to the man's house? Have I flirted outrageously with him? No. I'm not interested. I've never been interested. I wasn't interested when we were sixteen and he repeatedly asked me out back in high school."

Frances couldn't help it, she chuckled right along with Liz, who was no longer even trying to control her mirth. "Sounds to me as if she's protesting too much," Frances said.

"That's what I thought," Liz agreed.

"Does this mean you turned him down?" Frances asked.

"I did," Flo said, then scowled across the room. "But do you think that makes a bit of difference to those old biddies? They're acting like I stole the man right out of their clutches. And naturally they're blaming me because he's not here tonight, when I happen to know the only reason he didn't show up is because he's gone to Charleston with Mavis Johnson, who's obviously not as picky as I am about the men she dates."

"Sounds to me like another example when

playing hard to get works more effectively than flirting outrageously," Liz said. "Some might think that was your strategy."

"Well, it wasn't," Flo responded indignantly. "I wasn't playing games. Jake is not my type. And I assure you, he's not heartbroken. He's gone off on an overnight trip with Mavis, hasn't he?"

"What exactly is your type?" Liz inquired, fighting a smile.

"I always thought it was that he had his own teeth and could still move without a walker," Frances teased.

Flo looked from Frances to Liz, then shook her head, her lips finally curving into a smile. "My bar is somewhat higher than that," she assured them. "I wouldn't mind having an intelligent conversation from time to time, or maybe a spin around a dance floor."

"I thought spinning around a dance floor was how you broke your hip," Liz commented.

"It was line dancing," Flo retorted. "But I see your point. Maybe my agility is a bit compromised. I should probably accept that, but I've given up my high heels and that's as much as I'm willing to compromise for the moment."

"Okay, since neither Liz or I are angling

for a man," Frances began, casting a look toward Liz for confirmation. Liz nodded. "Then we're not your competition. So who in Serenity does appeal to you?"

"Besides Elliott?" Flo quipped.

"Taken and too young," Frances retorted. "Try again."

"I had a feeling you'd say that," Flo said, then leaned closer. "Promise you won't mention this to another soul. If it gets back to Helen, my staid daughter will probably have me committed."

"Not a word," Liz promised.

Frances sketched a cross across her heart.

Apparently satisfied, Flo said, "I've been seeing Don Leighton."

"At the post office?" Liz asked, her eyes wide. "He must be ten years younger than you."

"Twelve actually," Flo said with a grin. "We've gone over to Columbia to a few clubs. That man can do a Texas two-step like a youngster."

"Is that all you've been doing?" Frances asked, unrepentantly curious. While the idea of having sex at her age hadn't crossed her mind in years, she knew Flo well enough to imagine she was still interested.

Flo's cheeks turned pink. "That's the part that would flat-out kill Helen. When I mentioned leaving condoms in my bedside table when I left my condo in Boca Raton, she about had a heart attack. To think I might be having *S-E-X* right here, practically under her nose, would horrify her."

"I imagine it would," Liz said huffily, then grinned. "You lucky woman!"

Frances turned to her. "You're envious?"

"I most certainly am," Liz said, then sighed. "Not that any man is ever likely to see this saggy old body of mine again."

"I'm with you," Frances said with heartfelt emotion.

"Oh, just turn out the stupid lights and don't worry about it," Flo advised. "Do you think men our age look one iota better in their birthday suits?"

Frances choked back a laugh but was unable to stop it from erupting. Then Liz and Flo joined her.

"I don't know about you two, but I've lost all interest in playing cards tonight," Frances said. "I have a half-gallon of rocky road ice cream at my place if you're interested."

"Count me in," Liz said at once.

"Let's go," Flo concurred eagerly. "I think if we make a quick stop at Sullivan's, I can probably nab us a few brownies to go with that ice cream. Erik always puts a few aside for me, bless his heart. That's just one advantage to having a pastry chef as a son-in-law."

"Who needs men when there are brownies and ice cream?" Frances said, startled when both Flo and Liz shot disbelieving looks in her direction.

"Not the same," Liz said.

"Not even close," Flo agreed.

Frances just shook her head. Call her crazy, but it was about as much of an indulgence as she could handle these days.

The best part of tonight, though, was that neither Flo nor Liz had said a single word about her seeing a doctor. What a relief that had been, especially when she'd been dreading another argument. Instead, they'd shared a lot of laughter, and wasn't that the very best medicine of all?

Elliott had been avoiding his mother for a while now. Oh, he saw her on Sundays and when he picked Daisy and Mack up in the evenings, but with so many other people around, there'd been no time for the sort of cross-examination he knew she wanted to have about the state of his marriage. Karen had filled him in on the lecture she'd received. Since she'd apparently held her own, he'd felt no need to confront his mother about her meddling, especially since

241

that conversation would only open the door to a bunch of questions he didn't want to answer.

He thought he'd been fairly clever about evading her, but realized he'd only put off the inevitable when he looked up one day at the spa and saw her cross the exercise room with a determined glint in her eyes. He doubted she was there to register for a membership or to sign up for the seniors class.

"Excuse me," she said politely to his client. "Would you mind if I spoke to my son for a moment?"

Terry Hawthorn waved them off, looking relieved. "Take your time. I can catch my breath."

Elliott frowned at her. "Not if you do another circuit of the weight machines while I'm gone."

She sighed. "Slave driver."

"Fitness coach," he retorted, then reluctantly followed his mother to the patio out back. "Would you like a fruit smoothie from the café? Or maybe a muffin?"

"I didn't come to eat," she told him. "You've been avoiding me, Elliott Cruz. Oh, you come and go, but you never spend more than two seconds alone in a room with me." She held his gaze. "Why is that?" She didn't

wait for a reply before adding, "Because yo
do not want to hear what I have to say abou
fixing whatever problems there are in you
marriage."

"Because those problems, if there are
any," he said pointedly, "are between my
wife and me. It's up to us to resolve them."

"And my thoughts count for nothing?"

"Your thoughts will always matter to me,
but it's not up to you to fix my marriage."

"Then it *does* need fixing," she said, a
note of triumph in her voice.

"I didn't say that," Elliott retorted.
"Mama, please. Stop this. I'm a grown man.
I'm in love with my wife and, thank God,
she seems to love me, as well. We'll have
ups and downs and adjustments, but outside
interference won't help us to deal with
those."

"Karen wasn't so reluctant to listen," she
grumbled.

"Because she wants to please you," he
said. "She respects you as my mother, but
believe me, she's no more eager than I am
to have you meddling."

"Some people call it caring."

He sighed. "I know that's what you mean
it to be — I really do. But please, Mama, let
us be."

"I don't know what's come of this world

when children don't appreciate the wisdom of their own mother. First, Adelia, now you — you want no part of my advice."

Elliott frowned. "You've spoken to Adelia?"

"Of course. Even I can see that situation is a tragedy just waiting to happen. Your sister just tells me to butt out."

"And did you listen?"

"Of course not. I'm worried. That's what mothers do. We worry about the happiness of our children and our grandchildren, who will be affected by any rash decisions that might be made."

Elliott could see the depth of caring in her eyes, the concern she wasn't even trying to disguise. He wondered if she knew just how badly Ernesto was treating Adelia. He doubted it, because if she did, she might go tear him limb from limb herself. It was more comfortable for her to think that Adelia and Karen were the ones at fault if there were problems in their marriages. Years of conditioning from his father had taught her that was usually where any blame belonged.

"Mama, I'm keeping a close eye on Adelia. If she needs support, she knows she has it, not just from me, but from all the family. She wants to work through things on her own. We have to respect that." No matter

how difficult it might be, he conceded.

She gave him a disconcerted, frightened look. "How bad are things?"

"Bad enough," he said carefully. "Just make sure she knows you're there for her, Mama. Don't judge. Just listen. That's what Adelia really needs."

"I never liked Ernesto," she confided. "But he was her choice, and there was no talking her out of it. And then, of course, there was a baby to consider, and it was too late. Then more babies, one right after the other." She shrugged. "She seemed happy."

"I think she was," Elliott said. But he couldn't help wondering how long it had been since his sister had felt even a moment's happiness or contentment in her marriage.

His mother stood up, looking even more distressed than she had when she'd arrived.

"I'm sorry for interrupting you at work," she said. "I thought it was important that we talk."

He pressed a kiss to her cheek. "I'm glad you came by. And I'm sorry if you thought I was avoiding you."

She gave him a wry look. "You *were* avoiding me," she said. "But it's okay. I forget sometimes that you are a grown man who's

more than capable of solving his own problems."

"And anytime I can't, I'll come to you,
Mama. I promise."

"Then I'd better run along. I want to bake
gingerbread for the grandchildren, and
they'll be home from school soon."

"Thank you for treating Daisy and Mack
like family," he said.

She regarded him with surprise. "They
are family," she said simply.

He knew, that whatever issues she might
still have with his marriage to Karen, that
much was true. Daisy and Mack were family. He wished it always felt that clear-cut to
him.

12

Karen was taking a break in the kitchen at Sullivan's after a crazy Saturday lunch hour when the back door opened and Elliott came in with Mack in tow. Her son was only seven, but big for his age with a square body and sturdy legs. He still had the same impish grin he'd had as a toddler, and his eyes were filled with excitement.

"Guess what?" he called out as he ran across the room to hug her.

"What?" she asked, laughing at his exuberance.

"Elliott and me went to the park and all these kids were playing football and Elliott says I can play, too. Isn't that the best, Mom? It's just touch football for little kids, but we talked to the coach and everything. We have practice just like the big kids. And our first game is next week. Will you come?" He was all but bouncing up and down with excitement as he reported his big news.

Karen's gaze shot to her husband. "Football?" she asked quietly. "Without mentioning it to me?"

Elliott shrugged. "I took him to the park. The kids were practicing and he said he wanted to play. Travis, Tom and Cal are coaching the teams and they said he could play with the little guys. You heard him, Karen. They're playing touch football. There's no tackling."

"*So* not the point," she said tightly, not wanting to start a fight in front of Mack or to ruin her son's obvious excitement. All she seemed to do recently was put a damper on her family's enthusiasm for one thing or another.

"Mom, I'm even gonna have a uniform if they can find sponsors for the team," Mack said, tugging on her sleeve to get her attention. "Maybe Sullivan's could be a sponsor. You could ask, couldn't you?"

Apparently sensing that Karen would eat dirt before doing that, Elliott quickly stepped in. "Your mom doesn't need to do that, buddy. Remember, Mr. Sullivan said he could work it out."

"Oh, yeah," Mack said, then looked around the kitchen. "Did Erik bake cookies today? His chocolate chip cookies are the best."

Karen laughed despite her annoyance. She had no idea what secret ingredient Erik included in his cookie batter, but they were better than hers, or even Maria Cruz's. Leave it to her traitorous little boy to remind her of that.

"I think he saved a few just in case you stopped by today," she told Mack, tousling his hair as she went to look for the secret stash Erik always had on hand for the various kids popping in and out of the kitchen these days. She returned with two. "That's it, kiddo. And once you're finished getting chocolate all over yourself, make sure Elliott gets you into the tub when you get home. You look as if you've been playing in a mud pit."

Mack grinned. "Playing football is no good if you don't get dirty," he advised her. His eyes suddenly went wide. "Maybe I'll even get cut and need stitches! Timmy Marshall needed six stitches when he got slammed into the ground."

He sounded as if that were an incredibly desirable badge of honor. He obviously missed the concept that stitches required needles, something he despised.

Karen sighed. She'd hoped for a few more years before her son's athletic tendencies involved him in some of the more rambunctious sports. Why hadn't she mentioned that to Elliott? She should have known that her fitness-oriented husband would think football was a perfectly acceptable way for a seven-year-old to spend his Saturday mornings. Now she got to spend those days with her heart in her throat until she saw whether Mack got through the games without an injury.

Elliott hadn't started out the day with the intention of signing Mack up for football, but he hadn't resisted when Mack expressed interest. He hadn't played in any kind of formal league at that age, but he had hung out with neighborhood kids who were obsessed with the game. He'd had his share of bumps and bruises at Mack's age. It was all part of growing up, to his way of thinking.

He sighed, thinking about the look on Karen's face when Mack had made his big announcement. She obviously didn't see it that way. He knew that was going to come back to bite him in the butt.

When he'd dropped Mack off at his mother's so he could get to the spa for his afternoon clients, he spotted Cal in Maddie's office. He tapped on the open door.

"Do you all have a minute?"

250

Maddie looked up from the papers on her desk. "Sure. What's up?"

"Karen's not happy you signed Mack up for football," Cal guessed at once, giving him a sympathetic look.

Maddie looked startled. "You signed him up without talking it over with her? He's seven, for goodness' sakes."

"He wanted to play," Elliott said defensively.

"He's *seven*," Maddie repeated.

Cal chuckled. "Obviously it's a mom thing. Dads can't wait to get our kids involved in every sport out there."

"Because you seem to forget that those little heads aren't made out of concrete," Maddie said in disgust.

"They wear helmets," Cal reminded her. "And it's touch football. No tackling allowed."

"And yet they still get concussions," Maddie said. "I thank my lucky stars that all Ty ever cared about was baseball, and Kyle never was interested in playing sports at all."

Cal grinned at her. "But now we have a son who will probably go pro and play for the Falcons or maybe the Carolina Panthers," he said, speaking of their son who was little more than a toddler.

"Bite your tongue," Maddie said with feeling. "*If* our baby expresses an interest in playing football in high school, I'll consider it."

"Good players start in middle school," Cal told her. "Some start in the Peewee League."

"Then our son will be ordinary," she countered, her expression defiant. "I'm with Karen on this."

Elliott listened to the exchange, oddly relieved by it. "You really think she was upset because she thinks Mack's too young to play football?"

"Of course," Maddie said, giving him a puzzled look. "What did you think it was about?"

"I'm still a little fuzzy on the rules of being a stepdad," Elliott admitted. "I figured she was furious because she didn't think I had any right to make the call at all."

Maddie shook her head. "You're a fantastic stepfather. Karen knows that. Nope, if you ask me, it was all about making a stupid decision, not about your right to make it."

Cal chuckled. "My wife, the diplomat."

Elliott grinned, despite his overall mood. "Hey, I wanted her opinion. She didn't have to sugarcoat it."

"As if I would," Maddie retorted. "It's not in my nature."

"I can vouch for that," Cal said. He winked at her. "It's actually one of the traits I love about you, at least most of the time."

She gave him a considering look. "Okay, you're almost out of that hole you dug for yourself a minute ago. Keep going. What other traits do you love?"

Elliott backed out the door. "That might be too much information for my tender ears. Thanks for the input."

"Anytime," Maddie murmured, though she was already distracted because Cal had moved closer and was whispering who-knew-what into her ear. Whatever it was had put a smile on her face and a look in her eyes that Elliott recognized all too well. The man obviously knew exactly how to charm his wife. Elliott should probably ask for lessons.

"You signed him up without even asking me," Karen complained in a hushed voice to Elliott that night. "I thought we'd agreed that we needed to talk about things like this."

Elliott frowned at her words. "I could use a little clarity here. Is this about the possibility that Mack could be injured playing touch football, which is what I thought your objection was, or is it about me not consulting you?"

"Both," she said at once. "Mostly it's a problem because I'm his mother. I get to decide what he can and can't do." She spoke without thinking through the implication of her words. Only when she saw the immediate hurt in Elliott's eyes did she realize she'd taken entirely the wrong approach. He looked as if she'd slapped him. As annoyed as she'd been, she realized his reaction was totally justified, but before she could muster an apology, he was on his feet.

"I see," he said softly. He stood up and headed for the door. "I need to go out. I'll be back in a couple of hours."

Stunned that he would walk out in the middle of a discussion, she stared at him. "You're leaving now?"

"If I don't, we're both going to say things we don't mean. We need a time-out. Since I'm sure you don't want to leave *your* son and daughter, then I'm the one who needs to go."

Hearing her own ill-advised comment thrown back at her with so much pain in Elliott's voice snapped her out of her own anger. She hurried after him and caught up as he stepped outside.

"I'm sorry," she said, filled with contrition. "I didn't mean that the way it came

254

out. You're a wonderful father to Daisy and Mack in every way that counts."

"But you're the biological parent," he said stiffly. "Obviously I should keep that in mind."

She crossed the porch and touched his arm, felt the muscle quiver, saw the tension in the set of his shoulders. "I am so, so sorry."

Elliott sighed. "It's clear we have a lot more work to do on our communication skills, *querida.* We can't keep hurting each other like this."

"You're right," she said at once. "Can we table all of this for now? Frances is taking the kids tomorrow night. I'll fix a special dinner, and we'll talk. We need to decide how we're going to handle situations like this when they come up."

Elliott held her gaze. "What we need to decide is what my role is to be with your children," he told her. "I don't want to be an uninvolved father figure who's little more than a babysitter from time to time."

"Of course not," she said at once. "You've never been that."

"And we need to figure all this out before we consider having a baby of our own," he added. "We can't have one set of rules for our child and another for Daisy and Mack."

"Agreed."

He faced her, then held her gaze. "Before this dinner tomorrow, maybe you should think about whether you'd let me adopt Daisy and Mack. Their father hasn't been around in years. I think Helen could work out the legalities, if it's what you want. I *know* it's what I want. I've been telling you that for a long time, but you've brushed me off every time it's come up."

Karen regarded him with surprise. "I always thought you were talking theoretically. I guess I didn't realize how much it would mean to you. I should have understood."

"It's difficult being the outsider in the family."

Karen was genuinely stunned that she'd made him feel that way. "I've never meant for you to feel like an outsider. You're more of a father to Daisy and Mack than Ray ever was. That's how they think of you. You know that."

"And you?"

"It's how I see you, too," she insisted.

"That's not how it sounded just a few minutes ago," he said.

"I know it didn't and I'm truly sorry. I spoke without thinking."

"You know the irony of all this? Maddie

almost had me convinced you were only upset because you're a mom and moms have this ingrained fear of their kids getting hurt playing football, but obviously I was right all along. It looks to me that it has more to do with me not being entitled to go with my gut when it comes to parenting Daisy and Mack."

She frowned. "You discussed this with Maddie?"

"I did," he said with a hint of defiance. "I wanted another perspective. She and Cal were around when I got to the spa. They have experience with the whole stepparenting thing."

"Shouldn't you be talking to me about things like this, rather than our friends?" she asked, aware that she was being unreasonable. Of course, he'd talk to friends and seek advice, especially when they were likely to have worked through similar issues.

"I would have, but you were obviously upset and I didn't want to make it worse, especially since you were at work. I wanted to understand how I'd been in the wrong." He shrugged. "Obviously it didn't help, because Maddie got it wrong. It really is about me being a stepparent."

He looked her in the eye. "You know, if Ray were still in the picture, this wouldn't be an issue for me. I'd deal if I thought me acting like a dad was going to muddy the waters between him and the kids. That's not the case. How do *you* feel about me legally adopting them? The truth, Karen."

"I guess I haven't really considered it," she admitted. "I thought things were okay the way they are. They know you love them."

"But they also know you're the real authority figure."

She frowned at the characterization. "That's not true. They listen to you."

"Only when you're not around. Look, this doesn't have to happen, but I think it could be important for them to see that I love them as if they were my own. And it might clarify the situation when it comes to who gets to make the decisions or who disciplines them. We'll do it jointly. This may not matter now when they're so young, but the teenage years aren't that far away, at least for Daisy. It could matter then."

She saw the point he was making. "Jointly is good," she said at once, knowing that not only was he right, but that she'd been unfair to suggest otherwise. "I know it didn't come out that way earlier, but that was exactly my point. We need to talk about things and decide together. I'm not talking about whether they get ice cream after school or get a time-out for misbehaving. We have to be in agreement on the big things."

Elliott nodded. "Like football," he said.

She nodded. "Like football."

"Are you going to insist that Mack drop out?" he asked.

As badly as she wanted to do just that — he was only seven, after all — she wouldn't disappoint her son now that he had his heart set on it. Nor did she want to undercut Elliott's authority and prove the point he'd just been making about his decisions not counting.

"No, but if he comes home with cuts, bruises or broken bones, watch out," she warned.

"Duly noted," he said solemnly.

He came back inside then and pulled her into his arms. "Maybe we'll get this give-and-take thing down yet."

She touched his cheek, relaxing for the first time since the argument had begun. "I'm counting on it."

"And we'll talk some more about me formally adopting them?" he pressed.

She nodded. She had no idea why she'd been dragging her heels on taking a step that would give her children a greater sense of stability, but she knew deep in her heart that she had. She'd pretended that all those casual mentions had been theoretical because it suited her. She needed to figure out why she'd been reluctant, and then maybe she, Elliott and her children could finally move forward to become a totally united family.

Karen was surprised a few days later when Raylene tapped on the kitchen door at Sullivan's, then stepped inside, her expression chagrined.

"I know I promised I'd come by for coffee weeks ago, but my life's been a circus," she told Karen. "Is the offer still good?"

"Absolutely," Karen said. "And you picked a great morning. Erik made the coffee and left to pick up supplies. Dana Sue's not coming in for another hour."

She poured them both a cup, then gestured toward a stool beside her workplace. "I hope you don't mind, but I have prep work to do for lunch. I can talk while I chop, though. What's been going on that's kept you so busy?"

"Carter's been working all sorts of crazy shifts at the police department. Even though he's Serenity's chief now, he still takes shifts on the street. His sisters are involved in every single activity at the high school. Guess who gets to drive them there and back and sit in the audience and applaud when they have performances?"

"Quite a change for you from a couple of years ago," Karen said. "Are you coping okay?"

"Honestly, other than an occasional twinge of panic when I walk out the front door, I'm doing amazingly well with all the commotion. It's hard to believe there was a time I was too terrified to set foot outside the house." She shrugged. "It helps that my crazy, abusive ex is finally locked up for a good long time this time."

"I imagine that must be a huge relief. I don't know what I'd do if Ray ever got it into his head to wander back to Serenity. Not that he was abusive, but I have a huge amount of unresolved anger at the way he abandoned me to deal with his financial mess."

"Do you ever hear from him?" Raylene asked. "Does he ever ask about the kids?"

Karen shook her head. "It's as if they don't even exist." She thought of the role Raylene had been expected to step into with Carter's two younger sisters. "Can I ask you a question?"

"Sure."

"Has it been hard for you to figure out what role you're supposed to play with Carter's sisters?"

Raylene's expression turned thoughtful. "It was hard when we were first seeing each other and didn't know where our relationship might be going," she admitted. "I knew Carrie really needed a female influence in her life, but I didn't want to overstep. It got awkward from time to time." She grinned. "Now both girls just think of me as a big sister, I think, and Carter and I juggle things together. Maybe if Carter were their dad, rather than their older brother and legal guardian, it would be harder, but we're all adjusting to how to handle things, even Carter."

She gave Karen a penetrating look. "Why? Is Elliott having trouble fitting into the role of stepdad?"

"Actually he's incredible," Karen admitted. "I'm the one who seems to be having trouble adjusting to having a real partner who will share in the responsibility of raising my kids. Without intending to, I've made him feel as if he has no say."

Raylene frowned. "That's not good. Any idea why you might be doing that?"

Karen shook her head. "I keep going over it and over it, but I'm at a loss. He even wants to adopt them officially, but I've held back."

"Could it be because you're still scared of things not working out with Elliott?" Raylene speculated gently. "That might make you cautious about making him a permanent, legal fixture in their lives."

Karen frowned at the unexpected suggestion. Unfortunately, it sounded all too plausible. After being burned as badly as she had been by Ray, after cleaning up that mess, was she thinking that she didn't want to have to deal with all the ramifications if she and Elliott didn't make it?

"I hope not," she told Raylene. "I want this marriage to work more than anything. It's not just because I don't want another failure, either. I know how lucky I am to have found a man like Elliott, who's decent, kind and loving. Every time we hit a rough patch, though, I do panic, there's no question about that."

"Then that could be holding you back," Raylene said. "But if you think that refusing to let Elliott adopt the kids will protect them from any fallout if you and Elliott were to divorce down the road, you're fooling yourself. Their lives and emotions are already intertwined. All you're doing is depriving them of knowing that their stepfather loves them so unconditionally that he wants to make it legal."

Karen nodded slowly, seeing it all from a different perspective. She might not be quite ready to take that final leap of faith, but she knew she needed to get there, not only for her children's sake, but for her own.

She'd thought that marrying Elliott proved her commitment, but she saw now that there were more steps needed before she'd be fully invested in her marriage. It was an unexpected discovery and, with their recent share of ups and downs, it couldn't have come at a worse time.

Adelia walked into Ernesto's office at the development company he'd founded with two partners and turned into a regional success despite all of the dire economic forecasts in recent years. She walked right past his secretary, barely sparing her a wave. She could see the protest forming on the older woman's lips, but she pretended she didn't.

Ernesto was on the phone when she entered, leaning back in his chair, his expensively clad feet propped on the huge desk she'd helped him choose when she'd decorated his office in a way that would announce his success to any visitors. First impressions, she knew, counted for as much as reality in a new company starting out.

She paced while he finished his conversation, then moved to a leather chair in front of the desk when he hung up.

"This is a surprise," he said, his expression neutral. "What brings you by?"

"We need to talk," she announced with the determination she'd been stoking on the drive over here.

"Wouldn't it be better to have our personal conversations at home?"

"It would be, if you were ever there," she said. "And if our children weren't privy to every word. Selena's already upset enough about what's going on."

He frowned at that. "She eavesdrops? What is wrong with that child?"

"Nothing is wrong with her. She's twelve. She understands that our fighting can't mean anything good." She gave him a sharp look. "It doesn't help that she also knows all about your latest mistress."

He had the grace to look disconcerted by that. "How? Why would you tell her?" he asked angrily. "Do you want to ruin my relationship with her?"

"I've told her nothing. She's seen you with this woman." She gave him a scathing look. "What did you expect when you took up with someone just blocks away from our home? Didn't you know you were likely to get caught, or is that what you were counting on? Were you hoping I'd be so humiliated I'd finally cut you loose?"

He looked taken aback by her strong words. "You've always known about the other women. I assumed you understood that was the price for living in that big house and having all your needs met."

Adelia looked at him, wondering how she could ever have thought herself in love with this insensitive, self-absorbed man. "You truly believe what you're saying, don't you? That a big house and a few luxuries make up for being treated like nothing?"

"Not like nothing," he said heatedly. "You're the mother of my children."

"And nothing more," she said wearily, accepting that her role had been diminished to little more than caregiver to his children. "You're setting a terrible example for your son, Ernesto. I don't want him growing up thinking that it's acceptable for a man to treat a woman like this, with such little respect." She met his gaze. "And I don't want him or his sisters to see me as the kind of woman who finds that behavior acceptable."

He frowned at her words. "What is that supposed to mean?"

"It means that I expect you to spend your nights in our home, that I expect you to honor the commitment you made to me on the day we took our vows. If that means we spend the rest of our lives seeing marriage counselors, then that's what we'll do. We won't go on like this."

"And if I say no?" he asked, clearly confident that she had no fallback position, that she was trying to bluff him into changing.

"Then I will take our children and leave you," she said, holding his gaze. "And I will take you for every penny I possibly can, to assure that our children want for nothing. I haven't spoken to Helen Decatur-Whitney, but I'm pretty sure I have enough evidence to make sure the courts will give me everything I ask for."

He slammed his fist on the top of his desk. "There will be no divorce! Your mother will talk sense into you on that point."

"Don't count on it," she said mildly. "You see, I always worried too much about what Mama would say, but she's not living this lie that is our marriage. I am." She held his gaze. "And I'm done with the way things are."

Before he could reply, she stood up and walked out. Only after she reached her car did she realize how badly she was shaking. But for the first time in years she felt the first tiny shred of her self-respect returning.

13

Elliott felt as if he hadn't been home for ages. He'd been spending every evening after leaving the spa with whichever of the other men were available, working on renovations at the new gym. They were making good progress, but knowing that he owed money to his partners was weighing on him. Not that anyone was pressing him, but the sooner extra money started coming in, the better.

He had the added pressure of trying to keep his concern from Karen. She'd completely freak out if she realized that their obligation to the other partners hadn't been met, no matter how willing the other men were to let it slide until they opened the doors at the gym in a few weeks.

He took a break from hanging drywall and grabbed a bottle of juice from the refrigerator they'd installed in what eventually would be a small café area. It was actually a professional-grade refrigerator, bought used from Dana Sue, who'd conveniently decided it was time for a newer, larger unit at Sullivan's. He saw Ronnie's deft hand in encouraging that deal with his wife.

Travis came in and joined him. The ex-ballplayer-turned-country-radio-station-owner was covered in sawdust, but he'd never looked happier. "It's starting to take shape, don't you think?" he commented.

Elliott shrugged. "It's still hard for me to imagine it filled with shiny new equipment. Right now it looks like a big, empty space to me." He gestured around him. "And I'm still not convinced about this whole café thing. Do men care about something like that?"

Travis grinned. "You're in here having something to drink, aren't you?"

"But I'm . . ." His voice trailed off. "Hot, tired and sweaty, just like anyone who's been working out." He smiled as he realized that's exactly how their clients were likely to feel after a good workout.

Travis lifted his own bottle in a silent toast. "Exactly. I think we have to trust Maddie on stuff like this. And Dana Sue won't be stocking it with girly food like the muffins and salads they serve at the spa. I think she's planning some macho, yet healthy alternatives."

"Speaking of food, I could go for some right now," Elliott admitted. "Think anybody else would want to order a pizza?"

"Ronnie's already gone to pick 'em up," Travis said. "And as soon as I've had a slice, I need to get over to the radio station. I go on the air in an hour."

"The station's doing well, isn't it?"

"Despite my cousin Tom's dire prediction, yes," he said, grinning. "There's still room in the world for small-town, local radio. Advertising's been solid since the day we went on the air. Sarah and I won't get rich, but we can live comfortably. That's all I ask of life — that and having our kids healthy."

Elliott was tempted to ask him how he'd adapted to stepparenting, especially with Sarah's ex actually working for Travis at the station and underfoot all the time. Instead, he decided to focus on gym business, since Travis would be taking off for the station soon.

"Has Maddie talked to you about scheduling commercials as soon as we have our official opening date?" Elliott asked him.

"Not only has she talked to me, she managed to get me to cut my prices in half," Travis said, looking impressed. "I'm still trying to figure out how she pulled that off.

One minute I had control of the meeting, the next I was signing off on a deal that made my head spin when I looked at the figures later."

Elliott chuckled. "She's good, all right. I have to admit I'm happy to leave some of this business stuff in her hands. Of course, one of these days we'll all need to sit down and come up with a name for this place. We can't very well call it the anti-Dexter's."

Travis laughed. "But that would draw the customers in, I'll bet. You have all the equipment ordered?"

"And scheduled for delivery in three weeks," Elliott confirmed, then gazed doubtfully toward the main room. "What are the odds we'll be ready for it?"

"Ronnie says we will be, and he knows construction," Travis said. "He says Mitch Franklin has the plumber and the electrician scheduled for tomorrow, so we should be up to code by the end of the week with the locker room and showers just about completed, too. The finishing work and painting should be a breeze with all of us pitching in."

It should be, Elliott thought. It just meant that he was unlikely to spend any quality time with his wife or the kids anytime in the immediate future.

■ ■ ■ ■

Frances was sitting at a table in Wharton's, enjoying a rare genuine chocolate shake blended with real milk and ice cream the old-fashioned way, when Grace Wharton slid into the booth opposite her. Grace had a reputation for knowing more about what was going on in Serenity than anyone else in town. She didn't mind spreading the news around, either.

"You're friends with Elliott Cruz, right?" Grace said without preamble.

"Sure. He and Karen and the kids are like family to me," Frances said.

"What do you know about this gym he's opening over on Palmetto?"

"Just that it'll be a huge improvement over Dexter's," she said, then added, "No offense," because she knew Grace and Dexter had known each other for years. For that matter, everyone in town knew Dexter. They even liked him. They just believed he'd let that gym of his turn into a run-down dump.

Grace shrugged at the undeniable truth of her statement. "Any idea what they're going to charge for a membership?" She cast a surreptitious look over her shoulder in the direction of her husband. Neville Wharton was the pharmacist who ran the drugstore portion of Wharton's. "I'm thinking *he* could use a workout from time to time," she added in an undertone.

"You planning to give it to him for his birthday?" Frances asked, grinning at the thought of Neville's likely reaction to such a gift. Shock came to mind. He prided himself on the fact he could still get into his wedding suit, though the sad truth was he hadn't been able to buckle the pants in years, Grace had reported recently to anyone who'd listen.

Grace sat up straighter. "That's exactly what I'm planning to do. Nothing says I love you like a gift certificate to get your health back, don't you think so?"

"I'm not a hundred percent certain your husband will see it that way," Frances said gently. "How would you have felt if he'd given you a membership to The Corner Spa?"

Grace paused. "Insulted, I imagine, though I wouldn't have minded a gift certificate for some of those massages they give over there. *Whoo-ee,* do those things work the kinks out of my back after a day on my feet in this place!"

Frances smiled at the image of Grace crawling up onto a massage table and allowing herself to be pampered with scented oils and a massage. It wasn't something she'd ever expected of such a salt-of-the-earth, country-born-and-raised woman.

Grace gave her a wink. "I've picked up some pretty good gossip while I've been there, too."

Frances laughed. "Then definitely worth the cost. As for the gym, why don't I have Elliott stop by with a brochure? I'm pretty sure they're going to be available any day now. Or I'll grab one and bring it by next time I come in."

Grace nodded. "That'll do. Now, tell me this. How have you been feeling?"

"Just great," Frances said.

Grace frowned. "Really? I know some folks have been worried about you not being up to snuff."

Frances's mood, which had been upbeat only seconds before, sank. She knew once rumors started in Serenity, they took on a life of their own, especially once Grace got hold of them. She gave her friend an indignant look. "Well, you tell those folks, whoever they may be, that you just saw me and I'm in tip-top shape."

Grace looked disconcerted by her barely disguised hint of temper. "Well, of course, I will," she said at once. She reached for

274

Frances's hand. "You do know everyone in this town loves you. It's just concern, Frances, not an indictment or something. Nobody's ready to write you off, I promise you that."

Rationally, Frances understood that, but given everything that had gone on lately, it felt more as if people were making judgments about her, and she didn't like it. She didn't like it one bit.

With all the extra hours Elliott was spending at the gym getting it ready to open, Karen had hardly seen him. They'd always had a tough time finding time to be together, but it was even worse now with all these new after-hours demands on his time.

At the end of her shift at Sullivan's, she made a call to Maria Cruz and asked her to keep the kids overnight, then she put together a take-out order for two and headed to the gym. It would be the first time she'd seen it since the men had started the renovations.

Elliott was hanging drywall when she entered, the muscles in his arms and back stretched taut. With a sheen of perspiration on his olive skin, it was a sight to behold, she thought as she studied him appreciatively. He happened to glance over his

275

shoulder and caught her.

"Admiring the view?" he teased.

She pretended to be shocked. "Oh, it's you? I thought I was ogling some extraordinarily sexy stranger. Kicked my heart rate straight into overdrive."

He crossed the room and dropped a kiss on her forehead. "And why would you be ogling strange men, *querida?*"

"Well, you see, my husband has been away from home for a long time now, and I'm getting restless."

He laughed. "This may not be the best place for me to make that up to you," he told her, glancing around. "Too many interested third parties."

He spotted the bag she was carrying. "Is that takeout from Sullivan's?"

She nodded. "Unfortunately I only brought enough for you and me. I'm afraid the rest of the guys are out of luck."

Ronnie glanced over and spotted the Sullivan's takeout containers. "Why isn't *my* wife here with a take-out order?" he grumbled good-naturedly. "She's the owner of that restaurant."

"Which means she has to stay there and take care of the many, many paying customers," Karen reminded him. She turned back to her husband. "Anyplace we could have a little privacy? I'll feel guilty if we eat in front of all these starving men."

"You shouldn't. They just gobbled down three large pizzas," Elliott told her.

Disappointment spread through her. "You, too?"

"I had some, but you know I'm a bottomless pit, and whatever's in that bag smells wonderful. We can sit outside on the front porch steps. It's a nice night, or it was the last time I actually stepped out to breathe fresh air."

"It's a gorgeous night," she confirmed, following him outside.

As Elliott dug into the take-out, she studied him. Despite the long hours he'd been putting in, he looked good. Clearly the excitement of starting this business more than outweighed the stress and hard work of getting the doors open.

"How's it going in there?" she asked.

"You really want to know?"

"Of course I do. If it matters to you, it matters to me. Are you on schedule?"

"Ronnie says we are. I have my doubts."

She frowned at that. "Meaning?"

"The opening could be a week or two later than we originally anticipated, but there are always glitches in starting a new business. Tom and the others swear it's nothing to worry about."

She couldn't help the chill that swept over her. Nor could she seem to stop herself from asking, "Are you on budget?"

Elliott frowned at the question. "Karen —"

"Don't look at me like that. It's a reasonable question."

"But it's not your concern," he said, then flushed. "I take that back. Of course it's your concern, because we've invested our savings in this, but you need to trust me that we're okay."

"Would you tell me if there was a problem?" She could see by the way he avoided her gaze that he would not. "Elliott!"

"Yes, of course," he said eventually. "If there were a problem that could affect our finances, I'd tell you. There's nothing like that happening now." He held her gaze. "I swear it."

She knew she had to take him at his word. She owed him that level of trust. She couldn't keep undermining him by questioning every little decision he made, no matter how difficult it was for her to remain silent. "Okay, then. That's good enough for me."

He sighed and held her gaze. "Is it really, or is it always going to be this way when it comes to money?"

"I'm trying," she said, wishing she could promise that she was finally past all that ingrained panic.

He studied her intently, then slowly released a sigh. "I know you are, but you'll see, *querida,* I will always be here to take care of you and our family."

Though she knew he meant it to be reassuring — and it mostly was — she could also hear what she imagined to be the condescending tone of his father, the proud provider of all important things. It sent a chill down her spine.

"Elliott, promise me something," she said earnestly.

"Anything," he said at once.

"Don't ever feel you need to keep things from me. Even if something's bad, I need to know. I don't need you to protect me or leave me out. I can handle anything, as long as I'm not blindsided."

"I would never do that," he said, his tone mildly indignant.

She nodded, but the truth was, they both knew he would. It was the Cruz family way, at least for the men of the family. What they viewed as protection and taking charge, Karen saw as patronizing. She wondered if she and Elliott would ever see eye to eye about that.

"We need a family day," Elliott announced over breakfast on Sunday morning. "I've already told my mother we're not coming for Sunday dinner."

Karen stared at him, open-mouthed, with shock. "You're willing to ditch your mother? When did you get to be so brave?" she teased.

"It's not bravery. It's desperation," he declared. "We need some time together. We're going to pack up the car and drive over to the beach."

Even as Daisy and Mack whooped with delight, Karen still couldn't quite wrap her mind around the plan. "You're actually taking a day off? Now — with so much to do at the gym?"

"We've had no quality time together as a family since the renovations began," he said. "The men said they could spare me for today. That's the great thing about working with this group of guys. They understand the importance of family. We're all working two jobs essentially, so we've been rotating breaks to give everyone time at home. Today it's my turn, since you and the kids have the day off, as well."

"And we have the entire day to ourselves?" she said, still not quite believing it, but with anticipation finally beginning to kick in. "What did your mother say?"

"She said it was about time I took a break. I've had three calls from her in the past two weeks, telling me I was working too hard."

Karen grinned. "Yay for Mama Cruz!"

Elliott laughed. "I'm going to tell her that just this once you appreciate her interference."

"I do," Karen said. "And I'll be more than happy to tell her that myself." She turned to the kids. "Run and put a swimsuit, a towel and whatever toys or books you want into your backpacks. We're leaving . . ." She turned to Elliott. "How soon?"

"A half hour," he said.

She frowned. "That's awfully fast. I thought I could make fried chicken and coleslaw to take with us."

"Nope. We're going to grab lunch when we get there. Hot dogs for the kids and a whole passel of spiced shrimp for us. How does that sound?"

"Expensive," she said candidly, but refused to worry about the cost just this once. "And wonderful. Okay, kids, hurry. I get the sense that Elliott is impatient to get this trip underway."

The drive to the South Carolina coast was a long one, with the kids increasingly impatient about reaching the ocean. They'd only been once before, and so long ago, she doubted Mack even remembered, though he claimed he did, mostly to annoy Daisy, who kept telling him he'd been too little.

"Was not!" he said.

"Were, too," Daisy retorted. "You were a baby."

"Mom!" Mack protested.

Karen turned around. "The quickest way to get Elliott to turn this car right around and go back home is for the two of you to keep fighting."

Daisy and Mack gave each other mutinous looks, but at least they fell silent.

Karen leaned closer to Elliott and whispered, "I think I'm almost as impatient as they are. This is such a treat. Thank you for thinking of it."

"We all deserve it," Elliott said. "I want us to be a family that makes lots and lots of memories we can store away." He gave her a quick glance. "Did you bring the camera?"

"Of course."

A hopeful grin curved his lips. "And you're wearing your bikini?"

"Nope," she said, then grinned at his disappointed expression. "But I brought it!"

"The sight of you in that will be more than enough to make my day," he said with feeling.

As they neared the coast, Karen could smell the tang of salt in the air and feel the softness of the breeze. It was completely different from Serenity. Even before the sweet coconut aroma of sunscreen could be mixed in, just the scent of the air spoke of relaxation, vacations and fun, something that had been in very short supply during her lifetime. She realized now that she should have made more of a tradition of these day trips for the sake of the kids. Elliott was right. It was the sort of thing that made good childhood memories.

As soon as Elliott had parked the car, the kids tumbled out of the back. They'd worn their bathing suits under their clothes, so they headed straight out onto the sand with Elliott to choose a spot, while Karen went to a nearby restroom to change. Self-conscious about every stretch mark that showed when she donned her bikini, she covered herself with one of Elliott's T-shirts, then made her way to the beach to join them.

"Here comes Mom!" Mack shouted, filling a sand pail with water and racing toward her, obviously intent on getting her soaked.

"Don't you dare," she said as he lifted the pail, but her laughter only encouraged him to send the water flying in her direction.

"You're in trouble now," Daisy called out, giggling as Karen took off after her son, only to be scooped up by Elliott and carried out into the chilly water, then unceremoniously dunked.

Both Daisy and Mack were staring, wide-eyed, when she surfaced sputtering.

She stared at her husband, who was making no attempt at all to control his mirth. "You did not just do that," she said.

Elliott chuckled. "I believe there's evidence that I did. The question is, what are you going to do about it?"

In response, she dove beneath the surface, grabbed his ankle and hauled him under. She'd only accomplished it by catching him completely off guard, but the shocked look on his face when he came to the surface was priceless.

"Now we're even," she said, as the kids splashed into the water to join them, laughing and squealing about how cold the ocean was.

"I like the pool at Aunt Adelia's better," Mack said, shivering. "It's warm."

"Because it's heated, dummy," Daisy told him.

"You do not call your brother a dummy," Karen said, but she had little enthusiasm for disciplining them on a day like today. "Mack, if you're cold, go back to the blanket and wrap up in a towel. The sun will warm you right up."

"But I want to stay with you guys," he protested, even though his lips were turning blue, and he was shivering.

"I'll come with you, buddy," Elliott said, heading up to the beach with him.

Daisy turned to Karen. "Mom, you look happy."

Karen smiled. "I am happy." It occurred to her to wonder how she normally looked to her daughter. "I'm happy all the time," she said. "Doesn't it look that way to you?"

"Mostly, since you married Elliott," Daisy agreed. "You used to look sad or scared before that. Sometimes now you do, too."

"Grown-ups have lots of things on their minds," Karen told her. "Some of them are sad. Some things make us worry. But the bottom line is that you, Mack, Elliott and our life together make me the happiest I've been in a long time."

Daisy looked relieved. "I'm glad. I don't want you to ever get a divorce again. Mack and I love Elliott. And we love having a great big family with lots of aunts and

285

uncles and cousins and a grandma who bakes cookies."

"Hey, I bake cookies," Karen protested, teasing her.

"Not as good as Grandma Cruz's or as Frances's." Daisy's expression turned thoughtful. "Or as good as Erik's."

Karen knew she should probably be insulted, but how could she be when there were so many people in her life taking such good care of her children, filling them up with treats, and showering them with love? For way too many years she'd been alone and scared and overwhelmed by financial worries. She needed to take the time to remember, once in a while, just how far she'd come.

And she also needed to give herself credit for getting there mostly on her own, even if it had been with the support of an amazing circle of friends she was still learning to trust and appreciate. Whatever crises might lie ahead, it was reassuring to know she'd never have to face them alone again.

14

After a long morning on the beach, the kids were clearly starting to fade from the combination of sun, swimming and salt air. Elliott suggested they find a casual restaurant Dana Sue had recommended, then head on home since Monday was a school day.

"No," Mack protested, though he could barely keep his eyes open. "I want to swim and swim and swim."

"You turn blue every time you go in the water," Daisy said. "And all you do is complain about being cold."

"But it's still the best fun we've ever had," Mack enthused.

Elliott smiled at his exuberance. "And you, *niña?*" he asked Daisy. "Have you had fun?"

She nodded. "I can't wait to tell Selena. She's going to be so jealous. Ernesto never takes them to the beach." As if realizing that she'd touched on a sore topic, she frowned. "Maybe I shouldn't say anything, after all."

"I think you can tell Selena about what a great time you had," Elliott told her. "But maybe you could think about asking her if she'd like to come along next time. That way she wouldn't feel as if you'd left her out or were bragging about something she doesn't get to do."

Daisy's eyes lit up. "There's going to be a next time? And she could come?" she asked excitedly.

Elliott turned to Karen. "What do you think?"

Karen nodded at once. "I think we've started a new family tradition. Whenever we have the time for a special outing, this is what we'll do. Agreed?"

Elliott grinned at the enthusiastic shouts from the backseat. They'd needed a day like this, just the four of them. Whatever it had cost in terms of time and money was worth it. He hoped Karen truly understood that, so there could be future outings without her weighing the rewards against the expense.

At the restaurant, the kids barely made it through their late lunches before they were fighting to keep their eyes open. Karen's eyes, however, were still brimming with a delight he hadn't seen in a long time.

"It's been a good day, hasn't it?" he asked her.

"It has, and it's been a good reminder about how important it is to leave our cares behind every now and then. They'll still be waiting for us tomorrow, but they won't look as daunting after a day like this. I've been so cautious for so long, I didn't know any other way to be. Thank you for showing me that we can find a way to have some balance."

Elliott gave a nod of satisfaction. "Then I've accomplished my goal," he said. "I've put a smile on your lips and some color in your cheeks."

"You most definitely have," she said, then leaned forward to give him a quick kiss. "Thank you."

Almost immediately, though, she picked up another shrimp and studied it as if it were a specimen in a lab. "What spices do you suppose they used? These are delicious."

Elliott chuckled. "I knew you wouldn't get through the entire meal without wondering about that."

She winced. "I'm very predictable, aren't I?"

"In the best possible ways," he said,

"which is why I stopped on the way in and spoke to the hostess while you and the kids were in the restroom." He pulled a piece of paper from his pocket and held it tantalizingly out of her reach. "The chef's list of spices."

She regarded him with amazement. "You're kidding," she said excitedly, trying to grab it. "Most chefs won't divulge their trade secrets."

"But this one has a local cookbook and it's all in there. The hostess made a copy of the page, when I explained how fascinated you are with recipes."

"I knew that charm of yours would come in handy," she teased, once more trying to nab the piece of paper.

"Not just yet," he teased. "What's my reward?"

She grabbed him by the shoulders and gave him a kiss that had his blood stirring.

"Not bad," he said.

She frowned at his less-than-enthusiastic review. "That was an excellent kiss!" she protested.

"Where will it lead when we get home?"

She laughed then. "I didn't realize this was a negotiation. In that case, I imagine we could work out something that would be mutually satisfying."

"Okay, then," he said and handed over the piece of paper.

She was immediately absorbed in the list of spices, the tip of her tongue caught between her lips. With her brow knitted in concentration, she looked so intense and cute, it took every bit of restraint he possessed not to haul her into his arms and kiss her again, but with her promise still ringing in his ears, he could wait a little bit longer.

That didn't mean he didn't hurry just a bit to pay the bill, get Daisy and Mack settled in the car and get on the road. And if they made the trip just a little faster going home, well, he thought just this once the extra speed was justified. After all, who knew what the reward might be when she discovered he'd actually bought her a copy of the chef's entire cookbook?

Adelia had lost her last shred of patience with Ernesto. Her visit to his office had accomplished nothing, except perhaps to make him more defiant than ever. He obviously hadn't believed for a moment that she would end their marriage. And the truth was, as desperately as she wanted to reclaim her self-respect, she wasn't sure she could do it, either.

Just imagining the fallout with the family was daunting enough, to say nothing of what might happen if Ernesto somehow turned the tables in court and managed to slip out of any obligation to provide well for her and the children. She'd never held a meaningful job, and while she wasn't afraid of hard work, adjusting to a work schedule after being a stay-at-home mom would be a difficult transition. She couldn't help thinking she'd be shortchanging her children, and yet, other families did just fine with the mother working. Look at Karen and Elliott, for instance.

She knew she ought to make an appointment with Helen Decatur-Whitney, who had a reputation for winning big for her clients in cases like this, but that would make the whole possibility of divorce a little too real. On some completely unrealistic level, she kept thinking her husband would come to his senses. So far, though, there was no evidence of that happening. Either he didn't care or he was counting on her devotion to her faith to maintain the status quo, which clearly suited him just fine. She provided him with the perfect excuse to make no commitment to any of these women who wandered through his life.

In some ways the worst part of all this was

not having anyone she could confide in. Mama was out of the question, as were her sisters and Elliott. She thought of Karen, who'd offered more than once to listen without making comments or judgments, but after the way Adelia had behaved toward her sister-in-law before Karen and Elliott had married made just the thought of it too embarrassing. Still, that might eventually be her best option. Karen was certainly the only one within the family who had experience with divorce.

Adelia wished she'd maintained some of her friendships from high school, but once she'd gotten involved with Ernesto, she'd centered her life around him, then later around their children. She saw now what a huge mistake that had been. She had a lot of acquaintances from her volunteer work, but no one she felt close enough to that she'd be willing to confide her deepest fears and secrets to them.

"What I need," she decided one morning after the kids were off to school, "is a job." A part-time job would be the perfect transition just in case things progressed to the next level and she actually filed for divorce. She suddenly wanted the sense of independence that would bring.

However, just expressing the thought

aloud was so shocking, it took her a minute to absorb what she was considering. She had a degree from college in business, though the diploma was so dusty and her memories of her schoolwork so far in the past, she wasn't sure it mattered. Who would hire her based on that? What would she list on her résumé — a dozen school committees and volunteering at the library?

And who in Serenity would be hiring these days? The town had been hit by the economic downturn just like every place else, despite town manager Tom McDonald's best efforts to revitalize the community's downtown area. His cousin Travis's country music radio station and Raylene's boutique were the newest businesses on Main Street. She doubted either were hiring or that she'd be qualified for the work, anyway. Thinking about her lack of skills combined with the likely lack of opportunity was discouraging, which had her reaching for the cake she'd baked just that morning.

Sadly, that was another habit she'd gotten into — eating to stuff down her frustrations. She still had twenty pounds of so-called baby weight, even though her youngest was now in second grade.

"Well, I can't just sit here eating cake all day," she muttered, shoving the plate away in disgust. She needed to do something positive, something to boost her spirits, something she could control, since it was evident that for now the fate of her marriage was out of her hands.

"What I ought to be doing is exercising," she said, though the idea was utterly abhorrent to her. She'd never understood her brother's fascination with the joy of sweating. How many times, though, had he suggested that a good workout could relieve stress? Wasn't that what she needed as much as losing those extra pounds? Maybe she'd even splurge on a massage and a facial, while she was at it. At least if she eventually walked away from Ernesto, she could be in great shape and thumb her nose at him as she left.

Twenty minutes later she walked into The Corner Spa. She was hesitating in the reception area when Maddie Maddox stepped out of her office, smiling when she saw her.

"You're Elliott's sister, aren't you? Adelia, is it?"

Adelia nodded.

"Did you come by to see him? I think he's with a client, but he should be free in a minute."

"Actually I wanted to sign up for a membership and then maybe see if you have a personal trainer other than my brother who could work with me? Letting Elliott boss me around might be more than I can take right now."

Maddie laughed. "I can understand that, and I can certainly help with the membership. Jeff Matthews is our other trainer, and I'm sure he'd be happy to work you into his schedule. Why don't I start you on the paperwork, and I'll bring him in?"

She left Adelia filling out forms in an office that smelled of lavender and other scents that seemed to have a relaxing effect on her. Adelia couldn't be sure if it was those or just taking a positive step that had her feeling better already.

Twenty minutes later, she'd signed up for a six-month membership, scheduled her first session with Jeff for the following morning and made an appointment for a massage after that. She was on her way out when Elliott spotted her. He regarded her with surprise.

"Hey, sis, what are you doing here?"

"I signed up," she announced, thinking he'd be pleased that she'd finally taken a step he'd long ago recommended. "And Jeff's going to work with me."

Elliott frowned. "If I'd known you were interested, I'd have worked you into my schedule for free."

She shook her head at once. "Not what I wanted."

He grinned, finally getting her decision. "Does your baby brother actually scare you?"

"You have a reputation as a tough taskmaster," she admitted, "but it wasn't that."

"What then?"

"I was afraid you'd take pity on me and let me get away with it when I don't feel like doing something," she admitted. "I figure if I'm paying Jeff, I'll listen to him. I need somebody who won't cut me any slack."

"Good thinking," he conceded. "And Jeff knows what he's doing." He studied her with concern. "Mind telling me what brought this on? Ernesto hasn't said something about your weight, has he?"

"Ernesto doesn't speak to me about much of anything these days," she said before she could stop herself, then winced at Elliott's immediately angry expression. She held up a hand before he could respond. "Don't mind me. I was having a bad morning, and I just decided I wanted to do something positive. This was it."

"Do I need to —"

"Speak to my husband?" she finished, cutting him off. "Absolutely not."

"But if he's disrespecting you . . ."

"We both know he is and that he isn't going to change. I just have to figure out what I'm going to do about that. Now, please, leave it alone, okay?"

"I'm just saying —"

Again she cut him off, this time by pressing a kiss to his cheek. "Understood. Thanks for the offer of backup, but I'm dealing with this in my own way."

Though he didn't look happy about it, Elliott backed off.

She forced a smile. "I hear you, Karen and the kids ran off for a day at the beach on Sunday. Mama was surprisingly pleased about that. She didn't grumble once about you all missing Sunday dinner."

"I think she understood how badly we needed it. Next time you and the kids should come along. Being outside in all that salt air and sunshine was great. Daisy and Mack had a ball."

"So she told Selena."

Elliott frowned. "Selena didn't get upset or feel left out, did she?"

"No. In fact, she came home bubbling with excitement because Daisy said she could come along next time. It made me realize that I need to start looking out for my own kids. I think I take great care of them, but with everything that's been going on at home . . ." She shrugged. "It has to be taking a toll, though so far the only one who seems tuned in is Selena. She's very angry. I worry about what she might do. You know how rebellious she is already. What if some boy shows an interest and she does something crazy just to be noticed?"

Elliott's expression once again filled with concern. As the only man among the siblings, he considered it his duty to look out for not only his sisters, but their children, just as their father would have done had he lived.

"Have you talked to her about that?" he asked.

"Not that exactly, but I've told her she's not to even consider sex until she's at least thirty," she said, grinning. "Wishful thinking, I know, but maybe if I say it often enough she'll understand what a big deal it is. I certainly didn't. I got pregnant way too young, and I was almost twenty-one."

"Do you think you would have married Ernesto even if you hadn't gotten pregnant?" he asked.

Adelia considered the question carefully. "More than likely," she conceded. "I was crazy in love with him. I had no idea it would turn out the way it has."

Ernesto certainly hadn't been a serial cheater back then, or if he had been, he'd kept it well hidden. That wasn't something she intended to share with her protective brother. Elliott probably knew all about what was going on now. He'd certainly hinted that he knew, but she wasn't going to confirm it. He might feel compelled to have a chat with Ernesto, and no good could come of that.

"I'll see you tomorrow," she told her brother. "And you might want to warn Jeff that I'm a wuss when it comes to exercise."

He grinned. "A prediction? You'll be addicted in a month."

"And you, my dear brother, are a dreamer!"

She'd be lucky if she didn't collapse in exhaustion after the first session and never show her face here again.

Karen was beginning to really count on her morning visits with Raylene. They never lasted more than a few minutes, long enough for a cup of coffee and a quick conversation, but for the first time in her life she felt as if she had a real girlfriend. Best of all, she'd discovered that she and Raylene had quite a lot in common.

Both of them had had troubled relation-ships with their mothers. In Raylene's case, her mother had withdrawn and, as Raylene now realized, had shown signs of the same agoraphobia that Raylene herself had dealt with, keeping her confined to home. Karen's mother had been an alcoholic, who refused to see the devastating effect drinking was having on her or on her daughter.

Both of them were living in blended families, though the circumstances weren't the same. And both of them had overcome serious psychological issues and struggled to reach the point of living full and normal lives.

"When you look back a year, can you believe all the changes in your life?" Karen asked Raylene as she sat on a stool and watched while Karen chopped vegetables for the stew on the day's menu.

Raylene laughed. "No way. Every time I walk out the front door and make it all the way into town, I consider it a miracle. And then there's Carter. After the disaster that was my first marriage, he's like some fairy-tale prince — kind, considerate, sensitive." A wicked grin spread across her face. "And very, very sexy!"

Karen chuckled. "I landed one of those, too. There's absolutely no comparison between my first husband and Elliott. He's good to me. He's responsible. He's great with my kids."

Raylene studied her over the rim of her cup. "Mind if I ask you something personal?"

"Anything," Karen responded.

"Have you and Elliott talked any more about him adopting Daisy and Mack?"

"We've talked about it," Karen said, though she was aware of a certain tightness in her voice even as she said the words.

Raylene obviously picked up on it. "Then it's still a touchy subject?" she asked.

Karen nodded. "I've managed to avoid actually dealing with it. I just can't seem to make up my mind."

Raylene looked puzzled. "Why? Like I said before, I would think it would be great for the kids to know that Elliott loves them that much. Maybe it would be different if Ray — is that his name? — if he were still around, but he's not. Are you thinking he could turn up? Or does Helen think it would be hard to get him to relinquish his parental rights?"

Karen flushed guiltily. "I haven't even approached Helen. Ray did relinquish his rights when we got divorced, so it's probably not an issue."

"Then I really don't get it," Raylene said with the sort of candor that Karen had come to appreciate. "Not when you say yourself what a great stepfather Elliott's been."

Karen struggled to find an answer that would make sense to either of them. "I think you were right the last time we talked about this. A part of me keeps waiting for the other shoe to fall."

Raylene regarded her with understanding. "You're honestly afraid things might not work out with Elliott?"

Karen nodded. "Crazy, isn't it? Every day I thank my lucky stars for him, but there's this one tiny part of me that still thinks it's too good to be true."

"I'm in no position to give marriage counseling, but I do think marriage isn't something you can do by half measures. You have to be all in. Otherwise those tiny doubts can create a crack that will eventually turn into a huge fissure."

"My heart gets that," Karen responded. "It's a hundred percent onboard. It's my head. I can't turn off the part that questions my judgment. I made a terrible mistake once. What if I've done it again?"

"So, are you constantly looking for evidence that you made another mistake?"

Raylene asked, frowning.

Karen hesitated, then nodded. "That's exactly what I do," she admitted. Every little slip Elliott made — especially when it came to finances or evidence of macho behavior — triggered panic and went into some mental lockbox, stored away for some future time when they'd all be added together to prove that once again she'd chosen the wrong guy.

"You know that's not healthy, right?" Raylene asked, her concern evident.

"I know," Karen said bleakly. "I just don't know how to stop it."

"You saw the same shrink I did, didn't you?" Raylene asked. "Maybe it wouldn't hurt to talk this over with her."

The suggestion completely threw Karen. "I thought I was past the need for that."

"You probably are," Raylene consoled her. "Most of the time, anyway. But people like us who've been through traumatic ordeals should know better than most the value of asking for help *before* it's too late." She stood up and gave Karen a hug. "I've got to run. And please don't look so panicked. It's just a suggestion. I certainly don't mean to suggest you're unraveling or anything like that."

Karen forced a laugh. "Good to know.

And I do appreciate the suggestion. I'm beyond being able to see things clearly, so an objective point of view was definitely welcome."

But as Raylene left to run across the town green in time to open her boutique, Karen sank onto the stool at the kitchen counter in Sullivan's and worried that maybe she didn't have herself nearly as together these days as she'd thought she did. And what would Elliott think if she told him she thought she ought to seek counseling to work through some of these unresolved issues that were impacting their marriage? Though he'd never judged her for her near-breakdown in the past, would it shake his faith in the woman he'd married? Was she prepared for that?

With the last-minute crunch to finish the renovations at the gym, Elliott was usually the last to reach home. Thank goodness Dana Sue had been accommodating and had given Karen mostly day shifts, so the children weren't constantly left with his mom in the evenings. Not that she would have minded, but the child care would have come with increasingly strident lectures about them working too hard and neglecting not only Daisy and Mack, but each other.

When he came in at nearly midnight, he was surprised to find Karen waiting for him, a cup of coffee — hopefully decaf — in front of her.

"Hey, you," he said, dropping a kiss on her forehead. "Why aren't you already in bed?"

"I wanted to wait up for you," she said. "It feels as if it's been days since we've seen each other for more than a minute."

"Because it has been," he said wearily, pouring himself a glass of juice and joining her at the kitchen table. "Everything okay around here?"

"Fine," she said, though she looked as if it were anything but fine.

"Then you stayed up hoping you could seduce me?" he inquired hopefully.

She smiled. "While the idea definitely holds a lot of appeal, I was thinking we could talk."

"About?"

"Just talk," she said with a touch of impatience. "About what's going on, how we are, the normal stuff."

Elliott set his glass on the table and leaned forward. He took her hands in his. "Are you upset about something? Because I have to tell you, you'll need to spell it out for me. I'm too exhausted for guessing games."

She leveled a look into his eyes, her own eyes sparking with a surprising glint of anger. "That's exactly the problem," she said unreasonably. "There's never time for plain-old talking."

"Isn't that why we've been scheduling date nights?" he said, trying his best not to get drawn into an argument, especially when he couldn't figure out why they were fighting in the first place.

"And when was the last time we had one?" she demanded.

"I don't know. A week or two ago? You know how crazy it's been, getting these renovations done. And we just had an entire day to ourselves with the kids at the beach."

To his shock, her eyes welled with tears. "*Querida,* what's going on?" he asked, dismayed.

She swiped at her cheeks as the tears began to fall. "I'm being impossible," she said.

"You're not being impossible, but you're obviously upset, and I don't think it's about date nights."

She shook her head. "It's not. Raylene and I were talking this morning and she said something that scared the daylights out of me."

Elliott was at a loss. "What?"

"That maybe I should see my shrink again." She gave him a look filled with panic. "Do you think I'm losing it?"

"Losing it?" he asked incredulously. "No. Why would Raylene say such a thing? I thought the two of you were friends."

"We are, and it wasn't some kind of indictment. She just picked up on a few things I mentioned and said she thought an objective outsider might help me put things in perspective."

Elliott was still struggling to put the pieces together. Whatever had been said, it had obviously shaken his wife. "What things?"

She didn't reply right away. In fact, she was careful to avoid his gaze, but eventually she heaved a sigh. "I told her how scared I am that we might not make it."

Shock settled over Elliott. "Us? You think we're not going to make it? Why? Sure, we have our share of disagreements, but we're both committed to this marriage. Whatever comes along, we can handle it."

She gave him a watery smile. "You sound so sure of that."

"I *am* sure of that," he responded. "Aren't you?"

"Most of the time, yes, but then something happens and I start to question everything." She met his gaze. "It's crazy, I know. You're the best husband I could ever have hoped for. You're amazing with Daisy and Mack. It's almost as if it's too good to be true, so when we fight, it makes me question if anything so good can possibly last. Then I act crazy and wonder why you put up with me, like now."

Elliott stood up, gathered her into his arms, than sat back down with her cradled against his chest. He kissed the dampness on her cheeks.

"We're going to make it," he said, holding her gaze. "We'll have ups and downs like every other couple, but we'll get beyond them."

She sighed and tucked her head on his shoulder.

As he stroked her back, he said, "I thought Raylene was crazy in love with Carter."

"She is. And she was just trying to be a good friend. She said maybe my old shrink could help me figure out why I can't trust what we have a hundred percent."

"I can answer that," Elliott said without hesitation. "That idiot Ray made it impossible for you to believe that any relationship could be what it seems." He met her gaze. "But if you want to see your shrink again so she can tell you the same thing, it's fine with me. I'll even go with you."

She regarded him with surprise. "You'd do that? I thought you'd completely freak at the idea of seeing somebody."

"You're thinking of my father, I believe," he teased.

"Maybe so," she admitted.

He caressed her cheek, saw the fear in her eyes give way to something else. "Ah, *querida,* don't you know by now that there's nothing I won't do for you?" he murmured.

A faint smile finally played on her lips. "Does that include making love to me to-night?"

A full-fledged smile broke across his face. "You don't have to ask me twice."

He stood up with her still in his arms, flipped off the light switch with his elbow and headed out of the kitchen. After all, who needed sleep when he had a woman like this in his bed?

15

Though he still didn't entirely grasp why Karen had been so emotionally distraught the night before, Elliott took her seriously when she complained that their time together had been too limited. No job was worth paying such a high price that it affected his marriage. And even though the demands of a start-up were high, he figured this particular business would never work if he were worried about it destroying his relationship with his wife.

When he saw Frances at the seniors' exercise class, he approached her before class even started.

"Are you free tonight, by any chance? I know you usually play cards, but if you could pick the kids up after school and keep them, you'd be doing Karen and me a huge favor," he told her. "Feel free to tell me, though, if it's not convenient."

"Oh, I'd love to," she said at once.

"Then I'll call the school, so they'll know." He studied her closely. "And it won't be too much trouble for you to get them there in the morning? I'd ask my mother to keep them overnight, but she's got some sort of event at the church tonight. I know it's going to run late."

"Don't worry about it," Frances assured him. "I'll manage just fine. What about clothes for school tomorrow?"

"Karen or I will drop them off on our way out to dinner, if that's okay."

"Couldn't be better," Frances assured him. "I'll go home right after class and bake cookies for them."

Elliott chuckled. "I know they'll love that, but there's no need for you to spoil them rotten."

"I have to compete with Maria Cruz, don't I? I know how your mother spoils them."

"Sadly, that's true," Elliott said. "Thanks, Frances. You're a godsend."

"You know this is as much about me, as it is about helping out you and Karen. It's my pleasure."

As soon as the seniors' exercise class ended, he called Karen and filled her in on the plan.

"But what about the renovations?" she

asked. "Are you sure they can spare you?"

"Already cleared," he said. "And Frances, as you might imagine, is ecstatic about having Daisy and Mack to herself."

"Wouldn't she prefer to babysit at our house?"

"She's fine with having them for a sleepover," he reassured her. "In fact, I think she's looking forward to it."

"So am I," Karen said, her voice turning low and breathy. "You and me with a whole night alone! What will we do?"

"Oh, I'm sure I can think of a few things," he said. "See you later. Love you."

"I love you, too."

Elliott didn't give the matter another thought until four o'clock when the school principal called.

"I tried to reach Mrs. Cruz, but apparently she left work early," the woman explained.

"Is there a problem?" Elliott asked, regretting once more that they'd opted not to take on the expense of having cell phones. With the kids, Karen, especially, shouldn't be unreachable for any length of time.

"When you called earlier, you mentioned that Frances Wingate would be by for Daisy and Mack," the principal said. "School's been out for a while now and we've seen no

313

sign of her. The kids are still here, waiting in my office."

Elliott felt as if someone had just yanked his heart straight out of his chest. The kids were safe, so his immediate concern was for Frances. There was no way, short of an extreme emergency, that she'd fail to pick up the children. What if she'd collapsed after class at the spa? Or been struck by a car en route to walk the children home? A million and one things, none of them good, flashed through his head.

"I'll be right there," he assured the principal.

On the way, he kept trying to reach Karen. "Problem," he said at once when he finally caught up with her at home. "Frances never showed up at the school. I'm on my way to get the kids, but I think we need to trace her likely footsteps and go by her place to make sure she's okay."

"I'll start doing that," Karen said at once, her voice threaded with fear. "Could you see if Adelia could look after the kids, then meet me at Frances's apartment? I don't want them with us if . . ." Her voice broke before she could vocalize the same thought that had struck terror in him.

"Good idea," he said. "I'll be there as quickly as I can be. Wait for me, okay? Just in case." He left his direst thought unspoken.

At the school, Daisy and Mack looked perplexed, but otherwise seemed perfectly fine.

"The teacher said Frances was coming to meet us," Daisy said. "Where is she?"

"She was held up," Elliott told her, praying that it was no more than that. "I'm going to drop you off at Adelia's instead."

"Yay!" Daisy said eagerly. "Selena says she has a boyfriend and I want to hear about him."

"Selena's too young for a boyfriend," Elliott said automatically, but he didn't have time at the moment to worry about that crisis. The one he was facing with Frances was plenty big enough.

Frances had picked up the ingredients to make oatmeal raisin cookies, baked three dozen of them, then decided to take a few over to Liz and Flo, who agreed to meet her at Flo's apartment. She kept having this nagging thought that there was something else she was supposed to be doing, but there was nothing noted on her calendar.

As it usually did, her visit with Flo took the better part of an hour. Flo always had plenty to say, and her adventures usually kept both Frances and Liz in stitches, trying to imagine themselves behaving so outrageously at their age.

It was nearly five o'clock when she returned home to find Elliott and Karen pacing frantically on the sidewalk in front of her building. As soon as she saw them, comprehension dawned.

"Oh, my God, the children," she whispered as she walked toward them, tears in her eyes.

"I'm so sorry," she called out to them, only to have Karen race toward her and envelope her in a hug so tight it nearly knocked the breath out of her.

"We've been so worried," Karen told her. "When you didn't show up at the school, the principal called Elliott. We couldn't imagine what had happened to you. We've been looking everywhere."

Frances was weak-kneed at the thought of the terrible mistake she'd made. "I think we should go inside, if you don't mind," she said. "I need to sit down."

"Of course," Karen said at once, tucking Frances's arm through hers and walking her into the building.

Elliott took France's key and opened the door. "How about a glass of water?" he asked.

She nodded. "I'd love one. And there are cookies on the counter," she said, trying to make up for her memory lapse by playing the dutiful hostess.

She sat on the sofa, with Karen right next to her holding her hand as if she was afraid to let go. Only after Elliott had come back with three glasses of water and a few cookies on a plate did Karen meet her gaze directly.

"Frances, can you tell us what happened?" Karen asked gingerly, as if she feared even that simple question might be too much for Frances. "Where have you been?"

Under the circumstances, Frances understood her caution. She patted Karen's hand reassuringly. "I baked the cookies for the children, just as I told Elliott I planned to do. Then I decided to take some over to Flo and Liz." She drew in a deep breath before admitting, "I could lie and tell you I simply lost track of the time, but I didn't. I completely forgot about picking the children up at school. I didn't remember until I saw the two of you out front looking so frantic. Are the children all right?"

"They're at my sister's," Elliott said. "They're fine. No harm done."

Frances was aware that Karen was watching her closely.

"This isn't the first time, is it?" she asked. "You've forgotten other things?"

Frances nodded, seeing little point in lying to a young woman who'd been every bit as kind to her as a child of her own could possibly have been.

"Have you seen a doctor?" Elliott asked, his expression filled with so much concern it made Frances want to weep. This was exactly what she hadn't wanted, to have people worrying and feeling sorry for her. Accepting that from Flo and Liz was one thing. To have these two dear young people, who already had so much on their minds, adding her to their list of concerns wasn't right.

"I haven't seen my doctor yet," she admitted. "A part of me doesn't want to know what I'm dealing with. If you ask the majority of people my age, Alzheimer's is one of the things they fear the most." She was proud of herself for actually saying the word aloud.

"But Frances, there are other things that could be going on," Elliott said. "Maybe it's not as serious as Alzheimer's. Maybe there's just some sort of chemical imbalance that can easily be corrected. Maybe your meds are interacting adversely."

"You need to find out," Karen said, then

318

added decisively, "I'll call your doctor myself and I'll go with you."

"We both will," Elliott volunteered.

Fresh tears spilled down Frances's cheeks. "You're both so sweet to care so much."

"Nonsense. It's the least we can do after everything you've done for me, for us," Karen said. "Or, if you'd rather, I can call one of your children, tell them what's going on and they can come and see the doctor with you."

"Absolutely not," Frances said. "They'll have me in some retirement home faster than you can say old age. I want to manage as long as I can on my own. So far, I haven't burned down the apartment or gotten lost on my way to the senior center."

Her attempt at humor fell flat. If anything, Karen looked as if she were on the verge of tears. Frances gave her hand a squeeze.

"Stop looking as if this is the end of the world," she instructed. "Liz and Flo know what's going on. They'll see to it I don't do anything foolish. I intend to be around a long, long time, hopefully with most of my wits about me."

"But this is so unfair," Karen whispered. "You've done so much for so many people. You shouldn't have to face something like this."

"We all have our crosses to bear," Frances consoled her. Oddly, she found that comforting Karen eased her own panic. She couldn't imagine why, since today's incident was a clear and final indication that she could no longer put off getting answers.

Karen leaned into her side. It was hard to tell who was drawing comfort from the other.

"I want to see the doctor with you," Karen said again. "I know you have Liz and Flo, but you're like a mother to me, Frances. I want to do whatever I can to help."

"Just treat me as you always have," Frances said. "I want to hold on to every last shred of dignity for as long as humanly possible."

She saw Karen exchange a look with Elliott, but she couldn't quite interpret it. She also noted his nod in return.

"I'm staying here tonight," Karen told her quietly, though there was a note of steely resolve in her voice. "And tomorrow we'll see your doctor."

"I'm sure we won't be able to get in that quickly," Frances protested, still not ready for the medical verdict to be rendered.

"We'll get in," Karen said. "I'll put Liz on the case. Nobody says no to Liz once she's made up her mind about something."

Despite her anxiety, Frances chuckled. "No, they don't, do they? Okay, then. Tomorrow, it is, but you don't need to stay the night."

"You might not need me here, but I need to stay," Karen said.

"And I agree," Elliott added.

Frances gave them a wan smile. "Then I suppose that's that." She gave Elliott an apologetic look. "I'm sorry I spoiled your plans for tonight."

"You're far more important to us than a date night," he reassured her. "You're a part of our family. Now I'd better stop by the house and pick up a few things for Karen, then go over to my sister's to get the kids. Would you like me to bring them by to say good-night, or will that be too much for you?"

"Oh, please, bring them by," Frances said. "I'm sure they're wondering what on earth happened to me. I need to apologize and they probably need to see that I'm fine."

Karen nodded. "I think that's a great idea."

"Then that's a plan," Elliott said, then dropped a kiss on Frances's forehead before giving his wife a lingering kiss of her own.

Though she felt awful about ruining their night out, Frances couldn't help being grateful that Karen was going to be here. Despite her attempt to gloss over what had happened earlier, the incident had shaken her as none of the other minor memory lapses ever had. With the kids involved, things could have been so much worse. She'd be on her knees tonight, thanking God for keeping them safe at school. She knew in some cities with a less attentive school staff, they could have been left on their own to try to find their own way home. Who knew, then, what awful thing might have happened?

Karen didn't sleep a wink all night. Though Frances had shown no further memory issues for the remainder of the evening, Karen had been deeply shaken by her forgetting her promise to pick up the children at school. Whether it was Alzheimer's or something less dire, the lapse wasn't good. The thought of watching her friend go through a long, slow decline was heartbreaking.

After a restless night in the guest room, she finally dozed off near dawn and awoke to the scent of bacon frying and coffee perking. In the era of microwaves and coffeemakers, the two aromas of more old-fashioned preparation made her mouth water.

She found Frances in the kitchen, already dressed and smelling of her favorite lily of the valley scent.

"You look as if you slept well," Karen said.

"I did," Frances admitted. "Better than I have in a while." She studied Karen. "You, however, don't look as if you slept a wink."

"I couldn't seem to turn my mind off," Karen admitted.

"While mine doesn't seem to be operating at full tilt half the time," Frances quipped.

Karen stared at her. "How can you joke about this?"

"What else is there to do?" Frances said. "It's not as if I can change it."

"There are medicines," Karen protested, then realized she didn't really know that. She added with less certainty, "There must be."

"None that change the course of this," Frances said. "Believe me, Flo has been searching the internet for weeks now. There are a few promising things that could slow the progress, but they're not effective indefinitely."

"Has Flo looked for other possible diagnoses?" Karen asked, wanting to believe that her research had been incomplete, even though as the mother of the compulsively organized Helen Decatur-Whitney, it was unlikely there would be anything haphazard about Flo's approach.

"You'll have to ask her," Frances said. "She and Liz will be here shortly. They're joining us for breakfast."

"I wondered why you were making enough bacon for an army."

"We all figure we're past the age of worrying about our cholesterol," Frances said. "How many weeks or minutes can it possibly take off our lives at this late date? I've already had a full life. So has Liz. Flo probably has a few good years left in her before she accepts the inevitable the way Liz and I have."

"I wish you'd stop talking as if death is just around the corner," Karen said, shuddering.

Frances gave her an apologetic look, but she didn't pull back. "Sweetheart, we're all going to die. Once you get to my age, the only question is whether we'll go out with a bang or a whimper."

Karen fought down despair. "I expect you to go with a fight," she commanded.

Frances chuckled. "I'll do my best. Now, enough of this dreary talk. Do you know that Flo has a boyfriend?"

Karen couldn't help it. Her mouth dropped open. "Does Helen know?"

"Not if Flo's had her way," Frances confided. "She's pretty sure the knowledge would give her daughter a coronary."

"Then I certainly won't be the one to tell her," Karen said, sketching a cross across her chest. Impulsively, she stood up and gave Frances a fierce hug. "Is it any wonder I admire you so much?" she said. "You, Liz and Flo inspire me. I want to be you when I grow up."

"Oh, my darling child, you're your own woman and, if you ask me, you're pretty terrific just the way you are."

"And *that's* the other reason I love you," Karen said. "Until you came along, I never really understood unconditional love."

Frances regarded her with a sad expression. "Surely your mother . . ."

"You know better," Karen said. "But I do have you, and I count that among my blessings every single day."

And what on earth was she going to do if she lost that unwavering support, the woman who'd been her sounding board and fiercest protector through every crisis? The prospect was almost too much to bear.

Adelia jumped when the front door of the house slammed shut. A minute later, Ernesto walked into the kitchen, his expression stormy.

"What the hell is this?" he demanded, throwing a credit card bill onto the table. "Do you think I'm made of money?"

For too many years Adelia would have cowered under that glare of his and promptly offered to return whatever offending item had set him off. Not any longer. He might handle their finances, but she knew to the penny what was in their bank accounts.

"Is there a problem?" she inquired, keeping her tone even.

"You've spent hundreds of dollars at that spa where your brother works in the past week alone. Since I see no evidence that you've shed so much as an ounce, what have you been wasting it on?"

"Actually I've lost five pounds already," she said, unable to keep a note of pride out of her voice. Then, because she couldn't seem to resist, she added, "I thought I'd whip myself into shape for whatever — or whoever — comes along next in my life."

The comment clearly rocked him back on his heels. "Excuse me? What is that supposed to mean?"

"You've obviously moved on. Why shouldn't I?"

Color flooded his cheeks at the cavalier

remark. "If I discover so much as a hint that you're cheating on me . . ." he began.

Adelia held his gaze and dared him to complete the thought. "Yes?" she said eventually. "What will you do? Complain about the indignity? Divorce me? That ought to provide a lively courtroom experience."

He simply stared at her then. "What's happened to you?" he asked eventually.

"I've discovered I still have a spine," she told him with unmistakable pride. "I warned you it could happen. Now you have to figure out how you intend to deal with it."

He opened his mouth to speak, then shook his head, turned on his heel and walked out.

Adelia watched him go, a sense of wonder spreading through her. A few months ago, even a few weeks ago, she would have been terrified by having spoken so boldly, with such defiance. Now all she felt was a sense of triumph. It might be too late to get her marriage back, but it obviously wasn't too late to find herself.

Elliott had spoken to Karen earlier in the day, checking to see how Frances's appointment with the doctor had gone. Unfortunately there would be no definitive diagnosis without further testing, and he'd recommended a specialist in Columbia for that. It would be a couple of weeks before that happened.

He was still worrying not only about Frances, but about the impact of this on Karen when he walked from the spa over to the gym. When he entered, he was surprised to find that the walls in the main room had been finished and were now a cheery shade of sage green. If it had been up to him, they'd have been pale gray, but Maddie had convinced him that even men would appreciate a hint of color.

"If you go with gray, with all that steel gray and black equipment, it will soon look as dingy as Dexter's," she'd insisted.

As he glanced around, Elliott had to admit she'd been right. It looked clean and inviting. It was hard to believe that in another couple of weeks, the doors would be open. He'd finally have a business with a potential share of some decent profits. At long last maybe Karen would be able to put her worries over money behind her.

He found the rest of the guys on the back deck taking a break.

"What are you all doing out here slacking off?" he asked. "There's still work to be done."

Ronnie lifted a beer in a mocking salute. "We're brainstorming," he said. "The beer helps."

Elliott nodded, appreciating the concept. "Let me grab one and I'll brainstorm with you. What's the topic?"

"We need to come up with a name for this place," Cal said. "Maddie's having a cow because she can't finalize advertising or get a sign ordered without a name. She refuses to call it The Club, which was my suggestion."

"Gee, I wonder why," Travis said. "Even I can see that would have its drawbacks, such as not giving people so much as a clue about what kind of club it is. For all they'd know, we could be offering illegal poker games or smoke-filled cigar rooms."

Elliott grabbed his own beer, then propped himself against the deck railing. "Any other options so far?"

"What are we going to be?" Tom asked. "A gym, right? For men. So how do we put some kind of spin on that? It's pretty basic."

"The women were basic with The Corner Spa," Erik commented. "Spa says classy. The Corner Spa gives it a nice cozy, friendly feel. Turned out to be the perfect combination."

"Well, we're not on the corner, and I don't

think Middle of the Block Gym would cut it," Travis quipped.

"Dexter's was just Dexter's," Elliott noted.

"But he owned the place," Ronnie said. "We have a partnership."

Ronnie shook his head. "Who ever thought that naming this place would be harder than getting it renovated?"

"That's because renovations take brute strength, which we have in spades," Cal said. "A name requires finesse, which is maybe not our best attribute."

"Speak for yourself," Travis said, grinning. "I'm all about finesse. Ask Sarah."

"We could ask the women for their input," Tom suggested.

"And admit we're stumped?" Ronnie protested. "We'll never hear the end of it."

"I think Tom's right," Cal said. "We should buy them some tequila and margarita mix, let them have one of their infamous margarita nights and leave them to it."

"It'll be some girly name," Ronnie argued. "I guarantee it. They'll do it just to spite us."

"Do you have a manly alternative?" Cal asked him.

Ronnie gave him a sour look. "If I did, don't you think I'd have thrown it on the table by now?"

Elliott listened to the exchange with growing amusement. After growing up in a household of mostly women, he'd had only his father's example to go by of how men were supposed to behave. As Karen occasionally suggested, it was a macho style that could be objectionable to a more modern woman. These guys were showing him a different path. While their status as sexy, virile, strong men could never be questioned, they knew when to admit defeat and share the power with their other halves.

"You all seriously don't mind never hearing the end of it if we ask for help?" he inquired.

"We'll never hear the end of it if we get it wrong," Cal said with a shrug. "I say this way's better."

"Agreed," Tom said.

Travis, Erik and Elliott signed on as well, leaving Ronnie the only one with doubts.

"Oh, what the heck," Ronnie said eventually. "If you all can take the gloating, so can I. Now let's get back inside and do something that requires that brute strength someone mentioned earlier. My testosterone level needs a serious boost."

"Elliott, you'll speak to Maddie?" Cal asked as they went inside. "This may have been my idea, but I really, really don't want to be the one who has to admit to my wife that we're stumped."

Elliott laughed. "Nice to know you have some boundaries. I was getting worried there for a minute."

"Trust me, once you're married a few more years, you'll be more than eager to concede certain things to your wife," Cal said to nods of agreement from the others. "There's a nice ebb and flow to the balance of power. It generally works out in your favor in the end."

And once again, Elliott was struck by how different that philosophy was from the way he'd grown up. Definitely something to keep in mind when Karen gave him one of those looks that hinted he was treading all over her ability to think for herself.

16

"Emergency margarita night tomorrow," Dana Sue announced to Karen as they were closing up at Sullivan's. "Maddie just called. Apparently the guys have asked for our input on naming this new gym of theirs."

Karen stared at her incredulously. "Seriously? They're leaving it up to us?"

"I know," Dana Sue said with a chuckle. "I'm as shocked as you are. The only one who's not is Maddie. She said it's been obvious for a while now that they're clueless. She finally backed them into a corner and demanded a name so she can get going on advertising and signage."

"And we're supposed to come up with suggestions while we're looped on margaritas?" Karen asked, loving the idea of it.

"Apparently our success with The Corner Spa played into their confidence that we can do this better than they could. That and the fact that the only suggestion they've had so far was The Club."

"Isn't that some tool to keep people from stealing cars?" Karen asked.

Dana Sue laughed. "I hadn't even thought of that, but, yes. Obviously not the right name for this business, if we all imagine something different when we mention it."

Karen studied her. "You do know that we could probably each come up with a list and just hand 'em over to Maddie."

Dismay registered on Dana Sue's face. "What would be the fun of that? They've given us an excuse for a bonus margarita night only days after we were last together. They've even offered to buy the tequila and to babysit. Why on earth would we turn that down?"

"Good point," Karen said. "So being a good Sweet Magnolia implies seizing any opportunity for a get-together."

"Not just any get-together," Dana Sue corrected. "We have picnics and barbecues all the time that are not official Sweet Magnolia events. It only counts if it's a girls-only margarita night, where we get wild and crazy." Her expression turned thoughtful, and then a sparkle lit her eyes. "Or at least they think we do. It seems to make them happy to try to envision what goes on when we have these secret gatherings where they're not allowed."

"Including the possibility that we're mis-behaving?"

"Especially that," Dana Sue confirmed. "After all, that's how Helen, Maddie and I became such good friends back in the day. We were almost always in trouble in high school. I think that's why Helen became a lawyer. She figured sooner or later one of us would need legal representation."

Karen thought of what Frances had told her about Helen's mother having a new boyfriend and Helen's likely reaction to it.

"Can you tell me something I've been wondering about?" she asked Dana Sue. "How'd Helen turn out to be so different from Flo? It seems Flo pretty much goes with the flow, so to speak, while Helen is . . ." She searched for the right word.

"An uptight control freak?" Dana Sue provided with a grin. "She is by comparison to Flo, that's for sure, but Helen has her moments when she loosens up. That's part of what makes margarita nights so much fun. We get to see her lose her inhibitions."

Karen couldn't honestly imagine Helen ever loosening up that much. Then, again, she'd only been to one margarita night so far, and she'd had to cut out early. Maybe tomorrow night would be a revelation.

■ ■ ■ ■

Karen was the first to arrive at Maddie's. At Dana Sue's recommendation, she'd come with a tray of buffalo chicken wings and blue-cheese dip that she'd had time to prepare before leaving Sullivan's. Erik had put them on the menu as tonight's appetizer special, so she'd doubled the usual recipe and brought the extras along with her boss's permission.

She found Maddie looking surprisingly distracted, worry creasing her brow. Since Maddie was usually so in control of things, even with two toddlers and a teenager still at home, it was a shock to find her looking so out of sorts.

"Is everything okay?" Karen asked hesitantly, still not entirely comfortable in the role of friend, rather than just the wife of someone who worked with Maddie. "Is there anything I can do to help you get ready?"

Maddie immediately forced a smile. "Don't mind me. I just had a thoroughly exasperating conversation with Katie. Before I could get to the bottom of something, she flounced off and went to her room. Living with a teenager means living in the middle of a never-ending mood swing. I don't remember Ty or Kyle being nearly this impossible, though. Maybe it's just teenage girls."

Karen winced. "Gee, I can hardly wait. You make it sound like so much fun."

Maddie's expression turned rueful. "Sorry. It does have its moments of pure joy, too. I can vaguely remember a few of them."

"Do you need to deal with Katie now? I can answer the door when the others get here," Karen offered.

"Believe me, by now she has her earphones on and her music turned up. I won't get through to her till she calms down."

"Not that it's any of my business," Karen began, "but is there a problem at school?"

"I think so," Maddie said. "But she won't admit to that. She won't say if she's upset about a boy. Bottom line, she doesn't want to talk to me at all. With any luck, Cal will be able to shed some light. Working as a P.E. teacher and the high school baseball coach, he not only understands teenagers better than I do, but he's tapped into the school grapevine." She smiled at Karen. "Enough of that. Let's get these buffalo wings on a plate. They smell fabulous. A new addition to the Sullivan's menu?"

Karen nodded. "Erik persuaded Dana Sue

that chicken, in all its forms, is a Southern dish. It doesn't always have to be fried to qualify."

Maddie chuckled. "I'd love to have been there for that discussion. Dana Sue is very protective of the integrity of her Southern cuisine menu."

Within the next few minutes, as Karen arranged food on plates and Maddie carried them into the living room, the rest of the women arrived. Helen immediately went to work making frozen margaritas, handing them out as each batch was completed.

As soon as everyone was settled, the usual gossip started flowing, but Maddie clapped her hands. "Okay, ladies, no time for that. We're on a mission. We have to name this gym. Gossip to follow."

Suggestions poured out, from the fairly obvious, The Boys' Club — to one they all concluded was vaguely pornographic-sounding — The Blue Room.

"To say nothing of the fact that it's been painted sage green," Maddie said, shaking her head at the suggestion.

"Ooh, I love sage green," Jeanette said, immediately distracted. "It's so soothing. I wanted to paint the guest room that color, but somehow it wound up being dark blue, of all things. Tom painted it before I could stop him."

"Well, you can thank me for the green," Maddie said. "If they'd had their way, the entire place would have been industrial gray."

"Maybe we need to be more systematic about this," Karen said hesitantly. "You know, decide on one word first, like *gym*. Is that going to be part of the name for clarity's sake? Or fitness something?"

"Great idea," Maddie enthused. "What do you think of when you hear gym?"

"Sweaty clothes and Dexter's," Helen said, wrinkling her nose.

"Bad connotations," Maddie concluded. "Are we agreed about that?"

Everyone nodded.

"Then is *fitness* the right alternative?" Maddie asked. "Or some variation?"

"How about Fit for Life?" Raylene suggested, testing it out slowly.

Sarah's eyes lit up. "I like it. It sounds healthy and not too girly. It has a proactive ring to it."

"I don't know," Dana Sue said skeptically. "I'll bet there's already some chain of gyms with that name. We'd need to check, but I think we're on the right track. Any other spins on that?"

"I have one," Karen said. "What about Fit

for Anything?"

"Ooh, I really like that," Annie said. "It sounds young and hip."

Maddie looked around the room, a grin on her face. "Does it need anything tacked on? Club? Gym?"

"Nope. I think it works all on its own," Helen said. "A show of hands? All in favor?"

As every hand shot into the air, Karen grinned, pleased to have her suggestion approved. For the first time, she felt a tiny sense of ownership in the whole gym proposal.

"That's it, then," Helen said. Turning to Maddie, she handed over the cell phone that was never far from reach.

"Call Cal," she instructed. "Run it by the guys. I think they're all at Rosalina's having pizza with the kids. Some kind of misery-loves-company thing or babysitting co-op." She grinned. "Somehow Erik persuaded Ronnie to take Sara Beth with him, since Erik's stuck at Sullivan's till closing and I, of course, was needed here."

Maddie was on the phone for several minutes, while they waited. Her grin spread as she finally hung up.

"We have ourselves a name. The guys wholeheartedly approve."

"Great," Helen said briskly. "Now we can

get to the serious stuff. Who has good gossip?"

"Grace Wharton," Sarah commented wryly. "But she's not here."

Raylene nudged Sarah in the ribs. "But she tells you everything. Spill."

Karen had little to offer herself, but sitting back and listening, she couldn't help being amazed at how tapped in these women were. More fascinating, though, despite their salacious interest in the latest town news, there was an underlying note of concern for anyone who seemed to be going through a tough time. She didn't detect a single mean-spirited word, which told her a lot about their character.

They'd been chatting for the better part of an hour when Sarah turned to her. "There is something else I heard this week," she said, keeping her worried gaze on Karen. "Someone told me Frances might have Alzheimer's."

Helen nodded. "My mother mentioned something about that, too. She's worried sick about her."

Sarah kept her gaze on Karen. "I know the two of you are close. Is she okay? Are you holding up okay?"

To her dismay, Karen felt her eyes brimming with tears. "I don't really know. The doctor's sending her to see a specialist. Please don't say too much around town. I know that's like trying to stuff something back in a box after it's been taken out and assembled, but Frances is such a proud woman. She doesn't want people pitying her."

"We just want to help," Sarah protested. "She's always been there for everyone else."

"Nobody knows that better than I do," Karen said.

"I think we need to let Frances guide us," Helen said. "Once she knows what's going on, if she wants help, she'll ask for it. And my mom and Liz are going to be right there, too."

Karen nodded. "I know Frances will appreciate the fact that you're all so concerned, though. I'll definitely let her know. I think she forgets sometimes now many lives in this town she's touched."

Helen's attention remained focused on her. "What about you, though?" she inquired quietly after the others had moved on to different topics. "I know how much she means to you. You couldn't have had a more caring neighbor when your life was in turmoil."

"She was way more than a neighbor," Karen said. "If it hadn't been for her and you

342

back then, I really don't know what I would have done."

Helen nodded, not bothering to deny her own role in keeping Karen's world from spinning out of control. "Exactly," she said. "That's why I'm asking if you're okay."

"To be honest, I'm scared to death," Karen said. "You know what a lifeline she's been for me. The thought that she's in failing health has really shaken me." She sat up a little straighter and drew on some reserve of strength she hadn't been aware she possessed. "I guess it's my turn to return the favor."

"And we're here for backup anytime you need it," Helen promised. "Remember that. Alzheimer's is not an easy thing to face, not for the person who might have it, not for their friends or caregivers."

"I feel as if I've spent most of my adult life needing backup," Karen said. "Frances, you, even Elliott."

"That's what friends and family are for," Helen said. "Don't ever forget that. You'll have your chance to be there for one of us. It's the way life works."

"I guess it still comes as such a huge surprise," Karen admitted. "For so many years I felt not only terribly alone, but incapable of helping myself, much less anyone else."

Helen reached for her hand. "And now you're strong."

Karen smiled. "And now I'm strong," she echoed, savoring the knowledge.

Elliott had managed to carve out an hour or two the past few Saturdays to go with Mack to football practice. It hadn't been easy, but he knew if he wasn't on the scene and anything happened, he'd never hear the end of it. Karen continued to be unhappy about the fact that he'd signed Mack up. Though she was resigned to letting him play, she still refused to come to the games.

"You know I'll be one of those moms who runs onto the field and tries to dry his tears or kiss his boo-boos. I'll embarrass Mack to death," she'd explained stubbornly.

Though Elliott hadn't entirely bought her reason, he'd let it go.

Under coaching from Ronnie, Cal and Travis, the kids Mack's age were learning the fundamentals, but the rules were in a constant state of flux, and it was never entirely certain if the players would remember which goal line they were supposed to run toward.

Though the men stringently enforced that it was touch football, there were inevitably a few misplaced tackles that left cuts and bruises. Thankfully, so far Mack hadn't been among the victims.

Today, however, it seemed Elliott's good luck had just run out. He spotted a kid who was ten pounds heavier than Mack and several inches taller heading straight for Mack as he ran toward the goal line clutching the football. When a touch would have stopped the run, the kid aimed directly for Mack's stomach instead, knocking the breath out of him as they both tumbled to the ground.

Elliott was already on the field as Mack staggered to his feet. Expecting tears, he was stunned to see Mack take a swing at the offending player, catching him squarely in the jaw. It wasn't as if he had much force behind the punch, but it definitely must have stung. The kid started screaming as if he'd been mortally wounded.

"You're not supposed to tackle," Mack shouted at him as the other dad arrived just in time to witness the punch.

"You hit me!" the kid screamed, turning toward his father, who looked apoplectic.

"That boy needs to be thrown off the team," the father shouted at Ronnie, who'd left the other kids under Cal's care and was headed down the field to join them.

"Hold on," Elliott said to the father. "It was your kid who tackled him. My boy was just defending himself."

Ronnie arrived just then and tried to calm things down. "Okay, both boys were out of line," he said firmly. "They're suspended for the rest of the game."

"But that's not fair," Mack protested.

Elliott was inclined to agree, but he couldn't very well condone the punch Mack had thrown, either. Nor was he about to question Ronnie's authority.

"You know the rules," Elliott said quietly to Mack, a hand on his shoulder.

"You need to teach your kid sportsmanship," the other man said, still glowering.

Elliott had to rein in his temper. Fortunately Ronnie stepped in.

"You need to do the same, Dwight. This whole incident started because your son tackled Mack. It's not the first time he's deliberately tackled another player, either. Once more and he's out. Period."

"We'll make it easy, then," the man said defiantly. "I'll yank him now. This game is just for a bunch of sissies."

Elliott stared at him incredulously. "They're seven years old." He realized then that there was no point in engaging the man. He was clearly irrational.

But as he and Mack started to walk away, the man stepped in front of him, clearly not ready to concede the battle.

"I'm a little surprised at you, backing down the way you just did," he said snidely. "I thought all you Latino guys think you're hot stuff."

Evidence of prejudice of any kind in Serenity was rare, but it did happen. Elliott wanted to level the man on the spot, but the tiny part of his brain that wasn't engulfed in a red haze of fury held him back. He had to set an example for Mack. He could not allow this argument with an idiot to escalate.

"You don't want to go there," he said quietly.

"Actually I do," the man said belligerently. "You sneak over the border, live here illegally, steal jobs from honest Americans and then think you can teach your kids to bully other kids." He glanced at Mack. "Is he even your kid? Bet you didn't know your wife or girlfriend or whatever was stepping out on you, did you?"

Elliott had had enough. He was about to pop the guy in the jaw when Ronnie stepped squarely between them. "Dwight, go home," he said in a firm undertone. "It's not even nine in the morning and you're obviously drunk. You're embarrassing yourself and your son. Go home."

After an instant's hesitation, Dwight muttered an expletive, then turned and walked away, his kid trotting along behind him, still wailing and rubbing his jaw.

Ronnie shook his head as Dwight left, then turned to Elliott. "I'm sorry."

"Not your fault," Elliott said. "I could have defused the situation much sooner by walking away."

"It's hard to walk away from someone who's spoiling for a fight and will say or do anything to get what they want. Dwight's been out of work for a year now. It doesn't excuse anything he said or did, but it might give you some perspective."

Elliott nodded. "Thanks for telling me that. I'd like to say it makes what happened less personal, but it doesn't."

Ronnie gave his shoulder a squeeze, then went back to the game. Elliott forced a smile for Mack, who looked shaken by the whole incident.

"I think we need ice cream, buddy. What do you think?"

"Ice cream is good," Mack said, grinning. "Can I have a banana split?"

Elliott chuckled, knowing his eyes were considerably bigger than his stomach. "How about we share one?"

"Yay!" Mack said eagerly.

But even though the morning ended on a better note, Elliott couldn't shake Dwight's words. It wasn't so much the ethnic slurs that bothered him. He'd been born and raised right here in Serenity, after all. It was the slam that Mack wasn't his. It was just one more incident to remind him that he had only the loosest possible claim to the child he thought of as his son.

Karen had heard about the incident at the ball field by midmorning, but it was her night to work late at Sullivan's, so it was after eleven when she finally got home. Elliott was already in bed. He'd left a light on in the living room for her and a night-light glowing in the hallway for the kids.

After a quick peek to make sure Daisy and Mack were asleep, and a good-night kiss for each of them, she showered to rid herself of the scents that clung after a day in the restaurant kitchen. She pulled on one of Elliott's T-shirts, then crawled into bed beside him, hoping not to disturb his sleep.

He rolled over, though, and reached for her.

"I thought I heard you come in," he murmured sleepily, nuzzling her neck.

"Sorry. I was trying not to wake you."

In the faint light of the moon, she could see the smile on his lips.

"You can wake me anytime, *querida.*"

She knew that things could go any one of several ways now. With the right signal, they could be making love. With a question or two, they could be having one of the late-night talks that brought them each up to date on their days. Or she could kiss his cheek, murmur, "Good night," and Elliott would fall straight back into a sound sleep.

Though she was exhausted, the first option held plenty of allure, but before she could run a hand over his bare hip or along his solid abs, he pulled himself into a sitting position with pillows at his back.

"We should talk about something that happened today," he told her.

"I heard Mack got into a fight on the football field," she said, preempting his news. She knew he was going to feel guilty about Mack's slight injury after the production she'd made about him playing football. "He didn't look any the worse for wear when I checked on him just now, and Ronnie said he gave as good as he got." She frowned. "Not that I condone fighting."

"The incident was nothing," Elliott said, waving it off as if it were of no consequence.

"It was what happened after that's on my mind."

Karen hadn't been aware of anything that had happened after. "What do you mean?"

He frowned. "Ronnie didn't mention anything?"

"Not to me," she said.

"The father of this other boy —"

"Dwight Millhouse," she said, cutting him off. "I know him. He's having a tough time finding a job, and he's spending way too much of his time off drinking instead of looking for work."

Elliott nodded. "Okay, I'm trying to allow for that, for him being out of work and for him being drunk, but he said some things."

Karen regarded him curiously. "What kind of things?"

"Some were about me being Latino," he began.

She stared at him incredulously. "You're kidding me! If I'd been there, I'd have slugged him myself."

Elliott smiled. "I'm sorry you weren't there to stand up for me, then," he said, clearly amused. "But that's not important. He made a comment about Mack not being my son. I know he has no idea of our situation and he was just spouting off whatever vile thing he could think of, but it reminded me that we need to make a decision about whether or not you're going to allow me to adopt Daisy and Mack. I feel as if we're all in limbo."

Karen, who had been propped up on her side to listen, fell back against the pillows and closed her eyes. She'd known they'd get back to this eventually, but she was no more certain now than she had been before about the right thing to do.

When she opened her eyes, Elliott was frowning.

"You're still opposed, aren't you?" he asked, his expression dismayed, maybe even angry.

"Not opposed exactly. You're an amazing stepfather. The kids couldn't possibly have anyone better in their lives." She gave him a plaintive look. "Why isn't that enough?"

"Maybe you should ask them how they feel about that," he said tightly. "I'm not so sure they'd tell you they're thrilled not to have the clarity of knowing I will always be there for them. Kids need stability. Like I told you before, if Ray were around, I wouldn't push this, but he's not. He hasn't seen them in years. He hasn't even called or sent a birthday card."

"It's not about Ray," she protested.

"Then it's about you and how you feel,"

he concluded. "For some reason, you don't want to legalize my relationship with them. Do you like having them all to yourself and keeping me on the fringes of the family?"

She winced at the hurt in his voice and at the characterization that she'd deliberately made him an outsider. "You're as much the heart of this family as I am," she countered.

"It doesn't feel that way."

"And a piece of paper will change that?" she asked.

"For me, it will," he said. "And if you're honest with yourself, I think you know it will change it for Daisy and Mack, as well. We need to do this, Karen. Maybe not tomorrow or the next day, but soon, and definitely before we have any child of our own. And that's not just because it will make discipline more difficult if we have two sets of standards, two different authority figures, but because it will make Daisy and Mack feel less secure if they think I care more about our baby than I do about them, just because I fathered the baby."

Karen knew he was right. Her head was shouting at her that it was the right thing to do, but the part of her that still felt as if every day with Elliott was a gift she didn't entirely deserve, a gift likely to be snatched away, *that* part couldn't bring herself to take a step that would only be more difficult to undo when things eventually fell apart.

"Don't be mad at me," she begged him. "I just need a little more time to wrap my head around all the implications."

"Explain these implications to me," he requested.

"I will, once I've given this more thought."

"Please tell me it's not about the cost of hiring Helen to handle this," he said. "Whatever she charges, it would be a small price to pay for settling this matter once and for all."

"It's not the money," she said.

He studied her, obviously unhappy with her evasion, but eventually he nodded. "Just don't take too long, okay?"

"How long is too long?" she asked.

He met her gaze. "I don't know."

Left unsaid was what would happen if she decided she couldn't do as he'd asked.

17

Adelia was proud of herself for sticking to the routine of workouts at the spa several days a week. She only worked with the trainer one of those days, but Jeff kept a close eye on her when she was there for her additional sessions and always managed a minute or two to encourage her.

She'd lost ten pounds now and was almost ready for a smaller size in clothes, but she decided to wait a little longer before going on the shopping spree she felt she'd soon deserve.

"You look good," Elliott noted, stopping her on her way out one morning. He grinned. "So, are you addicted yet?"

"I have to admit I like the way I feel after an hour of exercise," Adelia conceded. "But I will never enjoy the workout itself."

"You wouldn't admit it to me if you did," he teased.

She laughed. "Probably not. How are you?

It's only another week before your fancy new gym will open. Are you excited?"

"You have no idea. Do you have time to take a quick walk over there? I'll show you around."

She could see the excitement in his eyes. "Of course I'll come."

The exterior of Fit for Anything was not dissimilar to that of The Corner Spa, a Victorian house that had been renovated and put to a new use. Inside, there were certain similarities, as well. The equipment was the same high quality, but the walls were a soothing shade of green, rather than the sunshiny yellow at the spa. It was clean and ever-so-slightly more masculine. New floor-to-ceiling windows let in lots of sunlight and a similar view of the woods and ravine out back. In place of the brick patio, there was a wooden deck with tables and chairs that were less fussy than the wrought iron at the spa. A café menu posted hearty soups and healthy sandwich wraps, rather than salads and smoothies.

"Elliott, it's incredible," she said. "How are the memberships going?"

"Maddie says we're already ahead of projections, and that's even before we have the open house this weekend. And I have a nice, solid client list here, in addition to the women I'll continue training over at the spa. Dexter's actually been sending people to me. It's very gracious of him, all things considered."

She beamed at him, happy to see him so enthused about his career. For too long he'd been a little defensive about his chosen field, probably due to entirely too much family torment.

"I am so proud of you."

He shrugged modestly. "It wasn't even my idea. Some of the Sweet Magnolia husbands came up with it."

"But they've made you a partner, and they're trusting you to make it a success," she said. "Congratulations! I know we all gave you a lot of grief when you said you wanted to be a fitness instructor and personal trainer, especially in a town the size of Serenity, but you've made it work."

"I've also taken on a lot of debt," he admitted. "It makes me nervous. We were all brought up to pay as we go. And it terrifies Karen. What if I wind up letting her down?"

"Doubts are understandable, especially before you get going, but from everything you just told me, all the signs are pointing to a huge success. Stay focused on that."

"I know once the cash actually starts coming in, I'll feel a lot better." He glanced at her. "Thanks for letting me admit how I'm feeling. I can't say a word about any doubts to Karen. She's scared to death as it is. I invested just about every dime we'd been saving for a baby."

Adelia couldn't keep herself from wincing at that. "No wonder she's terrified." She studied him. "And that's why you keep putting Mama and me off about when you two will have a child of your own."

He nodded. "That's one reason."

She frowned at his bleak tone. "And another reason?"

"I want to adopt Daisy and Mack officially before we have our own baby. I don't want them ever to feel they're not as important to me as a new child that Karen and I have together. There are other reasons, too, but I think they deserve that stability."

Adelia nodded. "Which is exactly why you're such an amazing stepdad. You put them first. Is Karen balking?"

"Yes, and I wish I knew exactly why. It's not about Ray being their biological dad. He's long since out of the picture. She's hesitant for some reason, and she won't get into it with me."

Adelia considered offering to talk to Karen, but once again felt it would be unwise given their shaky history. "You'll work it out," she said instead. "She knows how much you love Daisy and Mack and how much they love you."

"Yeah, I guess so," he said. He seemed to visibly shake off his dark mood and gave her a look of brotherly concern, one she knew was likely to precede a cross-examination about her life.

"Now, I'd better run," she said hurriedly. "I have an appointment."

Elliott regarded her skeptically. "Do you really? Or are you just trying to avoid my questions?"

She grinned at him. "Does it really matter? Either way, I'm out of here." She pressed a quick kiss to his cheek. "Love you."

"Love you, too," he called after her as she all but sprinted toward the front door.

Once she reached her car, though, she sat back with a sigh. There wasn't anyplace at all she needed to be, and it was hours before the kids would be home from school. Once the prospect of uninterrupted hours on her own would have stretched out like an unexpected vacation. Now it meant she'd have too much time to think about the sorry state of her marriage and how much more humiliation she intended to take.

She drove to Wharton's, picked up the local weekly from the newsstand and settled in a booth with a tall glass of sweet tea. Reading the paper took far too little of her spare time. She found herself glancing at the local classified ads. When she saw that Raylene Rollins was advertising for a clerk at her new boutique on Main Street, she glanced out the window and across the square.

It was right there, straight across the green. Was that some sort of a sign?

Before she could talk herself out of it or convince herself that she should at least go home and put on more presentable attire before going to a job interview, she took the shortcut across the grass and walked inside.

Raylene was handling a sale at the register, while several other customers browsed. Adelia recognized one of the women from a PTA committee at school.

"That red would look amazing with your coloring," she told Lydia Green. "Not everyone can wear a color that bold."

Lydia grinned at her. "I fell in love with it the minute I saw it, but I wasn't sure." She held it up in front of her. "You really think so?"

"I know so," Adelia said confidently. "Try it on and see for yourself. And I just saw the perfect scarf to accessorize it. I'll grab it and bring it to the dressing room."

Lydia gave her an odd look. "Do you even work here?"

Adelia leaned close. "No, but I'm hoping to. I'm giving it a test run with you. Maybe it will impress Raylene more than the lack of experience on my résumé."

Lydia laughed. "A very bold move."

Adelia brought her the scarf, but by then Lydia was already sold on the dress. She added the scarf and a bracelet that Adelia had also spotted.

When she reached the counter, Lydia told Raylene. "She's a very good salesperson. You need to hire her."

Raylene gave Adelia a startled look. "Are you applying?"

Adelia took a deep breath and nodded. "When you have the time, maybe we can talk about it. I'll just keep pitching in till you're free."

An hour and several sales later, Raylene led the way into her tiny office in the back.

"You're good," she complimented Adelia. "You have a real eye for what works and doesn't work with a woman's shape and coloring. Those women left here very happy. I know clothes and style, but matching them with the right people can be infinitely

361

trickier. You steer them in the right direction without offending them."

Adelia basked in the praise. "It was fun." She glanced down at her own attire. "Obviously my own sense of style could use a little attention. I was working out at The Corner Spa, stopped at Wharton's and saw your ad. I came over on impulse."

"It was a good impulse," Raylene said. "Are you seriously interested in the job? I know you're on lots of committees in town. Do you have the time?"

Adelia hesitated. "I need to work . . ." she admitted eventually.

Raylene looked puzzled. "I thought —"

"That my husband was a hotshot developer?" Adelia supplied. "He is."

"Then why do you need to work? You didn't say you wanted to. You said you *needed* to."

"My kids are in school. My days are increasingly empty. And I want something of my own. I'm trying to work on my self-respect."

Raylene nodded. "Those are all things I can understand." She hesitated, then smiled. "The job's yours if you want it." She mentioned the salary. "We can work the hours around your schedule and mine. Will that work for you?"

Adelia nodded eagerly. "I'll make it work."

"Want to start tomorrow? Say, when we open at ten? I'll have you here when I'm here initially till you're trained on the register and know the stock system. After that we'll divvy up the early and late shifts and Saturdays. I have a part-timer who fills in, as well."

"Thank you," Raylene said, trying to contain her exuberance. "Thank you so much."

"Hey, if you keep selling the way you were today before I even hired you, you're going to be a great addition."

"I'll do my best," Adelia promised.

When she left, it was all she could do to keep from skipping down the block. She'd gotten herself a job! It might not be a calling or a career, but it was one more step in the right direction. Pretty soon she was going to be able to look in the mirror and genuinely like the woman she'd become.

Karen was stirring the batter for an apple cake, one of the few desserts Erik would allow her to attempt, while Raylene sipped her morning coffee.

"I hired Elliott's sister Adelia yesterday," Raylene said, almost causing Karen to drop the bowl of batter.

"Adelia's going to work for you?" Karen repeated, just to make sure she'd heard correctly.

"She starts this morning, in fact," Raylene confirmed. "She walked in the door out of the blue yesterday and managed to sell two outrageously expensive dresses, a suit and some accessories while I was busy working the register. You should have seen her. She has an amazing instinct for what clothes make a woman look her best."

"Adelia?" Karen repeated skeptically. Not that her sister-in-law couldn't look stylish when she tried. She just didn't try very often.

"It was impressive, I'll tell you that," Raylene said. "If she keeps it up, my bottom line is going to be very, very good."

She studied Karen, then frowned. "Why do you sound so shocked?"

"Because the Cruz women — or Hernandez in Adelia's case — don't work. They stay home and care for their children. When Elliott and I were first together, believe me, that's all I heard. I was accused of neglecting my children by working to support them. Elliott's mother and Adelia were the most vocal."

"That's a pretty old-fashioned view," Raylene said.

Karen shrugged. "It works for a lot of mothers and, if it does, more power to them. I couldn't afford to stay at home. Somebody had to pay the bills."

"Why do you suppose Adelia had such a sudden change of heart?" Raylene asked, her expression thoughtful. "She mentioned something about wanting a job for her own self-respect. Any idea what she meant by that?"

Unfortunately, Karen had a pretty good idea of exactly what Adelia had meant. She was at least emotionally breaking free of Ernesto, or at least that would be Karen's guess. She wasn't about to share such personal information with Raylene, though.

Instead, she shrugged. "I'll bet a lot of women hit a point when they want their own identity aside from being a wife and mother."

Raylene nodded. "You're probably right. Bottom line, I am really glad she wandered in yesterday. I might finally be able to get a little more time to enjoy my own family life one of these days. Owning a business is a lot more demanding than I'd realized when I opened the boutique. At the time I was just so grateful to be able to leave the house and do something, I didn't give a thought to all the hours involved. Now I want at least a tiny bit of my freedom back."

"Adelia's smart. She actually has a degree in business. I think she'll be able to help you with a lot more than sales, if that's what you want," Karen said.

Raylene's eyes lit up at that news. "Lucky me!"

Actually, Karen thought, Adelia was the lucky one. Though she wouldn't have thought of her sister-in-law being anything other than a stay-at-home mom, she could see how this could be the perfect niche for her. And Raylene, who'd been through her own share of personal crises, would be the perfect support system for someone in Adelia's situation.

Ever since he and Karen had argued over his role in making decisions for Daisy and Mack and her refusal to make a commitment to allowing an adoption, Elliott's frustration with the situation had grown. Just yesterday Daisy had defied him over doing her homework, shouting that he wasn't the boss of her. Though he was sure other children uttered the same words, to him they carried an entirely different meaning. Later she'd apologized, but the remark had stung.

With an hour break in his schedule, he

made a quick call to Helen's office.

"Is she free, by any chance?" he asked Barb, Helen's long-time secretary.

"For another twenty minutes, she is. How fast can you get over here?"

"Two minutes," Elliott promised. "I'm already on my way."

He jogged around the corner and down the block, then up the front steps of the house Helen had recently bought and renovated into her new office. According to all reports, she'd been saying for months that she needed the extra space because she intended to bring in another legal partner. Given her determination to control every aspect of her life, no one, Elliott included, believed she'd relinquish a single client, even to some handpicked partner.

Helen was standing in the reception area when he arrived. "Is this about the partnership papers for the gym?" she asked. "They're all signed, sealed and delivered. Everything's nice and legal. And the loan agreement you had me draw up with the other partners is finished, as well. Everyone's signed off on that. You should have your copy in today's mail."

Elliott shook his head. "That's all great, but I'm here about something else."

Alarm immediately registered on her face.

"Come on in," she said, gesturing for him to go into her office, then closing the door behind them. "Please tell me you and Karen aren't thinking about getting a divorce, because I can tell you now, I couldn't represent you. She and I have a history. I'd feel obligated to represent her."

He smiled at her fierce sense of loyalty. "And that would terrify me, if it were why I'm here," he said frankly. "Actually, I'm wondering about what I'd need to do to legally adopt Daisy and Mack."

Her eyes lit up. "I've been wondering why you hadn't already done that. Anticipating this, I cleared the way when we got Ray to give up his parental rights in the divorce. Sadly, it wasn't much of a fight. He'd already moved on to a new life someplace in Nevada. I think he was busy conning some other poor woman. One of these days I'd like to file suit and go after him for all the back child support he owes Karen, but she wants to put all of it behind her. I don't think she has the stomach for another fight with him. I honestly can't say I blame her, but that money rightfully belongs to Daisy and Mack. It would make a tidy nest egg for their college fund."

"The man was a sleaze, no question about

it," Elliott said. "Karen's lucky to be rid of him."

"And even luckier to have found you," Helen said.

"Thanks for the vote of confidence."

"I do have a question, though. Why are you here, rather than Karen, or at least *with* Karen?"

He winced at the all-too-relevant question. "I was hoping you wouldn't see anything odd about that," he admitted.

Helen frowned. "Is she opposed to the adoption for some reason?"

He thought about the question. "Not opposed, exactly. She just seems hesitant about moving forward. She won't say why, but lately I've gotten the feeling that she still doesn't entirely trust our marriage to last. I suspect she thinks that my adopting Daisy and Mack would muddy the waters if we divorced."

"Has she said as much?"

He shook his head. "She won't say anything," he said, not even trying to hide his frustration. "She just pushes off the discussion to another time. I thought maybe if I talked to you, made sure there were no legal hurdles, I could convince her that it's time to move forward on this. Daisy, Mack and I are all a little bit in limbo about my real

369

role in their lives."

Helen nodded. "I can see how that could get complicated. Kids need to understand who the authority figures are in their lives. I saw it with Maddie and Cal, when they got together. Though Cal didn't adopt Katie, Kyle and Ty, he already had a role of respect in the family as Ty's baseball coach. Plus he's used to working with kids, and he had Maddie's unconditional support to interact with them as a disciplinarian. Even her ex didn't pull some kind of stunt and try to undercut him."

Elliott nodded. "I'd be happy to settle for being a stepfather, if Ray were in the picture, but he's not. I think the kids need to know they can count on me, that I'm in their lives forever. I think that's going to be even more critical if Karen and I have a child of our own. I'd never want Daisy or Mack to feel as if they're second-best in my affections."

"And you're willing to make that commitment? Even if something were to happen, if you and Karen were to split down the road, you'd expect to be a father to Daisy and Mack? You'd obligate yourself for child support, all of it?"

"Absolutely," he said without hesitation. "A split's not an option, but even hypothetically, yes, I'd want to remain in their lives as their father and support them. They were still very young when Karen and I began seeing each other. I feel as if I've raised them almost from birth, as it is."

"Then I'd say the only hurdle you face is getting Karen to agree. I think the legalities would go fairly smoothly. Get her on board, and we'll talk again," she said, standing up and coming around her desk. She gave him a kiss on his cheek. "You're a good guy, Elliott Cruz, but then, the smart women in this town have always known that."

Elliott couldn't help wondering if Karen would agree, especially when she found out he'd just gone behind her back. Again.

Karen picked the kids up from her mother-in-law's house, managing to avoid any sort of interrogation while she was at it. She arrived home feeling triumphant. She still had an hour to get dinner on the table before Elliott was likely to get home. Now that the renovations had been completed, they had a few free evenings before the gym's open house over the weekend and then the official launch next week, when his schedule likely would go crazy.

She managed to convince Daisy to go to her room to do her homework, but Mack trailed after her into the kitchen.

"When's Daddy coming home?" he asked, stunning her.

"You know your father doesn't live in Serenity anymore," she said carefully. It was the first time Mack had even mentioned Ray in a very long time.

"Not him," Mack said impatiently. "Elliott. I want him to be my dad. I want to call him Daddy." He gave her a plaintive look. "Please. I hardly even remember my real dad."

Karen drew in a deep breath. She knew Elliott would never manipulate her by planting such an idea in Mack's head, so her son had to have come up with this on his own. It was proof enough that Elliott had been right about how desperately her kids needed some clarity.

"You want Elliott to be your dad?" she asked. He nodded enthusiastically. "Daisy does, too."

"You're sure? She hasn't mentioned it to me."

"She doesn't want you to be sad," he said.

Karen held back a sigh at how her indecision had apparently been affecting Daisy and Mack. "Elliott and I will talk about it," she promised.

"Tonight?" Mack pleaded, his face lighting up.

"Tonight," she confirmed. "Now, take a juice box and go do your homework. I'll call you when dinner's ready."

It seemed that the decision about adoption was mostly out of her hands. How could she possibly deny her children and her husband something they all wanted? She'd never known her own father, so being without a male role model had just seemed the norm to her. With Elliott in the picture, her children understood what having a great dad could be like, yet she'd held the fulfillment of that dream tantalizingly out of reach with her doubts.

"No more," she murmured, resolving to give them all what they wanted. She'd manage to quiet her fears somehow.

While the water for pasta came to a boil, she glanced through the mail and saw an envelope from Helen. Unable to resist, she opened it and found what appeared to be loan documents associated with the deal Elliott had made with the other partners at the gym.

The documents themselves were no surprise. The amount of money involved, however, staggered her. Maybe twenty thousand dollars seemed like nothing to them, but to her it suggested years of debt. It had taken several years of scrimping and saving just to wipe out the few thousand that Ray had left her obligated to pay off.

She was still staring at the document in shock, when Elliott came in. He glanced at her, but went straight to the stove where the water had apparently boiled down to nothing. He turned off the burner under the scorched pot, then regarded her with concern.

"What's going on?"

She lifted her gaze and regarded him with a sense of betrayal. "Twenty thousand dollars?" she whispered, barely able to utter the words.

He winced at her tone. "You knew about the loan."

"But you never said it was for that much."

"Because I knew you'd freak out," he admitted. "Exactly like you're doing now."

"Elliott, how are we supposed to pay off that kind of money? It will take forever! And what about the baby you claimed was so important? We can't even think about that if we have this kind of debt hanging over us."

He sat down, reached for her trembling hands, but she pulled them away.

"You can't just talk this away," she said. "It's too huge."

"I can show you the numbers. Memberships at the gym are already ahead of projections. I have more private clients than ever before, starting next week. We'll pay this off in no time. And if we need to stretch it out, the terms are flexible."

"It's a twenty-thousand-dollar debt," she repeated. "Do you realize how long it could take to pay that off, even at a moderately quick clip? And what about interest? My God, Elliott, that alone will eat us alive."

"Stop it. You're getting worked up over nothing. There's minimal interest. And did you not hear what I just said about the memberships and the extra clients? We'll have at least a few hundred extra every week to pay down the loan."

She was past listening to reason. The thought that he'd done this, if not behind her back, at least deceptively, made her stomach hurt. She stood up.

"I can't talk to you right now," she said. "I need to think. I'm going for a drive."

He looked as if he might argue, but eventually he gave her a curt nod. "We'll talk more when you get back."

"You'll see that the kids have dinner?"

"Of course."

She left the house without a jacket. The evening air was brisk, but it felt good. She needed some kind of a shock to her system. Once in the car, though, she had no idea where to go. She couldn't dump all of this on Frances, not with everything going on in her life. And Raylene might have had a lot of other issues in her life, but she'd never faced financial woes the way Karen had. And she could hardly turn to anyone in the Cruz family. They'd immediately jump to Elliott's defense.

As she had years ago when she'd been in dire straights, she found herself heading for Helen's office, praying she'd find her there. When it came to clearheaded, nonjudgmental advice, no one in town was better.

18

The lights in Helen's office were still burning brightly, much to Karen's relief. The outer door was locked but opened quickly at her knock. Helen smiled when she saw her.

"This is an unexpected pleasure. What brings you by? Have you and Elliott made a decision about the adoption so quickly?"

Karen just stared at her. "Adoption?"

"That is why you're here, isn't it? I told him to work it out with you and I'd handle the paperwork. We shouldn't hit any snags, not since Ray gave up his parental rights in the divorce settlement."

"You've talked to Elliott about adopting Daisy and Mack?" Karen said, feeling as if she'd just taken another major hit below the belt.

"He was here earlier," Helen said, looking confused. "That's not why you're here?"

"No, that's apparently just one more thing

my husband failed to mention," she said, sighing heavily. "I'll add it to the list."

Helen looked chagrined. "I am so sorry. I just assumed. Dumb me, I should know better than to make assumptions. It's just that the timing seemed to be more than coincidental. You did know Elliott wants to adopt Daisy and Mack, right?"

Karen nodded. "That much I knew. In fact, earlier this evening I was leaning in that direction. Now . . ." She shrugged. "I'm not sure of anything anymore."

"That doesn't sound good," Helen said sympathetically. She led the way into her office and gestured toward a chair. "Sit down and tell me what's going on. Can I get you something to drink? I've dumped the coffee, but I could make another pot. Or I have sodas in the fridge."

"Nothing, thanks." Karen took a deep breath, then spilled out her shock at discovering the amount of the loan Elliott had taken out to start the gym. "That's over and above what he'd already taken out of our savings."

"The baby fund," Helen said.

Karen regarded her with surprise. "He told you that?"

She nodded. "He recognized how much faith it took for you to let him use that money."

"I'm not sure faith had anything to do with it. I just saw how much this gym meant to him, so I gave in, even though it went against every instinct I had."

"I've told you before that I don't think there's a real risk here, right?"

Karen nodded. "I guess that's why I came to you. You understand the circumstances and you have a better sense for this business venture than I do. You really believe they're going to make it, that Elliott's not throwing our financial future down the drain?" She gave Helen a frustrated look. "I know I've asked you this repeatedly, but it seems I keep needing to hear you say it."

Helen smiled. "I understand, and, yes, I really believe in this venture of theirs. I know how hard this is for you, Karen, but at some point you have to learn to trust your husband. He's not a selfish bastard like Ray. It's not about his ego. He wants to build a good future for your whole family — you, Daisy, Mack and whatever children might come along. Do you believe that much?"

Karen thought about it, then nodded slowly. "Intellectually, yes. It's just so scary to look at a piece of paper and see that dollar amount right there in black and white when I know what it represents in terms of scrimping and saving."

"Okay, let's say Elliott had decided against moving forward with this because of your anxiety. How do you see your future unfolding then?"

"We'd have gotten by," Karen said at once.

"And getting by would be enough for you?"

She saw the point Helen was trying to make. "Most people want more for their families, don't they? So the bottom line is that I might feel insecure now, but in the end, we'll have much more security," she admitted. "The potential benefit outweighs the risk."

Helen nodded. "That's how I see it. Life doesn't come without risks. You know that. If you're entirely happy with the status quo, then there's no reason to rock the boat. But if a little rocking will make things much better in the long run, then you have to be willing to take the occasional chance. See what I mean?"

"Then I shouldn't let my fear get the better of me," Karen concluded.

"It's always wise to be aware of your comfort zone," Helen corrected. "But it's equally smart to step out of it from time to time. You have to weigh those potential benefits realistically against the risks. I think this is one of those times when the potential wins out. Give Elliott the chance to prove himself. He's never let you down yet, has he?"

"No," Karen agreed. She even managed a weak smile.

"Here's one more bit of reassurance, if it helps. I do know you and your circumstances. And I do understand this particular type of business venture. If I'd thought for a single second that the men were in over their heads, I'd have stepped in. You know me, I can't keep an opinion to myself to save my soul. I'd have done everything I could to save them from themselves."

Karen actually chuckled at the truth of that. "I knew there was a reason I came over here. You've always been able to steady me."

"Glad to help anytime," Helen said. "Want to talk some about the adoption before you go?"

Karen shook her head. She might feel reassured about the business, but all the secret doubts she harbored about her marriage had risen to the surface once more. She wasn't quite ready to go home and forgive and forget, much less take the huge leap of faith that the adoption would require. That would take a little longer.

■ ■ ■ ■

Frances clutched the prescription she'd been given so tightly it was doubtful the pharmacist would be able to read it once she eventually turned it in to be filled.

"Are you okay?" Liz asked worriedly as they drove from Columbia back to Serenity.

"Not according to the doctor," Frances said in a halfhearted attempt at humor.

She'd been through a battery of tests recently, many of them simply to rule out things like a brain tumor or adverse interactions from the medicines she was taking. She'd undergone an MRI, all sorts of verbal testing and several memory tests, including a few more today. Though the results weren't in yet, all the evidence seemed to point to an early stage of Alzheimer's. At least that's what she'd heard in the mumbo jumbo from the doctor who'd had the bedside manner and clarity of a physicist who never left his think tank for human interaction.

"We still don't *know* anything," Flo consoled her. "*If* it is Alzheimer's, it's the very earliest stage. He said that."

"Did he really?" Frances asked wryly. "How could you tell with all that Latin being spouted as if I should understand what he was saying? He got impatient every time I tried to clarify something."

Liz chuckled. "He wasn't exactly a charmer, was he? But he did seem to know his stuff, and he said there's no reason to panic."

"Not yet," Frances said, her tone still dire.

"Stop it," Flo ordered. "The way I understood him, you're more likely to die of a heart attack than you are to reach the final stages of Alzheimer's, if that's even what you're dealing with. What was that other thing he mentioned, Liz?"

"Mild cognitive impairment," Liz said, referring to the notes she'd dutifully taken for precisely this reason. Frances had sat there in a haze throughout the appointment. "He definitely said it could be that."

"And it's not as bad as Alzheimer's," Flo said triumphantly.

Frances gave her a skeptical look. "Did you miss the part about it eventually evolving into Alzheimer's?" She'd locked onto that because it was the diagnosis she'd anticipated, despite her very best attempts to go into this with a positive attitude.

"You're almost ninety," Flo retorted. "It'll have to evolve pretty darn fast to be an issue."

Even Frances managed a chuckle at her wry sense of humor. "Then for the moment, I'll take some comfort from that," she said just as wryly.

"Well, I recommend we go to Wharton's for hot fudge sundaes," Liz said. "That always cheers me up." She gave Frances a chiding look. "We are not going to let you wallow in despair over this, especially before we have a final diagnosis. I choose to believe the doctor, that it's entirely likely that you'll have lots of wonderful experiences ahead of you."

"But will I remember any of them?" Frances quipped.

Flo chuckled, but Liz didn't.

"Stop that this instant!" Liz commanded. "I know making jokes is a defense mechanism, but the reality is, you're probably in better health than most of the people we know. If this cognitive-impairment thing or Alzheimer's does start to progress, we'll just deal with that when it happens."

"Better listen to her, Frances," Flo said. "You know how Liz is when things don't go her way. She turned this town on its ear years ago when she insisted that Grace's mother-in-law serve her maid at the counter in Wharton's. She's not too old to stir up another ruckus if you don't get with the program. Don't start acting feeble when anyone can see that you're not."

Frances looked from one friend to the other, then shook her head. "Thank God for the two of you," she said sincerely. "There's not a chance I'll give up with the pair of you as cheerleaders."

"We could get outfits," Flo offered. "Maybe pompoms. I think I'd look quite fetching in one of those short skirts, waving a set of pom-poms."

"You don't need to go that far. I've gotten the message," Frances told her, though she had to admit the image of Flo and Liz in short little pleated shirts and tight Serenity High School sweaters, shaking pompoms around, did make her smile.

"Good for you," Liz enthused, then paused before prodding, "Well? How about that hot fudge sundae?"

Frances grinned, her mood already improving. "That would be good, but you know what would be even better?"

"What?" Liz asked eagerly.

"One of those margarita nights that those girls — Maddie, Helen, Dana Sue and the rest of them — are always talking about," Frances suggested.

Flo's eyes lit up. "*Whoo-ee!* Count me in. I believe I'll call my daughter and tell her to watch out. The Sweet Magnolias will soon have nothing on the Senior Magnolias!"

"Do either of you know how to make a decent margarita?" Liz inquired, looking a little skeptical.

"Of course," Flo retorted. "Where do you think Helen got her lethal recipe?"

"Okay, then. Margaritas, it is," Liz said. "And we'd better have them at my place. Travis and Sarah are right next door, in case things get out of hand. They can drive the two of you home."

"And then talk about it on the radio tomorrow morning on that show of theirs," Frances said, giggling at the potential outrageousness of it. She'd spent every one of her nearly ninety years being thoroughly respectable. It was about darn time she kicked up her heels.

Elliott sat at the kitchen table after feeding the kids, jotting down numbers to show to Karen when she eventually returned home. Maybe if she saw the real figures, based on gym memberships and his increased number of private clients, she'd be able to relax. Even using the preliminary numbers before the real push began, he thought the addition to his income was impressive. Surely it would be enough to allay her panic.

He was still at it, when Mack wandered into the kitchen in his PJs, his expression hopeful.

"Hey, buddy, what's up?" Elliott asked.

Mack climbed into his lap, something he rarely did anymore, and snuggled close. "Did Mom talk to you?" he asked.

Now, there was a minefield. Karen had talked, but not about anything he cared to share with a seven-year-old.

"About what?" he inquired carefully.

" 'Dopting me and Daisy," Mack said, catching him off guard.

"No. Was she supposed to?" Elliott asked him.

"Uh-huh. I told her me and Daisy wanted you to be our real, forever dad. She said she'd talk to you about it tonight. She promised."

A huge weight seemed to lift off Elliott's shoulders. If the kids had independently gone to Karen to request this, he knew she'd never deny them.

"Well, something came up when I first got home, so it may have slipped her mind. We'll talk about it as soon as she gets back."

Mack sat up and looked him in the eye. "Would it be okay with you?"

Elliott smiled and hugged him tightly. "It would be great with me!" He knew better than to make promises, though. "It's a big deal, though, so your mom and I need to have a long talk about it. Can you be patient?"

Mack shook his head, all but bouncing with excitement. "I'm no good at patient."

Elliott laughed. "Me, either, buddy. Me, either."

Karen arrived home to find the kids in bed and Elliott waiting for her in the kitchen.

"I kept dinner warm for you, if you're hungry," he said. "Or if warmed-up pasta offends your culinary instincts, I can make you something else."

She tried to muster a smile for him, but she wasn't quite able to hide the hurt she was still feeling.

"I'm not hungry," she said.

"Can we talk?" he asked, a plea behind the words. He held up a lined pad of paper. "I've made some notes. I think the figures will reassure you."

Though she wanted nothing more than to crawl into bed and let sleep take her away from this conversation, she knew that the real work of marriage couldn't be put off. If Elliott was ready to talk, she needed to listen.

"Let me get something to drink first," she said.

"No, sit. I'll get it. What would you like?"

It touched her that he was trying so hard. For a man not used to apologizing for his actions, he was doing everything he could to show her he was sorry for the way he'd handled this.

"Any caffeine-free diet soda in the refrigerator?"

Elliott looked inside, nodded and grabbed two, another sign of just how nervous he was. He never drank sodas, caffeine-free or not. He popped the tops and poured the drinks over ice.

She forced herself to meet his worried gaze. "For what it's worth, I'm not furious anymore."

His lips curved slightly at that. "Good to know. You probably have a right to be."

"In some ways, I couldn't agree with you more. In others, I know I overreacted. Once again, I let the past dictate how I handled seeing those papers. You're not Ray. Our marriage is nothing like the one I had with him."

"But you're still a survivor of that experience," Elliott said. "I need to remember that and let it guide how I handle things. I'm just not used to answering to someone else,

389

I guess."

"It's the family way," she said, actually injecting a hint of amusement into her voice, though there was nothing particularly amusing about the situation. "You are your father's son, after all."

Elliott immediately took offense. "You know better."

She shook her head. "I love you, but the evidence proves otherwise. You act in a vacuum. I know you do it for all the right reasons, because you love us and want an amazing future for us, but we're a couple. And I, maybe even more than most wives and certainly more than your mother or sisters, need to be a part of the decisions that get made. I can't make myself any clearer than that. It's a deal breaker for me, Elliott."

He looked shaken by her words. "I'm not my father," he repeated. "When I've left you out, it's not because I don't value your opinion, or think my way's the only way. It's because I'm trying to protect you from the worry you feel where money's concerned. I've explained that before."

"And I've told you that silence is exactly the wrong way to fix that," she said. "If you explain things to me, show me those figures you say you have, maybe I'll see what you see and won't be so afraid."

He nodded. "Probably a valid point."

She smiled then. "Probably?"

"Okay, definitely." He pushed his notes across to her. "These are just the current figures," he cautioned. "Maddie's convinced the open house and launch next week will show a huge spike. That's what happened with The Corner Spa once word of mouth kicked in. I know I already have more men signed up for private training than I did women in the first few months at the spa."

Karen studied the numbers, blinking at the bottom line. She lifted her gaze to meet his. "Seriously? This is the income you're looking at already?"

He nodded. "The gym will get a cut the same way the spa does." He pointed to another figure. "But it's still a sizable boost for us. We can manage the loan and put money back into the baby account, Karen. You can see it's right there in black and white."

She breathed an audible sigh of relief and felt the tension in her shoulders finally begin to ease. "Helen told me it was going to be okay, but seeing it on paper like this really does make a believer out of me. Thank you for not brushing off my concerns or dismissing them as irrational."

"I never meant to do that, ever," he said. "I tried to protect you and only wound up making things worse."

"Which should be a lesson to you," she said.

"Full disclosure from here on out," he promised.

Karen nodded. It was another one of those midnight promises made with sincerity that she knew without a doubt she could count on.

"Something else came up while I was at Helen's," she said.

He winced. "She told you I'd been to see her about adopting Daisy and Mack," he guessed.

"You got it," she said, frowning. "Why would you do that?"

"I just wanted to be sure the legalities wouldn't get complicated," he said. "I had every intention of discussing what she told me with you tonight."

"And ironically, until I saw those loan papers, I had every intention of talking to you about the same thing. Mack and Daisy want this as much as you do. At least Mack does. I haven't sat down with Daisy yet, but I have no doubt that she's as eager as he is. I didn't realize they'd been discussing this."

Elliott studied her face. "How about you?

Are you ready to take this step?"

She caught the hopeful note in his voice, remembered the plea she'd heard from her son and nodded. "Can we not say anything to Mack and Daisy just yet, though?"

He frowned at the request. "Still hedging your bets. Karen?"

"I suppose I am," she said candidly. "I believe we made great strides here tonight, but the way we got here shook me up a little. It reminded me that there are still some big differences in the way we look at marriage."

Elliott hesitated, looking as if he were torn about how to respond. To her surprise, though, he finally nodded agreement.

"There are," he said, his expression somber. "But I have a hunch the ones I see are not the same as the differences you see."

"I don't understand," she said, undeniably shaken even without hearing exactly what he meant.

"You see marriage as a partnership, and you *think* I see it as some kind of benevolent dictatorship."

She couldn't deny the truth of that assessment. "True."

"Want to know the difference that concerns me?" he asked.

"Of course."

"Okay, then," he said slowly, as if gathering his thoughts. "I see marriage as a commitment I made to spend forever with you, through good times and bad." He held her gaze. "You're convinced there are term limits. Until you truly believe that I will love you until the day I die and can say the same, then you're right. We're on shaky ground. You'll view every mistake I make as a step on a slippery slope to divorce."

At the seriousness of his tone, Karen felt the earth shift under her. He sounded so sure that his love was undying. He'd felt that certainty from the very beginning. Why couldn't she take that same leap of faith? Was it past history? Was it his own recent actions? Or was there something wrong with her that she viewed love as something that always came with an expiration date?

All she knew for sure was that she needed to figure that out, and she needed to do it soon before she lost the most important relationship of her life with a man who was truly dedicated to loving her and her children — not just now, but forever.

19

When the phone rang at midnight, Elliott reached for it, hoping to grab it before it woke Karen. He should have known better. She was already sitting up, rubbing her eyes as he answered.

"What is it?" she murmured sleepily. "Nobody calls at this hour."

"It's Sarah," he said, muffling the phone with his hand.

Karen was instantly alert. "Why? What's happened?"

Smiling as he tried to listen to Sarah, even as Karen peppered him with questions, he finally laughed out loud and handed the phone over to her. "You need to hear this for yourself," he told her.

Regarding him with puzzlement, she took the phone. "Sarah? What's going on?"

Elliott watched the play of emotions on her face as Sarah apparently told her what she'd just told him — that Frances, Flo and

Liz were currently looped out of their minds on margaritas and singing in the yard that separated Liz's guest house from the main house she'd sold to Travis before his marriage to Sarah.

"Oh, dear," Karen murmured, though she couldn't seem to stop herself from smiling. "Of course I'll be right there."

When she'd hung up, she couldn't seem to bring herself to meet Elliott's gaze. "She told you?" she asked, lips twitching.

"Oh, yeah," Elliott confirmed. "I gather you want to go and pick up Frances."

"One of us certainly needs to. She'll probably be less embarrassed if it's me."

"You sure about that?"

"I'm like a daughter to her," Karen said.

"Precisely. What mother wants her daughter to see her making a fool of herself? Besides, she might require a little extra assistance getting home and into her apartment."

"True, but I can't help myself. I have to see this. And I gather Sarah has also called Helen to come after Flo. How can I miss that?"

Elliott chuckled. "It's a sight I wouldn't mind seeing, either, but obviously we can't both go. Will you bring Frances back here?"

"I suppose that depends. She may insist

on going home to be sure the kids don't get a glimpse of her like this."

Elliott nodded. "Okay, do whatever you think is best. Just call me if you're going to stay with her. I can handle things here in the morning."

"You can't say we don't lead interesting lives," she told him as she dragged on jeans and a sweatshirt. "Try to get some sleep. I know the open house is Saturday, and you have a million and one things that need to get done tomorrow. If I can help, leave me a note if I'm not back before you go in the morning."

"Will do." He rolled over and would have buried his head under a pillow, but a thought struck him. "Hey, Karen," he said just as she was about to walk out.

"What?"

"Take video," he said, barely containing a chuckle. "I think when she sobers up, Frances is going to want a record of this night. Something tells me it's been years since she's gone this wild."

"You just want something to hold over her head next time you're in dire need of her oatmeal raisin cookies," she accused.

"Absolutely not. Charm's all I need to get those," he boasted. "It still works on her."

In fact, he wished it worked half as well on his wife.

When Karen parked in front of Travis and Sarah's house, it looked as if they were throwing a party. Helen's car was already there, along with Carter Rollins's police cruiser, lights flashing. She gathered a neighbor had taken exception to the post-midnight concert from the three unruly seniors.

As she rounded the side of the main house, she overheard Helen's impatient voice. "Mom, what on earth were you thinking? Who gets drunk and disorderly at your age?"

"We were just having a little fun," Flo said defensively. "You girls have margarita nights all the time without anyone calling the cops."

"Mostly because we don't go outside and serenade the entire neighborhood," Helen said with unmistakable exasperation.

Karen spotted Frances seated on a concrete bench in the garden and crossed the yard to sit beside her. "Girls' night out?" she inquired lightly.

Frances blinked and regarded her with surprise. "What are you doing here?"

"Sarah called me. She thought you might

want a lift home or back to my place."

"Really? I was going to walk as soon as things stopped spinning."

"Probably not a good idea," Karen told her. "Just how many margaritas did you have?"

"I only remember one," she said, her expression bewildered. "Would one knock me on my behind like this?"

"If it was Helen's recipe, yes," Karen said, chuckling despite her determination to be sympathetic and nonjudgmental. "There's a reason we all describe them as lethal."

"Yes, I can see that now," Frances said, her head bobbing like one of those dolls.

"Are you ready to go?"

Frances shook her head, then winced, probably because it was pounding with a margarita-induced headache. "I really can't drink anymore," she murmured regretfully. "I could hold my liquor much better back in the day."

"I'm sure you could," Karen consoled her. "Do you think you're feeling steady enough to walk to my car?"

"Can't go," Frances said, gesturing toward Carter who was standing across the lawn next to Travis, both of them clearly trying to muffle laughter. She leaned closer to Karen and confided, "I think we're under arrest."

Frances sounded oddly pleased by the possibility.

"Let me check," Karen offered. "I'm pretty sure you're free to go."

She patted Frances's hand, then crossed the lawn. "Any reason I can't take Frances home?" she asked Carter, whose eyes were twinkling.

"None that I can see," the town's police chief said, grinning. "Assuming she can stay upright long enough to get to your car."

"I'll get her out there," Travis offered. "Will you be able to manage once you get her home?"

Karen nodded. "As long as she doesn't pass out on me, I'll get her inside. Worst case, I'll take her to my house, and Elliott can carry her in. She can sleep in the guest room." She regarded Travis curiously. "Any idea what brought this on?"

"According to Liz, who's in no better shape than these two, they saw Frances's doctor today in Columbia."

The last of Karen's humor at the situation fled. "Oh, my God, what did he tell her?"

"I'm a little muddy on that," Travis admitted, his expression sobering, as well. "I'm not sure if they were celebrating good news or drowning their sorrows. Chances are you won't get to the bottom of it until morning, when clearer heads prevail."

Karen glanced across the yard to where Frances was rocking back and forth on that bench, a woebegone expression on her face. Just looking at her, she had a hunch she knew what the news had been. And if it was as dire as she feared, morning would be soon enough to hear about it.

Frances had never been so embarrassed in her life. What little she could recall of the night before was mostly a blur of margarita-induced laughter, singing every Johnny Cash song they could remember, and then the arrival, first of Sarah and Travis, whom they'd obviously awakened, then of Carter Rollins, followed by Helen and Karen. Since she'd awakened in her own bed, someone had obviously brought her home. She was fairly certain she could thank Karen for that.

She sat up gingerly, waited for the room to steady itself, then stood slowly, holding on tightly to the nightstand beside the bed.

"Hmm," she murmured with surprise. "Not so bad."

She went into the bathroom, took a shower, washed her face and cleaned her teeth, then pulled on a comfortable pair of slacks and a blouse. When she walked into the kitchen and found Karen there, she nearly jumped out of her skin.

"I didn't know you'd stayed," Frances said. "You must have been the one who got me home."

"That was me," Karen confirmed, doing a halfhearted job of stifling a smile.

Frances winced. "Just how bad was it? I remember Carter showing up, but not much after that."

"Oh, I think the presence of a cop quieted things down pretty quickly," Karen said, then giggled as she reported, "You thought you were under arrest."

"But we weren't?" she asked, almost disappointed. Unlike Liz, who'd been arrested more than once during civil rights demonstrations, Frances had never misbehaved in a way that would land her in jail. She wondered if that was evidence her life had been far too dull.

"No arrests," Karen told her. "Just a stern warning." She gestured toward the kettle on the stove. "Do you want tea or coffee? How's your stomach?"

Frances considered the question. "Steady enough," she concluded. "I think coffee would be good. It might wipe away the last of this alcohol haze."

"So, whose idea was it to have a marga. night?" Karen asked as she poured the cc fee.

"Mine," Frances admitted. "The Sweet Magnolias always have such fun. Flo thinks we should be the Senior Magnolias. We had one once before, but it didn't end like this."

"I'm sure the others would be flattered you want to emulate them," Karen told her, "but maybe you ought to drink sweet tea instead."

Frances regarded her indignantly. "We might have gotten a little crazy last night, but we're not too old to handle the occasional margarita. At my age, who cares if we make fools of ourselves? It's called living, and I intend to do as much of it as I possibly can."

As soon as she'd spoken, she saw the worry on Karen's face. "Oh, don't look like that. I'm not going to do anything dangerous, though I've always wondered what it would be like to go skydiving."

Karen's eyes went wide with shock. "Frances!"

Frances chuckled. "Just teasing. Even I'm not that foolish. A fall walking down the street could land me in the hospital with a broken hip. Who knows what I'd break jumping out of a plane?" She shook her

d. "No, that's definitely not for me."

"What brought all this on?" Karen asked.

"Travis seemed to think you'd gotten a report back from the doctor in Columbia yesterday."

Frances nodded. "Nothing conclusive yet. It could be something called mild cognitive impairment, which is manageable, but which can also lead to Alzheimer's. Or it could be early stage Alzheimer's already. It's hard to be definitive, I guess. At least they ruled out a brain tumor and a few other things."

"So it was good news," Karen said, studying her.

"Better than it might have been, I suppose, but not a clean bill of health," Frances admitted candidly. "I have a prescription to be filled, and we'll see if that helps. At least it seems as if my children won't have to worry about shipping me off to a nursing home just yet."

Karen jumped up and threw her arms around her. "I'm so relieved," she told her. "And we'll all pitch in to do whatever we can to help out. If the time comes when you can't live here, maybe we could work it out for you to live with Elliott and me."

Frances was more touched by the offer than she could possibly say, and she knew it

404

had been made with the generosity of spirit that she'd always seen in Karen. She doubted her own children would make the same offer. Jennifer and Jeffrey loved her, no question about that, but she doubted they'd want her intruding on the busy, complicated lives they'd established for themselves.

With her eyes stinging with tears, she clung to Karen's hand. "You have no idea how much it means to me that you would even suggest such a thing, but hopefully we're a long way from needing to make that sort of decision. If and when that time comes, I'll not be a burden, Karen, not to you or my family. I'll make the decision myself to find a place where I'll get whatever care I need. With this much of a warning, I may even get Liz and Flo to help me start looking now. I've thought about this long and hard. I want to be someplace I've chosen, not whatever facility happens to be available when the time comes."

Karen regarded her with dismay. "Then you're reconciled to leaving your home here?"

"Eventually. It's something anyone my age needs to consider. I won't be happy about leaving this apartment or all my friends, but who knows? Maybe Liz and Flo will decide to come with me. I hear there can be some lively men in some of those retirement places. That ought to be enough to get Flo to take a look."

Karen chuckled. "She's a real live wire, isn't she? But I thought she was already involved with someone."

Frances nodded. "Oh, she is, but she'll never stop keeping her options open, if you ask me. It's wonderful to see, actually. She had a tough life. Helen's dad was gone early and Flo worked hard to make ends meet and make sure her daughter had all the advantages she hadn't had. It's nice that she's finally living life to the fullest after all those years of struggling."

"You're all remarkable, in my view," Karen said.

Frances smiled at her. "Okay, young lady, you've done your duty by me. You need to run along and check on your own family. I'll be just fine."

"Let me fix you breakfast first," Karen pleaded.

The chance to leave a meal in the hands of a chef who'd won her own share of kudos at Sullivan's was too good to pass up. "You know I can't turn that down," she told her. "Why don't you call Elliott and invite him and the kids to join us? It's still early enough, I think, that they'll have time before work and school."

"You wouldn't mind?" Karen asked.

"Of course not."

Karen grinned. "I know Elliott's dying to hear all about last night. He wanted to come pick you up himself."

"Well, we'll not discuss it in front of the children," Frances said flatly. "They're far too young to hear about my silly shenanigans. I'll fill Elliott in when I go to my exercise class next week."

"Are you going to the open house at his gym tomorrow?" Karen asked. "It's the only time they're letting women in to get a peek at it. You can ride over with me, if you like. I have to go early to oversee the catering from Sullivan's."

"Oh, I'd love to," Frances said. "Now call that man of yours and get them over here."

Despite all the craziness of the night before and her worries over what the doctor had — and hadn't — said, today was getting off to a surprisingly bright start.

Elliott had been pleased to find Frances so alert and cheerful. Though Karen had quietly cautioned him not to ask about the night before in front of the children, he'd seen the unmistakable twinkle in Frances's eye when he'd asked if she'd done anything interesting lately.

"Don't go there, young man," she said with a warning shake of her finger.

He'd simply laughed, relieved by her attitude.

He hadn't lingered long, though. He'd planned to see three of his regular clients at the spa this morning, then spend the rest of the day at Fit for Anything to make sure every detail was in place for tomorrow's open house. He knew it wasn't necessary, of course — Maddie had lists of her lists — but at least he'd be around if she needed him to follow up on anything.

He finished up at the spa by ten and was about to head out, when he ran into Ernesto on the street.

"I was just coming to see you," his brother-in-law said. "You going somewhere?"

"I'm heading over to the new gym to get ready for tomorrow's open house." He forced himself to ask, "Did you need something? You'll have to tell me while I walk over there. I've got a packed day ahead." And it didn't include a pleasant conversation with the man who'd been making his sister miserable. Keeping his opinions to himself was going to be a real test.

Ernesto regarded him with a dark look. "I need you to talk sense into your sister."

Elliott stopped in his tracks, frowning at his brother-in-law's tone. "What does that mean? What is it you think Adelia's done?"

"She's neglecting the children. She's throwing away money hand over fist. She's talking back to me. I don't know what the hell is going on with her. I do know she's not the woman I married."

Elliott had to calm his temper. "Maybe that's because you're not the man she married," he said quietly, his resolve shattered. "I promised I'd stay out of this, but you came to me. I know all about the way you've been disrespecting her, Ernesto. I'm sure half the town knows, since you've done nothing to hide your sleazy affair. The only reason I haven't tried to beat some sense into you is because Adelia asked me not to."

Ernesto didn't have the grace to look even remotely embarrassed that Elliott knew of his cheating. "I'm entitled to a little enjoyment after all these years," Ernesto said defensively. "Your sister was paying attention to the children, not me. She didn't take care of herself. You saw how she looked. She gained weight."

"Carrying your children," Elliott said incredulously. "You ought to be down on yours knees every day thanking God for the way she's taking care of your family, the support she's given to you so you could focus on making a successful career for yourself."

"I've given her a fine home. She has everything money can buy," Ernesto argued. "Is she grateful? No. Apparently that's not enough for her."

"I doubt it would be enough for any woman whose husband is cheating on her," Elliott said. "You said before that you're entitled to that. I'm here to tell you that you're not. Whatever Adelia's dishing out to you these days, trust me, I'm on her side. It's probably not even half what you deserve."

Ernesto scowled at him. "I'm not doing anything your own father didn't do," he said.

Elliott stared at him in shock. "You don't know what the hell you're talking about. My mother would never have put up with him cheating."

"She turned a blind eye to it, just the way most wives do," Ernesto said confidently. "Ask her, if you don't believe me. Or tell Adelia to ask her. I'll bet Maria would give her an earful about what a dutiful wife should do in this situation."

With that he turned and walked away,

leaving Elliott reeling. Surely Ernesto couldn't have been right about his father. It was true that his mother had treated his father like a king, leaving most of the family decisions in his hands, but cheating? She wouldn't have tolerated it. She had more self-respect than that.

Or did she? he wondered. Given how she felt about divorce, would she have sealed her lips and endured the situation?

Suddenly he found himself once again questioning all the values that had been drilled into him over the years. While he knew he'd never believe it was his right to cheat on Karen, how many other aspects of his father's attitude toward marriage had he inadvertently accepted? Was there more validity to Karen's charge that he was behaving just like his father than he'd wanted to believe?

He stepped into the gym and asked Maddie, "Can you spare me a few more minutes?"

"If you'll pick up a few things while you're out," she said.

"Sure."

He made a list of everything she wanted, then went back to the spa parking lot for his car. Five minutes later, he was parked in front of Raylene's dress shop on Main Street.

He felt completely out of place walking inside, then found himself grinning when Adelia stepped out of the back, looking great in a dress perfectly suited for her curvaceous figure.

"Don't you look like the height of fashion," he commented.

"I bought it with last week's paycheck," she said. "Every penny of last week's paycheck, in fact. I probably should have charged it to Ernesto."

"You probably should have," he said, his good mood fading. "I just had a little chat with your husband."

"Elliott, I asked you not to," she said, looking dismayed.

"Hey, don't blame me," he said, hands in the air. "He came to me. He wanted me to get you to shape up and behave the way a proper wife should."

She stared at him incredulously. "Are you kidding me?"

"Not so much," he said.

"In that case, I hope you told him off."

"I told him you probably weren't treating him half as badly as he deserved." He glanced around. "Are we alone here?"

"Unless a customer comes in, yes. Why?"

"Ernesto did say a couple of things that got to me," he admitted.

"About me?"

He shook his head. "No, one was about Dad. He said he'd cheated on Mom."

Adelia hesitated so long, he knew what she was going to say before she ever opened her mouth.

"I don't believe it," he said.

"She never said a word, but I knew," Adelia said. "I have no idea how long it went on or why she tolerated it." She shrugged. "That's one reason I know she won't understand why I'm so furious with Ernesto. She'll just tell me that's one of the crosses I need to bear to have a lovely home."

Elliott muttered an expletive.

Adelia smiled at his rare loss of control. "My sentiment exactly." She studied him. "Is there something else?"

He took a deep breath. "Am I like Dad?"

She regarded him intently. "You're not talking about being a cheater, I assume."

"Never," he said flatly.

"Then it's about his general macho attitude," she concluded. "And I'd have to say yes. It's the way you were brought up, just as our sisters and I were raised to think women were to stay in their proper place."

Elliott was shaken by her confirmation.

"Really? You think I'm like Dad?"

"In the best ways, yes," she said in an effort to console him. "Dad always put his family first. He didn't see cheating as the antithesis of that. Don't ask me why, but he obviously didn't. He made the decisions he thought were best for our own good. He worked hard, so he thought he deserved unquestioning loyalty. I've seen a little of that in you."

Before he could respond, she put a hand on the clenched muscle in his arm. "Don't take that the wrong way, because there's another side to you that balances it out. You're sensitive and compassionate in ways Dad never dreamed of being." She regarded him with concern. "Why are you asking about this?"

"Karen's called me on it a few times. I've always thought she was overreacting or misinterpreting what I was doing, but maybe she's not. Maybe I need to take a harder look at how I handle the decisions in our marriage."

"You mean share them with her?" she asked, amusement threading through her voice.

He winced at the accuracy of her guess. "Yes."

"It couldn't hurt," his sister agreed. "You

love her. She loves you. You know she's smart. Doesn't that lay the groundwork for a great partnership?" She shrugged. "Not that I'd know anything about how that works. Ernesto's world veers toward a dictatorship. He's having a little trouble with the fact that I'm changing up the rules."

Elliott regarded her with admiration. "Good for you. Any predictions for how it's going to go?"

"If he's running to you for backup, I've at least shaken him up," she said. "But I'm not counting on much more than a few seconds of guilt. He's not that introspective."

"Leave him," Elliott said, not sure which of them was more surprised by his impulsive words. "He doesn't deserve you."

"No," she said. "He doesn't." Then she sighed. "We'll see, though. There's a lot to consider."

"Whatever you decide, I'll back you up. I mean that, Adelia."

She gave him a hard kiss on the cheek. "And *that*," she said, "is what makes you different from Dad."

20

Elliott had been totally shaken by his conversation with Adelia, both in terms of her situation and what she'd told him about how he'd inadvertently patterned his own marital behavior on his father's. It was something he needed to correct, no question about it.

He realized now that he'd been so busy protecting Karen the way he thought a good husband should — at least in his mind — that he'd failed to acknowledge what she'd kept trying to tell him, that she wanted their marriage to be a real partnership. That meant sharing everything, even the worries. It would require a shift in thinking, but he could do it.

Now, though, he had to focus on getting the gym ready for tomorrow's open house. There was too much riding on it for him to be distracted over the next couple of days.

Once he'd picked up all the supplies on

Maddie's list, he went back to the gym, toted everything inside, then went in search of Maddie. He found a note on the desk in what would eventually be his office. For the moment, they were sharing it.

"Crisis at Katie's school," she'd written. "Back as soon as I can get here." She'd noted the time at 10:45, shortly after he'd spoken to her. It was now after noon.

Since he knew what needed to be done before tomorrow's event, he got started with the final checklist on each of the areas to make sure every piece of equipment was spotless, every square inch of the floor polished and swept. He even checked to assure the supply of brochures and membership applications at the reception desk was adequate and that there were plenty of pens.

He was about to run through the checklist for the café when Maddie finally arrived, Katie in tow. Judging from the scowl on Maddie's face, all was not well.

"Suspended," she said by way of explanation as she ushered her daughter into the office.

When she emerged a few minutes later, she released a heavy sigh.

"Want to talk about it?" Elliott asked.

"I would if I actually knew much. She was suspended for skipping class. Apparently it's not the first time. She refuses to say why. Cal tried to mediate, but the principal wasn't budging. Frankly, I don't blame her, especially since this is a repeat violation. I never knew about the first one, because Katie somehow forgot to bring the note home. How she kept the news from Cal is beyond me. He knows everything that goes on at that school."

"Would they fill Cal in, rather than your ex-husband?"

"No, but he didn't know, either. I called him to make sure." She gave Elliott a weary look. "Do we have any odious tasks left to accomplish around here? I want her to suffer, rather than sitting in my office sulking over the injustice of it all."

Elliott grinned. "Sadly, I'm afraid all the floors have been scrubbed and the locker rooms are spotless."

"Too bad," Maddie murmured. "Maybe I should take her over to The Corner Spa. Those locker rooms are always in need of a good scrubbing."

"Go ahead. I think everything here is under control, at least based on those checklists of yours that I found on the desk."

She gave him a grateful look. "Would you mind? I feel like I have to deal with this as quickly and firmly as possible. Katie needs to learn a lesson. She's always been such a good kid that this has come as quite a shock."

"Do what you need to do," Elliott said. "I'll call if I run into anything I don't know how to handle."

"Did you see that a reporter from the local paper is stopping by in an hour for a tour and an interview?" she asked. "Think you can handle that?"

"I'd rather eat dirt, but I'll manage," he said.

She laughed. "Get used to it. You're the very sexy face of this place now. I'm thinking billboards showing off those excellent abs of yours might not hurt at some point."

He regarded her with horror, certain she had to be teasing. "No way," he protested.

"Oh, yes," she said, grinning. "You are definitely the poster boy for fitness in Serenity."

Elliott groaned. "Heaven help me!"

"God's already done you many favors," she teased. "And you've made the most of them."

Elliott felt heat climb into his cheeks. "Get out of here, Maddie. You're embarrassing me."

"Garnet Rogers and Flo Decatur have said the same and more," she said, laughing. "Buck up and take it like a man."

He was still shaking his head, when she returned with Katie, who followed her from the gym, her expression glum. He watched them go, wondering if that's what the future held in store for him and Karen. Given what he'd already seen of Selena's behavior and now this, he was pretty sure Daisy was destined to follow along the same troubling path of rebellion. It seemed to come with being a teenager. And, from what he'd observed recently, girls were much trickier to manage than boys.

Dana Sue had assigned Karen to handle the on-site part of Sullivan's catering for the open house at Fit for Anything on Saturday. She'd obviously known Karen would want to be there to share in Elliott's big day.

Maddie had scheduled the event from ten in the morning to two in the afternoon on Saturday, so families could stop in, look over the facilities, chat with Elliott or her about memberships, and enjoy the mini-wraps and other hors d'oeuvres being served in the café.

To Karen's delight, the gym had been packed from the moment the doors opened. She'd barely caught a glimpse of Elliott, who'd been besieged by men wanting to sign up for personal training or asking about the various classes being offered early in the morning, during the lunch hour or in the evening to accommodate the schedules of working men. She'd had to call Sullivan's twice for refills on the wraps and other food. The second time, Dana Sue had come over herself.

She looked around at the crowd with a pleased smile spreading across her face. "I'd love to get close enough to Maddie to ask, but it looks to me as if this is going really, really well."

"That's what I thought, too," Karen said. "I don't know if even half these men are signing up, but if so, I may never see my husband again."

Dana Sue gave her a knowing look. "Are you feeling better about your investment now?"

"You have no idea," Karen said with genuine relief. "I should have trusted Elliott from the beginning."

Dana Sue nodded. "I do understand why you were nervous, though. I can admit now that I had a few qualms of my own."

"Gee, thanks for sharing," Karen said. "I felt as if I was out on the skeptical limb all by myself."

"You were scared enough without me adding to your worries," Dana Sue said. "I guess I understood how women would react to a place like The Corner Spa, but men? Who knew if they were this eager for a clean, state-of-the-art place to exercise? They could have been content jogging around the track at the high school."

"I could have filled you in on that point," a man said as he reached for a miniature chicken-caesar wrap and popped it into his mouth.

"Dexter," Dana Sue said, recognizing him at once. "How nice to see you! How are your plans for Florida?"

"Coming along nicely, thanks to this place opening," he said without even a hint of bitterness. "I know what everyone thought of my gym, but it filled a need in this town. Elliott, Ronnie, Cal and the others saw that. Men aren't that different from women. Plenty of 'em will exercise to stay in shape if there's a convenient place to do it and their friends go there. Give 'em an introductory discount, and they'll flock right in. That's what I told Maddie, and just look around you. That woman knows good advice when she hears it."

"She does, indeed," Dana Sue said. "I'm so glad you're excited about retirement. I know the guys were worried about driving you out of business."

"I'd have told 'em not to worry, if they'd asked. I was more than ready for this change. I can't wait to get close to those casinos," Dexter said. "I'm feeling lucky."

He popped another hors d'oeuvre into his mouth, then wandered away.

"He's quite a character," Karen said.

"But smarter than people ever gave him credit for, I think. He knew that gym of his would draw customers whether he ever put a dime into it or not. He recognized the need, even before Maddie, Helen and I did. I think he viewed The Corner Spa as the first step in his retirement plan."

"It certainly sounded that way," Karen replied just as Frances came over.

"I don't suppose you girls are serving margaritas," she teased.

"Not to you," Dana Sue responded, a twinkle in her eyes. "From all reports, you can't handle them."

"Just a minor miscalculation," Frances said, waving off the incident. "Next time we'll water 'em down a bit."

"Maybe you should just join us," Dana Sue suggested. "We can keep an eye on your intake."

Frances's eyes immediately lit up with delight. "Seriously? You'd let us be Sweet

Magnolias for a night?"

"If you ask me, you all were the original Sweet Magnolias," Dana Sue confided. "We just came along later and carried on the tradition."

"Oh, I can't wait to tell Liz and Flo," Frances said eagerly, hurrying off.

"You just made her day," Karen told Dana Sue.

Dana Sue chuckled. "But probably not Helen's. She's going to freak out when she hears the news." She shrugged. "However, in my humble opinion, it will be good for her to bond with Flo in a whole new way."

"I'm sure she'll appreciate your consideration," Karen said, not even trying to hide her amusement over the likely confrontation.

"I'm not worried," Dana Sue said cavalierly. "Ronnie will protect me. He likes a good go-round with Helen from time to time. And speaking of my husband, I'd better find him and congratulate him before I get back to Sullivan's. Call if you need anything else over here."

"It's already two o'clock. The party's bound to wind down soon," Karen said. "Especially if the food disappears."

"You have a point. I'll check with Maddie and see if she wants it to die out or if she wants the crowd to linger."

As Dana Sue headed off into the crowd, Karen walked around the café, checking on platters and taking away those that were empty, refilling a few others with the fresh supplies Dana Sue had just brought over.

When her body began to tingle, she knew Elliott was nearby even before she turned around and found him right behind her.

"Congratulations!" she said, giving him a kiss. "It looks to me as if you have a major success on your hands."

"It is going well, isn't it?" he said, looking around at those who continued to linger. "It's almost scary how well it's gone."

"I'm so proud of you," she said sincerely. "Not just for succeeding, but for sticking to your guns even in the face of my panic. You believed in this. I should have, too."

He seemed surprised by her words. "You mean that, don't you?"

She nodded. "You've never given me a single reason to doubt your intentions will always be for the good of our family. I owe it to you to trust you more than I did. I'm sorry."

"Thank you for saying that. I've realized a few things myself in the past couple of days. We'll have to have one of our date nights soon and talk about all that. You free tomorrow night?"

"I'll make sure of it," she said, then gestured around the gym. "After tomorrow, who knows when I'll be able to get on your schedule again."

He pulled her into his arms and rested his chin on her head. "I will always make time for you, *querida*. Always."

After the day's success, Maddie invited everyone over to her house for a private celebration for the gym's partners. Since kids were included, it was a mob scene in the backyard. Cal and Ronnie were flipping burgers on the grill, an activity usually claimed by Erik, but he was on duty in the kitchen at Sullivan's tonight.

Elliott joined the two men at the grill. Ronnie grinned at him.

"You must be feeling good about now," he said to Elliott.

"I feel a whole lot better than I did this time yesterday," he admitted. "Memberships are a lot stronger than we projected and I'm completely booked for the first six weeks we're open. I think we may need to hire another trainer, at least part-time. Jeff could probably spare a couple of hours a day, though he's picking up the slack for me at the spa, so maybe not."

"Up to you," Cal said. "We're just innocent bystanders from here on out. You and Maddie are running the place."

Elliott glanced around the yard, looking for some sign of Katie. She was nowhere in sight. "I don't mean to meddle in something that's none of my business, but are things okay with Katie? I don't see her here."

"Grounded," Cal said succinctly. "She's allowed down to eat when the food's ready, but otherwise she has to stay in her room. We've cut off access to her cell phone and her email. She's one unhappy teenager at the moment."

Ronnie looked surprised by the news. "What happened?"

"She cut class," Cal said.

"Any idea why?" Elliott asked.

Cal shook his head. "She's covering up something, but she won't give either Maddie or me a clue. And I haven't heard any rumors at school, so I can't put the pieces together, either. Maddie's beside herself since this is so unlike Katie. I can't say that I blame her." He shrugged. "We'll get to the bottom of it eventually. Sooner rather than later would be good. I don't like seeing Maddie so upset."

Just then Elliott spotted Karen coming through the kitchen door carrying a tray of hamburger buns. "Duty calls," he said and went to help her.

"Hey, haven't you done enough food service for one day?" he asked, taking the tray from her.

"I don't mind pitching in." She glanced around. "Where are Daisy and Mack?"

"Mack's in the front yard with some of the boys. Travis is out there keeping an eye on them. Daisy's right over there helping Helen look after the little kids."

Karen smiled at the sight of Daisy, sitting close to Helen on a bench under a tree. "I think Helen still misses her and Mack. Those weeks she took care of them for me formed a bond none of them are likely to forget. It was really hard on Helen when it was time for me take them back. I was so relieved to have them home again, I don't think I understood how difficult it was for her to let them go, but she did it without a single complaint. She truly is remarkable."

"She is, and she knew there was never any question that they belonged with their mom," Elliott said. "She understood that from the get-go. She just pitched in during a crisis."

"And I will always owe her for that," Karen said with emotion. She waved her hand. "Look at me. It still makes me cry thinking about how generous and unselfish she was. I'm so glad she has a daughter of her own now. She and Erik are wonderful parents. Sarah Beth is very lucky."

Elliott held her gaze. "So are Daisy and Mack."

She smiled at that. "They'll be even luckier when they officially have both of us."

Elliott stared at her. "Are you saying what I think you're saying?"

"I'm saying that I want to move forward and have you adopt them legally," she said. "It's time."

Elliott pulled her into his arms. "Ah, *querida,* I thought today couldn't possibly be any better, but you've just made it the best day of my life."

Karen and Elliott managed to find a few minutes alone with Helen before the end of the evening to fill her in on Karen's decision. A smile immediately broke across her face.

"I am so happy you've decided on this," she told them. "I'll get to work on it first thing on Monday morning."

Karen regarded her nervously. "Any chance there could be some kind of a glitch or is it okay if we tell the kids?"

"I can't foresee any problems," Helen as-

429

sured her. "Legal matters can always take an unexpected turn, but I think it would be safe enough to tell them."

Karen turned to Elliott. "We should do it when we get home."

"You're sure about that?"

She nodded. "I know how badly they want it. They should know."

Elliott's delighted expression was proof that she was making the right decision.

As soon as they arrived at home, she stopped the kids from running off to their rooms.

Daisy and Mack exchanged a worried look.

"Are we in trouble?" Mack asked.

Karen regarded him with a stern expression. "Is there any reason you should be?" It was amazing the things she sometimes found out by bluffing.

Mack shook his head. "Honest, Mom, I was good tonight."

"Me, too," Daisy said.

"Okay, then," Karen said, making a show of relenting. She smiled at them. "Elliott and I have good news we wanted to share with you."

"You're having a baby," Daisy said, bouncing up and down with excitement.

Karen stared at her, startled by her enthusiasm. "You want a baby brother or sister?"

"Well, sure," Daisy said. "I want a sister."

"A brother," Mack corrected. "Being a big brother would be cool. I could teach him stuff."

"So, is that the news?" Daisy asked hopefully.

"Not this time," Elliott said. "Your mom and I have spoken to Helen and we're going to move forward with me officially adopting you. Once the paperwork is handled, I'll be your dad." He studied each of them. "I hope that's what you both want, because it's what I want more than anything."

Mack was the first to launch himself at Elliott, but Daisy was right behind him, tumbling Elliott back onto the sofa in their exuberance.

Karen watched the three of them with tears stinging her eyes. "I gather you're happy," she said, laughing at the sight.

"This is the best news ever!" Daisy declared.

"The very best!" Mack concurred.

"Will I be Daisy Cruz now?"

Elliott glanced at Karen for confirmation, then nodded. "If that's what you want. How about you, Mack? Do you want to change your last name to Cruz?"

"Uh-huh," Mack said eagerly. A moment

later a puzzled expression passed across his face, followed by unmistakable concern. "Will that make me Latino?"

Karen regarded him with surprise. "Why do you ask?"

"Because sometimes people say mean things about being Latino, like Petey Millhouse's dad did."

Elliott sighed at the comment. "Changing your name won't change who you are, Mack. It won't make you Latino. That comes from your genes. You know me. You know my family. Do you think there's anything wrong with being Latino?"

"No way," Mack said with conviction.

"Then that's what matters," Elliott told him.

Karen ruffled her son's hair. "Sometimes people say mean things about other people for all sorts of reasons. It's usually because they're scared. What's important is what you know in your heart to be true, just like Elliott said. Cruz is a name you can be very proud to have." She held her husband's gaze. "I certainly am."

"And best of all, it means we'll be a real family," Daisy said. "We'll have a dad who's never ever going to leave us."

Elliott beamed at her. "You've got that right. You're stuck with me."

"Cool," Mack said.

Daisy's grin spread across her face. "Way cool!"

Seeing how secure her children clearly felt with the knowledge that Elliott was in their life for keeps, Karen regretted she hadn't taken this step sooner. Right now, this moment was the best thing she'd done for them since the day she'd married Elliott.

21

When Adelia got home after picking up the younger children from school, she found Selena locked in her room, her music playing so loudly it nearly shook the house. It was a sure sign that Selena was upset about something, no telling what. She pounded on her daughter's door.

"Turn the music down and let me in," Adelia commanded.

When there was no response, she took out the extra key she'd had made for just this situation and opened the door herself. She found Selena facedown on the bed, sobbing. When Adelia sat down next to her, Selena stilled for a heartbeat, then launched herself into Adelia's arms.

"Shh," Adelia murmured, holding her close. "It's okay. Whatever it is can't possibly be so bad. We'll work it out."

She felt Selena's faint shake of her head. "Not this. You can't fix it."

"Of course we can," she insisted. "[...] very good problem-solvers in this family[...]

Selena sniffed and sat up, her eyes re[...] rimmed, her cheeks damp with tears. "It'[...] too late. If you could make it better, you'd have done it before now."

Adelia had a terrible feeling about where the conversation was headed. "Does this have something to do with your father?"

Selena nodded. "I saw them," she said.

It was unnecessary for her to explain to whom she was referring. They both knew.

"Together," she added indignantly. "He brought her to my school when he came to pick me up. He said he wanted me to get to know her. He said he knew I already knew about what was going on and that I was old enough to understand."

She regarded Adelia with a dismayed expression. "But I *don't* understand. How can he do this to you? To us? It's so wrong!"

Incensed by Ernesto's insensitive behavior, Adelia had a few thoughts about that, none of which she could share with her daughter. She couldn't help wondering if subconsciously her husband was testing her, trying to see how far he'd need to push before he broke her.

She chose her words carefully, though. Whatever happened between her and sto, she wanted her children to come ough it believing their mother and father th loved them. "I suppose from his point of view he was paying you a compliment by thinking you're mature enough to handle this," she said, stroking Selena's long, dark hair. "But I'll talk to him, sweetheart. I'll make him understand that what he did made you uncomfortable."

"Not uncomfortable," Selena said furiously. "He made me mad. You're my mom, and she's *nothing* to me. I don't want to get to know her, not ever." She gave Adelia a disappointed look. "You know what else I don't get? I don't get why you're letting him get away with it. That's not right, either."

Adelia shrank at the hint of her daughter's disdain. She would not allow Ernesto — or her own actions — to ruin her children's opinion of her. "I told you I'll talk to him. He won't try to force this woman on you again."

"I don't mean what happened today," Selena said with impatience. "I mean all of it, the whole affair. He acts like it's normal to treat you like this, and you're letting him. Cheating is wrong, Mom. Even I know that much."

For a moment Adelia couldn't even form a coherent thought. As low as Ernesto had sunk up until now, she'd thought he would protect their children from having to deal with his infidelity. She was at fault for this. Apparently her revelation that Selena had already figured it out had given Ernesto the absurd notion that an introduction to this other woman would be acceptable.

Seeing the hurt and the lack of respect in her daughter's eyes just now was the final straw. Selena was right. If she continued to pretend that Ernesto's behavior was acceptable to her, then she didn't deserve her children's respect, either. And it was a terrible lesson for Selena to learn that women just sat back and looked the other way when it came to their husbands cheating on them.

"I'm done," she murmured under her breath.

Selena stared at her, clearly shocked by the implication of those two simple words. "Mom? What are you saying?"

"I'm saying that you're right about me putting up with your father's outrageous and disrespectful behavior. And I won't have him trying to draw you into the middle of it, either. I'd hoped . . ." She shrugged off the thought. "Never mind what I'd hoped. I'm finished."

"Like, you're divorcing him?" Selena asked in a small, scared voice. "What will happen to us?"

Clearly Selena hadn't expected her tirade to push things in that direction. She'd apparently hoped Adelia would view it as some sort of call to arms and force Ernesto back into line.

"I'm not sure if it will come to divorce," Adelia hedged, though she knew in her gut that was the only likely option. "But I am giving him an ultimatum. Then, we'll see." Again, she ran a hand over her daughter's hair, swept it away from her face. She cupped her chin and looked into her eyes. "And no matter what, we'll be just fine. I promise."

Selena sighed and looked away. "I hate that he's doing this to us," she murmured.

"Me, too, sweetheart." Adelia held her a little longer, then stood up. "Can you watch your brothers and sisters for an hour? I want to see your father, and it's best that we not have this conversation here."

Selena nodded.

As Adelia was about to leave, Selena called after her. "Mom, I just want things to be the way they used to be."

"I know, sweetheart. I'm just not sure that's possible," she said with real regret.

Twenty minutes later Adelia breezed past

Ernesto's protesting secretary and interrupted a meeting in his office.

He scowled at her entrance.

"Can't you see I'm in the middle of
something?" he said tightly.

"I'm in the middle of something myself,"
she responded. "Unless you want me to
share it with your associates, I suggest you
make a little time for me now." She gave the
other men an apologetic look. "I'm sorry
for the inconvenience."

"No problem," one of them said as they
all rose and departed quickly, clearly not
ready to sit in on a marital dispute of some
kind.

Ernesto's scowl deepened. "This had better be damned important."

"It is, if you expect your marriage to me
to last even one second longer," she said
with a calm she was far from feeling. "I'm
done, Ernesto. I have no idea what you were
thinking by introducing that woman to our
daughter, but I won't have it. This affair of
yours ends now and we work on our marriage, or you move out of the house and I
file for divorce. Those are your choices.
There's no middle ground. And you have
maybe two seconds to decide, because I'm
done being patient while you behave like an
overgrown adolescent who can't control his

hormones."

He regarded her belligerently. "I've told you before that I'm not walking away from this other relationship," he said defiantly. "I have needs you don't satisfy."

She almost smiled at that arrogantly masculine response. "And I have needs that you don't satisfy. I haven't gone chasing around town to fulfill them and deliberately humiliated you in the process."

"What needs?" he scoffed. "You have the house of your dreams. You have the family you wanted. You can buy whatever you want."

She leveled a withering look directly at him. "And the last time you showed me the tiniest shred of love or respect? When was that exactly?"

For an instant he looked taken aback by her quietly spoken query.

"I've given you everything you ever wanted," he finally replied, looking genuinely mystified.

"No, you've given me everything you thought would keep me quiet and let you get away with doing whatever you want," she corrected. "Sorry, but those days are over."

"You'll never file for divorce," he said, sounding very sure of himself. "It will give your mother a heart attack."

"She won't like it," Adelia agreed. "I'm past worrying about that. I need to set an example for our children that what's happening is unacceptable. Men shouldn't treat women like this, and women shouldn't accept it. Period. Selena's already questioning why I allow it."

"The church doesn't recognize divorce," Ernesto reminded her.

"Then I'll file for an annulment while I'm at it."

"And turn our children into bastards?" He looked stunned by the possibility that she would go to such an extreme.

"If that's the only choice," she insisted, though she, too, was more shaken than she cared to admit by the idea. It was the one thing she'd never understood about the church's stance, that they would grant an annulment that somehow negated all evidence that the marriage had ever existed, leaving children in some sort of limbo. How, she wondered, was that better than a clean and simple divorce in circumstances such as these?

She studied Ernesto's face, looking for even the faintest hint that there was one tiny shred of love left between them. He looked beleaguered but not sorry. That was

441

what convinced her that they were out of options.

Drawing in a deep breath, she held his gaze. "I'll have your clothes packed in a couple of hours. You can pick them up after the children have gone to bed. Come back tomorrow and we'll explain to them what we've decided."

"But nothing's been decided," he shouted as she walked out of his office.

She turned back and gave him a look filled with genuine regret for the life they might have had. "Yes, it has. It's over, Ernesto."

"We'll see about that," he said, but his voice rang hollow.

Adelia didn't stop shaking until after she'd reached her car and settled behind the wheel. She closed her eyes and drew in a deep breath. It was over. Done.

And surprisingly, she didn't feel half as awful about that as she'd expected to. If anything, she finally felt an overwhelming sense of relief that the decision had finally been made . . . and that she'd been the one brave enough to make it. All that was left was to deal with the repercussions.

All, she thought wryly. Her personal hell was probably just beginning.

Karen had Tuesday off. She spent the morning cleaning the house, then ran into Serenity to stop by Raylene's. She was having a sale, and she'd told Karen the day before that there was a dress at half price that would be perfect for her.

"I'll put it aside, but try to get by early. If sales are even half as brisk as I'm hoping, I'll be dragging out every last piece of inventory to meet demand."

Sure enough, when Karen walked into the boutique, it was crowded with shoppers, mostly women she knew from her rare attendance at PTA meetings at school. She had a hunch Raylene could thank Adelia for that. From what she'd heard, Adelia had been spreading the word about the shop to every committee she served on. Raylene said business had soared since she'd hired Karen's sister-in-law.

She spotted Raylene behind the register dealing with a long line of customers and Adelia acting like a traffic cop directing people in and out of the store's three tiny dressing rooms. Raylene beckoned her over.

"Mention the dress to Adelia," she said. "She knows where I put it. And you can try it on in my office, if the dressing rooms are backed up."

Karen nodded. "Will do." Before she approached Adelia, though, she glanced through the racks, blanching at the price tags. Even at half off, most of these clothes were far beyond her budget. Coming here had probably been a bad idea. It was going to be embarrassing to admit to Raylene that she couldn't afford anything, even at a bargain price.

She was thinking about slipping out, hoping that Raylene wouldn't notice her departure, but before she could edge toward the door, Adelia spotted her.

"Hi. Raylene told me you might be stopping by. She has the perfect dress on hold for you. Want me to get it out of the back?"

Karen shook her head. "I'm not sure I want to see it," she admitted candidly. "Everything in here is too expensive, even on sale."

Adelia nodded in understanding. "When was the last time you actually bought something special for yourself? You buy your kids clothes first, then shop at the discount stores, right?"

Karen nodded, surprisingly unembarrassed by Adelia's straight talk.

"Then I think you deserve to treat yourself just this once. Well-made clothes never go out of style. In the end they're less expensive than two or three cheap things that fall apart in the wash."

Karen grinned at her. "I think I see why Raylene considers herself so lucky to have found you. You're a very good saleswoman."

A genuine smile broke across Adelia's face, for perhaps the first time in Karen's memory. "Thanks. I have to tell you it feels really wonderful to discover I'm good at something besides getting dinner on the table and carpooling." She gave Karen a hopeful look. "Does that mean you'll at least try on the dress? What would it say about me if I couldn't even persuade my own sister-in-law to try something on?"

Karen hesitated, then shrugged. "I suppose it couldn't hurt just to try it on." She knew, though, that it was the first dangerous step toward leaving the store with something she couldn't afford.

"Great!" Adelia said. "I'll get it and meet you by the dressing rooms. I think there's one free, which is something of a miracle today. If not, I'll put you in Raylene's office."

A few minutes later Karen was wearing a dress that had originally cost as much as her weekly take-home pay. Even at half price, buying it was out of the question.

Still, she couldn't seem to stop herself from turning this way and that in front of the mirror, imagining the day when she

445

could afford even just one special-occasion dress that fit like a dream the way this one did.

"It's absolutely perfect," Adelia enthused. "And you may be one of the only people I know who can carry off that shade of sunshine yellow."

"You don't think I look like a daffodil?" Karen asked, needing to seize on an excuse to turn down the dress.

"If that means you look sunny, cheerful, springlike and sophisticated, then, yes," Raylene said, joining them. "It's as amazing on you as I thought it would be when I saw it."

"I do love it," Karen admitted, then sighed. "But I can't possibly spend this much on a dress. I wish I could. I'm sorry if you missed out on a sale by holding it for me."

"Not to worry," Raylene said briskly, giving her hand a squeeze. "You're not ever to feel pressured into buying something here."

"Not even by me," Adelia said. "I'm pushy, but reasonable."

Raylene laughed. "Excellent traits in a salesperson." She spotted another customer at the register. "Oops! Duty calls. Be sure to say goodbye before you go," she told Karen.

After she'd gone, Adelia lingered, her expression thoughtful. "Karen, would you consider letting me buy the dress for you?"

Karen stared at her in shock. "Absolutely not. I don't want charity from you."

Adelia frowned. "And isn't it sad that that's what you think it would be? It tells me how awful our relationship has been. I want to do this as my way of apologizing for the way I've treated you since I first found out that you and Elliott were seeing each other. I was judgmental and rude, even after Mama told me what you'd been through." She held Karen's gaze. "I'd like to make amends. Maybe start over."

Karen regarded her sister-in-law with curiosity. "Why now?"

Adelia shrugged. "I guess I've finally seen the error of my ways, that's all," she said, a defensive note creeping into her voice.

Karen had the oddest sensation there was more to the generous gesture, but Adelia wasn't the kind of woman who'd ever admit to anything she wasn't ready to reveal.

"Are you sure you want to do this?" she asked. "It's amazingly generous of you."

Adelia shrugged, her cheeks pink. "Maybe it'll make up for the drugstore shower gel I've been giving you for Christmas the past couple of years."

Karen laughed. "Did you think you were offending me? I love that stuff. It's a rare treat."

Adelia stared at her in disbelief, then began to chuckle. "I think I really do need to get to know you a whole lot better. You're a glass half-full kind of woman, and I am so not used to that."

"I haven't always been," Karen admitted.

"Even better," Adelia said. "You can show me how you got there. I know Elliott's working late at the gym tonight. Want to bring the kids over to my place for dinner?" She gave Karen an encouraging look. "Mama won't be there."

Karen hesitated.

Adelia seemed to have read her mind, because a shadow passed over her face. "Neither will Ernesto."

Karen had a hunch there was a story behind that. She wondered just how revealing Adelia might be. She knew, though, it was an overture she couldn't afford to pass up. When she'd first met the Cruz family, she'd desperately wanted their acceptance. She thought she was gaining it in tiny increments, but befriending Adelia would amount to a giant leap forward.

"We'd love to," she told her.

"And you'll take the dress?" Adelia

pressed. "Please."

"Definitely pushy," Karen murmured, though she was grinning when she said it. "Just like your brother. It's how he got me to marry him. He wouldn't give up."

"It's good that he didn't," Adelia said, surprising her. "I'm just beginning to see that."

"A dress, a dinner and a compliment," Karen summed up. "I'd say we're making strides."

Adelia leaned in close. "Don't tell my sisters just yet. They'll think I've gone over to the dark side. Mama, too."

Karen chuckled. "Are you having a midlife crisis of some kind?"

Adelia shrugged. "Could be, but I have to say it's starting to feel good."

Karen studied the color in her cheeks and the brightness in her eyes. "I can see that. Good for you."

Whatever was going on to bring about this dramatic change, she was happy for Adelia . . . and for herself. For the first time since her marriage to Elliott, she sensed the real possibility that she could be friends with one of his sisters. She'd known from the beginning just how much he wanted that. It was turning out to be quite a day.

■ ■ ■ ■

"Adelia actually invited you and the kids over for dinner?" Elliott said incredulously when he finally arrived home after ten o'clock. His days lately had been exhausting, and he cherished these late-night conversations with his wife. "I don't know which shocks me more, that she invited you or that you accepted. Had she locked away the knives?"

Karen gave him a chiding look. "It was fine. Everyone behaved very civilly. The kids had a blast in the pool and I had fun with Adelia."

"And Ernesto?"

"No sign of him. No mention of him, either." She shook her head. "Something's going on there, Elliott. Whatever it is, though, Adelia actually seems happy about it."

He paused while removing his clothes. "She didn't talk about it?"

"We're not quite to the stage of sharing intimate little secrets yet," Karen admitted.

"Then what did you talk about?" he asked, then grinned. "Me?"

"Your name was mentioned from time to time," she said, clearly amused by his assumption that he was the only topic they had in common. "Mostly, though, we talked about how much fun she's having working for Raylene, how well her diet and exercise program are going, and school stuff. She's trying to rope me onto half a dozen committees."

"Did she have any luck?"

"She talked me into one — baking cupcakes for the fall festival. Don't tell her, but I'd already promised Daisy I'd do it. Adelia took such joy in thinking she wrangled a commitment from me that I didn't want to spoil it for her."

Elliott laughed. "Watch yourself. She's sneaky when she wants something. Why do you think they put her on so many committees? It's because she can talk anyone into doing anything. She got me into more trouble as a kid that way."

"You let your big sister boss you around?" Karen teased. "I can't imagine it."

"Imagine it," he confirmed. "Like I said, Adelia was sneaky."

He crawled into bed next to his wife, studying her face up close. "You look happy."

"I am," she admitted. "I saw a whole other side to your sister today. It made me believe maybe we could be friends."

"You have no idea what that would mean to me," Elliott said. "Not just for my sake, but for yours. Having a sister would be good for you."

"Even a sneaky one?" she asked wryly.

"I'd say so."

Her expression sobered then. "There's something I haven't even told you yet. I'm not sure how you'll feel about it."

Elliott frowned at her somber tone. "What?"

"She bought a dress for me at Raylene's. I went by because Raylene said it was perfect for me, but the second I saw the price, I told them I couldn't afford it, even on sale. Adelia insisted on buying it. She said it was to make up for giving me so much grief. I know I should probably have said no, but she seemed to want to do it so badly. I thought maybe accepting would be the gracious thing to do, a first step, if you know what I mean."

Elliott's pride kicked in. His first reaction was to insist she take the dress straight back. It humiliated him to think that his wife thought she couldn't afford to buy anything she wanted. Worse yet, she'd admitted as much to his sister.

Gazing into her worried expression, though, he couldn't make himself utter the words. For once he needed to swallow his pride. Adelia had wanted to do something nice for his wife. It was a gesture he needed to applaud, not condemn. And Karen, no slouch herself when it came to pride, had accepted the gesture graciously.

"You want me to take it back, don't you?" Karen asked when he'd said nothing. "It's okay. I knew I shouldn't accept it."

Despite her quick offer, he saw the disappointment in her eyes. "No, you should keep the dress," he said, drawing her into his arms. "And I will take you someplace special to wear it."

It was, he thought, the perfect compromise between his willful pride and his love of his wife. Perhaps he'd taken that lesson about being less like his father to heart, after all, and was already putting it to good use.

22

Frances spread her cards out on the table at the senior center on Wednesday night. "Gin!" she announced triumphantly.

"You're kidding me," Liz said, sounding thoroughly disgusted. "Again?"

Frances grinned. "What can I say? I'm on a roll. Maybe we should plan a trip to Vegas, while I'm on this hot streak."

Flo's eyes immediately lit up. "Seriously? You'd like to go to Las Vegas?"

"No, she wouldn't," Liz said. "She keeps tossing out these outlandish ideas like some sort of bucket list she wants to accomplish before she dies. It's morbid. I think she just wants to test the waters to see if either of us is crazy enough to join her."

"Actually going to Vegas is a perfectly rational idea," Frances said, suddenly determined to pursue the vacation. "We all love to gamble. There are lots of shows we can see. Why shouldn't we go and have some fun?"

"You have my attention," Flo said eagerly. "Come on, Liz. Don't be a stick-in-the-mud. Senior Magnolias do daring things."

"It's the *Sweet* Magnolias who are daring," Liz corrected. "Seniors behave respectably."

"This from a woman who once staged sit-ins right here in Serenity," Frances scoffed. "When did you get old and stuffy?"

"Around the time I turned eighty and my kids started looking for any excuse to send me to a retirement home," Liz retorted.

"Well, Travis made sure that's not going to happen when he invited you to stay on in the guest house after he bought your property," Frances said. "He and Sarah will protect you. No one in your family is going to go up against those two. They'll use that radio station of theirs to stir up a *Free Liz* protest or something."

Frances watched as Liz struggled between her sense of decorum and her well-proven record as a risk taker. The twinkle in her eyes suggested she was close to making the more outrageous choice.

"Oh, come on," Flo prodded when she apparently couldn't tolerate the silence another second. "You know you want to. If anyone's going to jump all over this and rain on our parade, it'll be my Helen. We might not want to let her in on our plans."

"Stop that nonsense," Frances said. "We're old and we're bold. I think that needs to be our motto for whatever time we have left."

Liz stared at her incredulously, then chuckled. "I have to admit, I like that. Okay, ladies, let's get online and order those tickets. I'm thinking we should reserve a suite. How about you?"

"How wonderfully indulgent!" Flo said eagerly. "Let's do it."

Frances sat back, listening to them as they seized on the plan and ran with it. Who would have thought at this late stage of her life and especially after all she'd been through recently that she'd be looking ahead, instead of settling for old memories? Just thinking about it made her smile . . . and gave her hope. If she was going down for the final count, it wouldn't be quietly.

It was Helen who called an emergency meeting of the Sweet Magnolias.

"Do you have any idea what my mother, Frances and Liz want to do?" she demanded when everyone was settled in her living room. She hadn't even made the usual batch of margaritas. She'd served sweet tea.

456

Failing to stock a supply of tequila and frozen limeade was a sure sign that she was genuinely upset.

"They're going to Las Vegas," Karen ventured carefully, not entirely sure if that's what had Helen in such a state.

"Exactly!" Helen said, regarding her accusingly. "Why aren't you more upset about this?"

"When Frances told me, I thought it sounded like fun," Karen admitted.

"Three old women on the loose by themselves halfway across the country struck you as a great idea?" Helen said incredulously. "Are you nuts? Who knows what could happen?"

"They'll gamble, maybe lose a little money, see a couple of shows and come home," Maddie soothed. "I don't see why you're getting so worked up about it."

"Oh, let's see," Helen said, her expression still dire. "Frances is ninety and has some sort of memory issues, Liz is just as old, and my mother is recovering from a broken hip she got trying to learn line dancing. Am I the only one who sees the potential for disaster?"

She turned a fierce scowl on Dana Sue who'd dared to chuckle. "Not a laughing matter," Helen declared.

Dana Sue's eyes continued to sparkle with mirth. "You have to admit the image of them taking on Vegas is pretty funny. I'm not sure the Vegas strip is ready for those three. Come on, Helen. Lighten up. I doubt they're going to play high-stakes poker. I imagine they'll lose a few dollars in the slots and be happy."

Helen sighed heavily. "I should have taken the time to shop for tequila so I could make the margaritas. I could use one. You all are not being supportive."

"No, we're being rational," Maddie said, unmistakably amused by Helen's rant. "Something you rarely are when it comes to your mother."

"Because she's impulsive and reckless," Helen said.

"No, she wants to actually live her life," Maddie corrected gently. "You need to let her. When you brought her back here, you were terrified she was going to be dependent on you. Now that she's behaving independently, that's driving you nuts, too. You can't have it both ways. Let her do what makes her happy."

"I agree," Karen said, risking another sour look from Helen. "I know Frances isn't really my family, but I think of her as if she were. I want her to have every single minute of joy she can grab. I suspect there comes a time when everyone wants to put their parents or grandparents into a nice, safe environment to protect them from harm, but isn't it better to let them live while they can? The time will come soon enough when they'll have no options. If Frances, Liz and Flo want to make this trip and think they can, I think we should be supporting them, not looking for ways to hold them back." She wavered under Helen's dark look, but then added, "Just my opinion."

"And mine," Dana Sue added supportively.

Maddie offered Helen a consoling look, then suggested with a sly twinkle in her eyes. "If you're that worried, you could go along. Chaperone them."

"Great idea," Dana Sue enthused before Helen could recover from her obvious shock. "I'll go, too."

Helen groaned. "Oh, sweet heaven," she murmured, looking from one to the other. "You're serious?"

"I am," Dana Sue confirmed.

"Come to think of it, I haven't had a girls-gone-wild weekend in a very long time," Maddie said. "Count me in, too." She glanced around at the rest of them. "Anyone else?"

Sarah, Raylene, Jeanette and Karen shook their heads.

"As much as I would love it, there's no way I can get away," Sarah said. "Though I'm thinking we should do live daily updates on my morning radio show. Travis will love the idea. It's bound to be a ratings bonanza. Grace can tune them in on the radio at Wharton's."

"What a fantastic idea!" Raylene added. "Oh, I wish I could come along."

Helen stared at them. "You want to take my humiliation public?"

Maddie patted her hand. "What your mother does is no reflection on you," she consoled her.

Helen rolled her eyes. "In Serenity? Who are you trying to kid? This trip will be the talk of the courthouse for weeks. I won't be able to look a single judge or opposing attorney in the eye without blushing."

"Oh, please," Dana Sue said. "You're tougher than that. At least that's what you're always telling us. A little gossip isn't going to be your undoing. Isn't that what you told Maddie when the whole town was up in arms over her dating Cal?"

Helen merely buried her head in her hands.

"So, you all just have to take lots and lots

of video on your cell phones, too, and send back daily reports to the rest of us," Karen said innocently. "I'd suggest keeping that just between us, but if our seniors really do go wild . . ." She cast a wicked grin in Helen's direction. "We can put the video up on YouTube and make them famous."

Helen glanced up, a look of horror on her face. "This was not at all how I planned for tonight to end," she lamented.

"Oh, buck up," Maddie said. "It's going to be fun."

"Or the death of me," Helen murmured.

Despite all Helen's grumbling protests, Karen envied her. It was a trip she definitely wouldn't mind sharing with Frances.

"You're so lucky," she told Helen.

Helen continued to look skeptical. "Lucky?"

"There will come a time when these memories will mean the world to you," she told her.

Helen shook her head, but her lips were finally twitching ever so slightly into a smile. "You are such a little optimist."

Karen nodded. "Kind of a miracle, don't you think?"

Certainly to her way of thinking, it was.

Elliott heard about the trip to Las Vegas from Cal and Ronnie, who claimed they were tempted to go along just to keep the women out of trouble.

"Don't you think Helen will do that?" Elliott asked. "She's a lawyer and she has a good head on her shoulders."

"Not when she's under the influence of our wives and margaritas," Ronnie said, a twinkle in his eyes. "It's actually a joy to behold when she cuts loose and lets herself have fun."

"Which is why Erik has begged Dana Sue to close Sullivan's for a couple of days so he can tag along and keep an eye on his wife," Cal said, chuckling. "The way this is going, the entire town might have to shut down so we can all trail out there to watch the fireworks."

"I wonder why Karen didn't mention any of this to me," Elliott said. "If the trip was Frances's idea, I'm sure she'd love to be there."

Of course, even as he spoke, he knew the answer. She would never spend that kind of money on something as frivolous as a trip to Las Vegas. She wouldn't even spend it on a dress she'd fallen in love with for herself. It gave him an idea of just what he could give her for her upcoming birthday.

"Do you think the women would mind one more?" he asked. "I'm thinking this trip would be the perfect birthday present for Karen, especially if Erik convinces Dana Sue to shut down Sullivan's for a few days."

"Let me have a talk with my wife," Ronnie said. "I think she can be persuaded to close down for a good cause. We're talking a couple of days. It'll be good for her, Erik and Karen to get away from that pressure cooker. Once the glowing reviews for Sullivan's started appearing all over the state, she's been working nonstop for the past few years. So have they."

Cal gave him a wry look. "I suppose that means you'll shut down the hardware store, too."

Ronnie shrugged. "We're talking about a weekend. No big deal."

Cal turned back to Elliott. "I'm thinking you and I are going to be stuck here holding down the fort. I am not hauling the kids to Las Vegas, especially not with Katie still grounded. And I can't ask Maddie's mom to babysit them for an entire weekend. Paula's okay with the kids once they're teenagers, but I think our two preschoolers scare the daylights out of her. They move too fast and are still a little short on conversational skills."

"I'm sensing it will be a big weekend for fast food and pizza," Elliott agreed. "I'd better get to my next client if I'm going to pay for this trip. Keep me posted on the dates and how things are working out with Dana Sue, so I can surprise Karen."

"Will do," Ronnie promised.

Elliott knew the impulsive gift was not without risks. He was going to have to show Karen copies of their bank statement, check stubs to prove the loan was being paid off and his latest receipts from his private clients before she'd accept the gesture. Still, he thought it would be worth it to give her this once-in-a-lifetime chance to do something with Frances before it was too late.

Three days later, the arrangements had been made for the trip. Elliott had bought the airline ticket for Karen, put it in a box wrapped in baby-shower paper — the only kind he'd found in the house — and tied it with a big red bow left over from Christmas.

He took Karen to Rosalina's for dinner. He'd wanted to take her someplace a little more special, but he figured he'd be on shaky enough ground with the gift. An

464

expensive restaurant would probably have her reeling.

When their drinks and pizza had been served, he raised his glass. "Happy birthday, *querida!* I hope it's just one of many, many happy ones we share together."

She'd worn her new yellow dress and had taken time to style her hair with more loose curls than usual. Her cheeks were pink and her eyes sparkling. He thought she'd never looked more beautiful. As always, when she smiled at him, she took his breath away.

"Thank you," she said. "I have a gift for you."

Elliott frowned at that. "For me? But it's *your* birthday."

"I know, but this surprise came my way, and I wanted to share it with you."

"That sounds mysterious," he said, genuinely puzzled.

Suddenly she looked incredibly nervous. "I know we had a plan, that we were trying to stick to a plan . . ." she began, but her voice trailed off.

Elliott's heart suddenly began to race. "You're not . . . we're not . . ." He could barely speak, partly from being overwhelmed with joy, partly because he was afraid he'd gotten it wrong. "Are you pregnant, *querida?*"

She nodded, clearly embarrassed. "I didn't mean for it to happen. We've been so careful." Color bloomed in her cheeks. "But not always, I guess." She studied him intently. "Are you mad?"

"Mad?" he asked incredulously, barely containing a whoop of joy that would lift the restaurant's rafters. "I'm thrilled. I thought I came here tonight with a pretty darn good birthday gift, but I can't top this. How soon? Do you know? Have you seen the doctor?" He regarded her intently. "Are you sure?"

She nodded. "Very sure. Four home pregnancy kits sure. I haven't been to the doctor yet because I thought you might want to come with me. You won't be able to see anything. It's too early for an ultrasound, but still . . ." She regarded him hopefully. "You do want to come, right?"

"To every single appointment," he confirmed. "You look happy. I hope you are, because I'm overjoyed. I can hardly wait to tell everyone."

"Not just yet," she cautioned. "These early months can be tricky. Let's get through them first, okay?"

"Whatever you say," he said at once. He'd have given her the moon just then if she'd said she had a craving for the green cheese it was supposedly made of. He regarded her worriedly. "I don't want you panicking about money, you hear me? You've seen how well the gym is doing. We may be ahead of schedule on the baby plan, but we're okay, Karen."

She nodded. "I know that. And the minute I found out, for some reason, I just felt myself relax about all of it." She reached for his hand. "We'll be all right. I know we will."

"We will be," he confirmed.

A grin spread across her face as she clung to his hand. "Okay now," she teased, then challenged, "Top that for a birthday surprise."

He reached into his jacket where he'd stuffed the long, slim box. He couldn't help chuckling as he handed it to her. "I thought the baby paper was a tacky substitute for birthday paper, but it's certainly turned out to be on the mark."

"And the red bow's exactly the festive touch the night deserves," she said, laughing.

Elliott held his breath as she opened it and looked at the envelope inside. As she removed the plane ticket to Las Vegas, her eyes grew wide and delight spread across her face.

"You bought me a ticket to go to Vegas

with the girls?" she asked incredulously.

"And don't say that I told you, but Frances is reserving a room for you as her gift. She's absolutely thrilled that you're coming along."

For just a heartbeat, her excitement visibly dimmed. "But can we afford this?"

"Bought and paid for," Elliott confirmed. "And I have bank statements back home that prove we can. You might have to raid Mack's piggy bank for gambling money, but I think it won't even come to that. I've gotten some nice tips, and I've put a little aside just for you to fritter away on the slots."

"Maybe I'll hit a jackpot, and our money worries will be over forever," she said with surprising optimism.

"Heaven knows, I'm feeling lucky," Elliott told her. "Want to know why? Because for the first time I can remember, you don't look absolutely terrified by the prospect of spending a little extra to do something special. I think we're finally over that hurdle in our marriage."

"Maybe not over it," she warned. "But it's not nearly as high and scary as it was a few months ago."

She frowned again. "What about Sullivan's? If Dana Sue and I are both going, Erik and Tina can't run it alone, even for a couple of days."

"She's shutting it down for the weekend. Erik's coming, too. He's hoping to keep Helen sane."

Karen laughed. "I don't envy him that task. She's totally freaked out."

"Just so you're not," he said, squeezing her hand. "I want you to go on this trip and have the time of your life. You deserve to run a little wild. Just don't go picking up any handsome strangers in the casinos."

She held his gaze. "Why would I want to when I'll have the sexiest man on earth, the father of my child, waiting for me back here?"

As celebrations went, Elliott thought this had been the best of his entire life, not because of what he'd given his wife, but the gift of pure joy she'd given to him.

After the euphoria of her birthday celebration, Karen's mood sank the next morning when she opened the door to find Adelia on her doorstep, her expression dark. She was obviously shaken. Even after their recent detente, the visit came as a surprise.

"Adelia, is everything okay? You look upset."

Though Adelia stepped warily inside, she couldn't seem to bring herself to meet

Karen's gaze. There was no hint of the friendliness of a few days ago. Instead, she asked tersely, "Is Elliott here?"

"No, he's already at the spa," Karen said. She took a closer look and realized that her sister-in-law had been crying, though she'd tried to hide her swollen eyes with makeup. "Why don't I pour you a cup of coffee and we can talk. Elliott made it, so it's strong the way all of you like it."

Adelia shook her head and backed toward the door. "I should go."

Karen reached out and put a hand on her arm. "You're obviously upset about something. I'm happy to listen. I can do it without judging or giving advice, if that's what you want."

"You'll think I'm an idiot," Adelia said, clearly embarrassed.

"Why on earth would I think such a thing?" Karen asked, genuinely shocked. "I thought we made some progress the other night toward being friends."

"We did, or at least I hoped we had," Adelia said, "but still, after all of the commotion I stirred up over you being divorced, how can you not laugh when I say I'm leaving my husband?"

After blurting out the words, Adelia couldn't seem to bring herself to look at

470

Karen. Karen knew what it had cost her to make that admission, especially to her.

"I'm sorry," she said softly to her sister-in-law. "I know it couldn't have been an easy decision for you."

Adelia seemed startled by Karen's compassion. "You really mean that, don't you?"

"I promised you no judgments," Karen said. "I'm certainly in no position to make them, not about this."

Adelia sighed heavily. "Mama is going to have a coronary. I doubt the rest of the family will be any better."

"Probably not," Karen said candidly. "But they're not the ones walking in your shoes, are they?"

As Karen's careful choice of words sank in, Adelia stared at her. "You know, don't you? You know Ernesto has been cheating on me?" She sank onto the sofa and buried her face in her hands. "I knew he hadn't been even the tiniest bit discreet, but I was hoping the word wasn't all over town."

"I don't know that it is all over town," Karen said. "Selena said something to Daisy. Daisy didn't totally understand, but she told me."

"And my brother knows, too," she guessed, sounding resigned. "I thought he did. More than once I've had to warn him

471

not to have a talk with Ernesto. I was hoping it was only because he knew I was unhappy."

Karen nodded. "Yeah, I've had a little trouble reeling in his temper myself. I told him it would only humiliate you to have him interfering."

Adelia nodded. "Thank you for that."

"Now, please, come into the kitchen. Let's have that coffee. I can call Elliott, if you'd like. I'm sure he'd come home if you want to talk. Or you can use me as a sounding board. I'll just make a quick call to the restaurant and let Erik know I'm running late."

"I didn't mean to come over here and disrupt your day," Adelia apologized. "I'm not even sure why I came. I actually threw Ernesto out days ago, but I woke up this morning and it hit me that my husband is gone and I have an appointment this morning to see Helen."

"Would you like me to go with you?" Karen asked at once.

Adelia managed a weak smile. "God, what did I do to deserve your kindness?"

Karen grinned. "You bought me a dress."

"I'll buy you twenty if you'll stick by me once Mama starts ranting and raving about what a terrible person I am."

"You're not a terrible person," Karen said.

"But I was so superior and mean when Elliott first brought you home. I didn't want to hear any of the reasons behind your divorce. The church said it was wrong and that was enough for me. Now here I am with my marriage falling apart and I'm pouring out my troubles to you and you're actually being sympathetic."

"Did you want me to throw you back onto the street?"

"I probably deserve it," Adelia said.

"You're family," Karen said simply. "Lately I appreciate more than most what that means." She set a cup of coffee in front of Adelia, then offered her a slice of the pie she'd baked the night before.

"Are you sure divorce is the only option?" she asked gently. "Knowing your convictions, maybe you should think it through a little longer."

"Too late," Adelia said. "Not only has he been cheating on me for a very long time, but he acted as if I had no right to be angry about it. He said it was just the way things were, that all men eventually cheat. He said I should be happy that he was providing a roof over our heads and taking care of our children. And he had the gall to introduce Selena to the current other woman." Her temper visibly stirred. "She lives in the same neighborhood. Did I mention that?"

Karen winced. "Selena told Daisy, so I knew."

"My poor child," Adelia said sorrowfully. "She's scared and confused and furious with me and with her father."

"Why you?" Karen asked.

"She blames me for letting him get away with it. I think that's when I finally realized I could no longer look the other way. I don't want my son to think what their father is doing is acceptable, and I don't want my daughters to think a woman has to take such disrespect."

Karen was still trying to absorb the idea that Ernesto thought it was his right to have affairs and rub his wife's nose in them. "I'm trying to come to grips with what you said a minute ago. He actually said that you should accept him cheating?"

"And more about how boring I am in bed," she admitted. "Maybe it's true. I don't know. Whether it is or not, it was humiliating."

"No wonder you want to kick him to the curb," Karen said with feeling, horrified on Adelia's behalf. "That's unacceptable."

Adelia met her gaze for the first time. "It

really is, isn't it? I don't have to put up with it."

"Of course, you don't," Karen said. "Now, tell me what Elliott and I can do. You have an appointment with Helen, so that's under control. We all know what a barracuda she can be in these circumstances. Do you need a place to stay? It would be a tight fit, but you'd be welcome here with the kids."

Adelia regarded her with amazement. "There you go again, catching me by surprise. Thank you for offering, but we're okay. I'm not budging from the house. That was the first thing Helen told me when I called to make the appointment."

"Well, why don't you at least hang out here until it's time to see her? I need to leave for work, or I could stay a little longer if you want to talk some more."

"No, you should go," Adelia said. "If you don't mind, though, I will stay for just a little while. I can't seem to think straight at my house. There are too many memories crowding in."

"Stay here as long as you like," Karen told her.

For the first time, Karen felt like a real member of the Cruz family. Even more important in many ways, she felt as if she was worthy of helping someone else after so many years of needing help herself.

There was another positive side effect of this bleak situation, as well. Listening to Adelia had reaffirmed just how lucky she was to have a man as solid and dependable as Elliott in her life. For all of their recent ups and downs, he was clearly a treasure she hadn't appreciated half as much as she should have.

23

Flo had two men vying for her attention as she played one of the slot machines lined up in the casino they'd chosen for that night's action.

"Just look at her," Liz said with a grin. "What is it about her that has men fawning all over her?"

"She lives her life every second and enjoys it," Frances said. "I think all of us our age, men and women, like to be around that sort of energy and optimism."

Liz laughed. "If only we could keep up with it." Her expression sobered as she studied Frances. "Are you okay? You look a little tired."

"The flashing lights and noise are starting to bother me a little," Frances said. "I think I might head back to the room, if you don't mind."

"Of course not. I'll come with you."

"No need," Frances said. "Stay here and

have fun. I'll get Karen to walk back with me. I don't think she enjoys throwing money into these slot machines nearly as much as the rest of us do. She'll be relieved to have an excuse to stop."

"Okay, if you're sure," Liz said, though there was unmistakable worry in her eyes.

Frances squeezed her hand. "Very sure. Have fun."

"Well, there is a machine over there that looks to me as if it's due for a big payoff. I've had my eye on it for a while now."

"Then get over there and claim it," Frances encouraged. "Bring home a jackpot!"

Just then bells and whistles seemed to go wild nearby. Lights started flashing, followed by an incredulous whoop of excitement and laughter.

"That voice sounds familiar," Frances said.

"Let's look," Liz said, leading the way toward the commotion. Even Flo left her gentlemen to trail along with them.

As they turned down the aisle, they spotted Karen in the middle of the Sweet Magnolias as a machine seemed to be in the throes of flashing mechanical ecstasy. Karen spotted Frances and ran toward her, her eyes alight with excitement.

"I won!" she said, catching Frances in a

hug. "Can you believe it? I hit a jackpot! I actually hit a jackpot! It was my very last quarter, too. I'd promised myself I was going to stop."

"How much did you win?" Flo asked excitedly.

Karen's expression went blank. "I have no idea. A lot, I think."

A casino employee joined them. "Ten thousand dollars," he said, handing her a ticket to be cashed out.

Karen turned pale. "No way," she murmured, looking shocked. She turned to Frances. "Did he just say ten thousand dollars?"

"He most certainly did," Frances said, laughing at her delight. "And nobody in this group deserves it more." She looked around at the others. "I'd say that makes this trip a rousing success."

Even Helen looked pleased. "Want me to come with you to cash in the ticket? There are probably some forms you'll have to fill out for taxes and so on."

"Uh-huh," Karen said, clearly dazed. "And then I want to call Elliott. He's never in a million years going to believe this. We have a big chunk of our baby fund back."

"So you can finally get started on your plan to add to your family," Frances said happily. "How wonderful!"

The color in Karen's cheeks deepened.

Helen gave her a slow, intuitive once-over. "You're already pregnant!" she guessed. "That's why you've turned down every margarita we've offered."

Karen nodded sheepishly. "It was supposed to stay a secret a little longer."

"But not from us," Dana Sue said. "Sweet Magnolias should know everything before anyone else in town."

Karen's eyes widened. "You can't put any of this in tomorrow's radio report. Elliott will have a cow if his family finds out on the radio before we can tell them the news ourselves. Please, swear to me this is just between us."

Flo looked especially disappointed. She'd been the self-appointed reporter who'd been talking to Sarah and Travis on the air live every morning. She told everyone she was the only one awake that early without a hangover.

"We are so never going to hear the end of this trip," Helen had moaned the first time she'd heard her.

"Oh, stop it," Flo teased. "You're secretly loving every minute of this, and at least you get to go back to your room with a hunk every night. The rest of us are all flying solo."

"Thank God for that," Helen murmured. "I've seen some of those guys who're hitting on you. Please tell me you know better than to invite any of them back to Serenity."

Flo winked at the rest of them. "You never know."

Helen frowned at the taunt. "You're saying that just to make me crazy, right? They're wearing polyester, Mother!"

"I'm sorry if they offend your sense of fashion. They're all very nice men."

Frances decided to step in. "Helen, weren't you going with Karen to help her with her winning ticket?"

With obvious reluctance, Helen tore her gaze away from her mother and turned a fierce look toward Frances and then Liz. "Just keep her away from the Elvis impersonators and the wedding chapels, okay?"

Liz chuckled. "I think we can promise that much." She linked her arm through Flo's. "Come on. Stop tormenting your daughter and let's go win some money. Hopefully Karen's luck will have rubbed off on one of us."

Frances went with Karen and Helen. As soon as they'd taken care of the paperwork and accepted a check for the winnings after taxes, Karen turned to Frances. "I'm ready to head back to the room. How about you?"

"I was planning to head back an hour ago, but I got caught up in all the excitement," Frances admitted.

"I'll see you both in the morning, then," Helen said, giving them each a hug. "Don't tell anyone else, but for all my complaining, I'm having a blast. I think I'm going to see if I can persuade my husband to go back to the room and do a little private strip show for me," she confided.

Frances chuckled as Helen walked away. "I don't think she'll have any problem getting Erik to do whatever she wants, do you?"

"Not even a tiny hint of opposition," Karen confirmed. She studied Frances as they walked the two blocks back to their own hotel. "Is this trip everything you wanted it to be?"

Frances thought about the fun and laughter that would linger for weeks in the retelling. She thought about the delight in Karen's eyes at the jackpot that would provide some relief from her financial burdens.

"Everything," she confirmed, smiling. "And then some!"

To Karen's surprise, Adelia had managed to keep her plans for divorcing Ernesto a secret for a couple of weeks now. Even after Karen's return from Las Vegas, the news still wasn't out. She couldn't very well blame her sister-in-law for wanting to put off the inevitable outcry.

"I know I'll have to break the news soon," Adelia had admitted the day after Karen got back. "Helen's going to have Ernesto served with divorce papers this week and he's not going to take it quietly."

"Then maybe you should break it to them first," Karen had advised her that morning. "Maybe you're not giving them enough credit. Your mother, your sisters and Elliott love you. They all want you to be happy."

Apparently Adelia had taken her advice, because when Karen got home from her shift at Sullivan's that night, she found her house filled with members of the Cruz family. Their voices were raised so high, they didn't even hear her when she entered. It was Elliott's mother who saw her first.

"How dare you tell my daughter to get a divorce?" she shouted accusingly over the others.

At that, everyone fell silent and turned on Karen, apparently awaiting a reply. She looked toward Elliott for support, only to find that he looked as angry as everyone else. She scowled at the whole lot of them, refusing to be intimidated.

"Adelia came to see Elliott a while back," she explained, avoiding her sister-in-law's gaze. Adelia looked as if she were close to tears. "She was obviously distraught. I didn't tell her to get a divorce. She'd already decided that it was what she needed to do. All I did was offer her support. If that's a crime, then I'm guilty. Frankly, though, you're her family, and it seems to me, her feelings should be your first priority, not yelling at me or blaming her when Ernesto gave her no alternative."

Once more, noisy chaos erupted. She eased over to her husband. "Where are Daisy and Mack?"

"When people started turning up here in a frenzy, I called Frances. Flo brought her over, and they took them out for burgers and then to Frances's place for the night."

She nodded. "Good idea. They didn't need to be in the middle of this."

"And you?" he asked. "Did you need to be in the middle?"

She frowned at the accusatory note in his voice. "Was I supposed to turn your sister away? You know the situation as well as I do." She leveled a look into his eyes. "Do you actually think she should stay with Ernesto?"

Rather than answering, he evaded. "You should have called me that day. I would have come home. Perhaps I could have calmed her down before she did anything rash. Divorce is a huge step, especially in this family."

"Do you think I don't understand that?" Karen said. "It's a huge step for anyone. If it's not, then they don't understand what's going on or what it's likely to do to their family."

Elliott looked momentarily taken aback by her fierce tone. "You think Adelia understands all of this?"

"And then some," she said. "You need to talk to her and listen to what she says."

He frowned. "I know about the cheating, but is there more?"

"Ask your sister," she said. "You wanted me to get out of the middle, remember?"

He studied her intently, his expression grim. "Has he ever hurt her?"

"Physically? Not that I know of."

"Well, that's something at least."

Karen stared at him incredulously. "Please don't tell me that's the bar for a divorce in your view. There are lots of ways for a marriage to be destroyed. If you ask me, repetitive cheating with no hint of remorse ranks right up there."

Elliott closed his eyes at her implication. "Then this affair of his wasn't something new, a one-time thing?"

"No. He's shown her the most humiliating disrespect possible over and over again."

"I see," he said at last.

"If you do, then you need to settle your family down, make them see her side of this. She shouldn't be made to feel guilty for standing up for herself. Look at her, Elliott. Your mother and sisters are battering her right now emotionally just the way Ernesto did. How is that fair?"

"They're expressing their beliefs," he said, still defending them. He drew in a deep breath, though, and nodded, "But you're right, all the yelling isn't getting us anywhere."

"Don't make Adelia an outcast over this," Karen pleaded, feeling sympathy for her sister-in-law in a way she'd never expected to. "You never made me feel that way, even though you knew my history. I'm sure you disapproved of me being divorced as strongly as your family did, but you were able to see my side. Show Adelia the same respect."

He smiled at her then. "I haven't shown you nearly as much respect since then, have I? That's really what so many of our fights have been about. I'm just seeing that clearly."

Karen regarded him with an even deeper sense of hope. She was surprised he'd realized the real root of their problems, when even she had been focused on his actions, not the underlying disrespect when he shut her out of important decisions or even the small ones. It was all of a piece — the lack of communication, the high-handedness and the financial disagreements — all stemmed from a disrespect for her strength and intelligence.

"I'm not sure even I saw it so clearly until just now," she said. "Identifying the problem is the real first step to solving it. Now maybe we can really turn those midnight promises we've made into a new reality."

Elliott's expression immediately brightened, all thoughts of his sister's situation and the surrounding chaos apparently forgotten. "How about I shoo these people out of here?" he suggested. "We have some serious making up to do."

She glanced around at the squabbling members of the Cruz family and chuckled as she tried to envision that ever happening. "Good luck with that. If there's one thing your family loves more than great food, it's a lively debate."

"Then they can have it elsewhere," he said, clapping his hands to get their attention. "Go home," he said, when they fell silent. "Karen's right. Every one of us needs to be on Adelia's side, no matter what." He gave his mother a pointed look. "You, too, Mama. You know this situation must be serious for Adelia to risk offending you by taking such a drastic action. Talk to her and find out what really happened."

His mother looked taken aback. "You think divorce is justified?"

"In this case, I think you owe it to your daughter to find out," he said staunchly, crossing the room to kiss his sister's cheek.

To Karen's surprise, Mrs. Cruz looked from her to Elliott and back again, then nodded. "I know you would not say such a thing lightly. Adelia, come home with me. We'll talk."

"Really, Mama?" Adelia asked skeptically. "Because to be honest, I'm not up to a full-court press from you and the entire family. If that's your intention, I think I'll hide out right here with Elliott and Karen." She glanced at them. "Sorry. I'm sure you have better things to do."

Elliott nodded. "We most definitely do, but you're the first priority for now."

Maria Cruz seemed startled by her daughter's show of defiance. A hint of sympathy softened her expression. "Just you and I," she promised. "And no yelling. Only a mother listening to what's breaking her daughter's heart."

Instantly misty-eyed, Adelia stood. "Thank you, Mama." She pressed a kiss to Karen's cheek, then one to Elliott's. "Thank you for everything."

"Anytime," Karen told her, giving her hand a reassuring squeeze.

With that settled, everyone trooped out, leaving Karen alone with her husband.

"You know I will never cheat on you, *querida,*" he said, pulling her into his arms. "I would never disrespect you in that way." He held her gaze. "Or in any other way. Never again."

"From now on, we talk things over," she said.

"And work them out," he agreed.

"Compromise," she suggested, unable to keep a hint of amusement out of her voice. It was a concept with which Elliott was only marginally familiar, but at least he seemed eager to learn.

"Compromise," he agreed, then grinned. "And then we make up in bed."

"Definitely a good plan," she said with enthusiasm.

"Starting now?" he inquired hopefully.

Laughing as he scooped her into his arms, she replied, "No time like the present."

She had a feeling tonight hadn't been their last argument, but if they could end each one like this, they'd make it. She thought of Mrs. Cruz's admission that she and her husband had always ended a day of tension with a kiss. They'd had nearly fifty good years together. If she and Elliott could match that, even with a few rough patches, she'd count herself lucky.

Sugar and spice, she thought, recalling the way she and Elliott had once been described. As a cook, she understood the differences and the dangers.

She also knew just how well they could blend if they were used with careful thought and a delicate touch. If that worked with food, then surely she and Elliott could make the same ingredients work to create an amazing, solid marriage that would last forever.

And a baby born of that combination? She simply smiled at the amazing thought of it. The months ahead promised to be the best of her life . . . so far.

490

DISCUSSION QUESTIONS

1. Karen's world was nearly destroyed by the mountain of debt left behind by her ex-husband. As a result, she's terrified by any financially risky decision made by Elliott. Have you ever struggled with financial decisions in your marriage? How did you resolve them?

2. Often communication issues that arise in a marriage happen because some topics were never discussed *before* the wedding. Did you and your spouse have pre-ceremony conversations about potentially difficult topics such as finances, family size or even how to divide up your holiday and vacation time between his family and yours? If you didn't, has it caused problems for you? Were you able to settle these issues in a way that satisfied both of you?

3. Marriages are often overwhelmed by bag-

gage from past relationships. Have you ever carried issues from the past into your current relationship? How did you manage to leave the past behind? Or have you?

4. The ability to compromise is often the cornerstone of a strong marriage. Is there a particularly difficult issue that you and your spouse have been unable to resolve through compromise? How do you handle it when it arises?

5. The Cruz family has a deeply ingrained religious conviction regarding divorce. If you or someone you know has such deep beliefs, what would you do if faced by the situations that Karen and now Adelia have faced?

6. Do you know men like Ernesto who believe that cheating is their right as long as they're providing for their family? How do you think their wives should deal with it? Is it ever okay to stay with such a man strictly for the sake of the children? Or for financial security?

7. Adelia has been a stay-at-home mom for her entire marriage. Even though she holds a degree in business, she's scared

about trying to find a place in the work force. Have you ever been faced with that situation, having to return to work unexpectedly? How did you feel when it happened? How has it worked out?

8. When the incidents of forgetfulness start piling up, Frances is terrified that she might have Alzheimer's, so terrified that she puts off going to the doctor for as long as possible. Have you ever been faced with a medical scare of any kind? What was your first instinct, to see the doctor and find out, or to delay seeking a diagnosis? Who persuaded you that it was better to know?

9. For many seniors and their families, Alzheimer's is one of the scariest possible diagnoses they can receive. Do you feel that way? Has anyone in your family been diagnosed with Alzheimer's? How has your family coped? What was the most difficult part of dealing with this disease?

ABOUT THE AUTHOR

With her roots firmly planted in the South, **Sherryl Woods** has written many of her more than one hundred books in that distinctive setting, whether it's her home state of Virginia, her adopted state, Florida, or her much-adored South Carolina. She's also especially partial to small towns, wherever they may be. A member of Novelists Inc. and Sisters in Crime, Sherryl divides her time between her childhood summer home overlooking the Potomac River in Colonial Beach, Virginia, and her oceanfront home with its lighthouse view in Key Biscayne, Florida. Sherryl also loves hearing from readers. You can join her at her blog, www.justbetweenfriendsblog.com, visit her website at www.sherrylwoods.com or contact her directly at Sherryl703 @gmail.com.

The employees of Thorndike Press hope you have enjoyed this Large Print book. All our Thorndike, Wheeler, and Kennebec Large Print titles are designed for easy reading, and all our books are made to last. Other Thorndike Press Large Print books are available at your library, through selected bookstores, or directly from us.

For information about titles, please call:
  (800) 223-1244

or visit our Web site at:
  http://gale.cengage.com/thorndike

To share your comments, please write:
  Publisher
  Thorndike Press
  10 Water St., Suite 310
  Waterville, ME 04901